HIGHLAND KISS

Eric turned to face Bethia and found her staring at him. He wondered if she intended to stop him before he even stole one kiss. When he slid his arm around her tiny waist, tugging her close to him, and she did not resist, he breathed an inner sigh of relief.

He started in surprise when, as he slowly lowered his mouth to hers, she suddenly wrapped her slender arms around his neck and yanked him even closer.

"Ye must be confused, lass," he said as he released her mouth and began to kiss her throat. "That was a morning kiss."

Bethia giggled, then sighed with delight as he moved his hands over her back. "There are different kinds of kisses for different occasions, are there?"

"For us—aye."

"Then what sort of kiss would ye give me if I told ye that I wasnae ready to go to sleep yet?" She cried out softly in surprise when he abruptly turned, pinning her firmly beneath his lean, hard body.

"That would require a kiss that asked, nay, begged for something," he said in a soft, rough voice as he brushed his mouth over hers.

The kiss he gave Bethia sent all of her senses reeling. She realized that he had been treating her gently, restraining himself. With his tongue, he ravished her mouth, then he pulled it back, tempting her to follow with her own, so the dance would begin all over again. He released her mouth only briefly, just long enough for her to take a breath, then started all over again until she was aware of nothing but the taste of him . . . .

Books by Hannah Howell

ONLY FOR YOU

MY VALIANT KNIGHT

UNCONQUERED

WILD ROSES

A TASTE OF FIRE

HIGHLAND DESTINY

HIGHLAND HONOR

HIGHLAND PROMISE

A STOCKINGFUL OF JOY

HIGHLAND VOW

HIGHLAND KNIGHT

HIGHLAND HEARTS

HIGHLAND BRIDE

HIGHLAND ANGEL

HIGHLAND GROOM

HIGHLAND WARRIOR

RECKLESS

HIGHLAND CONQUEROR

HIGHLAND CHAMPION

HIGHLAND LOVER

Published by Zebra Books

HIGHLAND PROMISE

Hannah Howell

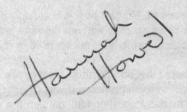

Zebra Books
Kensington Publishing Corp.

http://www.zebrabooks.com

ZEBRA BOOKS are published by

Kensington Publishing Corp.
850 Third Avenue
New York, NY 10022

ISBN: 0-8217-7984-2

First Printing: July, 1999
10   9   8   7

Printed in the United States of America

Chapter One

Bethia Drummond watched the two sweating men throw the rock-strewn dirt on top of her sister's body and held her tiny nephew James a little closer. Orphaned before his first birthday by the greed of his own kinsmen, he was going to need a lot of love and, much more importantly, a lot of protection. Bethia swallowed her tears and tossed a few sprigs of white heather onto her sister's grave. Her heart found it hard to believe that her womb sister Sorcha was gone forever, but her mind knew that Sorcha now lay entwined forever with her love, her husband Robert, beneath the deepening dirt. Put there, she thought with a rising fury, by the avarice of Robert's family.

She stared across the slowly filling grave at Robert's uncle William and his two sons, Iain and Angus. They were Drummonds only by name, never by blood, William having taken the name when he had married Robert's aunt Mary. The barren Mary had willingly taken William's two small sons as her own, but none of her kindness and love had penetrated their thick, evil hides. The woman had, without doubt, clasped a whole nest of adders to her bosom and paid dearly for her charity. The woman's death, barely a year past, had been a slow and agonizing, and very suspicious, one. Now two more obstacles to the lands and wealth of Dunncraig were gone and she held the last. William and his two hulking sons would never get James. Bethia swore on her sister's grave that she would see all three men dead first and that they would be made to pay for all of their crimes.

When William and his sons approached her, Bethia tensed. She resisted the urge to turn and run, taking the happily gurgling James far away from the three dark men. It would be neither safe nor wise to let them know that she was suspicious of them.

"Ye need not fear for the laddie's care," William said in his rough voice as he lightly ruffled the little boy's bright red curls. "We will care for the wee bairn."

Bethia wanted to scrub the man's touch off the boy, but forced herself to smile. "My sister asked me to care for her child. 'Tis why I came here."

"Ye are a verra young lass. 'Tis sure that ye dinnae wish to waste your life caring for another woman's child. Ye should be away making a few wee bairns of your own."

"Caring for the bairn of my womb sister could ne'er be a waste, sir."

"Mayhap this isnae a good time to discuss this." William forced his thin-lipped mouth into a parody of a sympathetic smile and patted Bethia on the shoulder. "Ye are still wrapped too tightly in your grief o'er your poor sister's death. We will talk of this later."

"As ye wish."

It was hard not to yank herself away from William's chilling touch, but Bethia forced herself to smile at the three men once again. She then turned and walked back to the keep with a hard-won calm. Bethia wanted to scream out her suspicions, wanted to unsheath her dagger and plunge it deep into William's black heart, but she knew that would gain her nothing except one brief, pleasant taste of revenge. The man's sons would quickly and bloodily avenge his death, killing both her and James. In truth, she would probably accomplish no more than giving them a ready explanation for the boy's death since she could not be sure she could even kill William.

Defeating William and his sons and making them pay for their crimes required care and planning. Bethia needed to subdue the emotions twisting her insides into a painful knot. She knew that she would also need some help and she could not count on finding any amongst the cowed people of Dunncraig. William had a tight grip upon all who lived at the keep and on the lands—one Robert had either not seen or been too often away at court or fighting in France to break. Robert's naivete or neglect had cost him and Sorcha their lives. Bethia had no intention of allowing James to join them in their cold grave.

"Your father was all that was brave and honorable," Bethia told little James as she entered the small, dark room they shared, "but he should have watched his home fires much more carefully, laddie."

She settled the yawning child in his cradle and sat on the edge of her small, hard bed to watch him. Sorcha's brilliant green eyes blessed his sweet little face and his hair was only a little brighter than his mother's. The envy Bethia had sometimes suffered over her sister's often acclaimed beauty now seemed petty and sad. She might have a duller, browner hair color and the curse of mismatched eyes, as well as a far less womanly figure than her sister's, but she was still alive. Sorcha's highly praised beauty and charm had always seemed such a blessing, but they had not saved her.

And she was stronger, Bethia decided as she watched the fair James fall asleep. Sorcha had been like a candle admired for its light and warmth, for the beauty of its color-rich flame, but also easily snuffed out and left cold, lifeless. She had always been more wary than Sorcha, more able to see the evil in people. It had surprised her when Sorcha had sent word asking her to come and help with James, for Dunncraig was filled with women eager and able to help care for their laird's son and heir. Bethia now wondered if, finally, some hint of suspicion or fear had crept into her sister's loving, trusting heart.

She sighed and vigorously wiped away a tear. If it had, it had come far too late. It did, however, explain Sorcha's odd choice of words in her missive. Sorcha had asked her sister to come and watch over James. Not nurse him, play with him, visit him, or aid his mother, but to watch over him. And that was exactly what Bethia intended to do.

Every breath she took, every whisper of her skirts over the rush-covered floors, made Bethia's heart skip painfully as she crept along the shadowed halls of Dunncraig. She knew how to be quiet yet that skill appeared to be failing her miserably. No outcry came, however, as she made her way through the keep and out into the bailey. It had taken her three torturous days to find a way out of Dunncraig, one she could possibly get to unseen, and it felt as if it was taking her almost as long to get to it. And every step of the way, she was terrified that James, so sweetly oblivious to the danger he was in, would make some sound that would give them away.

For each minute of those three days she had wavered between doubting her suspicions and searching for a way to flee unseen. The death of James's little puppy had brutally ended all of her doubts and suspicions. Bethia doubted she would ever know why, after blissfully eating and drinking everything brought to her and James the first day after the funeral, she had suddenly felt compelled to test the food on the second day. When the puppy had died after tasting the food, she had wept out of guilt for using the poor, trusting animal in such a way and a strange mixture of fury and fear because all of her dark suspicions had been so gruesomely proven right. The fact that she had not been able to give the little animal a burial worthy of his sacrifice only added to her anger. She now knew that the slow, painful deaths of Sorcha and Robert had been caused by poison and not by some unnamed wasting sickness as was claimed.

Finally, Bethia reached the spot she had been seeking: a small break in the wall behind the reeking stables. Robert had not only been unaware of the deadly enemies within his keep, but of the crumbling state of his keep as well. If he had seen how poorly the place was kept, he never would have left William in control of the accounts. Bethia was not sure what William and his sons were doing with the money from the lands and tenants but they were certainly not maintaining the keep they were so willing to kill for.

As she squeezed herself and James through the opening a few pieces of the crumbling wall clattered noisily to the ground. She held herself still within the opening, holding her breath as she waited for the outcry she was sure would come. It surprised her a little when there was none. Such a noise should have caused one of the men at arms to at least glance her way. As she cautiously slipped out into the night and hurried toward the woods at the far end of the surrounding fields, she felt a little more confident about her chances of escape with every step she took. The men guarding Dunncraig were obviously as lax in their duties as William was in keeping Dunncraig strong.

It was not until she entered the frightening yet welcome shadows of the forest that Bethia dared to breathe a sigh of relief. She knew it would not be long before a pursuit was begun, but she had taken the first step toward freedom and safety and she allowed a touch of hope to enter her heart. A horse would have been a great help but she had not dared to try to steal one, not even dared to retrieve the sweet little mare she had ridden in on. She would never have gotten the animal out through her tiny bolt-hole. Bethia silently promised the little mare that she would not leave her in that rotting stable any longer than necessary. Without a horse, however, if she was going to put any distance at all between herself and James and their enemies, she was going to have to do a lot of walking.

James shifted in the blanket sling resting against Bethia's chest and she idly rubbed his back as she started to walk. "Be at ease, my bonny wee laddie." She took one last look at Dunncraig, wishing she could have bid a final farewell to Sorcha, but promising that she would return. "I will see that those swine who feed out of your father's trough will soon be choking on their ill-begotten meal. And may God heartily curse all men who seek to fill their pockets with the riches of others," she whispered as she marched deeper into the wood.

"Are ye sure ye ought to go and face these people?" Balfour Murray asked his young foster brother Eric as he sat down at the head table in the great hall of Donncoill and began to fill his plate with food.

Eric smiled at Balfour, then winked at his brother's wife Maldie, who just rolled her eyes and began to eat. "We have tried every other means to gain my birthright, but everything we do is either contested or ignored. This game has been played out after thirteen long years. I grow heartily weary of it."

"I still cannae see how confronting the fools will change anything."

"It may not, but 'tis the only thing we havenae tried."

"There is still the king to turn to."

"We have tried that too, although mayhap nay as ardently as we might have. Howbeit, I think our liege would prefer nay to take any side in all of this. The Beaton lairds may have been swine, and still are, but they have ne'er angered or offended the king. The MacMillans, my mother's clan, are also on amiable terms with the king, considered loyal and able fighters. I believe I may be the proof they cannae deny. I carry the Beaton mark upon my back and many have said that I carry the look of my mother and her kin. Mayhap 'tis past time the Beatons and MacMillans see the proof with their verra own eyes.''

"Do ye think the Beatons will heed the truth e'en if ye bare your back and force them to see the mark there?'' asked Maldie.

"Nay, mayhap not, but it cannae hurt to try,'' Eric replied. "I have heard nay ill about the MacMillans. Unfortunately, I have yet to meet with one during my times at court. They may but heed the lies told by the Beatons too closely. Mayhap I can finally make them see the truth.''

"Ye must take someone with you,'' insisted Balfour. " 'Tis a pity Nigel went to France.''

"Gisele has now born him three bonny bairns. 'Twas past time they were shown to their kinsmen in France.''

"Aye, I ken it. If ye can but wait until my work is done, I could come with ye or Nigel may have returned.''

"This is my fight, Balfour, and mine alone.''

It took Eric the rest of the evening and most of the next day to convince Balfour that this was indeed something he had to do alone. Neither of them feared any real threat from the Beatons or the MacMillans, for they and their quarrels were all too well known to the king. Any harm coming to Eric on the lands of either family would bring a swift and harsh response and both families knew it. There were other dangers in traveling alone, however, and Balfour did not hesitate to list them in gruesome detail.

He was still listing them three days later when Eric was leading his packed horse out of the stables. "A mon to watch your back wouldnae be a bad thing,'' he said, frowning as Eric just smiled and mounted his black gelding Connor.

"Nay, it wouldnae,'' agreed Eric, pausing to tie his long, thick reddish gold hair back with a wide strip of blackened leather. "Howbeit, ye have more need of able-bodied men than I do. I can care for myself, Balfour. I dinnae go to do battle and I think I can fight off a thief or two or e'en outrun them. Cease mothering me,'' he added gently.

Balfour grinned. "Go on your way then, but if ye meet with more trouble then ye can deal with, pause at an inn and send back here for a mon or two. Or return and we will set off in more force when the work in the fields is done."

"Agreed. I will be certain to send word of how I fare."

" 'Tis best that ye do, for if we havenae heard from ye in what we feel is too long a time, we will come hunting for you. Go with God," Balfour added as Eric rode through the gates.

Eric waved, then continued on. He was torn many ways about what he was doing. What he sought was indeed his birthright, yet it galled him to have to go and beg for it. Balfour had gifted him with a small peel tower and some land to the west of Donncoill. At times he felt strongly inclined to cease trying to get what was not willingly being offered, to just go and make a life at the peel tower. Then his sense of what was right and fair rose in his breast and he went back to struggling to gain his birthright.

There was also the often ignored fact that he was not a Murray by blood. The ties were as strong and had been deepened by his half sister Maldie's marriage to Balfour, but legally the Murrays owed him nothing, did not have to provide for him in any manner at all. But they did. They called him brother and they meant it. That made the refusal of the Beatons and the MacMillans to accept him as kin all the more infuriating. Eric had a right to all that had been his mother's and his father's. In his heart he knew he could never be anything but a Murray, but he intended to retrieve all that had been stolen from him by the lies of the Beatons. If his blood kinsmen wanted to fight over it, then fight he would. For thirteen years, since they had learned the truth about his birth, they had clung to the gentle, diplomatic way. Now was the time for confrontation.

It took him only a few hours to reach the gates of the Beatons' keep. Although he was not surprised when they refused him entry, refused to even speak to him, he was disappointed. His father's cousin had slipped onto the lands within days after his father's death and clearly intended to stay. Sir Graham Beaton was as cruel and as clever as his father had been and, if only for the sake of the long-suffering people who lived in and around the keep, Eric would like to see the man unseated from his stolen lands, but it was clear now that that would take a fight.

As he rode away, struggling to ignore the insults flung from the walls, he decided to continue on to the MacMillans'. If he could win his battle for recognition there, he would have more men, more power, and more money with which to fight the Beaton usurper. Eric suspected that Sir Graham knew the truth and thought that, by refusing to look closely or heed any of the calls to surrender the stolen lands, he could hold on to his riches. An alliance through blood with the more favored MacMillans might be just enough to force the man to admit the truth, to concur with all he fought to deny and decry as lies. Eric became even more determined to win the favor of his mother's kinsmen. It now meant more than the legal winning of his birthright. It could easily mean the final ousting of a long line of despicable Beaton lairds.

"Maman?"

Bethia swallowed a sudden welling of tears as she held the ornate silver quaich up to James's mouth and let him sip at the water it held. The small, shallow drinking cup, its two handles beautifully carved with an old Celtic design, had been her sister's wedding cup. Their father had spent a great deal of money on it and had searched long and hard for the best craftsman to make it. To hear Sorcha's child ask for his mother as he drank from that treasured memento made Bethia's heart clench with a sorrow she had not yet had time to deal with.

"I fear I must be your maman now, laddie," she whispered as she ruffled his silken curls and gave him a small piece of bread to chew on. "I ken that I am nay as good as the one those bastards stole away from you, but I shall do the best I can.''

A small voice in her mind murmured that she would at least keep James alive, something his mother had almost failed to do; then she cursed herself for having such a disloyal thought. In the two days she had been creeping through the wood, inching her way toward home and safety, she had found herself suffering more and more unkind thoughts about her sister and her husband. She cursed their weakness, silently derided them for their blindness, and wondered how such a sweet child could have two such fools for his parents. Each time she thought such things, she felt overwhelmed with guilt.

"I need time to sit and look into my heart," she said to the boy, then idly chewed on a piece of bread. "I am so angry, and 'tis odd, but most times I am angry at your poor parents. They did naught but get murdered, which isnae their fault, not truly. Aye, they could have been more alert, more cautious, mayhap looked at those around them instead of at each other all of the time, but those arenae really faults.''

"Maman?"

"Nay, laddie, no maman." Bethia kissed her nephew's forehead. "She is gone. 'Tis just me and ye now. Mayhap that is why I feel so angry. Sorcha should still be here. She was young and hale, nay ready for a cold grave. I fear I can think of too many things she and her bonny husband could have done to save themselves and then I become angry that neither of them did any of those things. There is only one mon I should curse— William. Aye, and his two brutish sons. That is where I must direct all of my anger, eh?''

"Baba.''

"Baba? What is a baba?" She smiled, then sighed. "We dinnae ken much about each other, do we, James? I dinnae think that fleeing men who wish to kill you will give us much time to do so either. Mayhap when we get to my home, to Dunnbea, we may take the time to learn of each other and your grandmere will be most eager to help. Aye, and your grandpere. Ye willnae be alone, sweet James, though none of us can replace those ye have had stolen away from you. There will be loving and caring aplenty and mayhap that will ease the loss ye have suffered. 'Tis a blessing that ye are still such a young bairn for the loss and pain may nay be so deep or painful.''

Bethia knew that she was fortunate in one thing. James was a very even-tempered child who did little fussing or crying. He had his mother's sweet nature—Sorcha's ever flowing happiness with life and the world around her. It served Bethia well as they ran for their lives, but she was determined that Sorcha's son would learn the value of a little wariness and caution.

She was just preparing to pack up their things and continue her long walk home when she heard a soft noise. Cursing herself for not watching more closely, she drew her dagger and stood in front of the child. Two men slipped out of the shadows of the surrounding trees. She frowned slightly, for they did not look like William's men.

''Ye willnae take the bairn,'' she said firmly.

''We dinnae want the bairn,'' the taller of the two men said, briefly glancing at her dagger and then at the silver cup James still held in his tiny hands.

''Ye are naught but base thieves.''

''Weel, 'tis certain we arenae what ye were expecting, but we arenae base thieves. We are verra good ones and it looks as if luck has smiled upon us.''

Bethia knew that she ought to just let them take what they wanted, that fighting with the men would only endanger her and James, could even get them killed. What the thieves wished to steal from her, however, was all she had left of Sorcha. Her mind told her to pick up the baby and run, but her heart, still

raw and aching with grief, was determined that these rough
men would never touch Sorcha's things.

"Ye willnae take what is mine without a fight, sirs," she
said coldly, praying that they were abject cowards.

"Now, lassie, are those few things really worth your life or
the bairn's?"

"Nay, but the question should be, are they really worth
yours?"

Chapter Two

The sound of voices pulled Eric from his thoughts. He tensed in his saddle and listened more carefully, finally determining the direction they came from. He had decided it was best to take the less traveled routes to his mother's family to avoid any trouble, yet it appeared that he was about to ride into some.

Cautiously, he edged his mount toward the voices. He briefly considered dismounting and approaching on foot, but decided to remain mounted. If there was trouble ahead and it was more than he could deal with, he wanted to be able to get out of its reach as fast as possible.

When he first saw the people through the trees, he had to resist the urge to rub his eyes in disbelief. A tiny, slender, chestnut-haired woman with only a small ornate dagger stood facing two sword-wielding men. Eric stared at the bairn behind her for a full moment before he believed it was really there.

"Now, lassie, are those few things really worth your life or the bairn's?" Eric heard the taller of the two men say.

And the little woman replied, "Nay, but the question should be, are they really worth yours?"

Brave, Eric thought. *Foolish, but brave.* The woman's question was enough to make the two thieves hesitate and Eric decided their indecision gave him the perfect opportunity to help the woman. As the two men assumed a fighting stance, Eric boldly rode into the small clearing. He had to smile at the way all three people gaped at him as if he was some apparition formed by the mists of the forest.

"I think the lady wishes to keep her things, sirs," he drawled as he drew his sword. "If ye wish to keep your brutish heads upon your cowardly shoulders, I suggest ye run—now—verra fast and verra far."

The men hesitated barely a heartbeat before stumbling back into the wood. Eric watched their flight until he could no longer see them and then turned to look at the woman. She still stared at him as if he was a ghost and he took full advantage of her openmouthed confusion to look her over carefully.

His brothers' wives were small, delicately built women, but he suspected this one would look small even next to them. Her hair was thick and long, hanging in soft waves to her small yet shapely hips. It was a rich, deep chestnut color; the sunlight that broke through the cover of the trees decorated it with glimpses of red. Her face was small, vaguely heart shaped, with the hint of a stubborn chin, a small straight nose, and an invitingly full mouth. What grabbed and held Eric's attention, however, was her eyes. Wide, thickly lashed, and set beneath delicately arched brows, they did not match. The left one was a rich, clear green and the right was a brilliant blue.

After swiftly examining her form from her small but tempting breasts to her tiny waist, he glanced at the baby behind her. The little boy had strikingly red curls and green eyes. Eric suddenly found himself keenly interested in whether or not the child was hers and where the father was. He looked back at the woman and smiled as she began to shake free of her shock.

Bethia had been stunned when the tall, lean knight rode in and sent the robbers fleeing for their meager lives. It took her a long time to shake aside her astonishment. She knew he was studying her and found herself carefully studying him back.

He was a beautiful man, she mused, knowing there was no other word to describe him. His long, reddish gold hair fell below his broad shoulders; it was so thick that even tying it back could not fully contain or hide it. His face was one of the most perfect she had ever seen, with its smooth, high forehead, high, wide cheekbones, long, handsomely unbroken nose, strong chin, and mouth that even she, in all of her innocence, recognized as dangerously sensuous. Deep, rich blue eyes were framed by surprisingly long brown lashes and set perfectly beneath faintly arced light brown brows.

His face was not all that was beautiful either. His body, attired handsomely in a crisp white linen shirt and a plaid she did not recognize, was tall and leanly muscular. Broad shoulders, a trim waist and hips, and long, well-shaped, muscular legs were enough to make any maid's heart beat faster. It was not surprising that she had thought him a vision. Men like him did not simply ride out of the trees and save one's life.

That started Bethia wondering what he was doing there, at this spot and at this opportune time. She held her dagger at the ready as her suspicions began to grow. Just because he was a pleasure for her eyes did not mean he was a good man. He could be working for William. She might not have been rescued at all—she might simply have changed one danger for another.

"Who are ye, sir?" she demanded. "I dinnae recognize your plaid or your clan badge."

"Such a sweet thank-ye for my aid," he murmured.

Bethia refused to let his soft reprimand over her apparent ingratitude embarrass her. There was too much at stake to be overconcerned with courtesies. "I am nay sure I have been rescued yet."

Eric bowed slightly in the saddle "I am Sir Eric Murray of Donncoill."

"I dinnae recognize the name or the place, so ye must be verra far afield, sir."

"I seek out my mother's family. And what are ye doing in the depths of the forest with naught but a bairn and a dagger?"

"A fair question, I suppose."

"Verra fair."

She eased her wary stance only a little, trying not to let the man's deep, attractive voice lull her suspicions. "I am taking my nephew to his family."

The word *nephew* made Eric a little happier than he thought it should. "With no one to aid or guard you?"

Bethia tensed again as he sheathed his sword and slowly dismounted. There was nothing threatening in his movements, but she dared not trust anyone. James's life was at risk and that was something far too valuable to gamble with.

"There was no one I felt I could trust with his life." She backed up, planting herself firmly between James and Eric as he took a small step toward her. "I think ye may understand that, at this moment, that also includes you, sir."

"Ye dinnae recognize my name or my clan, lass. I cannae believe ye dinnae ken exactly who your enemies are and 'tis clear that I dinnae number amongst them."

"Not yet."

Eric smiled faintly. "I have told ye who I am, but ye havenae returned the kindness."

Bethia wished the man would cease smiling at her. That beautiful smile threatened to steal away her wits, soften her wariness, and make her ready to believe he was truly her savior. His deep voice was almost like a caress, making her feel unforgivably rude for not trusting in him immediately. He might not be one of William's men, but she began to think he could be dangerous in many other ways.

"I am Bethia Drummond and this is my nephew, James Drummond, laird of Dunncraig."

"Dunncraig?"

"Ye ken the place?"

"Only that it is but one of the many I must pass to get where I am going."

"Weel, depending upon which way ye ride, ye may have already passed it."

"I ride to the MacMillans of Bealachan."

Bethia knew the family well, but that only eased her wariness a little. The man might not be going to them as a friend. "Why?"

"They are my mother's kinsmen."

"Yet ye speak as if this is the first time ye travel there."

"It is, but the reasons for that make for a long, sometimes dark tale and I cannae say I feel inclined to relate it whilst a dagger is held to my throat."

Even as she did so, Bethia knew it was a mistake, but she glanced down at her dagger to see where it was pointed. It angered her, even frightened her, but it did not surprise her when his long fingers wrapped around her wrist and he easily snatched the dagger from her hand. She waited tensely for his next move and frowned a little when he simply released her and turned to smile at a happily gurgling James.

" 'Tis wondrous to see such unconcern. 'Tis the blessing of being a bairn." Eric glanced at her as she edged around him until she stood next to the boy. "Children can trust so easily."

" 'Tis because they are still innocent of the evil in the world." Bethia quickly pulled James up into her arms and glared at Eric over the child's curls.

He straightened up and stepped closer to her, pleased when she did not step away. It showed him that, despite her angry wariness, she might yet come to trust him. The way she spoke of trusting no one with the child's life told him that she was in danger or certainly thought she was. Eric was determined to help her and he strongly suspected that urge had a lot to do with beautifully mismatched eyes and a full mouth he already ached to taste.

"Which is why they require others to watch o'er them," he murmured.

"That is what I am doing," she snapped.

"And ye think ye need no help in that?"

The man stood so close it made her head swim. She was much too aware of how only James's tiny body seperated the man from her. Her gaze was filled with his beauty. Worse, he had lowered his voice, the rich seductiveness of it making her heart beat so fast and loud she could barely think over the pounding of it. The man seemed to affect her much like a too large tankard of hearty wine.

"Mayhap I could use a wee bit," she grudgingly agreed, "but that doesnae mean it must be from you."

"Oh, but I think it must." Eric reached out to ruffle the child's curls, inwardly smiling when his fingers brushed against Bethia's stubborn little chin and she jerked her head back as if his touch had burned her. "Where are ye headed?"

"To Dunnbea," she replied without hesitation, then cursed herself for her lack of guile.

"Which is but another of the places I must pass by as I ride to meet with my kinsmen."

"Aye."

"The MacMillans of Bealachan arenae feuding with the Drummonds of Dunnbea, are they?"

"Nay. They have long been allies."

"Then we ride the same path."

"I go by a verra twisted route. It may slow your pace."

"Nay, for I too go by a verra twisted, hidden route. As ye can see, I ride alone. I seek to avoid trouble during my travel."

She almost smiled. "Then I should leave me far behind, kind sir, for there is a great deal of trouble following me about."

Bethia was not sure why she was being so elusive, so reluctant to accept Eric's aid. It was true that she did not know the Murrays of Donncoill, but she suspected that was because there was not much to hear, at least not much that was bad. Tales of evil done by men traveled far and wide, but, if people behaved themselves, only their most heroic deeds were spoken of. The MacMillans were his kinsmen and they were close, long-standing allies of her own family. He certainly had the look of a MacMillan. He was going in the same direction she was. He had just saved her from what could have been a deadly confrontation, and although he had taken away her dagger, he had still made no threatening move toward her or James. Good sense demanded that she ask his protection.

"Come, lass, put aside your pride and accept an honest offer of help," Eric said.

" 'Tis nay just pride which makes me hesitate, sir," she replied.

"Have I not just shown ye that I mean ye no harm?"

"Aye, but 'tis nay just myself that I must consider in any and all decisions I make."

"I would ne'er hurt a bairn."

There was a taut note in his lovely voice and Bethia almost smiled. She had just insulted him. Oddly, that eased a great many of her suspicions and doubts. Although she still felt uneasy, she began to think it was not because she did not trust him to help her, but because he was such a dangerously attractive man. She had never been as unsettled by a man as she was by him. That danger would be her own to fight or succumb to, however, and she had to think only of James now.

"Then, sir knight, I ask ye, upon your honor, to get me and the bairn safely to Dunnbea," she finally said and inwardly shivered with a delight that almost frightened her when he smiled at her.

"A promise easily made, m'lady."

"Easily made, mayhap, but ye may find it nay so easy to fulfill."

"I am nay without skill with the sword I carry."

"I am sure, but there may be many a mon trying to stop me and this lad from reaching my family. Sir, ye have just stepped into the midst of a deadly fight. On one side, at this moment, stands just me and this wee bairn—and now you. On the other is a black-hearted mon named William and his two grasping sons, Iain and Angus, and all the men they can force and pay to chase us."

"Why?"

"Because William seeks to steal what is rightfully this child's. He has already set his wife in her grave, then murdered my sister and her husband. But the day before I left in the dead of night, he tried to murder me and the bairn with poison. I believe that is his preferred weapon. The mon seeks to hold Dunncraig, to claim through marriage and death what was ne'er his."

Eric kept his expression calm, but inside he was heartily cursing. He bore little similarity to the men Bethia was fleeing, but instinct told him that she would not like his reasons for traveling to the MacMillans. He decided to wait to tell her the truth. She barely trusted him now and he wanted to prove himself to her a little more before he told her something that might well smother that newborn trust.

"Ye have found yourself a mon with some knowledge of such flights. My brother and his wife fled across France, running from men who wished to hang her for a murder she had not commited. Mayhap I can finally put to use some of the tales he told me."

"Why is your brother nay traveling with you to meet your mother's kinsmen?"

"Because his mother isnae mine." He almost laughed at the confused frown that darkened her pretty face, swiftly followed by a look of intense curiousity. "Another long tale. Best we save such things for later. 'Tis a long journey ahead of us."

"I ken it. And I suppose we had best get started."

Bethia hesitated when Eric held out his arms for the boy; then, her heart pounding with unease, she placed James in his arms. It was the first time James had been out of her grasp since his mother had died and she fought the urge to immediately snatch him back. If she was going to trust the man with their lives, she certainly ought to be able to trust him to hold the child for a few moments.

Eric watched as she collected up her things, pausing to smooth her hands over the little silver cup before putting it into her bag. "I think the mon asked a good question, lass," he said quietly. "Were those things really worth risking your life or the bairn's?"

"Nay," she answered easily as she stood up. "At least, that is what my mind screamed, but, I fear, at that moment, my heart spoke even louder. The cup was my sister's wedding cup. She was my womb sister and she has been dead barely a week. I couldnae let that mon take it or any of the other things I managed to cling to and slip out of Dunncraig. It was foolish. I ken it."

"Aye, but eminently understandable." He took her by the arm and led her over to his horse. "Your grief is too new."

"I am nay sure it will e'er grow old," Bethia whispered.

"No two people can be closer than those who have shared a mother's womb. But life has a way of dulling the sharp edge of such loss. Ye ne'er forget, but ye learn to accept." He handed her James and attached her small bag to his saddle as she settled the little boy in the blanket sling she wore. "And she left ye the best of memories of herself."

"True enough," she said as she briefly combed her fingers through James's curls. She frowned at the horse. "Are we all to ride him then?"

"Aye," Eric replied as he lifted her up into the saddle.

"The weight of a big mon and two others may be more than he can bear." Bethia frowned at Eric when he laughed and mounted behind her. "What amuses you?"

"Ye calling me a big mon."

"Weel, ye are."

"Mayhap to a wee lass like ye, but—trust me in this, lass—
I am nay so big."

"And I am nay that wee," she grumbled, then inwardly
cursed when she heard him chuckle.

"Ye were the second born, werenae ye?" he asked as he
nudged the horse into a slow amble.

"Aye, and aye, I was verra small and sickly, but I grew
bigger and stronger."

"Oh, aye, ye are a veritable mountain of a woman."

"Ye make jest of me."

"Mayhap, but meaning no unkindness. Believe me, little
Bethia, when ye see me next to another mon, ye will ken that
I understand exactly how ye feel. 'Tisnae easy to be the runt."

"I am nay a runt," she snapped, then pressed her lips together
when Eric just chuckled.

Bethia knew that was exactly what she was, but she did not
like to hear it said. Neither did she believe Sir Eric ever felt
small. He certainly did not feel small to her as he wrapped his
long arms around her and took up his reins. She felt completely
enfolded within his embrace. In fact, she felt smaller and more
uncertain than she had in a very long time.

Slowly, she became aware of the fact that he was nuzzling
her hair. She tensed and tried to pull away from his long body,
but his arms allowed her little room to move. Although she
did not fear for her life or James's, she no longer felt completely
safe.

"Sir, what are ye doing?" she demanded, and inwardly
grimaced over the soft unsteadiness of her voice.

"Smelling your hair," he replied.

Her eyes widened, for she had not expected such honesty.
"Weel, ye may cease such play this verra moment."

"Kind of ye to give me leave to cease, but I am nay sure I
am of a mind to."

Eric knew he was acting outrageously, but he felt an urge to see how far he could push her. He wanted her, faster and more fiercely than he had ever wanted a woman, and he was curious to see if there was any response in her, no matter how small. Bethia fascinated him and made him hungry, and he wanted her to suffer likewise.

"Weel, ye can just try to put your mind to it now."

"If I must."

"Aye, ye must."

"I but flatter ye, lass."

"Weel, I have more important things to think about now than some mon's flatteries. I think I shall have to make ye give me another promise."

"And what would that be?"

"That ye will treat me with the respect due a lady of my birth."

"Oh, aye, that I can do."

Bethia tried to turn her head to look at him, but could not get a clear view of his expression. She had a feeling that she should have worded her request more carefully, that the man had not promised what she had wanted him to. She stared ahead of them and tried not to feel anything as he held her close in his arms.

It was going to be a struggle to ignore his allure, she realized. Something deep inside of her responded hotly and immediately to his touch, his smile, even his voice, and she suspected it was a very heedless part of her. Sir Eric Murray might have arrived just in time to save her and might well keep his promise to get her and James safely to Dunnbea, but Bethia began to think that was all he had and would promise. She could not change her mind now, she thought as she looked down at a dozing James, but she began to think she had just traded a deadly danger for a far more subtle one.

Chapter Three

"Sit, lass," Eric ordered in a soft voice as he urged her toward the fire he had just built. "Tend to the wee lad and I will do all the rest."

"I should help," Bethia murmured even as she sat down.

"Ye are. I can tend the horse, make camp, and prepare us a poor but hearty meal. I cannae tend to a bairn."

She nodded as he set her bag down next to her. Exhaustion weighted her movements as she spread out the changing rags she had washed earlier in the day, hoping they would finish drying by the fire. Bethia did not understand the deep weariness that had infected her. She had not been walking all that long before Sir Eric had found her, barely two nights and most of two days. Then she had enjoyed the ease of riding for the rest of the day yet she felt as if she had not slept for weeks. As she changed James's rags and spread out his bedding, she tried to shrug off her weariness, at least enough so that she could stay awake through the meal and ask Sir Eric Murray a few hard questions.

What troubled her the most was how she seemed to have relaxed the moment she had accepted Sir Eric's kind offer of aid. It was shortly after she had climbed up on his horse that her deep weariness had begun to creep over her, swamping the rigid wariness she had maintained since her arrival at Dunn-craig. Sir Eric had wrapped those slim, strong arms around her and she had ceased to fight. Since she did not really know the man, Bethia felt that was dangerous. His beauty and his deep, rich voice might make her innards flutter, but she could not allow that mindless warmth to burn away all of her good sense and caution. If it was only her own life at risk, Bethia knew she would allow herself to be lulled by his beauty and apparent kindness, but she could never forget that there was James to consider in all she did.

As Eric sat down by the fire and began to prepare some porridge, he caught Bethia covertly eyeing him and inwardly sighed. She had been quiet, weariness stilling her suspicions, but she had obviously shaken some of that exhaustion aside. There would be questions now, ones he would have to answer cautiously. He knew he had every right to go after his inheri-tance just as he knew she would treat such a quest with suspi-cion. It was not fair, but it was completely understandable. Eric found it easy enough to set aside any sense of insult over her wariness. He hoped he could set aside any dangerous questions she might ask with as much ease.

He needed to win her trust before he told her the whole truth. Saving her from those thieves was not really enough. Somehow he had to make her believe he was not an enemy and never would be. Even then he knew the truth could seriously damage his cause, but if she discovered the truth now, he would probably have to make her a prisoner to keep her with him.

In the hope of diverting the questions he could sense were trembling on her tongue, he asked, "Are ye certain the mon William is a murderer?" He dished her out some of the thick oatmeal into a rough wooden bowl.

Bethia frowned as she accepted the food. "I am verra sure, Sir Eric." She blew gently on a small spoonful of the porridge and then fed it to James. "Do ye think me some faint-of-heart lass who sees evil lurking around every corner?"

"Nay, but murder is a hard crime to hang about a mon's neck. Aye, it can e'en set a noose there."

"I ken it. Sir William and his loathsome spawn deserve to be hanged from the highest tree."

"If they have done as ye have claimed, they do."

" 'Tis nay so strange for a mon to kill to gain riches."

"True. Greed is a common motive for crimes as is vengence or passion. But ye dinnae speak of throats cut in the dark of night or a dagger slipped between a mon's ribs. Such acts are easily seen as murder and can be loudly decried." He sighed and shook his head slightly. "Ye speak on poison—a black, subtle method of murder. Verra hard to prove. There are a few poisons which leave a mark, quickly seen, and weel kenned. Others work in a way that could easily be claimed as naught but a malady of some sort."

Bethia reluctantly nodded. " 'Tis why I now run to my family, race to seek their protection and aid. Weel, that and the fact that the people of Dunncraig are so cowed that none there would help me. Nay, not e'en if William slaughtered us all afore their verra eyes."

"Ye implied that your sister and her husband had but recently died, yet the keep is already beneath William's boot?"

"Oh, aye." Bethia took a long drink from the wineskin and then handed it to him. "I fear my sister Sorcha and her husband Robert were, weel, nay too wise. Mayhap they were too newly wed, then caught up in the joy of the bairn." She shrugged. "Whate'er it was, something kept them blissfully unaware of how their lands were being bled dry, their keep left to crumble, and the loyalty of their people stolen away. Fear grips the people of Dunncraig and all could see that Robert and Sorcha were too weak to free them from William's ever tightening

grip. I didnae ken Robert that weel. Mayhap he was cowed by
William as completely as all of the others were.''

"Harsh words.''

"Verra,'' she agreed in a near whisper, sadness weighting
her words. ''At times I hate them both for the trust and weakness
that allowed them to be murdered, for leaving me no tale of
martyred bravery and honor to console myself with.''

Eric moved to sit by her side and put his arm around her
slim shoulders. It pleased him when her stiffness at his touch
rapidly faded. Some of her initial wariness had already begun
to fade. She needed help and was wise enough to know it. That
could only work in his favor.

"That would indeed be finer,'' he agreed. ''Howbeit, for
each death met in glory, there are many that are not. Ye must
forgive them their blindness and their weaknesses. In the end
they acted, did they not? They sent for ye to come to the aid
of their son.''

"Aye, I believe they did. I didnae understand at first. 'Twas
nay until I saw them buried that I realized Sorcha's message
to me had held a warning. She bade me come to watch o'er
her son. An odd choice of words I thought until I saw how
matters stood at Dunncraig. I but wish she had lived long
enough to tell me what she may have seen or heard, to tell me
what finally warned her. It may have led to some proof of
William's guilt.''

"No one else spoke out against him and his sons?''

"Nay. I told you, they are all cowed, fearful for their verra
lives.''

"Who can blame them if they too ken that William has killed
their laird and his wife? After all, if he can strike those so high
with apparent impunity, he would find no qualms about striking
the common ones down in an instant.''

"Aye, there is a sad truth in that.'' She sighed. ''And the
only one they see who could take the laird's place is a barely

weaned bairn. And I suppose they could nay be sure that I could gather any strength of arms to stand against the mon.''

"Can ye?"

"Aye. My kinsmen will heed what I say and act swiftly to protect this wee lad. Sorcha was much loved. Many will be outraged by her murder. Our allies will most certainly join with us.''

"Allies like the MacMillans?"

"Aye." She struggled to smother a huge yawn. "Many will be eager to save Sorcha's son's birthright." She finished her food, then gave James a small drink of her rapidly waning supply of goat's milk. "When Sorcha was taken to court, it was immediately clear that she could have made a marriage that would have allied our clan with some of the most powerful ones in all of Scotland, but she wanted Robert, a distant cousin of ours. Nevertheless, she made many friends and her beauty and sweet charm aided my parents in making many new friends and allies. There is no judging how many may be eager to help us avenge her death. She won so verra many hearts." James curled up on his blanket, sleepily sucking on his fingers, and she began to rub his back.

"Ye must have won some hearts as weel," Eric murmured, unable to resist the temptation to tangle his fingers in the heavy blanket of her hair. She had left it unbraided and it still hung to her slim hips in rippled waves, begging to be stroked.

"Oh, I didnae go to court."

"Nay? Ye were ill?"

Bethia tucked a small blanket around a now sleeping James. "Nay. 'Twas decided all monies should go to making sure Sorcha shined at court, e'en though all said she would shine e'en if she was dressed in rags. Sorcha was also able to win hearts with but a smile." She sent Eric a brief, shy smile. "I fear I have a sharp tongue, dinnae hold a firm rein on my temper, and dinnae trust as easily as Sorcha did. Sorcha saw only good in everyone."

Eric did not like the portrait painted by Bethia's words. Sorcha had clearly been the favored child, seen as the better of the pair. Even Bethia spoke of the woman as if she had been but one smile away from sainthood. Bethia had obviously been set in her sister's shadow and left there. Eric suspected Bethia had not only had to fight to survive being the smallest at birth, but probably struggled continuously just to be noticed once in a while.

" 'Tis wondrous when someone can remain so pure of heart, their eyes unclouded by suspicion, but walking in that blessed state didnae keep her alive, did it?" he said.

There was a hint of anger in his voice, a shade of sarcasm, and Bethia frowned at him. "Nay, it didnae. Robert was much akin to Sorcha. Bonny, trusting, and charming. 'Tis a pity such sweetness and beauty seems unable to survive long in this harsh world."

"There is truth in that, but a wee pinch of wariness is what keeps a person alive. If one is going to skip through life bonny, charming, and trusting, one best have a solid, wary, dour mon always at one's back."

She smiled faintly. "Aye. One of us should have considered that," she said, her sadness quickly returning. "We sent two sweet bairns into a wolf's lair without a shield." She lightly touched the sleeping James's bright curls. "This bairn will be watched. He will also be taught how to watch his own back. The lad has the same sweet nature his parents had, and whilst I dinnae wish to destroy that, I do mean to temper it."

"Ye will do that? I should think that your parents would take on the care of the lad."

"Oh, my parents will love him, for he is a part of Sorcha, but"—she grimaced, feeling a little guilty for what she was about to say—"they loved and raised Sorcha too, didnae they? They fall too easily beneath the allure of that sweetness and beauty and feel all others do as weel. Caution, wariness, the ability to look closely beneath a smile were ne'er taught. Thus they raised Sorcha and thus they will try to raise James. Nay, 'twill be my sad lot to tell this bairn that, sometimes, that smile hides a lie, or, worse, a dagger aimed at your heart. Mayhap Bowen will help.''

Bethia felt Eric's fingers clench briefly in her hair, and she eyed him curiously. It was, perhaps, a good time to tell him to stop caressing her hair, but the words would not come. The way he combed his long fingers through her hair, caressed it, toyed with it, occasionally even lifted it to his face to smell or kiss it was, oddly, both comforting and exhilarating. Bethia ruefully admitted to herself that she did not want him to stop. It was a little wanton of her to let a man she had only just met touch her in an almost seductive way, but, she sighed, he was such a beautiful man. If she let it go no farther, what harm could there be?

"Who is Bowen?'' Eric asked, hoping he sounded only mildly interested, that none of the startling surge of jealousy he had felt was revealed in his voice. He did not really understand why it troubled him so to hear her speak another man's name with something that sounded suspiciously like affection.

"One of the men-at-arms at Dunnbea. He and Peter were mercenaries hired by my father near to ten years ago when we were suffering mightily from raids by the English and an old enemy. They stayed when the worst of the fighting had passed, for they had proven their worth many times over. Both men were verra patient with me, for I often trailed along behind them like a faithful puppy. Me and my cousin Wallace, who is my uncle's bastard and but two years older than me. Bowen and Peter taught Wallace and me a great deal. The four of us were verra close, but when my father realized that there would be no more children, he claimed Wallace as his heir and I didnae get to play with the lad much after that. He was too busy being trained to be a knight and a laird.''

"As ye were being trained to be a lady, 'twas most like for the best.''

Bethia grimaced slightly, realized she was leaning against Sir Eric, sleepy and at ease in his arms, then decided she was too weary to concern herself with the lapse. "I fear I didnae do weel in that training. Mayhap I was left too long with the men, allowed to romp free like some lad. Mayhap 'twas just that Sorcha was so graceful, so quick to learn all the arts of a lady, that none saw the need to force me to continually stumble and fail."

Eric was sure there had been good in Sorcha, but he thought that if he heard much more about her wondrous perfection he would gag. He was not sure why he was so angered by the image of rejection Bethia so blithely painted, but he accepted the feeling. It was possible that he felt such a swift, strong bond with her because he too had been rejected. The love and acceptance of the Murrays had certainly softened the blow, but the sting of such disregard by one's own blood could never be fully erased. He wondered if Bethia was truly blind to how poorly she had been treated or if she simply fought to ignore it because it hurt.

Or even worse, he wondered with a sudden frown, she might believe it was deserved. Bethia might truly believe that her twin had been so much more perfect than herself. Such a lack of confidence, fed and nurtured over the years, could make seducing the woman very difficult indeed and Eric knew he would be doing his utmost to seduce her. His hunger for her was strong and getting stronger. He was just no longer sure how he would do it. Flatteries would certainly be scoffed at. Then he looked at the way she rested against him, clearly enjoying the way he stroked her hair. Perhaps flatteries would not be needed.

A flicker of guilt rippled through him, but he ruthlessly pushed it aside. It was wrong to seduce a wellborn maiden, but he knew arguing such things as honor and respect would not stop him. He simply decided that, if she succumbed, if she relinquished her maidenhead to him, he would marry her. His brothers would think him mad to decide such a thing when he had known the lass for mere hours, but to his surprise, he felt no qualms at all about his decision. Perhaps, he mused with a faint smile, the instinct to mate had finally been roused in him.

Eric became aware of how heavily Bethia was leaning against him and, relutanctly, but gently, pushed her into a seated position. "I think ye need to bed down now, lass."

Bethia blinked, rubbed her hands over her face, and realized she was more asleep than awake. "Aye, I am weary." She staggered to her feet. "I will just slip away for a moment."

Even as she stumbled into the shadows, Eric hastily moved to the far edge of their camp and relieved himself. As quickly as he could, he laid out their bedding side by side. He sat down and was removing his boots when she returned.

Barely a foot from the fire, Bethia stopped abruptly and stared at the bedding. It took her sleep-dulled mind a full minute to accept what she saw. Her bedding was spread out next to Eric's. She glared at him.

"Now, lass, why are ye looking at me as if I am some adder poised to strike?" Eric asked, lying down, tugging a blanket over himself, and crossing his arms beneath his head.

"Mayhap because ye look much akin to one at the moment," she replied. "I will sleep on the other side of the fire."

"A fire already so small it gives off verra little warmth."

"We have blankets to give us warmth."

"Bethia, ye need not fear me."

"Nay? Are ye sure ye arenae thinking to, weel, convince me to thank ye for your aid in some way?"

"One thing I learned ere I was e'en old enough to care was that a mon always heeds a lass's nay." He patted the bedding next to his. "Come and rest. Ye can wrap yourself tight in your own blanket. Use it as a shield, if ye wish. 'Twill still be warmer for the both of us if we sleep side by side. Aye, and set the bairn atween us. He will also be in need of some warmth."

There was no arguing that. James would not only be warm nestled between them, but protected. Although Bethia was nervous about sleeping so close to Sir Eric, she realized that she was not truly frightened by the idea. She could not make herself see him as a threat. After setting James in the middle of the bedding, she sat down and removed her boots, praying all the while that the man's bonny face was not dulling her wit.

After a great deal of fidgeting and arranging, Bethia settled down on her side facing the fire, then softly cursed. She should be facing James, her arm lightly encircling the child so that she would be warned if he tried to leave the bed. After some more fidgeting, she got herself turned round and curled protectively around the sleeping child. Despite her best efforts to close her eyes and ignore the man lying so close to her, she looked at Eric, not surprised to find him grinning at her.

"Settled now, are ye?" he asked, idly reaching out to brush a stray lock of hair off her face and ignoring her frown.

"Aye. Ye cannae fault me for being cautious," she said, cursing the defensive tone of her voice. She had every right to wonder if he played some game with her.

"Weel, ye may ease your fears. The bairn separates us."

"He isnae much of a barrier."

"Nay, but I swear to you, Bethia, the word nay is all the shield ye will e'er need with me."

"Good, for if ye think I will be giving ye any favors just because ye are helping me, ye had best think again."

"I dinnae need to think on it e'en the once. Nay, I dinnae want ye to fall into my arms because ye feel gratitude."

"Then we are in agreement."

She tensed when Eric raised himself up on one elbow and leaned over the baby. His face was suddenly much too close to hers. Bethia looked at his mouth, knowing it was a mistake, but unable to stop herself.

"Aye," he said softly. "When ye come to me 'twill be because ye wish to share my passion. The last thing I wish in my bed is gratitude. Weel, mayhap a wee bit after I pleasure ye wouldnae be amiss.''

Bethia gasped softly, but was not sure if it was only because his words shocked her. Just hearing the word *passion* on his lips set her heart racing. Her surprise kept her from jerking away when he touched his lips to hers. Then the feel of his warm mouth against hers was enough to hold her in place as he gave her a short, seductive kiss. Even as she regained enough of her wits to untangle her arm from her blanket, fully intending to shove him away from her, he lay back down on his side of their rough bed.

"What did ye do that for?" she whispered, clenching her hand into a tight fist to stop herself from touching her lips in wonder over how such a gentle caress could make the blood pound so hotly through her veins.

"I was but saying good sleep to you."

"Weel, next time try just saying the words."

" 'Tis nay as much fun."

Bethia pressed her lips together, refusing to say anything else. It would only give the impossible man another chance to speak and further unsettle her. She closed her eyes. Looking at him was equally as dangerous.

The words he had said, however, were not so easily ignored. He wanted her to share his passion. She was not fool enough to think that passion was just for her, but that realization was not enough to cool her sudden interest. There was a far too large part of her that was intrigued, indeed, strongly tempted, to discover what Eric's passion was like. Bethia suspected that a man as beautiful as Sir Eric Murray had a great deal of experience in the art of passion and was probably very skilled.

Such curiosity, she decided, was not truly bad. What worried her was the strong possibility that the feelings stirring within her went far deeper than mere curiosity. Bethia lightly touched her lips, still feeling the warmth of his. His kiss had not been very passionate—a slight pressure of his mouth, a brief tease of his tongue—but it had sent sharp, hot feelings spilling throughout her body. Sir Eric was indeed a threat to her, but she could not leave his side for she needed his help too much. Bethia could only pray that he would not betray her to her enemies and that she would have the strength not to betray herself in his arms.

Chapter Four

Bethia knew glaring at the river they had to cross would not make the rough water flow slower or run lower, but she did it anyway. For three long days they had slunk over the countryside, William and his sons hot on their heels. A few times they had even seen their enemies and nearly been seen themselves. Bethia heartily wished she could raise an army right now, ride out to confront William, and cut him and his loathsome sons down. The fear and the constant need to hide were driving her mad. She desperately wanted to feel safe again, wanted James protected and warm.

A quick glance at the man standing next to her made her silently curse. Sir Eric might be doing a fine job of keeping her and James alive, but he was also driving her mad. He said good night each night with a kiss and woke her each morning with another. The night kisses were almost chaste, but the morning ones were pure, heated seduction. Fool that she was, she never found the strength to refuse either. As they rode, he belabored her heart and mind with caresses and words that stirred her passions. She felt tense, irritable, caught between wanting to beat Eric senseless and hurl him to the ground to force him to finish what he had started. The man was indeed pushing her into madness.

"I am nay sure we can cross safely here," she said, forcing her thoughts to the important problem of eluding the men hunting her and James.

"It can be done." Eric idly stroked his horse's neck. "I would prefer to stay upon dry ground, but that isnae possible. And William is so close at our backs that we havenae the time to wander about looking for a better trail."

"And if there is one, he or some of his men probably crouch there."

"Aye. Ye can swim, I pray."

"Oh, aye, verra weel. Bowen taught me." She smiled faintly. "In truth, he and Peter decided to teach Wallace, and I demanded that they teach me as weel. Bowen finally agreed, saying that since I was such a sharp-tongued wench 'twas certain some mon would try to drown me one day."

Eric laughed softly yet felt a twinge of sadness as well. Whenever Bethia spoke of her childhood, she spoke of Bowen, Peter, and Wallace. Her father and mother were rarely mentioned unless she spoke of Sorcha. It was good that Bethia had found someone to care for her, yet that should have been her parents. Every tale Bethia told revealed that she had been treated much as her cousin Wallace had for a while, as some bastard child they were forced to take in. Even worse, in his mind, was the growing evidence that the wondrous Sorcha never did anything to change matters. The situation was beyond his comprehension.

"Weel, 'tis best to get this done." Eric made sure James's sling was firmly secured high on the saddle.

"Would it nay be better if one of us carried the lad?" Bethia asked as she hitched up her skirts to free her legs.

"We will need all of our limbs free to fight the strength of the water. And Connor is far taller than either of us. Set here as he is gives the lad a better chance of keeping his wee head clear of the water.''

"And Connor will head straight for the opposite bank?''

"Aye, and then wait there. He has proven himself a strong swimmer, unafraid of water, time and time again.'' He held his hand over the horse's flank. "Ready?''

"Aye.''

Bethia fought back a sudden surge of panic when Eric slapped the horse and the animal plunged into the water. James quickly began screaming as the cold water penetrated his sling and splashed his face. Bethia took a deep breath and dove into the water, Eric swiftly doing the same. The cold made her curse, but she gritted her teeth and began to swim, her gaze fixed upon the horse. The water was rough and littered with debris, the current strong, but the horse never faltered and quickly reached the other side. Connor shook the water from his coat and caused James to scream all the louder. Bethia closed her ears to the child's distress and concentrated on getting to the other side. By the time she reached the bank, she was shivering from the cold and the strain.

Sitting down, oblivious to the mud, she looked for Eric. A scream of warning and terror erupted from her throat when she saw a tree branch whirling his way. She leapt to her feet even as it slammed into him. For one heart-stopping moment, he disappeared beneath the water. Even as his head reappeared, Bethia saw his arm curled around the branch. He did not start swimming again, however, and she realized he was now simply fighting to keep from drowning. Unless he regained his strength, that was already a lost battle.

Grabbing the horse's reins, Bethia hurried along the bank, keeping Eric constantly in view and frantically trying to think of some way to help him. A few yards down the river the wood he clung to became tangled in a small dam formed by other debris. Eric managed to pull himself a little farther out of the water, but Bethia could see how weak he was. He could even have been hurt when the branch struck him. The small dam shifted and bounced in the current and she knew it would not hold for much longer.

Bethia stripped off her soaking clothes until she wore only her thin linen shift. The weight of her clothes had wearied her during her first swim and she dared not risk letting them sap the rest of her strength now. She grabbed the rope Eric kept looped on his saddle, tied one end of it to the saddle horn, and then draped the rest of it over her shoulder. As she took a deep breath and prayed for strength, she leapt into the icy water and swam toward Eric.

"Lass, ye fool, what are ye about? Go back," Eric demanded when she reached his side, but the hoarse faintness of his voice stole most of the power from his command.

"I intend to save your bonny hide," she said as she tied the rope around his waist.

"I doubt I look verra bonny at the moment."

She noticed how pale he was. His lips were tinged blue with cold, and blood from a graze on his forehead was smearing the side of his face. "Nay, ye do look a wee bit pitiful. Now how do I get your horse to pull us out of this mess?"

"Just tell him to pull. He will ken what to do."

After slipping her arm around his chest, Bethia yelled the command at Connor. It took one more bellow before the horse began to move. Bethia quickly turned onto her back, her body submerged beneath Eric's. She fought to keep both of their heads above water and to ward off the trecherous debris swirling around them as they were pulled toward the shore.

Once on the bank, Bethia let the horse drag Eric onto the shore and then removed the rope. As Eric lay gasping for air and shivering, Bethia took a few moments to rub herself dry, dress, and then change James. Collecting what she felt was needed to attend Eric, she hurried back to his side.

Despite Eric's dire need to be dry and warm, Bethia found

it disturbing to undress the man. He was certainly not looking his best, the cold stealing all of the life from his skin, but he was still fine enough to make her hands tremble slightly as she rubbed him dry. His chest was broad and smooth. A thin line of fair hair started at his navel, dove down to his groin, where it blossomed slightly, then fanned out to lightly coat his long, muscular legs. It annoyed her a little that he even had nice-looking feet.

"Considering that I am frozen to the verra marrow of my bones, I doubt I look verra monly just now," Eric said with a rueful glance at his groin, the cold he still felt making his voice tremble.

Bethia gave him a slightly disgusted look as she started to tug on his dry clothes, then drawled, "Why, nay, sir, ye look as bonny as James. Ne'er kenned a mon could be so cute down there." Despite her worry for his health, she was almost able to laugh at his shock.

Eric started to laugh, then winced and clutched at his aching head. "God, woman. Like wee James? Cute? God's bones," he said and laughed again, but with a little more care this time. "How ye wound me."

"I believe your vanity will survive." After wrapping him in a blanket, she leaned over him to more closely examine the wound on his head. " 'Tisnae deep enough to require any stitches," she murmured as she wiped the blood off his face with a scrap of cloth.

"Some hint of mercy at last."

Bethia just smiled faintly as she put some salve on his wound, then wrapped a bandage around his head. He had ceased to shiver so bad that his teeth clicked, but he still looked pale. She knew he was very weak too, for although he had tried to help her get him dressed he had been able to do little more than tug down on his jupon a little.

"Dinnae look so fretful, lass," he said as he slowly forced his aching body into a seated position.

"Are ye sure ye can move?" When he stood up and swayed, she quickly put her arm around him to steady him.

"Enough to get on my horse. We cannae sit here, lass. Those dogs chasing you and the bairn were verra close the last we looked. 'Tis why we crossed here, if ye recall."

"Aye, but ye are verra unsteady, Eric."

"Just get me in the saddle. I will sit behind you and hang on whilst ye take up the reins."

"Will Connor let me?" Bethia asked, eyeing the huge horse warily as she helped Eric stumble over to the animal.

"Aye, since I will also be on his back."

It was not going to be easy to get Eric there, she mused, as they reached the horse. "Just let me gather the bairn and what little I have unpacked," she said.

"Do that. I will just slump here against old Connor and prepare myself to be hoisted up into the saddle."

There was something very similar to petulance tainting his rich voice and Bethia had to bite back a smile. Eric clearly did not like to be dependent upon a small woman—probably on any woman. She quickly picked up the few things scattered around on the bank, including their very wet clothes, then settled James in a dry blanket sling across her chest.

It was not easy getting Eric up into the saddle, but, after some pushing, it was done. Bethia took a deep breath to steady herself, then mounted in front of him and took up the reins. Although she considered herself a good rider, she had never handled a warhorse before, nor even any horse as big as Connor, and she was not sure how well she would do. The moment Eric wrapped his arms around her waist and was resting steadily against her back, she nudged Connor into a slow amble.

"We could go a wee bit faster, lass," Eric said, a little concerned over how slowly the warmth was returning to his body.

"Nay, not until I get to ken this beastie a wee bit better," she replied. "Do ye think William is nigh?"

"He would have to be in France ere I ceased to think that he was too nigh. Nay, e'en that would be too close."

"Aye. I wouldst prefer him and his loathsome sons dead and buried."

Eric smiled weakly against her wet hair. "Ye always call them his *loathsome sons.*"

"All ye would have to do is see them once and ye would understand. They are huge, dark, hulking beasties with cold eyes that clearly reveal their bone-deep meanness. William feels that he has a sound reason for murdering people. His sons dinnae want or need one." Bethia sighed and shook her head. "Dunncraig would probably be knee-deep in bodies, save that William holds a tight rein on that evil pair. They do, however, abuse the lasses within their reach with impunity. I saw that soon after my arrival. Aye, and did so despite the weight of my grief. It did puzzle me some that Sorcha ne'er did."

It was getting harder not to offer a rather sharp, unflattering opinion upon Sorcha. Eric suspected the woman would never have seen the plight of the women on her lands simply because she probably never really noticed who did all of the work. If the woman was unable to see the sad plight of her own twin for years, she would certainly never notice some poor maid's distress. That was more truth than Bethia would want to deal with now, however. Eric was not sure she would ever wish to do so.

Holding his tongue concerning Sorcha was going to prove difficult if he and Bethia got married. Eric was forming a picture of the woman as vain, completely self-concerned and selfish, and probably irresponsible. It was possible for the woman to have been all of those things and worse, yet still appear sweet and charming. It was becoming clear that no one had ever denied Sorcha anything. Sorcha Drummond had been able to trip through her, admittedly, sadly shortened life happy and smiling disarmingly, for people had scurried to remove all obstacles from her path or she had simply ignored them. Someday Bethia was going to relate one tale too many revealing her sister's charming disregard for all around her and Eric feared he might feel compelled to tell her a few cold truths. Perhaps, he thought with a wry smile, the constant battle to allow Bethia her delusions about her twin would be the penance he had to pay for seducing her.

Too exhausted to keep talking, Eric clung to Bethia and tried to regain his strength. His head throbbed and his body ached all over from the battering it had taken in the river. There was a painful knot too low in his throat to clear away and his lungs ached with every breath he took. Eric feared he had not cleared all of the water from his body.

A few more miles passed before Eric realized that he needed to stop moving. He was not going to get the rest he needed to recoup his strength sitting on the back of a horse. What he needed was a bed, no matter how rough, perhaps a little food, and a long rest. It was not safe to pause for too long while Robert Drummond's murderous kinsmen dogged their trail, but without a good rest, Eric knew he would collapse, and could easily become too ill to move for days. They were close to Dunnbea, but not close enough. That was true of the little village he had been riding toward as well. Even if he could cling to health and conciousness until the village, the chill damp in the air told him that a storm was brewing. Another soaking could well finish him.

"Bethia, we must halt soon," he forced himself to say, ruthlessly beating down that prideful part of him that longed to keep on going.

"Ye wish to eat or"—she blushed—"see to some other need?"

"Nay. It shames me to admit it, but I need to rest. I need to lie down near a warm fire."

" 'Twould be best if ye did that. I just wasnae sure ye would heed me if I said so."

"If ye had said so whilst we shivered on the riverbank, I

probably wouldnae. I was determined to shake off the battering that twice-cursed river gave me as easily as I shook the water from my hair, but that was prideful nonsense. My head throbs so fiercely it causes my stomach to churn and I dinnae think there is one part of me that doesnae ache.''

"It wouldnae hurt me and James to take a wee rest either," Bethia said, "and I dinnae say that just to soothe your poor wee pride."

"A mon's pride isnae a poor wee thing, lass."

She ignored that. "James and I may have made the crossing safely, but we were both soaked to the skin. Aye, and I am feeling a wee bit battered myself. And our clothes and a few other things could do with being dried out. So we will stop and rest as soon as I see a suitable place to do so."

"Try to find something that isnae too easy to see, yet will provide some shelter."

"Ye wish to be hidden."

"As hidden as possible, aye. A roof of some sort may be needed as weel, for I scent rain on the air."

Bethia nodded. "I can feel a storm moving o'er us too."

It was a good two hours later before Bethia found something. Set against a rocky hillside, nearly obscured by trees and the hill itself, was a surprisingly well-built shieling. The little shepherd's hut had walls of rock seamed with hard clay and what appeared to be an intact thatched roof. Either it was newly built or the builder was skilled at a lot more than herding his animals. Next to it was a shallow well in the hillside that would serve perfectly to stable the horse, even sheltering it from the storm now blackening the sky overhead.

Such a sturdy house was sorely needed, Bethia thought, as she fought the urge to nudge Connor into a gallop and race toward the shieling. In the last hour, Eric had begun to rest more heavily against her, obviously losing the battle to stay concious. What troubled her more, however, was how warm he felt against her, too warm if she was any judge. If she could get him bedded down by a fire so that he could rest easily, she might yet stave off the fever she feared was seeping through his body.

"Bethia?" Eric muttered when he felt the horse stop. He had to fight to overcome the grogginess that clouded his mind.

"I found us a place to rest," she said as she dismounted. "Just stay there until I can make sure 'tis empty and that the inside looks as good as the outside."

As he clung to the pommel of the saddle, Eric stared at the little hut. Bethia was right. It did look good, promising them a sturdy, dry shelter. In truth, it was finer than some of the crofter huts he had seen. Whoever had built it evidently did not want to suffer any discomfort while watching over his animals, might even have thought to make this a permanent home someday.

Still marveling that the tiny hut had a proper, heavy wooden door and not simply a heavily oiled drape of animal hide, Bethia stepped inside and murmured with delight and satisfaction. Greased leather tightly covered the two small windows and, along with the door, had insured that no animal had gotten inside to make a home. A sturdy, somewhat large wooden bed was set against one wall. Dirt had been scraped away to reveal the rock beneath giving the hut an uneven but surprisingly clean stone floor. What truly amazed her, however, was that, instead of a hearth set in the middle of the floor, there was a roughly built fireplace in the wall opposite the bed. A table and two stools were set to the side of it. The place was more of a home than a temporary shepherd's shelter.

After a quick but thorough check of the thick straw mattress on the bed to ensure that it was clean and free of vermin, Bethia set James down on the bed and hurried back to get Eric. " 'Tis a wondrous little place, Eric," she said as she helped him dismount.

"Do ye think someone still lives here?" he asked, silently cursing his weakness as he slumped against her.

Staggering a little beneath his weight, Bethia pulled him into the hut and urged him down to lie on the bed next to James. "Nay, but I am nay sure 'tis only a drover's hut."

"Mayhap a hunting lodge for whate'er laird rules o'er these lands?"

"Aye, or mayhap the drover who built it plans to live here once he is too old to be a drover."

"Or it could be some laird's wee love nest."

"It seems a lot of work to go to just to enjoy a tussle now and then."

Eric grinned briefly. "Some men like to do their tussling in comfort, lass. Or the lass he is tussling with is too weel kenned and an illicit tryst too dangerous."

"Weel, no matter. I dinnae expect anyone will come along, so we should be safe." She frowned at Sir Eric, who still looked dangerously pale. "Can ye keep an eye on James for just a wee while so that I might tend to a few chores?"

"Aye." Eric laughed softly when he looked at the child lying beside him gnawing on his plump little toes. "That much I can do."

Bethia hurried out to get their things. She then unsaddled Connor and secured the horse in the small stable. Once back inside the hut, she strung Eric's rope across the room and draped their wet clothes over it. She got a small fire going, fetched water to boil, and then hurried away again to search out as much dry wood as possible before the rains began. Seeing that both James and Eric were asleep, she took the small bow and arrows she always carried with her and slipped away to try to do some hunting.

The smell of roasting meat brought Eric out of his deep sleep. Then he recalled that he was supposed to be watching James and, slightly panicked, looked around. He breathed a sigh of relief when he saw the child sleeping peacefully in a rough blanket-lined box upon the floor by the bed. His gaze then rested on Bethia, who slowly turned the spit upon which the meat roasted.

"Rabbit?" he asked, wondering why his throat was so sore.

A soft gasp of surprise escaped Bethia and she turned to look at Eric. He had been sleeping soundly for the whole afternoon and most of the evening, but he still did not look that well. His voice was very hoarse. She prayed he was only suffering a mild chill from his near drowning, but did not say so.

"Aye, this wee valley fair teems with game," she said as she quickly moved to plump the pillow she had made from moss and soft grasses wrapped in one of her shifts so that he could lean against the crude headboard of the bed with a little comfort. "Whilst ye were merrily snoring away the day, I collected my wee hunting bow and arrows and went to fetch us some meat."

Eric touched the strange yet comfortable pillow set behind him. "Ye have some odd skills for a weelborn lass."

"As I have said, I spent a lot of time forcing my company upon Bowen, Peter, and Wallace."

"I doubt it troubled them verra much." He took a sip of the water she served him, savoring the way it soothed his sore throat.

"Nay, I think not, although they found much pleasure in complaining about it. Are ye hungry?" she asked, taking the cup back after he had finished the drink.

"Oh, aye. 'Twas the smell of food that roused me." He cautiously sat up on the edge of the bed, still a little groggy, but confident that he could do at least one thing without her aid. "Has the rain come?"

"Come, gone, and, I believe, thinking of pouring down on us again verra soon. Where are ye going?" Bethia asked when he slowly stood up.

"I may be as weak as a bairn, but I must insist on doing at

least this one thing without your help." He smiled faintly when, after scowling in thought for a moment, she gasped softly and blushed. "Exactly."

"I will get ye some food whilst ye are out," she mumbled, hurrying back to the fireplace.

Eric was sweating and shaking slightly when he returned, but fought to hide it. He did not understand why he was so weak. When he crawled back into bed and sagged back against the pillow, he began to fear that one day of rest was not going to be enough to cure what ailed him. A frowning Bethia set a small dish of rabbit and porridge in front of him and he realized that he was no longer very hungry.

"Eat as much as ye can," Bethia urged. "Ye cannae regain your strength on an empty belly."

"Nay. I just dinnae ken what ails me," he muttered and slowly began to eat.

"Ye were cracked o'er the head by a branch and nearly drowned in some verra cold water. 'Tisnae something ye can just walk away from. Ye may have also taken a chill."

"Ye havenae."

"I didnae get my head split open or nearly drown."

"True."

He finished the meal but Bethia could see that it had been a struggle as she took the bowl and handed him another cup of water. "Dinnae worry o'er it. There is plenty of food, water, and wood for the fire. We can set here until ye are hale again."

"Your enemies are searching for you."

"I ken it, but this place is weel hidden. There is also a wee path to the top of the hill this place crouches next to. I went up there and one can see all about for what looks to be miles. And when ye decided we needed to rest, I moved off the trail we followed by a wee bit."

"Ye got lost."

"A wee bit," she reluctantly admitted. "Rest, Eric. That is what will heal you."

When he just closed his eyes rather than argue further, Bethia felt uneasy. The man was certainly unwell and she was not terribly skilled as a healer. After securing the hut and banking the fire, Bethia slipped into bed beside him. It was scandalous to share the bed, and it held more temptation than she might be able to deal with, but there was no other choice. Between James and Eric all the blankets were taken. Bethia lightly touched Eric's face, felt the warmth there, and softly cursed. He was feverish, although he did not appear to have a very high fever. She prayed he would recover quickly and not just because she needed his protection. To her dismay, Bethia realized it would tear her heart out if he died.

Chapter Five

"Ah, I am still alive."

That deep, slightly hoarse voice right next to her ear startled Bethia awake so abruptly she had to scramble not to fall off the bed. Slowly she turned to face Eric and lightly placed her palm on his forehead. Cool. She breathed a sigh of relief.

" 'Twould appear so," she drawled, fighting to hide her elation over his recovery.

"How long have I forced us to linger here?"

"Four days. Ye developed a verra bad fever, Eric."

"Four days," he muttered, ran a hand through his hair, and grimaced in mild disgust over how dirty and tangled it was. "Have ye seen anything of your enemies?"

"Nay. In truth, I have seen no one. The rain would have washed away our trail and it has been raining for most of the time ye were ill. William would have had no trail to follow. And he likes his comforts far too much to be out riding o'er the countryside in this poor weather."

"Good. We should leave here." Eric tried to sit up, but

found even that meager action almost more than he could accomplish. Bethia needed to put only one hand on his chest to hold him in place.

"Nay. Ye couldnae get your strength back that first day we rested here because the fever had already gotten a grip on you. Now ye will rest and eat. A day, mayhap two, and then we shall be on our way."

" 'Tis dangerous to stay so long in one place."

" 'Tis even more dangerous to try to ride out when ye are so weak ye will fall off your horse ere we have left the valley."

"Ye do ken how to wound a mon's vanity."

She just smiled and slipped out of the bed. Keeping her attitude cool and aloof, she helped him see to his needs, ignoring his muttering. Once he was back in bed, she began to make him some porridge. At his insistence, she left him struggling to eat without help and saw to a now awake James.

It was late in the afternoon, after Eric had slept and remained clear of the fever, that Bethia conceded to his demands to have a wash. She left him with two buckets of heated water and, taking James with her, went to climb to the top of the hill. Setting the boy down and letting him play on the grass, she stared out at the surrounding countryside. To her relief, there was still no sign of any riders. For now they were still safe.

With a sigh, she sat down, idly accepting James's gifts of bugs, rocks, and most anything else he found on the ground. Now that she was out of Eric's sight, she allowed the deep relief she felt over his recovery to show. For four long days she had lived in fear that he would succumb to the fever. Now that the weight of that fear was lifted from her shoulders, she felt exhausted.

The time she had spent nursing him and praying for his life had forced her to face a hard truth. She loved the man, deeply and probably incurably. It frightened her. A man like Sir Eric

Murray was not for her. She was facing only heartbreak, but she knew there was no turning back now.

Time and time again, as she had sat by his bedside, bathing his brow, she had thought about his wish to have her share his passion. He gave her no words of love, no hint that there would ever be anything more than passion. Bethia had scolded herself again and again, repeated all the dire warnings given to young maids of good birth, but none of it made any difference. As she had sat there, terrified that he would die, she had cursed herself for not succumbing to his seduction.

"Fool," she muttered.

Now that he was alive, now that she knew how much she loved him, temptation was back in force. What she needed to do before he recovered fully was decide if she would give in to that temptation. It would ruin her for marriage, but then none had been offered or arranged for her. Shortly after Sorcha's marriage, Bethia had begun to think that her parents had no intention of seeing her wed, had never even given the matter a thought. She did almost all of the work around the demesne and they obviously did not want to give that up. It was a lonely life with little joy and no thanks. It was the life waiting for her when she returned to Dunnbea. Did she really want to go back to it without tasting the passion she and Eric could share at least once?

The answer that rang in her head was a very loud no, but she told herself not to be hasty. As she picked up James and headed back to the hut, she warned herself to be cautious. Eric Murray had actually told her little about himself. Each time she had begun to ask him questions, he had adeptly turned the conversation back to her or the trouble dogging her heels. It was time the man told her a few truths about himself and about why he was riding over the countryside all alone. Only when she had them could she make any sort of decision about what she may or may not take from him.

*   *   *

Bethia woke to the sharp demand of passion. She curled her arms around Eric's neck as he kissed her. He gently nipped her bottom lip, and although still unsure about such deep kisses, she opened her mouth to the invasion of his tongue. She shivered in his arms as he stroked the inside of her mouth with his tongue. His beautiful hands moved over her body in a caress just short of intimacy yet still creating a heady warmth.

For a few moments, Bethia simply took what he had to give, enjoying the heat flowing through her veins, the taste of him in her mouth, and the feel of his long, strong body pressed to hers. Beneath her growing passion lay a flicker of fear, but that only added to the excitement. Then he slid his hand up her rib cage and covered her breast. The sharp want that tore through her when he brushed his thumb over her already hardening nipple brought her to her senses concerning the danger she was courting. With a soft cry of alarm, she flung herself from his grasp and scrambled out of the bed.

The man's health was certainly improved, she thought dazedly as she stood by the bed and stared at him. In the two days since the fever had broken, his recovery had been little less than amazing. Bethia realized it had been a mistake to keep sharing the bed, then soothed her guilt by reminding herself that there had been no other place to sleep. She took a deep breath to try to steady herself, fighting to still the faint tremor of want that still rippled through her body, and grabbed for her gown.

" 'Tis warmer in the bed," Eric murmured as he stretched out on his back and crossed his arms behind his head.

Too warm, Bethia thought as she felt an irritating tension replace the warmth his touch had left her with. As she laced up her gown, she looked at him. He was not as calm and relaxed as he wanted to appear. There was a tautness in his fine body, a heat glittering in his eyes. He wanted her. It was a heady knowledge—so heady that she was tempted to crawl back into bed with him. The fact that a man like Sir Eric would feel passion for her, a skinny little wench with mismatched eyes, made the temptation he presented almost more than she could resist.

She grasped frantically at some sensibility and strength as she hurried to light the fire. She had not had any of her questions about him answered yet. Bethia knew she had allowed concern for his health let her be diverted from her determination to find out more about him. But, she thought as she heard him dress and slip outside, his health was restored. They would leave tomorrow and she did not know much more about him than she had when he had first ridden into view.

Once they had broken their fast and she had tended to James's needs, she carried a stool over to the bed and sat down. Eric, sprawled on his back on the bed and looking far too fine for her peace of mind, turned his head and eyed her warily. He would talk to her now or she would do her best to see that he did not get any more chances to steal even the smallest of kisses.

Eric studied Bethia's small face and inwardly grimaced. Several times since he had roused from his fever, she had gently tried to get him to talk about himself. It was clear that she would no longer be gentle. He felt the sharp bite of frustrated need in his body and sighed. It was something he supposed he ought to get used to, for after he answered her questions, she would probably be even harder to seduce than she was now.

"I think ye ken more about me than anyone outside of Dunnbea," Bethia said, "yet I ken verra little about you, Sir Eric. Dinnae ye think that should change?"

"Mayhap I havenae said much because I am certain ye willnae like what ye hear," he replied.

"Probably not, but I think I need to hear it. Why is it that ye dinnae seem to ken anything about your mother's kin?"

"A good start," Eric muttered. "My father thought I was a

bastard got upon my mother by the Murray laird. I was still warm from my mother's womb when he had me taken to a hillside and left to die.'' He smiled grimly when Bethia gasped and paled. ''Aye, the laird of Dubhlinn was a hard bastard. He was also a fool. If he had but taken a good look at me he would have seen that I was indeed his spawn. The mark on my back?''

''That wee heart?''

''Aye, 'tis something only the Beaton laird could have given me. 'Tis how my brother's wife Maldie and I kenned we were brother and sister, equally cursed in our father. She was but one of many girl children he had sired, walking away from them when he saw that the woman he had seeded hadnae given him the son he sought.''

''The son he had tossed away,'' she whispered, unable to truly understand how anyone could do such a thing to a tiny baby. ''How did ye survive?''

''A Murray mon found me and took me back to Donncoill. It was accepted that I was the Murray laird's bastard, for he and my mother had feared that the child she carried was his. I was thirteen, convinced I was a Murray, happy in that knowledge, when I had to face the truth. Maldie had come to kill her father. Her dying mother had made her swear to do it to avenge her and I think Maldie needed to avenge the fact that he had deserted her too, not just her mother. She had had a hard life with a bitter mother—a woman who became a whore and tried to get Maldie to be one too.''

''She must have been so angry,'' Bethia said quietly as she pulled her stool closer to the bed and rested her arms on the mattress. ''Please dinnae tell me she did it, for no one should have such a black sin upon her soul. So sad that her own mother would ask something of her that would so taint her.''

''Nay, she didnae.'' Eric smiled faintly when she sighed with relief and he smoothed his hand over her thick braid. ''My mother was dead, killed along with her midwife because my father couldnae bear that she had betrayed him. That is why I ne'er kenned my mother. I have learned what I can about her kinsmen o'er the years and sent them word, but they have continued to believe the Beatons. They think I am naught but a bastard.''

"But e'en if ye were, ye are the bastard of their kinswoman. Ye would think they would at least wish to see you.''

Knowing what he was about to say could push Bethia so far away he would never be able to pull her back, Eric softly cursed. "I seek what is mine by the rights of my birth." He sighed when she tensed beneath his hand and pulled back. "I am the true heir to Dubhlinn, but another Beaton slipped into the place and now denies me. The king doesnae wish to be troubled with all of this, so we cannae get aid from him. Also, there is whatever my mother had. I ken why Beaton wishes to keep me marked a bastard, for I would take everything he clutches, but I am nay sure why it matters to the MacMillans. All I can think is that they dinnae wish to anger the Beatons. And, mayhap, they are shamed by what they see as their kinswoman's misdeeds."

"And ye are willing to fight for this?"

" 'Tis mine. For thirteen years, I have tried to settle this with no more than words, petitions, months at court discussing it with the king, and many another calm, peaceful way. They willnae heed me. Now I mean to confront them." Eric watched Bethia steadily as she slowly got to her feet. "I am no William trying to kill and steal my way to land and coin."

"Of course ye arenae," she snapped, but was too distracted to pay much heed to her swift and sharp defense of Eric. "I must think about this."

"Aye, I understand."

At least he tried to, he mused as he watched her leave. It seemed all very clear to him. He was the rightful heir. For years he had struggled peacefully to gain what was his, and no one would relinquish it. It was the Beatons and the MacMillans who pushed for a confrontation.

James's soft gurgle brought Eric's gaze to the child. The
baby lay in his rough little bed sucking on his fingers and
slowly going to sleep. His parents were dead and someone
wanted him dead as well. Bethia was probably still too locked
in her grief and fear to be completely reasonable. She was
viewing the matter through pure emotion. He tried to take
comfort in the swift, sharp way she had refuted his fear that
she thought he was like William.

Eric got up and started to pack their things. They would have
to leave in the morning. He had felt that they could leave this
morning, but Bethia had convinced him that one more day of
rest would ensure the fever would not return. He had to admit
that he had not looked forward to riding for a whole day. Eric
grimaced and glanced toward the door. He had hoped to spend
the day furthering his attempt to pull Bethia into his bed. Instead,
she had pushed for the truth and he had given it to her, saying
the one thing that could keep her out of his arms. Although he
wanted her more than he had ever wanted a woman, he was a
little surprised at how much that thought distressed him. Perhaps, he mused, while Bethia was struggling to sort out her
thoughts, he ought to take a longer, harder look at what he was
thinking and feeling, besides the need to bury himself in her
warmth.

Bethia sighed with weariness when she reached the top of
the hill. It was a hard climb to make twice in such a short span
of time. She sat on the grass, staring out at the surrounding
land, but seeing little. Eric's words had shocked her deeply.
The only way to give them the thought and consideration they
required was to get away from him, away from his bonny face
and seductive voice.

Emotion was disordering her thinking and she knew it. For
a moment, all she had been able to think of was that the man
she had turned to for help was yet another seeking land and

coin at the expense of others. The fact that she had refused to allow him to compare himself to William, or think that she did, revealed that at least some common sense was still at work within her disordered thoughts. Bethia took several deep breaths of the crisp air. She needed to calm herself and think, needed to grasp reason and push all emotion aside.

Unlike William, Eric had a right to what he sought. Bethia did not think she was being foolishly quick to believe his claims. The tale he had told was too dark, too wild to be anything more than the truth. And no matter what she felt about what he was doing, she simply could not make herself believe that Eric would lie to her. In fact, if he was given to lying, he would never have told her a tale that he had to know could push her very far away.

What troubled her the most, she realized, was the implication that he was ready to fight for what he considered was his. Bethia had the sinking feeling that her unease over that had little to do with the trouble she now faced. It was very possible that she simply did not like the idea of Eric going to battle over anything.

Slowly standing up, she decided she had reacted badly to his news. She had sought the truth and now had to deal with it. It was not so bad. He sought only what was his. Somehow she would get over her distaste for battles fought over land or money. In truth, she thought with a sigh as she studied the landscape, it might not matter if she did or did not. Eric might want to bed her, but there had been no talk of any deeper feelings or a future. It was quite possible he would leave her at Dunnbea and ride away.

Just as she started to turn to go back down the hill, Bethia caught sight of a group of riders. She quickly flung herself to the ground so that she would not be seen and watched the men riding slowly toward the hill. Even from a distance, she recognized the hulking forms of William and his two sons. Theirs were distinctive shapes and equally distinctive poor riding styles. Squirming back toward the path on her belly, she finally stood up and scrambled down the hillside. Their time of rest and quiet had come to an abrupt end. She prayed she and Eric could get away before they were seen.

Eric looked up when Bethia stumbled into the hut. Her obvious distress was all the warning he needed. He quickly yanked on his boots and reached for his sword.

"How near are they?" he demanded.

"On the far side of the hill." Seeing that he had already packed their things, she reached for James, using the blanket he had been sleeping on to make his sling. "They appear to be in no hurry, so I dinnae think they are following any trail."

Eric grabbed their packs and started out the door. "Take a moment and see if ye can clear away some of the signs that we have been here."

Bethia did what she could, but was not sure it was enough. The ashes could even still be warm if William and his men arrived at the hut too quickly. There was also the smell of a fire and recently cooked food in the hut. She fanned the door for a moment, but was not sure that would bring in enough outside air to get rid of the scent of recent habitation. All she could do was pray that William had no time or inclination to look closely or even that he simply never found the place.

Eric rode up on Connor and she hurried to mount behind him. He made no comment on the fact that she added James's little bed to their baggage. She noted the branch he had tied to the poor beast's tail in hopes of brushing away their trail even as they rode along. Wrapping her arms around his trim waist she hung on as he nudged his horse into a gallop. If they could get out of the little valley before William entered it they might have a chance of getting away.

They rode hard for several miles and then Eric stopped. Bethia struggled to catch her breath, stolen by fear and the speed of their retreat, as Eric removed the branch from Connor's tail. She knew it was too soon to relax but she took some

comfort from the fact that they had heard no outcry or sounds
of pursuit.

"Do ye think we have eluded them?" she asked as he gave
Connor some water.

"For now. 'Tis a shame I never got to the top of that hill,
for I would have been able to judge how far away they were
when ye saw them." He handed her his waterskin, idly brushing
the dust from his clothes as she drank. "I am a little surprised
that ye sought my aid when ye saw them."

As she handed him back the waterskin, she smiled faintly.
"Nay, you arenae." She caught the flash of his grin just before
he took a drink. "Besides, I needed your horse."

"Ah, and here I thought it was my skill as a knight and my
charm that brought ye hieing back to my side."

"Such vanity." She sighed, the moment of jesting swiftly
passing. "I think, after so many days of not seeing that bastard,
that I had nourished the hope that we had lost him."

"Ye cannae really lose him, nay completely. The mon has
to ken that ye would make your way back to Dunnbea."

"Of course, and so only needs to ride in that direction."
She frowned as Eric mounted in front of her and started them
on their way again. "He cannae think to confront my whole
clan."

"Nay, I dinnae think so. He must hope he can stop ye ere
ye get there, but mayhap he thinks he can talk his way out of
your accusations."

"He cannae. I may nay have the proof needed to hunt him
down and hang him, but my family will believe my tale. They
will protect James."

Eric nodded. "They would have more claim to his care than
William anyway."

"Aye, for William isnae blood kin."

"He does hold Dunncraig, however."

"For now."

"And what will ye do next? Fight for what is rightfully James's?"

Bethia muttered a curse and did not answer him. That was exactly what would happen if William did not give up his hold on Dunncraig, but she did not want to think about it. Land and riches were not worth people's lives. She did not understand why she seemed to be the only one who felt that way.

It was late in the afternoon when Eric suddenly veered off the trail he had been following and urged her to dismount. Bethia winced as she stood up, her muscles protesting the long ride. The long rest at the hut had stolen away the toughening she had gained before their trouble at the river.

"Where are ye going?" she asked when Eric did not dismount, but turned his horse back toward the trail.

"I want to go back a ways and see if William is close on our heels. We just passed a hillock that should give me enough of a view of the land."

"And ye want me to stay here?"

"Aye," Eric said and bent down to steal a quick kiss. "If he is close, he may see me and I shall have to move fast. I may e'en be able to pull him away from ye, lead him off in another direction."

"Aye, and he could catch ye."

"Then ye must go on to Dunnbea. It isnae that far away. There is a wee village up this road. A half day's ride at most. From there 'tis a few hours to Dunnbea. Nay more than ye had already traveled when I found you."

That was true but she did not want to travel it without Eric. She took a deep breath to still her fears. Although she did not want him to risk his life in even the smallest way, she could tell by the set of his jaw that he would not be deterred from his plan.

"How long should I wait ere I start out on my own?" she asked, staring down at the packs he dropped at her feet and struggling not to cry.

"If I havenae returned by dawn, go on alone.'

"I didnae nurse ye through a fever to have ye get yourself killed by William and his loathsome sons."

"I have no intention of letting those fools get me."

She watched him disappear back along the way they had just come and cursed softly. "Ye may have no intention of it, but 'tis pure vanity to think it cannae happen," she grumbled.

For a while it was not so hard to wait for Eric. Bethia filled the time caring for and playing with James. As each hour crept by and he did not return, however, the waiting became more and more unendurable. Bethia discovered that she had a fierce imagination, was too easily able to conjure up more gruesome deaths for Eric to endure than she could tolerate.

Bethia knew it would not only be a fierce heartache she would suffer if anything happened to Eric, but a deep, abiding guilt. William and his sons were her enemies, not Eric's. She had dragged him into the middle of her troubles, blindly and willingly allowed him to share her danger. In truth, he risked far more than she did at the moment. All she had to do was hide.

Feeding James some cold porridge she had set aside for just such an emergency, and ignoring his almost comical faces of distaste, Bethia tried to find the strength she needed to do as Eric had told her to. That strength would be especially important if he did not return. Glancing at the child, she tried to calm herself with the reminder that he was the most important one. James was totally unable to care for or protect himself. No matter how much she might ache to go after Eric, to try to discover his fate if he did not return by dawn, she knew she could not. She would have to set out on her own, would have to push all grief from her mind and heart and think only of getting Sorcha's son to Dunnbea.

Chapter Six

The sound of a horse breathing was the first thing that penetrated Bethia's exhausted, fear-frozen mind where she sat crouched in the dark. As the sun had set, she had moved herself and James into the shelter of some thick, uncomfortably prickly bushes. The darker it had grown the more afraid she had become—for herself and James and especially for Eric. She had not dared to light a fire as she had sat in the dark, huddled in blankets, praying diligently for Eric to come back to her. Now that she heard someone approach she had to fight the urge to run out into the open calling Eric's name. She pulled out her dagger and waited to see who had invaded her refuge.

"Bethia?" Eric called softly.

He looked all around the place where he had left Bethia and the child but could see nothing. For a brief moment, he feared that he had gotten lost for the first time in his life, had returned to the wrong place. Then he was afraid that William had somehow found them. He quickly shook away that chill fear as well. Eric had no doubt that he had led the man off in the wrong direction.

A soft rustling noise made him tense in alarm. He drew his sword and nearly gaped as Bethia stepped out of the shadows. Eric sheathed his sword and wondered how he could have missed seeing her if she had been close enough to hear his soft call. The woman was proving to have some very unusual skills.

"Where were you?" he asked as he started to unsaddle Connor.

Clenching her hands together in front of her as she fought the urge to fling herself into his arms, Bethia answered, "James and I were tucked up in the bushes o'er there." She pointed to a shadowy spot just behind her. "Are ye all right?"

"Aye, lass. I have set a false trail for the bastard that may be enough to get us all the way to Dunnbea safely." He moved to the center of the small clearing and prepared a spot to make a small, sheltered fire. "Ye have a true skill at hiding, lass. Did your friend Bowen teach ye that too?"

She nodded and collected the sleeping James from his hiding place. "When he was still a new mon at Dunnbea and we were dreadfully besieged with raids and fighting. Anyone caught outside the walls was at risk, and since I was let to run free, he decided I should ken how to hide. For such a wee lass, he felt it was the best protection, although later he did show me how to wield a dagger."

"Ye learned your lessons weel, lass. I had no hint ye were still here. I feared ye had fled or been taken."

"It helped that James is such a sweet-natured child."

Eric smiled faintly as he nursed the fire to life. "And one who appreciates a nice sleep."

Bethia laughed softly as she set James down and fetched the blankets to lay out their bed. "Aye, he does. 'Tis good, for although he doesnae cry too often, when he is awake his happy babbling can get quite loud." She lightly touched James's soft curls. "He is going to be a bonny lad." She grinned at Eric. "So bonny he may e'en be able to challenge you."

" 'Tis glad I am that I will be too old by then to care," he drawled and smiled when she laughed.

"Do ye think William found our wee refuge?" she asked a moment later, her good humor gone.

"I dinnae ken, lass. 'Tis possible he was but plodding along the route to Dunnbea hoping he would stumble upon us. He may have the cunning for poisoning a few unsuspecting people, but I dinnae think he kens how to actually fight for what he wants. The few times I watched him and his men, it didnae seem as if anyone was actually looking for us or for any marks of our passing."

"I just wish that made him less dangerous."

Eric said nothing, just prepared them some porridge. Bethia was right. It did not matter how poorly William Drummond did the job. The man wanted Bethia and James dead. That intent alone made him a serious threat. Even a complete fool could get lucky and accomplish what he had set out to do. The only way to end that threat was to kill the man and, quite probably, his sons as well. Until he had Bethia and the child safely behind the walls of Dunnbea, however, Eric knew he could not indulge in that solution.

"Mayhap I should just hunt the mon down and kill him," Bethia said, scowling into the fire.

It was not easy, but Eric managed to swallow the mouthful of water he had just drunk without choking. He wondered wildly if the woman could read his thoughts, then told himself not to be such a fool. Bethia was a clever woman. She had simply come to the same conclusion he had.

"Ye cannae do that," he snapped.

"And why cannae I?"

"Because ye are a wee lass."

"Nay that wee."

"Too wee to chase down a mon who has already killed three people to get what he wants—and his loathsome sons too. And what do ye plan to do with James whilst ye are on this hunt? Keep him slung o'er your back?''

Bethia stared at Eric in surprise. He seemed almost angry. It had not been a particularly good idea, but she was not sure it deserved that amount of irritation in response. Then Bethia recalled the times when she had presented Bowen with what she had thought was a good idea, but had, upon further consideration, turned out to be anything from silly to quite dangerous. Bowen had often responded in the same way, with angry sarcasm and a hint of frustration. Obviously, men lacked the calm reason to simply discuss the good and bad in a plan.

''I can see that ye dinnae want to discuss the matter,'' she murmured.

''Actually, what I want is for ye to nay e'en think about it.''

A stubborn part of Bethia wanted to sharply refuse Eric's wish, the part that bristled at his tone of command. What right did he have to tell her what to do? A moment later, she sighed. He had the right of her protector, her champion, a place she herself had willingly set him in. There was also the fact that she had already decided that hunting down William was a bad idea, holding far more chance of danger than success. She could concede this time, for she was not actually losing anything and Eric might think that she was a biddable lass. Men liked biddable lasses.

''As ye wish,'' she said quietly and accepted the bowl of porridge he held out to her.

''So meek.'' Eric laughed softly and shook his head before he began to eat. ''Ye concede naught.''

''How can ye say so? Did I nay just agree with what ye asked of me?''

''Aye, most prettily, *after* ye had decided nay to do it anyway.'' He chuckled at the cross look that flickered over her sweet face. ''Ye werenae a verra obedient child, were ye, Bethia?'' Eric frowned when she looked a little hurt, a little sad.

"Nay, I wasnae." Bethia pushed away the sudden memory of her parents' blatant disgust and disappointment with her. "Bowen often despaired of me when he wasnae laughing. My mama and papa often said that Sorcha had gotten all of the sweetness whereas I got all of the stubborness." Bethia paused briefly in sipping some water, for beneath the pain of those words and so many similar ones stirred a small voice that decried those words as unnecessarily cruel, as untrue.

"Something wrong?" Eric asked, thinking that she looked a little startled by her own thoughts.

"Nay, I am just weary." Bethia took their bowls and cleaned them out with a little sand and water. "I shall seek my privacy for a moment and then get some rest. Ye should rest as weel, Sir Eric. 'Tisnae that long since ye were abed with a fever."

He nodded and watched her slip away into the shadows of the surrounding trees. The weariness he felt was almost a blessing. It would make it easier to lie beside Bethia and do no more than sleep. After banking the fire, he slipped away for his own moment of privacy, idly wondering if he could stay away until Bethia fell asleep without causing her any undue alarm.

Bethia stepped back into the small clearing just in time to see Eric disappear into the shadows. She sighed and moved to the rough bed they would soon share. Slowly, she stripped to her chemise and wondered what she should do now. Twice, when the fever had gripped him so tightly and when he was trying to mislead William, she had faced losing Eric. Now approached the third time. There was this night and perhaps one other before they reached Dunnbea. Bethia was sure that, once there, Eric would leave her and he would not be returning. He had his own quest to fulfill.

She wanted Eric. Just once she wanted to be held in his arms, to give him the love she dared not speak of. Looking into her future she did not see much chance of finding another man to love even if she could ever forget Eric. She wanted to know what passion was. Eric had given her a taste of it with his kisses, his seductive words and caresses, but she wanted to know the full of it.

Glancing at James, snugly sleeping in the blanket-lined box they had taken from the hut, she realized that one small impediment was removed. Without James nestled between them, she and Eric would be sleeping side by side, just as they had done in the tiny house. Bethia wondered if that had occured to Eric when he had so amiably allowed her to add the box to their supplies. As she slipped beneath the blankets, she next wondered if the easiest thing to do would be to just wait until Eric kissed her and then not pull away as she had each time before.

There were a lot of things wrong with what she was contemplating, but Bethia found it difficult to be too concerned about any of them. Her maidenhead should go to her husband, but she was almost twenty and none had yet been presented to her. No one had ever even wooed her. There was also the simple fact that she loved Eric and he made her ache. Some man her family chose for her, if they ever did, would probably not stir her blood the way Eric could with just one smile.

By the time Eric returned from the wood, stripped to his braies, and threw his plaid over them for some added warmth, Bethia was almost decided. She briefly feared that her feelings were prompted too much by the fact that he was so breathtakingly handsome; then she shook that fear aside. There was no doubt in her mind that she could never again have such a beautiful man express desire for her, but that was not all that stirred her desire. It did, however, add to her feeling that she would be a fool not to grasp the opportunity with both hands and worry about the consequences and the heartbreak later.

Eric turned to face Bethia and found her staring at him. He wondered if she intended to stop him before he even stole one kiss. She had said nothing more about his plans to seek his rightful inheritance, but William's appearance could have been all that had prompted her to run back to him. When he slid his arm around her tiny waist, tugging her close to him, and she did not resist, he breathed an inner sigh of relief. She might be troubled by his plans, but she was not going to let that stand between them.

He started in surprise when, as he slowly lowered his mouth to hers, she suddenly wrapped her slender arms around his neck and yanked him even closer. This time when he nudged her lips with his tongue, she readily opened to him. He shuddered from the strength of his need when she timidly returned the prods and strokes of his tongue even as she curled her long fingers in his hair.

"Ye must be confused, lass," he said as he released her mouth and began to kiss her throat. "That was a morning kiss."

Bethia giggled, then sighed with delight as he moved his hands over her back. "There are different kinds of kisses for different occasions, are there?"

"For us, aye."

"Then what sort of kiss would ye give me if I told ye that I wasnae ready to go to sleep yet?" She cried out softly in surprise when he abruptly turned, pinning her firmly beneath his lean, hard body.

If any other woman had said such a thing, Eric would have seen it as a blatant invitation to share her bed and he would have been right. He could not be sure with Bethia. Although her kisses were now good enough to make his bones melt, she was still a complete innocent. If he guessed her meaning wrong, he could go too fast and frighten her—or hold back and miss the chance to gain the prize he had ached for since first seeing her. Somehow he would have to find the strength and wit to walk a fine line somewhere between the two until he was certain what she wanted.

"That would require a kiss that asked, nay, begged for something," he said in a soft, rough voice as he brushed his mouth over hers.

The kiss he gave her sent all of Bethia's senses reeling. She realized that he had been treating her gently, restraining himself. With his tongue, he ravished her mouth, then pulled it back, tempting her to follow with her own, and then the dance would begin all over again. He released her mouth only briefly, just long enough for her to take a breath, then started all over again until she was aware of nothing but the taste of him.

Eric shifted his body to one side, then slid his hand up her rib cage and covered her breast. Bethia softly groaned into his mouth as he rubbed his thumb over the nipple until it hardened, pressing almost painfully against her linen shift. There was a heated, gentle swelling between her legs, a moistness she did not understand. Eric moved his leg between hers, and with a murmur of confusion and desire, she rubbed against him. When he enclosed the aching tip of her breast in his mouth, gently nipped at it, then suckled, Bethia clung to him and felt the urge to tear away the linen that seperated them.

Suddenly, Eric stopped. She could sense him looking down at her even before she opened her eyes. Even in the dim light of the banked fire and the waning moon, she could see the tautness of his features. His broad chest heaved as he took several deep breaths. There was a faint tremor in his lean body. Bethia felt her desire soar as she realized that he wanted her, that he was caught as tightly in passion's grip as she was.

"Lass," he said, his voice a little unsteady. "If ye mean to stop this, 'twould be a kindness to do so now."

" 'Twould also be wise," she murmured and slid her bare foot up and down his hair-roughened calf.

"Oh, aye, verra wise."

"I dinnae feel particularly wise just now."

" 'Tis flattered I am to ken that my kisses could so disorder your thoughts, but it also means that ye probably dinnae ken what ye are pulling us toward with all your willingness." He started to move off her.

Bethia wrapped her arms and legs around him tightly, holding him on top of her. "If ye move away now, I just may have to hurt ye, Sir Eric."

Her words echoed in the complete stillness that followed her outburst. Bethia could not believe that she had said such a thing or that she had grabbed the man as if she intended to wrestle him into submission. She took one look at the stunned expression on his face, groaned in embarrassment, and clapped her hands over her face. She was certainly no lady and now Sir Eric could see that very clearly.

"Sweetling," Eric said in a choked voice, "I mean ye no insult, please believe me, but—"

He went off into gales of laughter so loud Bethia nervously glanced at James to be sure that he still slept. Eric was laughing so hard he rolled off her, and Bethia turned on her stomach, pressing her blush reddened face against her crossed arms. Her night of passion was not turning out as she had planned. She had imagined sweet words of acceptance and encouragement, fevered kisses and caresses, and had seen herself gracefully, yet with the appropriate amount of shyness, taking that final step into womanhood in the arms of the man she loved. Instead, she threatened him, then had to endure his laughter. The only thing that eased the sting of the shame she felt, though not by much, was recalling his apology before he had started laughing. There was a small chance that he did not think she was a complete idiot, and a brazen one as well. Bethia tensed when she felt the gentle pressure of his hand on her back and the touch of his lips on her hair.

"Come, my own, I meant no ridicule," he said, a hint of laughter still enriching his deep voice. " 'Twas funny. If ye were nay involved, ye would think so too. I have had women woo me, lure me, beg me, buy me—"

That remark caught Bethia's attention so sharply she abruptly ceased sulking over her ineptitude and stared at him. "Buy you?"

"Aye." He gently but firmly nudged her onto her back and

sprawled on top of her. "A verra fat purse she offered me too."

"Did she think ye were just some poor carpet knight?"

Eric had to smile over the outrage Bethia revealed for his sake, as well as her somewhat crude term for a man who pleasured the ladies while other men went off to fight. "Nay, nor some lowly knave. She just kenned that I was rather poor at the time and thought money would lure me more than pretty smiles and kisses. Mayhap she didnae think I would respond to either when they came from her." He smiled gently as he began to trace the delicate lines of her face with soft kisses. " 'Twas tempting."

"Eric, ye didnae, did ye?"

"Aye, I fear I did. I was verra young and in need of some coin so that I could continue at court." He winked. "I fear I also felt that, if she was so foolish as to pay dearly for something she could have gained with a little seduction, who was I to thwart her?" He was relieved when Bethia grinned, for only after he had begun the tale had he realized that she might not find it as amusing as his family did. "I found out later that she made a habit of buying young knights, paying them handsomely to warm her bed for a night or two."

"Weel, men pay for it. Mayhap she saw it as a reasonable way to go about it."

"Mayhap, but 'tis an old, somewhat sordid tale. I wish to think upon other things." He started to tug off her shift, then paused, allowing her one last chance to change her mind. "Are ye sure, Bethia? There will be no going back."

Eric knew that she did not understand the full implication behind his words, that she thought he referred only to her chastity. It was not fair, but he decided not to be more specific. Later, once he had made her his, he would make her understand that this possession was final. Eric knew that he was about to enjoy something special, intense and wondrous, and he had no intention of letting her walk away afterward and share it with another.

Bethia slid her hands around his neck and touched her lips to his. "I ken it. It may not be wise, but 'tis what I want."

He quickly kissed her, then tugged off her shift and tossed it aside. As he crouched over her, looking his fill of her slim form, he cursed the dim light. What he could see, from her small firm breasts to her slender hips, was exquisite, igniting his passion so swiftly and strongly he was afraid he might lack the patience she needed. He tore off his braies and quickly settled his body on top of hers. The way she immediately moved against him made him shudder. It was definitely going to be hard to go slowly.

"Skin like white silk," he murmured as he traced her collarbone with soft, nibbling kisses.

She would have liked to return his flattery in kind, but Bethia found it difficult to speak. The way he lightly kneaded her breasts with his elegant hands, teasing her nipples into hard, aching points with his thumbs, robbed her of the ability to form any coherent words. When he touched his warm lips to her breast, she cried out softly and arched into his body in unthinking surrender. She could not keep still as he lathed and suckled the tips of her breasts, increasing the tense, restless feeling low in her belly with each hungry tug of his mouth.

Her increasingly frantic movements came to an abrupt halt when he slid his hand over her trembling stomach and then between her legs. He kissed her and, with a few skillful strokes of his fingers, pushed away her shock over such an intimate touch. Eric thrust his finger inside her, his tongue in her mouth imitating the movement, and Bethia was lost. She clung to him, moving her hands greedily over his warm, hard body, willing to let him do what he pleased as long as he did not stop, as long as the feelings tearing through her did not stop.

Bethia was only partially aware of when he began to slowly join their bodies. He kept her drugged with kisses as he eased himself inside her, then with one quick thrust shattered her innocence. Bethia gasped as a sharp pain cut through the haze of desire she was sunk in. She knew her nails were digging into the skin of his shoulders, but he said nothing, and it took her a moment to gather enough wit to ease her grip. As she took several deep breaths to calm herself, she realized that the pain was already easing. She also realized that Eric was not moving.

Slowly, Bethia opened her eyes and met his steady gaze. She felt herself blush. Knowing the man she was looking at was intimately joined with her made her feel shy and uncertain. A close look at his taut features told her that it was costing Eric dearly to hold still within her and her embarrassment began to ease.

Eric held himself up on his forearms, fighting so hard to remain still he hardly dared to breathe. His whole body shook with the strain. Sweat beaded on his forehead as his mind struggled to keep his body from moving as instinct and aching need demanded it to. He wanted to give her slender body time to adjust to his invasion, but the feel of her tight heat surrounding him made him feel almost maddened with need.

"I think there is more," Bethia said quietly, slowly kneading the taut muscles in his back.

"Oh, aye, my heart, there is," he whispered as he grasped her by the calves and gently pushed her legs up until her knees were bent.

When he pressed deeper within her, she shuddered and then realized he did the same. He pulled back and she swiftly wrapped her arms and legs around him. "Dinnae leave me."

"I couldnae leave now if William stood round us with the whole of the king's army at his back." Eric laughed shakily. "I might conjure up just enough wit to ask them to wait." Bethia giggled and he had to kiss her.

Eric began to move, a slow, measured pace that soon threatened to drive her mad. Her body was taut with expectation,
but she was not exactly sure what it demanded, only knew that
Eric could give it to her. She slid her hands down his back
and began to caress his taut buttocks. His movements quickly
became fiercer and she groaned out her gratitude. Just as she
began to think that something had gone wrong, that she was
too tense, too frantic, Eric slid his hand down to where their
bodies were joined. He touched her, just one quick, gentle
touch, and she screamed as the tension within her body shattered, waves of blinding delight flooding her body. A small
part of her passion-dulled mind was aware of Eric plunging
once, deep and hard, into her trembling body, and calling out
her name as he jerked and shook in her arms. She murmured
a welcome when he collapsed on top of her, smoothing her
hands over his body as she savored the tingling pleasure that
still rippled through her.

Not sure how long he had sprawled in her arms, mindlessly
sated, Eric eased out of her body. He smiled when she made
a soft sound of regret. Propping himself up on his elbows, he
studied her as he idly brushed her tangled hair from her face.

Bethia was his now. It was not just a matter of honor
demanding that he wed the wellborn maid he had just seduced.
It was not even the fact that the passion he had found in her
slim arms was beyond compare. The moment he had entered
the warm shelter of her body, he had known that she was his,
known it in his heart, his mind, even in his soul. By allowing
him to make love to her, Bethia had sealed her fate. Eric
wondered how long it would take her to accept that and how
hard he would have to fight to make her do so.

When Eric turned onto his back and pulled her into his arms,
Bethia eagerly snuggled up against him. She felt a little tender,
a little dazed, but the sweet satisfaction humming through her
veins more than made up for such inconvenience. For tonight,

and perhaps tomorrow night, Eric was hers. Making love with Eric had shown her the true beauty of the act, shown her just how deeply she loved the man. When they parted at Dunnbea her pain would probably consume her, but she refused to think about that now. Right now, held close in Eric's arms, she was happy, and she meant to cling to that for as long as she could.

Chapter Seven

" 'Tis market day," Bethia murmured, staring at the large boisterous crowd in the village streets she and Eric had begun to ride down.

"Aye. I think it may be best if we dismount," Eric said and nimbly slipped out of the saddle. "Connor is verra even of temper, but there may be too much noise and activity here even for him to abide with calm. If I lead him through the crowds there will be less chance of trouble."

After Eric helped Bethia dismount, he gave her a hand in shifting James's sling from the back of her body to the front. She fell into step behind him as he began to slowly make his way down the street. James's soft curls brushed against her chin again and again as he twisted his head back and forth, his eyes wide as he stared at all the people.

The town was filled to bursting with people and animals; the noise of the sellers hawking their wares, people gossiping and arguing prices, and animals squealing was nearly deafening. It all made Bethia very uneasy. Such a crowd meant there may not be a room for them. It could also allow her enemies to slip close to them by using the crowds to hide themselves. So many people also meant a lot of eyes seeing her, Eric, and the child; thus a lot of people could point the way for William.

"Mayhap we should just continue on to Dunnbea," Bethia said, hurrying forward to walk by Eric's side so that he could be sure to hear her over the noise.

"I am nay sure we could make it ere night fell," Eric replied.

It was a small lie and, he felt, a harmless one. If they rode steadily, with only a little hurrying, they could reach Dunnbea while it was still light. He had no intention of rushing her back to her family, however. It might not be wise, considering the danger that lurked at their heels, but he wanted one more night, alone, with Bethia. He needed to strengthen the bond of passion between them, needed to reaffirm his possession of her. Once they reached Dunnbea, once she and James were safe behind those walls, he had to travel on to the MacMillans. Eric wanted to be sure he left behind a woman who knew exactly who she belonged to.

He winced as he thought of his reason for seeking out the MacMillans, allies of Bethia's clan. Not a word had been said about his quest since he had revealed the truth, and he was reluctant to bring the matter to the fore again. The fact that Bethia had become his lover eased his concern. She clearly had not turned away from him completely. Eric was not fool enough to think that the matter was settled, however. It just gave him hope that they could find a solution to the conflict between what he had to do and her feelings about the whole matter.

"Oh, I didnae think it was that much farther away," she said.

"Ye have ne'er been here?" Eric thought that a little odd, for it was not so far from her home.

"Nay, I ne'er left Dunnbea."

"Never?"

"Nay." She frowned up at him. "Why do ye sound so shocked?"

"I would have thought ye would have traveled at least once to a village fair or market day or e'en to the keeps of your allies."

"Someone had to watch o'er Dunnbea when my parents and Sorcha left."

"Mayhaps that was true when ye were grown, but ye were left behind e'en when ye were a child?"

Bethia did not like Eric's questions. They required her to recall painful times, made her look too closely at things she had tried not to be resentful or angry about. It was still a struggle; anger and hurt were still too easily roused. Long ago she had dried her tears, buried her pain, and forced herself to accept her life. There had obviously been something about her that her parents could not accept, so she had become a dutiful daughter. She did not appreciate Eric chipping away at that facade.

"I was a clumsy child," she said, unable to keep all of her annoyance out of her voice. "Aye, and sickly too. 'Twas thought best if I stayed secure at Dunnbea." She could tell by the look in his dark blue eyes that he found that a paltry explanation, but unable and unwilling to challenge his opinion, she simply looked away. "When I was older, they all felt that I was more use at Dunnbea, for at a young age, I took o'er most of my mother's work. She is a delicate woman, ye ken, and needs to take great care of herself."

Eric opened his mouth to proclaim that all nonsense, then quickly shut it. Bethia was not stupid. She had to know, deep in her heart, that it was all wrong. It was clear, however, that she chose to either ignore it or to deceive herself. Whether it was a game she played with herself to avoid pain or to keep peace within her family, he could not be sure; he was not even sure that Bethia would know herself. It would serve no purpose at the moment to open her wounds, of which he began to think she had many. There was one more question he needed to get answered, however.

"They must have been concerned when ye suddenly decided to go to your sister," he said.

"Sorcha asked me to come. It was enough."

"They didnae wish to travel with you?"

"They werenae close at hand when word came. I left quickly with a small guard. Those men would have returned to Dunnbea with the news of Sorcha's death, but didnae ken my feelings that it was murder. My parents are probably sunk deep in grief."

"Ye will be able to soothe some of that when ye bring them her son," he murmured, unable to think of anything else to say.

Bethia sensed the insincere courtesy of Eric's words and wondered at it, but her thoughts quickly turned to James. She prayed her parents would adore the child she brought into their care. He was certainly sweet and bonny enough for them to love. Yet they had been so fierce in their pride and devotion to Sorcha, she had sometimes wondered if they had any left for others. James was a part of Sorcha and that should be enough, but Bethia was not so sure. She kissed the top of James's head and promised the child that, no matter which way her parents turned, he would never want for love. Bethia swore that she would always be there for him.

Once at the inn, Bethia waited patiently outside with the horse and their goods. When Eric did not immediately return to her, she felt her hopes rise. It would be nice to stay in a proper bed again. Their brief time at the little cottage had spoiled her. Despite the joy she had found in Eric's arms last night, she had not been pleased to be sleeping on the hard ground again. She also wanted a decent meal with meat and wine and a hot bath. Her fears of discovery and concerns about James were quickly pushed aside when Eric stepped out of the inn, a big smile upon his face.

"We have a room?" she asked, unable to hide her excitement.

"Aye, and"—he kissed the tip of her nose and ruffled James's curls—"I have already ordered a bath."

"Oh, thank you. Ye are the best of men. And food?"

Eric laughed as he led his horse to the stable, giving the stable lad a coin but waving him away for he wished to tend to Connor himself. "And food. Enough meat and wine to please a king. While ye bathe, wee James and I shall seek out some bread, cheese, and wine to take with us on the morrow."

"Ye need not waste your coin. 'Tis nay such a long ride from here to Dunnbea."

"Nay, but we shall feast for every mile."

"Poor Connor," she drawled and laughed with him as he led her back into the inn.

It only took a few words from the innkeeper's wife for Bethia to realize the woman thought she and Eric and James were just a young family in need of a room for the night. She could not really believe Eric had lied outright to the kindly woman, but Bethia suspected he had done nothing to correct her errant assumptions when they were made. Bethia smiled and did the same. She felt she would rather do a penance for that small lie than risk losing the chance of a hot bath.

The maids were already filling a huge tub in the room with hot water. It was set before a warm fire to ensure that she did not take a chill. One of the maids sprinkled a handful of herbs over the water and the scent of lavender filled the room. Bethia took a deep breath as she removed James from his sling and handed him to Eric.

As the two fulsome maids left the room, Bethia saw the way they looked at Eric, their smiles blatantly inviting. She quickly looked at Eric and felt her pangs of jealousy ease. He was too busy making funny faces at a giggling James to even notice the lures sent his way.

"I shall leave you to your bath, m'lady," Eric said, bowing low with James in his arms and making the child laugh.

"Aye, please do." Bethia laughed and pushed him out the door. "And be quick about it ere the water cools."

"Be sure to lock the door behind me."

"I will."

The moment the door shut behind him, Bethia made sure that it was securely bolted, then began to strip off her clothes. She left them behind her in a trail from the door to the tub. The moment she stepped into the hot water, she sighed with delight. It had been too long since she had enjoyed such a luxury, and as she sank up to her neck in the gently scented water, she intended to savor it.

As the heat of the water soothed her aching muscles, Bethia found herself thinking about the maids and how the women had looked at Eric. She and Eric had been alone as they traveled to Dunnbea, and Bethia realized that, although she had easily guessed that women would be drawn to Eric, she had never really considered or understood how true that was. Until now. Despite the presence of ones they assumed were the man's wife and child, the two maids had tried to catch Eric's eye, to give him warm, inviting looks. Bethia had no doubt that the women would have offered him a toss in the hay right in front of her face. It was not only infuriating—it was astonishing.

A moment later, she struggled to shake away her concern. How women reacted to Eric would not be her problem after tonight. What mattered was that, for tonight, Eric was all hers. The complete disinterest he had revealed in the maids proved that. Bethia was determined not to spoil their remaining time together with petty jealousies and fears.

That determination faded abruptly only two hours later. Eric had returned but moments after Bethia had finished dressing and a bath was quickly prepared for him by the same two maids. Their eagerness to please him with a swiftly prepared, hot bath was almost painful to watch. It was when they cooingly offered to help him bathe, right in front of her, his supposed wife, that Bethia decided she had had enough. They were tainting her last night with Eric with their vulgar flirtations and she could not allow that.

When one of the maids reached out to unlace Eric's shirt, Bethia was there first, dropping several of James's soiled rags into her hands. "If ye have such an urge to scrub something, try these. I would like it done—quickly."

Biting back a smile, Eric politely but swiftly shooed the maids out of the room, then turned to look at Bethia. She looked gloriously furious and he was pleased. He had not purposely set out to make her jealous, but he would gladly accept the results of the maids' foolishness. Here was the proof that her feelings already ran deeper than passion alone.

"Is it always like that?" Bethia asked as the door shut behind the two maids.

"Like what, my heart?"

Bethia gave Eric a disgusted look for his attempt to act as if he had not noticed. "They did everything short of tearing off their clothes and jumping on you, and I begin to think that e'en that would have happened if we had waited long enough."

"They were unusually brazen."

" 'Twas as if I wasnae even here."

And that, mused Eric, was probably the worst of it. Bethia had spent far too much of her life being ignored, being treated as if she was not really there. The maids were very forward, but that had happened one or two times in the past. It would undoubtedly happen again, as brazenly as that or more subtlely. He could not do anything about it. He did not think he was vain, but he knew that women liked how he looked. Until age or injury marred his looks, women would probably flirt with him, undeterred by the fact that he was taken. Disinterest had rarely stopped them in the past. Somehow he was going to have to make Bethia so certain of him that such impertinences did not worry her too much. Eric sighed as he started to unlace his shirt. That might prove to be a larger task than he could handle.

" 'Twas just rudeness of a sort, lass. Aye, and a sad blindness to the utter disinterest I felt." He suddenly smiled at her. "Are ye going to stay and help me bathe?" He tugged off his shirt and tossed it aside.

The sight of his bared chest was enough to make Bethia's heart skip. She was tempted to take him up on his suggestion. It was time to retreat.

"I am taking James and we are going to find some goat's milk."

"Coward," Eric said, laughing as she hurried away.

"Best ye lock this door," she called after herself. "I should hate to return to find your poor body being ravished."

"Dinnae worry, lass. I mean to save it all for ye."

Bethia smiled, then sighed as she passed the two maids on her way out of the inn. Perhaps it was for the best that she and Eric would part soon. It would drive her mad to constantly watch women try to lure him into their arms. She would be doomed to spend her days wondering which invitation he would finally accept. Surely no man could be so beset by willing women and not succumb to the temptation eventually. If, by some miracle, Eric took her as his wife, Bethia feared she would end her days as a babbling fool, driven insane by fear and constant jealousy.

"And I have too fanciful a mind," she muttered, then turned her attention to finding James some of the goat's milk he so loved.

When Bethia returned to the room at the inn, she could smell the food even before she opened the door. She stepped inside the door, took a deep breath, and savored the smells of roasted meat and fresh bread. A soft laugh drew her gaze to Eric.

"I was thinking of hollering out the window for you," he said as he moved toward the well set table placed by the fire. "They brought this in but moments ago and one sniff was enough to make me ravenous. I feared I wouldnae be able to wait for your return ere I set upon it like some starving wolf.''

"Oh, I dinnae ken what to eat first," she said as she sat down at the table, James on her lap, and gazed at all the food on the table. "If we eat all this, Connor shall ne'er be able to carry us to Dunnbea.''

Eric just laughed, then sat down. He cut Bethia a thick slice of bread and then a smaller one for James. As soon as he had savored a large piece slathered with thick honey, he began to cut the meat. It took only a few more bites of food before their manners were completely cast aside, much to Eric's delight. Even little James giggled and cooed with pleasure as he stuffed his little face like some greedy piglet.

Finally, knowing she could not eat another bite no matter how much she was tempted, Bethia slumped back in her chair. She looked down at James and was torn between laughter and dismay. Sticky with honey, the child was covered with various pieces of the food he had eaten.

"What a messy wee piggy ye are," Bethia said as she helped James to a drink of goat's milk.

"Aye, he will need some scrubbing." Eric refilled their tankards with wine. "There is a bowl and ewer of water o'er by the window. It looks as if most of the food is on his clothes.''

Bethia nodded and started to strip the child. Despite her care, some of the food on his clothes got onto the squirming, giggling boy. Playfully scolding him, she took him to the water and washed him clean, then readied him for bed. After setting him in his little box set near the big bed, she stared down at her nephew for a moment. Soon they would be back at Dunnbea and he would no longer be only hers.

"Ye willnae lose him, lass," Eric said as he stepped up beside her and draped his arm around her shoulders.

"Soon he will be in my parents' care," she said, leaning against him and enjoying the comfort his strength gave her.

"Aye, but he will still be yours. He already calls you mama.''

"I ken it." She grimaced. "When he does I feel so pleased. Then I feel verra guilty o'er that pleasure. I shouldnae feel happy, nay when it means that he has forgotten my sister already, forgotten his true mother."

"He isnae old enough to have many strong memories of her. And if he was often in the care of a nursemaid, there could be even fewer memories."

Bethia winced and returned to the table to pick up her tankard. "He had a nursemaid. I talked to her some about the child and, God forgive me, gave little thought to how she would feel when I fled with the boy."

"If she cared for the lad at all, she was probably pleased that someone had the wit and strength to try to save him."

"Aye, she had the care of him a lot and 'twas clear to see that she loved him dearly." Bethia smiled shyly at Eric when he picked up his tankard of wine, then half sat, half sprawled on the bed as he took a drink. "I was a little surprised to learn just how often James was left in the woman's care, but then Sorcha was still rather newly wed and blindly besotted with Robert, unable to leave his side for verra long. At least Sorcha chose weel. Once this trouble has ended I shall see if the woman wishes to come to Dunnbea to help care for the boy."

"That would be kind." Eric patted the bed beside him. "Come to bed, lass."

Although Bethia moved to sit beside him, she said, "We are still dressed."

"At least we dinnae have our boots on."

"How verra weel mannered we are," she drawled, then tensed slightly as he set his tankard down on a table by the bed and began to unlace her gown. " 'Tis verra bright in here."

"Aye, and I am glad of it. Last night I was heartily cursing the darkness," he said, taking her wine away and setting it down next to his so that he could more easily divest her of her gown.

"Weel, I was verra pleased with it."

"Ah, my own, ye are bonny."

He kissed her, and for a while, she forgot how much light there was in the room. Eric kept her so bemused with his kisses she offered no resistance as he skillfully stripped them both of their clothes. Then, suddenly, she was sprawled on her back on the bed with him crouched over her. There was such warmth in his eyes as he looked her over that she felt almost beautiful even while she blushed with embarrassment.

In an attempt to distract herself from the unease she felt over being seen naked, her lack of womanly curves all too plain to see, Bethia looked at Eric. She had seen him naked before when she had nursed him through his fever, but she knew she would never tire of looking at him. His warm smooth skin stretched taut over hard muscles was a pure delight to see. Then her gaze rested upon his groin and her eyes widened. She had never seen him aroused. Bethia was glad that she had not had a chance to see him in that state last night or she would have lost all interest in becoming his lover. She was amazed that he had managed to get that inside of her without causing her a great deal more pain than he had.

Seeing the direction of her wide-eyed stare, Eric grinned and laid down in her arms. "It isnae that horrible a sight, I pray."

"Nay, I was just thinking that it was for the best I didnae see it last night. I cannae believe it fits," she whispered.

" 'Tis nay any bigger than any other mon's and, aye, it fits, beautifully so." He took her hand and placed it on his manhood, closing his eyes in pleasure as she shyly stroked him. "Are ye sore, my heart?"

"Nay. Should I be?"

"Some women claim that the pain lingers for a while. I dinnae ken much about it, in truth, for I have never lain with a virgin."

"Never? Truly? Was that some sort of rule?"

"Aye, that it was. I have weel and truly broken it now, havenae I?"

"I am sorry," she murmured, then wondered why she was apologizing.

Eric laughed softly and kissed her on the tip of her small nose. "And so ye should be for being such a sweet temptation, more than any sane mon can bear." He gently removed her tormenting little hand. "Enough of that."

"I was doing something wrong?" Bethia was a little disappointed, for she had enjoyed touching him.

"Nay, ye were doing verra weel indeed. Too weel."

Before she could ask what he meant, he kissed her. Bethia decided that he did that a lot, but it was such a pleasant way to end a discussion, such a sweet diversion, she decided not to complain. This was how she wished to spend the night, soaked in the pleasure only Eric could give her. It was the last chance she had to fully love the man and she did not intend to waste a minute of it.

Bethia allowed her greed for Eric—her need to try to sate herself on the feel and taste of him—to push aside all hints of modesty and embarrassment. She matched him kiss for kiss, touch for touch, although he skillfully eluded her attempts to stroke him as intimately as he did her. Soon she was so eager, so hungry for him, she tried to force him into her embrace. This time when he laughed, she did as well, for she knew that he shared her frenzy, that his amusement was born of the joy they made each other feel.

When he finally joined their bodies, Bethia cried out in pure delight. Her passion was quickly dimmed when he did not move, however. She looked up at him, shivering a little beneath the hot intensity of his gaze.

"Eric?" She slid her hands down his back to caress his buttocks, but although he groaned and trembled, he still did not move.

"Ye are mine, Bethia," he said, suddenly desperate to try to make her understand that this was more than simple love games, much more than a night of fevered lovemaking followed by a polite farewell.

"Weel, aye, since I am splayed out beneath ye like a filleted haddock, I think I might be," she murmured.

Eric laughed, despite how tightly knotted with unassuaged hunger he was. "Such a loving way ye have to flatter a mon," he drawled; then he grew serious again. "Nay, I dinnae mean just now, while I lie buried in your sweet body. I mean that ye are mine, all mine. Say it, Bethia. I need to hear ye say it."

Although Bethia was not sure what he meant, or what his expressed need for such words might imply, she decided to give him what he asked for. He could not know it, but it was the simple truth. She was his, would always be his no matter what happened to either of them in the years ahead. His mark was upon her, and even if she tried, it would never be removed. He held her heart and her happiness in his elegant hands, but she could never tell him so. By admitting that she was his, however, she could at least hint at that sad truth. It might ease some of the sorrow of unspoken words in the cold, lonely years ahead of her.

"Aye, Eric," she replied quietly, reaching up to stroke the fine lines of his face. "I am yours."

It was not all he wanted, but it was enough for now. It gave them a spoken bond. There was a look of confusion in her passion-dark eyes, but he could not yet say what was needed to ease that. Now was not the time to speak of marriage. He had too much left unfinished. Bethia would also think he asked only out of a sense of honor, only because he had taken her chastity. He needed time to make her believe that it was so much more than that which drove him to want to tie her firmly to his side.

Eric began to move, a slow, tantalizing rhythm that soon had Bethia feverish with need again. She was his, irrevocably his, and she wondered how he could not know it, could not feel it in her every touch or hear it in her every cry. As her release swept over her with blinding strength, she felt Eric move only twice more before he joined her in that state of bliss. Even through passion's haze, she heard him call out, but it was not her name upon his lips. He cried out the word *mine* as he sprawled in her arms. Bethia wondered dazedly if Eric too suffered from some doubts. She held him close, lazily kissing his shoulders as she fought to recover her strength and wits. If Eric had any doubts about how firmly she felt bound to him, by the end of the night, when they were finally too exhausted from their lovemaking to even wriggle their toes, all of his doubts would have faded.

Chapter Eight

Cold steel caressing his throat was an unwelcome way to greet the day, Eric decided as he slowly opened his eyes. He tightened his arm ever so slightly around a still sleeping Bethia. They had been found and it was all his fault. Eric felt weak with guilt and twisted with frustration and rage. It seemed too cruel of fate to make his last thought in life be the realization that he had so utterly failed Bethia and James.

"Cousin, ye had best open your wee eyes, and be it the blue or the green one, cast an eye at this laddie ere I skewer him," said the tall young man holding the sword to Eric's throat.

Cousin. Eric did not think the word had ever sounded so sweet. Bethia stirred against him and he kept his grip on her firm. She was naked and he did not wish her to start awake, unthinkingly displaying herself to the four men crowding their room.

He gently closed his hand around her shoulder and squeezed as he studied the men watching him with intense dislike. The man standing by the bed still holding the sword point far too close to him for comfort had to be Wallace. With his green eyes and dark red hair there was some family resemblance. The other three men were older and dark in coloring. Eric had the sinking feeling that two of them were Peter and Bowen. This was not the first impression he had wanted to make upon the men who had been so important to Bethia throughout her lonely childhood.

"Eric?" Bethia murmured as she started to stretch, then realized that he was holding her firmly to the bed.

"Caution, lass. We have company."

Bethia was briefly terrified as she opened her eyes and looked around the room. As she recognized Wallace, Peter, Bowen, and a man called Thomas, her terror rapidly changed to intense embarrassment. She could not believe they had found her and in such a compromising position. Then she saw the sword pointed at Eric and, with a soft curse, pushed it aside.

"What are ye doing, Wallace?" she snapped. "There is nay need to threaten the mon."

"The mon is lying naked in a bed with you, cousin," Wallace replied angrily but he lowered his sword. "Are ye going to tell me ye are wed to him?"

"Why dinnae ye all step outside and let us get dressed and then we can talk about this."

"Ye didnae answer me, cousin. Are ye wed to this pretty rogue?"

"I dinnae mean to have this talk whilst I am still undressed."

"Five minutes," growled the largest of the men, his dark brown eyes cold as they settled on Eric.

"Bowen," Bethia protested.

"Five minutes. We will be outside the door and Thomas will be set below the window."

"We best hurry," Bethia said the moment the door closed behind the four men. "When Bowen says five minutes, 'twill most like be four."

She cursed softly to herself as she and Eric got dressed.

Bethia wanted to talk to Eric before the others returned but Bowen was not going to give her the time. It was sad that her last night with Eric was ending so badly, but she put aside her disappointment. She was going to have to be very careful in what she said next or she and Eric could find themselves in a great deal of trouble.

"Eric, I am so sorry," she began, then winced as the door slammed open so loudly it startled James and he began to cry. "Oh, have a care," she snapped. "Ye woke the bairn, Bowen."

She picked up James and rubbed his back to soothe him, then turned and looked at the men. Her clansmen encircled a remarkably calm Eric. Bethia stared at them all in some surprise because even Wallace, the shortest of the three men, was a bit taller and broader than Eric. Bowen and Peter had always seemed especially large to her, but she began to think Eric had been right to say that, next to most men, he was not particularly big. Then, seeing the anger darkening her clansmen's faces, she began to fear for Eric's safety.

"Ye dinnae need to crowd him like that or glare at him so," she said as she hurried over to Eric's side.

"Nay? Who is the bairn?" demanded Wallace.

"James, Sorcha's son. What are ye doing here anyway?"

"That is nay important. I want to ken why ye were in bed with this bonny laddie!"

"Weel, I think it is important to ken how ye found us."

Eric almost smiled at the way the three men cursed and turned their glares on Bethia. He could sympathize. She was doing a good job of diverting them, but he knew it could not last for long. The big, dark man called Bowen looked stubborn enough to outlast her.

"We were here for the market day," replied Bowen. "We stopped in the inn to break our fast ere we returned to Dunnbea. One of the maids was gossiping about some guests they had. She was most taken with the bonny laddie but complained that he didnae seem to notice her. It confused the lass since the woman he had with him was such a skinny brown lass with the oddest eyes. How could such a fine mon want such a curveless lass whose eyes didnae match? she asked. Weel, that caught my interest. So I called the maid o'er and had a wee chat with her.''

''Fine,'' Bethia said between clenched teeth. ''If ye are intending to repeat the whole of it, do ye think ye could reconsider and leave out the insults to me?''

''I am nay sure, lass. It might make it hard to ken how we decided to come have a wee peek.''

After glaring at Wallace, who was grinning widely, she returned her cross look to Bowen. ''Ye could have at least knocked.''

''Nay. Ye would have slipped away if we had given ye any warning. I taught ye too weel.'' Bowen scowled at Eric. ''Weel, at least in most things. It seems I should have told ye a wee bit more about nay falling for the sweet words of pretty laddies.''

''Sir Eric Murray has kept me and James alive. I think that is the most important thing.'' Seeing that she had their full attention, she told them about her suspicions and how she had had to flee. ''So since ye are now here to help me and the bairn get safely to Dunnbea, I think we can just allow Sir Eric to be on his way, dinnae ye?''

''Nay,'' said Wallace, and then he frowned at Eric. ''Murray? Ye have the look of a MacMillan. Aye, and there is a fine lot of seducers in that clan.''

''He is Sir Eric Murray,'' Bethia said, but the men refused to allow her to distract their attention from Eric again.

Eric smiled faintly as all three men looked at him. He found it interesting that Wallace thought he was a MacMillan. That gave him hope that the meeting he would soon have with his mother's kinsmen might not go as badly as he had feared. It had to go better than this one, he mused with an inner sigh.

He knew what would happen now. They were going to demand he do what was right by Bethia. This was not how he had wanted it to happen, but there would be no stopping it. Somehow he was going to have to make Bethia understand that, although her kinsmen were forcing them before a priest, he had no objection to being there.

"Are ye wed, lad?" demanded Bowen.

"Nay," replied Eric.

"Betrothed?"

"Nay."

"Weel, ye are now. Ye are betrothed to the lass and ye will be wedding her verra soon."

"Nay!" Bethia protested, chilled by the thought of Eric being forced to marry her.

"Dinnae be a fool, child. Ye are a weelborn lass and ye were a virgin."

"Nay, I wasnae." She scowled when Bowen gave her a mildly disgusted look and then looked at Eric, one dark brow raised in silent query.

"Aye, she was," Eric quietly answered the unspoken question.

"Eric!" Bethia could not understand why he was being so complacent.

"I cannae let ye blacken your name, can I?"

Once marriage was demanded and Eric had agreed, Bethia could say nothing to get the men to change their minds and just let Eric go. Bethia soon found herself mostly ignored as their things were packed and they all left the inn. Worse, her clansmen very neatly kept her separated from Eric so that she could not even talk to him. It was going to be hard to find a way to free him if she was not even allowed to speak to him.

The ride to Dunnbea did little to lift her spirits. She and James were set behind Wallace while Bowen and Peter flanked Eric. All anyone would allow her to talk about was the trouble with William. Bethia found some comfort in the fact that her clansmen believed her talk of murder and threats without hesitation. She wished they would be so accommodating when she tried to talk them out of dragging Eric before a priest.

As they rode through the gates of Dunnbea, Bethia found her thoughts and concerns pulled away from Eric for the first time since their rude awakening at the inn. Now she would confront her parents. She was suddenly uneasy, not certain that they would believe James was in danger. As she was hurried off to her room so that she could clean herself and James up before seeing her parents, she also dreaded what they would have to say about Eric.

"What a bonny wee laddie," her maid Grizel said as the young woman hurried into Bethia's bedchamber and gazed at James, who lay on the bed playing with his toes.

As she tugged off her gown and began to wash up, Bethia eyed her maid. Grizel and she had known each other for nearly ten years. They were almost friends. Bethia suspected that, if her parents and Sorcha had not kept the woman rushing around from dawn to late at night, she and Grizel could actually have been very good friends. There simply had not been time to really get close. The slightly plump, brown-haired woman was only a few years older than her and had but recently married Peter. If Peter loved her, Grizel had to be the good, kindhearted woman she appeared to be, and Bethia wondered if there might be some help to be had there.

"Oh, nay. Nay, I willnae do it," Grizel said, looking at Bethia over James curls with wary brown eyes as she hugged the baby.

"I havenae asked ye anything yet," said Bethia.

"I ken it, but my Peter warned me. He said that if ye start staring at me, steady and hard, and there is a considering look on your face, I should just say nay and keep saying it. He said ye are at your most dangerous when ye are considering something."

Bethia wondered if she had time before meeting with her

parents to go and smack Peter. "Where have they put Sir Eric Murray?"

"Weel, they took him in to meet with your parents for a wee bit and then put him up in the east tower."

"And locked him in, nay doubt."

"Aye. Oh, lass, that is one fine looking mon."

"He is, but his bonny looks arenae going to get him out of that tower, are they?"

Grizel put James down and hurried over to help Bethia into a clean gown. "Nay, and neither are ye."

"Grizel, they are forcing that mon to marry me."

"And so he should after bedding ye and dinnae try to deny that he did, for my Peter told me how they found ye."

"Ye did a lot of talking ere ye rushed in here."

"Peter can talk verra fast and he told me most of it as I ran here. That mon had to ken that this could happen when he seduced you." Once Bethia was dressed, Grizel moved to clean up James. "Ye are a lady and were a virgin. Honor demands he wed ye."

"Mayhap I dinnae want a husband who was forced by honor to wed me."

"Considering what the two of ye were doing at that inn, I would say there is a wee bit more atween ye than honor. Dinnae look so sad, Bethia. He isnae yelling, isnae angry at all. Fact is, he was most pleasant. Went to the tower chatting most amiably with Bowen and Wallace. He didnae look at all like a mon being forced to do something he doesnae want to do."

Eric's friendly complacency had troubled Bethia a little. The few times she had looked his way as they had ridden to Dunnbea, he had seemed relaxed, had even smiled at her. She was not sure how a man forced to marry would act, but she did not think Eric was behaving quite as one would expect. She wished she could talk to him, find out what he was thinking. Bethia had the sinking feeling she was not going to have a chance to say one word with him until they were already securely married.

"Weel, since ye dinnae seem ready to help me—"

"Not in this. Ye have been seduced. The mon must do right and wed ye. Come, Bethia, he is a fine-looking mon and ye have had no other offered for a husband. If all had been as it should have with you, a husband would have been chosen for you. Take this one, for believe me, ye are probably getting a far better one than your parents would have chosen. He is fair, young, and ye obviously like how he warms your bed. I dinnae believe your parents would have e'er willingly wed ye off to any mon."

"Why?" Bethia asked, thinking the same, but unable to understand.

"Ye do all their work for them. Ye are verra useful. I am nay the only one who thinks they planned to keep ye here to see to all their needs and run this keep. Here is your chance to get away from them, to have a husband and some bairns of your own. Take it, lass."

"A sensible lass would, wouldnae she? A sensible lass wouldnae be hoping the mon would have asked her to be his wife because he cared for her and accept honor and vows said as good enough. And a sensible lass wouldnae worry about wedding a mon that the lasses chase after like hounds after a hare." She smiled faintly when Grizel laughed. "Weel, it doesnae matter, truly, for 'tis clear that neither I nor Eric will be given much choice."

"Nay, lass. None. Shall we take this laddie down to meet your parents?"

"Aye, 'tis best to get such confrontations o'er with as fast as possible."

Bethia fought to grasp some confidence and calm as she walked to the great hall, where her parents waited, but the moment she stepped inside and saw them, she lost what little she had gained. Grizel marched over to her parents to hand Lady Drummond her grandson and Bethia reluctantly followed.

She stood unnoticed as her father and mother studied James

as if he was some strange object, then handed the baby right back to Grizel. Bethia inwardly frowned, for there had been little sign of delight over the child and only one or two cool remarks about how James looked a little like Sorcha. It appeared, for the moment, that poor little James was not going to be smothered in appreciation just because he was part of the much adored Sorcha. The thought that the child might find himself treated as she and Wallace had been chilled Bethia to the bone, but she was not sure what she could do about it.

Then her parents turned their matching green eyes on her and Bethia had to crush the sudden urge to run. She felt like a scared, unhappy child and she hated it. Not only had she left Dunnbea but she had bedded down with a man. She had given them a great deal they could berate her with, and Bethia had the sick feeling that this scold was going to make all the past ones look insignificant.

"So ye took it upon yourself to bring the child away from its home," Lord Drummond said, slowly drumming his plump fingers against the arm of his heavy oak chair.

"Did Wallace nay tell ye the danger James was in?" Bethia asked.

"He told us that ye believe the lad was in danger, but ye have always had too fanciful a mind."

"This was nay fancy, Father. The food they brought us was poisoned. It killed James's puppy. Nay, this is no game," Bethia said forcefully even though her heart was pounding with fear. She had never stood up to her parents before, but the need to protect James gave her the strength. "William Drummond wants the lad dead and I am certain that he killed Sorcha and Robert."

"Of course he shall be made to pay for the death of our daughter, if what ye believe is true."

But nay for trying to kill James, Bethia thought and inwardly shook her head. Bowen and Wallace believed her. They would help her keep James safe even if her parents refused to accept her tale. And whether Eric wanted to be or not, soon he would be bound to the family. He also believed her, had been at her side as they had fled from William and his men. She did not need her parents to understand or believe her.

"Whatever danger ye think there might be doesnae excuse your behavior," Lady Drummond said, clasping her plump hands in her lap. "Did ye nay think of the shame ye would bring us ere ye decided to play the whore?"

"I do hope this young mon was the only one ye bedded down with," her father said.

For a moment, Bethia just stared at them. She could not think of one thing she had ever done that would make them think that, the moment she broke free of the walls of Dunnbea, she would be tossing her skirts up for any and every man. Bethia began to wonder if they knew her at all. Then she tried to soothe her hurt feelings by telling herself that they were just shocked and angry, that they did not really mean all they said. Making excuses for them was an old trick, but it was not working as well as it always had before, and Bethia wondered what had changed.

"I was wrong to lie down with Sir Eric, but he is the only mon I have e'er been with."

"Weel, after tomorrow ye will be his problem," her mother snapped. "If ye have taken up whorish ways, he will have to beat them out of you."

"Did ye give no thought to us at all?" demanded her father. "Ye have work to do here, yet now ye must leave us with no one to take your place. I cannae believe we have raised such an inconsiderate child. But then ye have always done as ye pleased, havenae ye?"

"Nay like your sister, God rest her blessed soul," her mother added, sniffing loudly. "Nay, our Sorcha kenned how to make her parents happy and proud. But she is dead and yet ye are still here. I shall ne'er understand how God could take our angel and leave ye here. It—"

Whatever her mother had been about to say was lost, for James suddenly began to scream. Bethia immediately took the child from Grizel and hugged him, rubbing her hand over his back to soothe him. When James quieted, leaning heavily on her shoulder and sucking on his fingers, Bethia noticed that he was scowling at Grizel. She glanced toward the maid and decided that Grizel looked far too innocent. It was unusual for James to suddenly start yelling and Bethia began to think Grizel had somehow prompted it. Holding James close, she looked back at her parents and caught them looking at James in mild distaste and confusion.

"Are ye sure he is Sorcha's child?" Lord Drummond asked. "I cannae recall our wee angel making such a horrible noise."

"This is Sorcha's son," Bethia replied. "He can be sensitive. 'Twas probably the anger in the room that started him wailing," she murmured and kissed the top of James's head to hide her face in case the lie she had just told was visible there.

"Weel, she did send us word that she had borne Robert a son, so we must believe ye, must we not?"

"Ye wouldnae try to foist some by-blow of yours off as Sorcha's bairn, would ye?" her mother asked, squinting at James as if she sought some clue in the child.

Bethia could not believe her own mother could say such a thing to her. She had always wondered why her parents had not rushed off to visit with their new grandson. Now she knew. They simply were not interested. It was probably even worse than that if they were so willing to mark James as her bastard just because he was not as perfect as his mother.

"This is Sorcha's son, and if I must, I will drag every person at Dunncraig before ye to testify to the fact."

"There is no need to speak so sharply to your mother," her father said in a cold voice. "Enough talk about the bairn. Ye will be wed on the morrow. I have sent Peter to fetch a priest. He will hear your confession, and let us pray that he can give ye absolution for all your sins, and then he will marry ye to Sir Eric Murray.''

Bethia feigned a curtsy, and even though she had not been formally dismissed, she hurried out of the great hall, Grizel close behind her. She prayed that she would not have to face her parents again. Her insides churned with a mixture of hurt and fury. Of all the things she had envisioned them saying, she had never once imagined such a cold disregard for James.

''I thought they would love him as they loved his mother,'' she said quietly as she entered her bedchamber and set James on the bed.

''Aye, I rather thought the same,'' Grizel agreed as she sat down next to the baby and watched Bethia pace her room. ''He is such a bonny child and sweet.''

''Except when someone pinches him,'' Bethia murmured, glancing at Grizel and smiling faintly when the woman blushed. ''Ye must cuddle him now so that he forgets it or thinks ye didnae do it apurpose.''

Picking the child up and holding him on her lap, Grizel sighed. ''I wanted her to shut her mouth.''

''She did. It hurt to hear it, but I wasnae surprised that she wished it was me buried at Dunncraig and nay Sorcha. Howbeit, I must set aside such hurts and set my mind to the care of this lad.'' She stepped over to the bed and lightly ruffled James's curls. ''I will raise him and I will protect him.''

''What of the mon ye are about to marry? Will he be willing to take on a bairn as weel as a wife?''

''I may nay ken how Eric feels about being dragged before a priest, but I have no doubt at all that he will accept the charge of James without hesitation. He loves the boy,'' she murmured and tried not to feel jealous. ''Aye, we will be a family. I just pray to God that I have the strength and wit to make it a good and loving one.''

* * *

Eric looked up from the meal he was finishing when Bowen entered the tower room. He leaned back in his chair and sipped his wine, watching closely as the big man shut the door and leaned against it. The look on the man's rough face told Eric he had not come just to see that he was comfortable in his prison. He had been expecting the man, however. Bowen was more family to Bethia than either of the plump, coldhearted people he had met upon his arrival at Dunnbea.

"Do ye want the lass?" Bowen asked abruptly, his brown eyes narrowing as he closely studied Eric.

"I would have thought that was obvious," Eric drawled.

"I mean for a wife, ye rogue."

"I am to be wed to her tomorrow."

Bowen grimaced and dragged his fingers through his long dark hair. "Aye, that is the plan."

"Are ye here to offer me another choice?"

"I have kenned the lass since she was little more than a bairn staggering with her first steps. Ye met her parents. Cold bastards who saw only the bonny Sorcha. Little Bethia was naught to them but an annoying shadow that occasionally crossed their path. The much loved Sorcha didnae treat her any better. Me, Wallace, and Peter talked this o'er and we dinnae want her going to a mon who, once the heat has cooled in his blood, will treat her nay better. At least she kens the way of it here and has made a place for herself."

Eric smiled faintly. "And so ye will let me go if ye dinnae think I can care for her as she needs to be cared for."

"Aye."

"I will marry Bethia. She is mine. I wish I could have had time to make her believe that I want her, but I shall have to deal with that after the vows are said and nay before."

"Do ye love the lass?"

"I am nay sure what I feel. Running from men trying to kill her and the bairn didnae give me much time to puzzle o'er my feelings. All I ken is that she is mine. The first time I held her, I kenned that I would ne'er allow her to leave me. I kenned the bond in my heart, my mind, my soul. When she became my lover, she sealed her fate. She just doesnae ken it yet," he added with a slow smile, pleased when Bowen grinned back with perfect male understanding.

Chapter Nine

"He will be here in but a moment, lass," said Bowen.

"I suppose it would take a wee bit of time to remove the chains," she muttered, scowling at the people gathered in the hall, then at Bowen when he grinned.

"Lass, ye bedded down with the mon."

"That doesnae mean I wish to have him for a husband. Mayhap I just thought he was bonny and decided it was time to take a lover."

"Aye, and I am about to retire to a monestary." He patted her on the shoulder. "I ken ye too weel, lass. Ye may nay wish to say it aloud but ye had to love that lad ere ye would bed him. He is a good lad and he will make ye a fine husband."

Bethia nodded and idly smoothed her hands over the deep green velvet surcoat she wore. Grizel had found some of the gowns Sorcha had left behind, and after a little stitching to make the gowns fit her slimmer shape, Bethia was dressed finer than she had ever been before. Her hair hung loose and a braided gold netting was draped over it. Her parents had made a few sharp remarks about her audacity in wearing her hair as if she was still a maiden bride, but for once, Bethia was able to ignore their disapproval. Eric liked her hair loose.

A murmur amongst the crowd warned her of Eric's arrival. She watched him as he walked toward her, dressed in his plaid and a fine linen shirt. He was such a beautiful man. Bethia could not help but wonder how he could be happy about this when he could do so much better than her for a wife.

Eric smiled crookedly as he took Bethia's hand in his and brushed a kiss over her knuckles. She looked nervous and a little sad. She needed assurances from him but now was not the time nor the place to give her any. He kept her hand clasped in his as he looked at Bowen, glancing only briefly at Bethia's parents who sat on the dais at the head of the hall.

"They ne'er came to speak with me again," he said.

"Nay. 'Tis settled in their mind," answered Bowen.

"For all they ken, I could be taking her to a wee shieling in the hills."

"They have offered ye no dower for me?" asked Bethia.

"Nay, lass, but I am nay needing one." He kissed her on the forehead.

"Weel, that is verra gallant of you, but whether ye need one or nay, they should have offered one."

"Dinnae fret yourself o'er it. Come, they are waving us forward. 'Tis time to kneel afore the priest."

"Eric," she began as he started to pull her toward where the priest waited for them.

"Ye said ye were mine, didnae ye, my heart?"

"Aye, I did."

"Weel, we are about to make that a true fact, sanctioned by the church."

She had no more chance to talk with him. Bethia tried to take comfort in the fact that she felt no reluctance in him. He might not have chosen her, but he did not appear to abhor the idea of being bound to her. As the priest muttered over them, she prayed she was not about to plunge herself into a lifetime of heartache.

The wedding feast was not as bad as she had feared. Her parents concentrated on the vast array of food set out before them and paid little attention to her. The people of Dunnbea seemed to be genuinely happy for her. Wallace, Bowen, and Peter sat across from her and Eric, ignoring her parents' disapproval over two men-at-arms sitting so high up the table, and they kept conversation going. Bethia relaxed a little when she saw that Eric and the three men were very friendly.

"Ye arenae eating much," Eric said as he offered Bethia a slice of apple.

"I was a wee bit nervous," she murmured.

"Ye are looking verra beautiful, Bethia."

"Sorcha left some of her gowns here and Grizel did them o'er to fit me."

"Are there others?"

"Aye, nearly a dozen. Why?"

"Weel, I would prefer to buy ye your gowns myself and I can afford to, but ye may have need of some finery ere we can get some in the usual way. Can Grizel make some others o'er to fit ye?"

"Certainly, but why?" She sipped at her wine as she frowned at him, for he was looking very serious.

"I may have to go to court e'en before I can take ye to meet my family."

"Court?" Bethia nearly choked on her wine. "I cannae go to court."

"Of course ye can. Ye are my wife now. Where I go, ye go, at least most of the time." Eric inwardly grimaced, for he had not had time to tell her about his planned trip to the MacMillans.

Bowen and Wallace drew his attention away from her and Bethia tried to calm herself. The mere thought of going to the king's court put her into a panic. She had never been trained for such things. There would be rules and courtesies to follow that no one had ever taught her. Bethia was terrified that she would shame Eric and wondered if there was any way she could get him to leave her behind when and if he had to go.

The time soon came for her and Eric to retire to their bed-chamber. He took her by the hand and led her to her parents so that they could politely take their leave. Bethia held her breath and prayed that her parents would just mutter some bland courtesy and let them escape.

"I think ye could have asked us if ye could ruin Sorcha's gowns like ye have," her mother snapped.

Bethia sighed, then frowned at Eric. His grip had tightened almost painfully on her hand and he looked coldly furious. She placed her other hand over their joined ones in a silent bid for peace.

"I didnae wish to shame ye by coming poorly dressed to my wedding," she said.

Lord Drummond scowled at Eric. "I suppose ye will be taking her away from here."

"As soon as I am able, sir."

"Weel, I hope ye have the wit and strength to make her a more obedient and respectful lass. We could ne'er do anything with her. She will be your burden now."

"Aye, all mine. We wish ye good sleep, laird, m'lady."

Bethia barely had time to feign a curtsy to her parents before Eric was dragging her from the hall. She caught up her skirts in one hand so that she would not trip as she hurried to keep up with his long strides. Only once did she force him to halt, yanking on his hand as they started to walk past Grizel just inside the doors of the great hall. The grinning maid held James and Bethia gave the boy a kiss on the cheek. Eric paused to do the same, then started towing her along again. Only a few rowdy bellows followed them out of the hall and Bethia thanked God for the reticence the people of Dunnbea showed.

When they reached the bedchamber that had been assigned

to them, Eric gently pushed her inside, slammed the door, and immediately went to the table that held the jug of wine and two goblets. Bethia stood where he had left her, wringing her hands as she tried not to be distressed by his sudden anger. He had a right to it, she told herself firmly, and she should not allow herself to be hurt by it.

"Eric," she began, wondering how one could possibly apologize for something that would affect the rest of his life, "I am so sorry."

Eric finished his drink, refilled his goblet, and poured one out for Bethia. "Lass, I have a feeling ye are apologizing for the wrong thing." He handed her the goblet, smiled briefly, and took another drink.

"Ye are angry. Ye have every right to be angry. I dragged ye into the midst of my danger and now ye have been weel and truly trapped."

"I dinnae feel trapped, my heart. I wasnae angry because of the wedding. I have ne'er been angry about that. Nay, I was angry at your parents."

"Oh. Weel, aye, they could have been a wee bit more courteous to you."

"I am the mon who seduced their daughter. If naught else, they should wish to wring my neck. Nay, 'twas the way they treated ye that stirred my rage. Ye have no idea how close I came to putting my fist in your father's face." He smiled at her look of shock. "That is why we left so abruptly, although getting ye into this bedchamber was reason enough."

Bethia quickly took a deep drink of her wine. She had been shocked, but not by the fact that Eric had wanted to hit her father. What had stunned her was the swift strong wish that he had done so which had swept over her. There was an anger in her that was becoming harder to keep buried. There may be a few things wrong with her hurried marriage, but Bethia began to think it was for the best if she left Dunnbea as soon as possible. Eric would take her away, and perhaps this anger that seemed to have been bred in her would leave before it made her do something she might regret.

"They are still grieving o'er Sorcha's death," she said. "It makes them unhappy and thus they are unkind."

Eric did not believe that for a minute and he had the feeling that, more and more, Bethia was finding such excuses hard to accept. He would never let her know that her parents had almost sent him away, that they had expressed astonishment that he would even bed the lass. It was Bowen, Peter, and Wallace who had insisted upon the marriage. The only feeling he had gotten from her parents was that they were highly annoyed to be losing their servant, the one who kept the keep running so smoothly.

"Soon ye need not try to explain their unkindness, for ye willnae have to deal with it anymore," he said as he set down his goblet and began to unlace her gown.

"Eric, about James," she said, wanting to get something said about her nephew before passion made her forget everything but Eric.

"He will stay with us." He slipped her surcoat off and began to unlace her corset. "I asked Wallace how they acted toward the lad and what he told me was enough to make me ken that we cannae leave him here with them. If Wallace was already the laird, I wouldnae worry, but nay them. They dinnae even believe that he is in danger."

Bethia hugged him. "Thank ye, Eric. They called him an it," she whispered. "They even, briefly, questioned if he was truly Sorcha's child."

"Whose else's could he be?" he asked, then tensed and pulled her away from him enough to look at her face. "Nay, they didnae ask if he was your bastard, did they?" He cursed when she blushed and nodded.

"Weel, they had ne'er seen Sorcha's son, so they couldnae recognize him as hers. And my having been caught abed with you made them question my morals." Bethia frowned.

"Although I dinnae ken where they thought I had been so that I could get with child, hide the fact, and then have the bairn. Or why I would hide him for a year, then brazenly bring him home. Howbeit, I had shamed myself the once and they were, mayhap, nay so wrong to wonder if I had done so before."

"Hush," he said, his voice hoarse with anger. "Nay another word."

"Eric?"

"Nay, we arenae going to talk about those fools at all. I fear that, if I hear any more of what poison spills from their lips and how ye try to find excuses for it, I shall say something we may both regret."

His blue eyes were dark with fury and Bethia decided she would abide by his wish to be silent concerning her parents. His outrage on her behalf warmed her. A small part of her still tried to excuse her parents, tried to convince her that they did not deserve Eric's anger, but it was easily smothered by the delight she felt over his defense of her.

When Eric got her stripped down to her fine linen shift, Bethia nervously finished off her wine and let him take her goblet away. He started to tug off her shift and she closed her eyes. She was still not comfortable with him seeing her naked, but he was her husband. It was his right, and he seemed to enjoy it.

A soft gasp escaped her when he picked her up in his arms and carried her to the bed. She lay there, watching through her lashes as he disrobed. This time the sight of his aroused manhood only excited her and she reached out to stroke it as he climbed onto the bed beside her.

"I am glad ye left your hair loose," he murmured against her throat, slowly running his tongue along the pulse point in her neck and making her shiver.

"Weel, I wasnae a maid when we said the vows, but ye are the only mon I have e'er been with, so I thought I could pretend without stirring up too much comment." When he framed her face with his elegant hands, she sighed. "I will try to be a good wife to you, Eric. I ken that ye could have done much better than me for a wife."

He brushed a kiss over her lips, then slowly covered her breasts with his hands as he kissed his way toward them. "I could have found a lass with more dowry, mayhap a wee piece of land." He rubbed her nipples into hard points with his thumbs, then took the taut peak of one deep into his mouth. "I could have also found a lass with bigger breasts." He smiled against her midriff when she gasped softly. "And fuller hips."

"Aye, ye could have, so why did ye bed me?" she asked sharply, even the passion he was stirring in her unable to ease all the pangs of jealousy she felt.

"Because ye are mine." He kissed the soft brown curls that sheltered her womanhood, holding her tightly in place when she tried to pull away in shock. "And I dinnae think, in all of Scotland, I would have e'er found one sweeter."

Bethia's whole body grew taut with shock when he kissed her, pressing his warm lips against a place she did not even have a polite name for. Barely a heartbeat later, however, shock was replaced by passion. She shuddered beneath the deep intimacy of his kiss, curling her fingers in his hair to hold him close as he drove her mad with his tongue. He kept her poised on the edge of her release for so long she started to curse him and tried to pull him back into her arms. Suddenly, he relented, joining their bodies with one swift thrust. It was all she needed and she cried out as she was swamped by waves of pleasure.

Eric felt her body clench around his, watched her release transform her face, and felt himself dragged along for the ride. He groaned out her name as he spilled his seed deep within her womb. Slumping down on top of her, he wondered how she could fail to see how perfect they were together. Her innocence had to be what kept her blind to the rarity of the passion they shared, to how beautifully they were matched.

"Ah, Bethia, my own," he murmured as he rolled over onto

his back and tucked her up to his side, "I have nay been a celibate, nay, nor even verra cautious with the ladies, but I have ne'er kenned it to be so wondrous." He sat up enough to dampen a rag in the bowl of water sitting next to the bed and, ignoring her blushes, washed them both clean before lying down again. "Trust me in this," Eric said as he pulled her back into his arms.

Bethia idly caressed his chest and tried not to think of how many women he had known, but it was impossible. "I suppose ye have a vast experience to call upon when ye make this judgment."

He smiled against her hair and then kissed the soft waves. "I fear I do. I was verra greedy when I was young, then grew more, weel, discriminating. But, aye, I have bedded a lot of women. I wish I could have come to this marriage bed as pure as you, but I cannae change the past. I was a free mon, no one held my heart or my name, so I took what was offered. Because of that misspent youth, however, I ken that this is beyond compare. I ken that I keep saying ye are mine, but believe me, my wee wife, I am yours as weel."

"Only mine?" she found the courage to ask, although her voice shook a little.

"Only yours. If I had thought I couldnae hold to the vows I just took, I would ne'er have taken them."

It was no pledge of undying love, but Bethia found comfort in his words. If Eric remained true to her, took his vows seriously, that would give her the chance to make him love her. Surely, if the passion was as fine and rare as he said it was, then it was not beyond hope that love would follow? Bethia prayed that was so, because she dreaded spending her life loving a man who could not love her in return.

"Where do we go from here, Eric?"

He sighed and rubbed his hand up and down her slim back. "I fear ye will stay right here for a wee while, although I would prefer to get ye out of here as soon as I can."

She looked up at him. "Ye are going somewhere?"

"To the MacMillans." He felt her tense against him. "Many of your people have asked me if I am a MacMillan. The look is there. 'Tis time I let my kinsmen see it."

"And do ye mean to do it alone?"

"Ye may still be hunted. Getting to Dunnbea may not be enough to stop William's deadly plots. And although I dinnae forsee any trouble with the MacMillans, whether they accept me or nay, who can say? Nay, 'tis best if ye and the lad stay here until I sort this out."

"And what if they dinnae accept ye as one of their own?"

"I dinnae ken yet."

"Will ye fight them for what is yours by right of birth?"

He cupped her face in his hands and brushed a kiss over her lips. "I dinnae want to, but I willnae lie and say that I will ne'er do so."

Bethia pressed her cheek against his chest. "I ken ye have a right to what ye seek. 'Tis just that I cannae believe 'tis right for people to fight and die o'er money and land."

" 'Tis what sets most people to fighting. That and honor."

"Oh, aye, and look what concern about your honor just got ye."

Eric slid his hand between Bethia's legs and caressed her, enjoying the soft gasp that escaped her. "Aye, it got me this." He slipped a finger inside her and sighed with contentment. "Ah, lass, I do love the feel of you." He moved his hand to the small of her back and held her close. "I can only promise that I will try to solve all of this without a fight."

"That must be enough and I thank ye for the promise."

She slowly moved her hand down over his stomach and then to his groin. The low sound he made caused her to smile, for it held a note of pure masculine contentment. She stroked him, fascinated by the way he twitched and hardened beneath her fingers. Glancing up at him, she saw the light flush of a growing passion on his high cheekbones and realized that she was not completely without power. Eric could drive her nearly mad with desire. Mayhap, she could do the same to him.

Eric trembled when he felt the warmth of her lips on his inner thighs. He clenched his hands into fists at his sides, fighting to keep his desire under control and allow her the chance to test her own budding skills on him. It would do her good, might even give her some measure of faith in herself, if she could see that she could stir him so deeply. When she touched her lips to his swollen member, he shuddered with the force of the pleasure that tore through him. He knew he was not going to be able to let her play her game for very long.

"Lass, are ye trying to drive me mad?" he asked in a thick voice as he threaded his fingers through her hair.

" 'Tis what ye do to me," she murmured. "Pure madness. And mayhap I have some dark motive."

"Ye?" Eric had hoped that talking to her would help him control his desire, but the way her breath stroked him intimately as she spoke, the way her lips moved against him, only made control more difficult. "I wouldnae have thought ye would e'er have a dark motive."

"Ye are leaving me tomorrow to go to the MacMillans."

"Aye, I must. Want to get the business done. Jesu," he groaned when she covered the tip of him briefly with her mouth.

"There will be a lot of lovely lasses at Bealachan. The MacMillans are said to breed some bonny women."

"I have ye."

"Aye, ye do. Howbeit, I have seen the way the women are drawn to ye, Sir Eric Murray."

Each time she ceased talking, she slipped her mouth over him, slowly, tauntingly, and he was not sure he could form a coherent word anymore. "I willnae e'en see them."

"Weel, just in case ye do espy one or two, and just in case they try their wiles upon you, I thought I might send ye on your way with such a warm memory of me that ye scoff at their attentions and think, 'Why should I dally here when I can find such pleasure at home?' "

"Ye will be able to hear me scoff all the way back here."

"Good. I shall be listening."

She said no more and turned all of her attention to sending him into a frenzy with her mouth. Eric tried to maintain some sense of sanity, aching to enjoy the pleasure she brought him for as long as possible, but he quickly succumbed to blind need. With a growl, he grabbed her beneath her arms and dragged her up his body.

Bethia gasped with a mixture of shock and delight when he set her down on top of him, entering her body in one clean stroke. She sat there straddling him for a moment as she savored this new position. Teasingly, she moved up and down on him once, very slowly, and smiled when he groaned and clutched at her hips.

"For a lass who is still verra innocent, ye are a verra fast learner," Eric said in a hoarse, unsteady voice.

"I am glad." She grinned at him, the pleasure rushing through her veins making her feel almost euphoric. "I begin to think there are many ways to play this game."

"Oh, aye, and I am going to enjoy teaching ye each and every one." Eric moved her on him and murmured his pleasure over the feel of her. "Ride your mon, my heart."

She readily obeyed his command. To Eric's delight and surprise, she proved to have a true skill. Bethia kept them both stretched taut on passion's rack for a long time before she drove them over the top. He caught her in his arms as she collapsed on top of him even as he savored the last shivers of his own release.

"I think we need to rest, lass," he said as he tucked her up against his side. "We may have slept apart last night, but we fair exhausted ourselves the night at the inn."

She covered a yawn with her hand and sleepily rubbed her cheek against his chest. "Aye, we are a greedy pair."

Eric felt her grow heavy against him, her breathing slowing in sleep, and closed his eyes. There was some trouble ahead for them, and not only the possible further threat from William. There was the whole matter of his rightful inheritance, for although he might not have to fight with the MacMillans, he knew the Beaton laird would demand one. There was the need to get Bethia away from the poison her heartless parents dealt her in such large doses. There was the king's court to visit to further his pleas and then he had to take her to Donncoill to meet his family. And while he was trying to show her that she had worth, that she mattered to him, there would be the women from his past to contend with. He was embarrassed by how many there were, and he had the sinking feeling that Bethia would, in some way, make him pay a penance for each and every one.

Bethia tried very hard not to yawn while she stood watching Eric prepare to leave Dunnbea. The last thing she wanted her clan to think was that she had exhausted herself in her new husband's bed. That was exactly what she had done, but it was none of their business. She did not like to see Eric leave. He would be on his own again, temptation hurled his way at every turn, not that her presence was enough to stop the women from languishing over him. He would also be alone to think about what he had been dragged into: danger and marriage. There was always the chance that he would decide she was not worth all of the trouble and just stay away.

Eric stepped up to her and gave her a light kiss on the lips. "I am nay sure I will be able to sit my horse for the ride to Bealachan since my wee wife wore me out."

Although she blushed, she said sharply, "Good. Then ye willnae be able to ride anything once ye get there."

"I should tell ye not to worry, scold ye for your jealousy even, and try to assure ye that, e'en if we had nay but kissed last night, I would ne'er turn to another woman. But''—he gave her a sweetly lecherous grin—"I think that might just make me a fool. Be at ease, my heart, I shall nay be gone that long. And''—he caressed her cheek with the back of his fingers—"dinnae forget that ye are now my wife, no longer anyone's daughter or sister or servant, but my wife.'' He mounted and rode out through the gates of Dunnbea.

Bethia turned around, saw that her parents stood right behind her, and suddenly understood Eric's parting words. He had seen her parents there and had probably spoken as much for their benefit as her own. As she slipped by them and started toward her bedchamber, she prayed Eric would not be away for too long. It was definitely time to leave Dunnbea, definitely past time for her to begin a new life.

Chapter Ten

"Murray?" The burly man at the gates of Bealachan scowled at him, a look of confusion in his gray eyes. "Are ye sure? Ye have the look of a MacMillan."

Eric almost laughed. It was amusing to have so many people question him this way, but it also made him feel as if he had erred in staying away from his mother's people for so long. If the resemblance was so strong that the Drummonds and now the MacMillans themselves saw it, one look might well have been enough and he could have saved himself years of tiresome petitions and diplomacy.

"Aye, the name is Sir Eric Murray. I will confess this much. There is a question concerning my birth. I will also assure ye that your laird and his wife will recognize my name. Assure them that I have come alone. I but wish to speak with them."

The man curtly ordered another man to watch Eric and went into the keep. Eric sat calmly on Connor, making no move that could be considered even the slightest bit aggressive or threatening, but it was hard. He wanted to get the meeting done and over with. With so many people recognizing his MacMillan blood, he wanted the laird himself to see it. He also wanted the matter dealt with favorably or unfavorably as quickly as possible so that he could return to Bethia. Favorably would be best, for then, at least in this case, he would not have to decide on whether he fought for what was rightfully his—and risked Bethia turning away from him—or gave up completely and tried not to feel as if he had been cheated.

The man returned and quietly led Eric into the keep. There was a tense alertness to the guard that told Eric he had not truly been welcomed, but he had to wonder if the guard had mentioned his likeness to the MacMillans and that was why he was finally being allowed an audience. A quick glance around as he was shown into the great hall told him that the MacMillans were certainly not refusing his claim because they were poor. There were more chairs than benches in the great hall, tapestries lined the walls, a huge fireplace dominated the far end of the massive hall, and there was a lush carpet on the dais where the laird and his wife sat.

Eric approached the dais, acutely aware of the armed guard close at his side, and bowed. As he straightened up, he watched the laird's eyes widen. The man grew so pale that his wife cried out and grasped him by the arm.

"Dear sweet heaven, 'tis my sister Katherine," he whispered and took a long drink from the silver goblet in front of him.

"I thought ye had the look of us," the guard grumbled and he relaxed at Eric's side.

"I am Sir Eric Murray of Donncoill," said Eric.

"I ken the name. Ye have plagued us for thirteen years with petitions and letters and the like." The laird waved to a seat to the left of him. "I have the ill feeling that I have been lied to and nay by ye as I have always believed."

"Nay, sir, not by me," Eric said quietly as he sat down and accepted the wine a page poured for him. "Graham Beaton holds Dubhlinn and means to continue to hold it. It is to his benefit that no one aid me.''

"He said ye were some bastard who tried to claim he was the child Katherine had born, a child who died.''

"Ah, so he didnae just tell ye that I was her bastard.''

Lord Ranald MacMillan shook his head. "If that was what we had been told we would have taken ye in. 'Twould have been hard to accept that my sister had commited adultery, but it would nay have been hard to accept the child of that sin. Nay, Beaton, Katherine's husband, and now Graham, have always claimed that ye are just some impostor, a liar and a thief who smells easy gain.''

"And he made it verra clear that he wouldnae consider us allies and friends any longer if we allowed ye near us to try to play your game,'' said Lady Mairi MacMillan.

"And ye ne'er questioned why, if I was but some impostor, he would care if ye got a look at me?'' Eric asked.

Lord Ranald winced. "It was easier to believe that than to believe my sister had born a bastard. Her husband—''

"Was a beast and a fool. He wanted a son, spent most of his miserable life begetting children on every lass he could get his hands on, but they were all girls. The mon thought I was the son of his wife's lover and tossed me out.''

"Tossed ye out?''

"He had his men take me into the wood and leave me on a hillside to die. Then he had your sister, my mother, and her midwife murdered or did it by his own hand—I was ne'er sure.''

"Tell me the whole tale.''

" 'Tis an ugly one.''

Lord Ranald laughed shakily and refilled his goblet. "I begin to see that.''

Eric sighed and began. Most of what he said he had tried to tell them in his letters and petitions, but he began to think they had not even read them. He watched Lord Ranald pale with each word he said and realized the man had never seen the true depth of evil in his sister's husband. Eric smiled faintly when he saw tears glistening in Lady MacMillan's eyes. Bethia had looked much the same when he had told her the story.

"And this Graham is of the same ilk?"

"Weel, I believe so. Life for the poor souls at Dubhlinn doesnae appear to have gotten any better under his rule. 'Tis one reason I havenae given up on gaining hold of Dubhlinn. I believe the people there deserve a better life for a change."

Lord Ranald watched him closely as he said, "Ye are Beaton's heir and a true MacMillan, yet ye continue to call yourself a Murray."

"And I believe I probably always will." Eric shrugged. "I was raised for thirteen years thinking I was a Murray bastard. I still felt like a Murray e'en after I found out I was no bastard. 'Tis true that no one would be pleased to claim Beaton as his father, but I dinnae think that is all of it. Balfour and Niger had the raising of me. Mayhap we arenae bound by blood but we are bound in every other way. I owe them my verra life."

"Aye, ye do." Lord Ranald reached out and briefly clasped Eric's hand in his. "Will ye stay a while? There are others to meet. Aunts, cousins. I should also like to tell ye about your mother."

"I am but newly married, sir." Eric briefly told them about Bethia and how he had met her, smiling a little when their eyes widened at the tale.

"The Drummonds havenae asked for aid, or are ye here to tell us that they have?"

"Nay, I dinnae think Bethia's parents believe the tale."

"But ye do?"

"Aye. The only thing I am nay sure of is how the mon will act now that Bethia and the bairn are safe at Dunnbea. Have ye e'er met my wife?"

"A time or two when we went to visit the Drummonds."

"She was ne'er brought forward," Lady Mairi said. "One

occasionally bumped into her or caught word of some mischief she had gotten into. I think she wasnae treated verra kindly," Lady Mairi said cautiously.

"Nay, she wasnae. I should like to get her away from that place and her parents as soon as I can."

"Can a week or two more make all that much difference?" Lord Ranald asked.

Eric hesitated. He already missed Bethia and he was a little worried about leaving her to her parents' untender mercies, for they could easily ruin what little gain he had made, stealing away the hints of spirit and confidence he had begun to glimpse in her. But after so many years of trying to get the attention of the MacMillans, he had it and he had complete acceptance. Not only would it be wise to strengthen that tentative connection, but there was a lot they might be able to tell him about Beaton that could help him later.

"I will stay for a week, two at the most, and then I must return to Dunnbea," he said and smiled crookedly at the delight his newfound uncle and aunt could not hide.

"I will fetch a mon to take a message back to Dunnbea for you," said Lady Mairi. " 'Twill ease your wife's mind."

Eric hoped so. Bethia might try to understand, but he knew she was not sure of him yet. He took some comfort in the fact that she was safe behind the walls of Dunnbea, so, at least for now, he did not have to worry about her safety.

Bethia sighed as she sat on a grassy spot in the rear of the bailey and watched James stumble around. His walking was improving each day, but he still tried to go too fast and tumbled a lot. Letting him practice on the soft grass kept his bruises to a minimum.

She missed Eric and she tried very hard not to. He had every right to stay away for a while. The MacMillans had accepted him and wished him to get to know his kinsmen better. Although it had only been a fortnight, however, she was eager to see him again. She did not sleep well without him by her side and her dreams were tormented with visions of him enjoying the company of beautiful women, women who might lure him away from her forever.

"Cease your sulking," said a cheerful voice from beside her as Grizel sat down on the grass.

"I am nay sulking," Bethia replied.

"Aye, ye are. Ye are missing that bonny husband of yours."

"Mayhap." Bethia sighed when Grizel snorted in disgust over her false haughtiness. "If it will make ye happy, then I will confess that I am worried about the women he must be seeing at Bealachan."

"Aye, I thought ye might be being just that stupid."

"Are ye sure ye are just a maid?"

"Dinnae try to put me in my place. That haughty tone willnae work with me. We have practically grown up together and I am wed to Peter, who is nearly an uncle to you."

"If ye try to make me call ye aunt I believe I will strike ye."

"I am trembling in my slippers. Lass, why do ye think your husband would be sniffing the flowers in another field?"

Bethia stared at Grizel for a moment and then laughed. "What a strange way to put it." Then she sighed and grew serious again. "Ye havenae seen how the lasses slather and drool o'er him. The maids at the inn near to ravished him before my verra eyes."

"Aye, I think I can believe that. He is a fine-looking mon. Some of the lasses here were doing a wee bit of that slathering and drooling."

"If ye are trying to make me feel better, ye are failing miserably."

Grizel laughed. "Sorry. I fear ye have just got to get used to it. Ye cannae blind all the lasses in Scotland."

" 'Tis a thought."

"Nay, ye could ne'er be so cruel. I dinnae ken what to say. I really didnae get the feeling your lad was one to spit on his vows. It would seem to me that ye are being unfair to him. Until he gives ye reason to believe he is unfaithful, ye shouldnae be accusing him of it in your thoughts."

Bethia nodded and caught James in her arms when he stumbled up to her; then she laughed when he immediately started off in another direction. "I ken it. I should just trust him until he gives me cause to do otherwise."

"Aye, and heed this. A mon doesnae mind a wee touch of jealousy in his woman, but only a wee touch. In truth, ye are rather impugning his honor each time ye think he will succumb to the temptation of willing lasses."

"Oh." Bethia grimaced. "I ne'er really thought of it that way."

"Try. If ye let such thoughts plague ye in your mind, soon the cross words come slipping out of your mouth. Next ye ken, ye are accusing him of bedding all the lasses within a day's ride, and if ye accuse him of it often enough, ye just may push him to it. That sort of mistrust and jealousy can be a poison to a marriage, Bethia. I saw it in my mother and father, so I ken what I speak of."

"Oh, I am sorry."

"Nay, 'tis in the past. It taught me something though, and although I cannae say I dinnae get jealous when I see a lass smiling at my Peter, I look to him first. Does he smile back? Is he in my bed every night? Does his passion still burn hot? I still get an aye to all of those questions and it eases the jealousy. Of course, that doesnae stop me from hunting down that forward wee slut who was making eyes at my mon and smacking her." She laughed along with Bethia.

"There is one problem with asking those questions about Eric right now. He isnae in my bed every night."

"True, but ye ken where he is and he has sent ye a message near every other day."

Recalling that, Bethia smiled. "Aye, he has. And he calls my some verra pretty names. My heart and my own."

"Weel, lass, if he is calling ye things like that, I think I should worry less about what he is being offered by the lasses at Bealachan and prepare myself to reward him mightily for refusing them all." Grizel stood up and brushed off her skirts. "I think we had best get that laddie in to have some food and ye are past due for another lesson in courtly manners."

Bethia softly cursed as she stood up and collected James. When she had expressed her dismay over the possibility of going to court with Eric, Wallace and Grizel had begun to train her. Although she began to feel that she would not put Eric to shame, she did think that the king's court was not going to be terribly enjoyable. There were too many rules to remember even about whom to curtsy to and how deep one should do it. The only thing she had enjoyed at all was learning how to dance, but she could not be sure she would ever get a chance to do so.

It was early afternoon when Bethia found herself alone with James with nothing to do. She decided to go and find some herbs. Recalling how helpless she had felt while Eric was fevered that time, she had decided to learn some of the art of healing from Old Helda, the clan's healing woman. Now she was trying to put together her own collection of herbs and medicines.

She briefly wondered if it was wise to go outside of the walls of Dunnbea, then shook aside her fear. From all she had heard, William was now trying to get Dunncraig by petitioning the king and her parents to become James's guardian. Since the messages he had been sending had come from Dunncraig, he could not even be close by. For now, Bethia felt she could venture outside in some safety and she went to find Bowen.

Bowen disagreed. "I think ye ought to stay right where ye are."

"I need to get away from these walls for just a wee while," she said, following him as he walked into the stables.

"A grave will feel even more confining."

"Bowen, the mon isnae even near here."

"How can ye be so sure of that?"

"Because he is sending his messages here from Dunncraig."

Bowen leaned against a stall and frowned at her. "Aye, so it is said. 'Tis just that the mon wanted ye and the lad dead. I have no reason to think he has changed his mind."

Bethia sighed. "Neither do I and that is why I asked for two armed men to go with me. I cannae see what the fool would gain by harming me or James now, but I also ken that he may not have the wit to ken that or he just may want us dead for ruining his wondrous plan to steal Dunncraig. Howbeit, all signs point to the fact that the mon has returned to Dunncraig."

"All right. Two armed men and ye are to return ere the sun sets."

She stood up on her tiptoes and kissed his beard-roughened cheek. "I dinnae think I will be gone even that long."

As she and the two men at arms rode out of Dunnbea, Bethia pushed aside her lingering worries. It was a surprisingly warm, sunny day and she intended to enjoy it to its fullest. James sat in his sling across her chest and looked all around him, babbling and pointing at everything. Bethia hoped his skill with words would improve as quickly as his walking, for she was interested in what he was trying to say.

She glanced in the direction of Bealachan and was a little disappointed not to see Eric riding toward her, then told herself not to be silly. He would return when he was able. Having been tossed aside by his father and left to believe he was a bastard, then rejected time and time again by his true kinsmen, Eric had more right to try to learn what he could about his newfound family than any other person she knew. This acceptance by his mother's family also meant that he would not be fighting over his rights with the MacMillans. Since that would have set him against her clan, she should be glad that he wanted to stay and visit.

Nevertheless, she wanted him home and not just because she sorely missed him in her bed. Even doing as Grizel advised and trusting him until he did something to destroy that trust, she could not stop worrying about him. Him she could trust with just a little effort. The women she did not trust at all and she could not forget that Eric was a lusty man.

"Nay, stop it, ye fool," she scolded herself. "Ye are venturing too close to nay trusting him again."

"Did ye say something, m'lady?" asked the man riding at her side.

"Nay, Dougal, I was just talking to the lad," she replied and sighed when Dougal nodded in understanding.

Bethia smiled faintly. There were some unseen advantages to having a child. One could do silly things and claim one was just playing with the child. One could also talk to oneself a great deal and save oneself from looking foolish by claiming one was talking to the baby. Glancing down at James, she decided she should be a little more careful in what she said around him, however. More and more words were slipping into his happy babble and she did not want to risk him repeating something she might wish to keep secret.

They had ridden just short of a half hour when Bethia had them stop. This was the place Old Helda had said had the best pickings for herbs and medicinal plants. Dougal helped her dismount, then joined the other man in standing guard while she searched out what she wanted. As she struggled to keep James from stuffing any plant she picked into his mouth, she began to collect some of the plants Helda had recommended.

It did not take her long to fill the little bag she had brought, but Bethia felt her hunt had been successful. She turned to the two men with her to tell them that she was ready to leave, and then cried out in fear. Dougal grunted and, wide-eyed with shock, fell on his face, revealing an arrow in his back. The other man screamed as another arrow slammed into his chest so hard it sent him crashing back into the tree he had been standing in front of.

Holding James tightly against her, Bethia stared in horror as nearly a dozen men rode out of the surrounding trees. She recognized three of the men immediately and frantically wondered how William and his sons could have arrived here from Dunncraig so quickly. Their latest pleas for guardianship of James had only arrived yesterday.

As William dismounted and walked up to her, she realized her wits had gone begging. They had all believed that William was back at Dunncraig, but the only one to have given them that idea was William's own messenger. Instead of sitting at Dunncraig trying to steal what was not his by right of birth, William and his men had been lurking around Dunnbea just waiting for a chance to get at her. *And I have just walked into his arms,* she thought angrily.

"Are ye mad?" Bethia demanded, trying desperately to hide the cold fear that was curling itself around her heart.

"Mad?" William frowned as if seriously considering the matter. "Nay, I dinnae think so. I tricked ye into coming outside where I could get you, didnae I?"

"I didnae come here to watch ye murder two good men. I certainly didnae come here because ye somehow lured me to this place."

"I ken it. But I am still the reason ye are here and ye have brought me wee James. I kenned that ye wouldnae be able to stay confined for verra long. All I had to do was allay suspicions about where I was and wait for ye to leave that keep."

"Ye do think ye are so much cleverer than ye are, dinnae ye?" *And I am very stupid,* she thought despondently.

"Oh, I am clever, for, I ask ye, who has won?"

Before she could say anything he drew back his fist and punched her in the face. Bethia knew one horrible moment of fear and pain, then nothing more.

*   *   *

"Bowen," Wallace yelled as he stumbled into the stables. "Ye had best come quickly."

Bowen hurried after the young man and pushed his way through a crowd of people staring at something on the ground. When he finally saw that they looked down at Dougal bleeding from a hole in his chest, he swore. He crouched down next to Grizel and Old Helda who worked to stop the bleeding.

"What happened, Dougal?" he asked, praying the gray-faced young man could stay awake long enough to tell him what he needed to know.

"We were attacked in the wood," Dougal said, his voice a hoarse thread of sound. "Robbie is dead. They thought I was too. 'Twas that William fellow. He took the lass and the bairn."

"Did ye see which way they rode?"

"West."

"Good lad." Bowen glanced at the two women as he stood up. "Do your best by the lad," he murmured and they both nodded.

"Did he say west?" Wallace asked.

"Aye."

"That willnae take the mon back to Dunncraig."

"Nay, it willnae. I think he wants to leave the bodies where they willnae point toward him. Men and horses, lad. If we move fast, we may just have a chance to save them."

Wallace roared out the orders, and as men hurried to obey, he turned back to Bowen. "I hope we can get her and the bairn back ere that mon of hers finds out what has happened."

"Too late," Peter said as he stepped up beside Bowen and pointed toward the man just riding into the bailey.

Chapter Eleven

"Where is she?" Eric demanded.

Bowen grimaced and dragged his fingers through his hair as he looked at Eric. "We think that bastard William has taken her."

Eric stared at the man. He had sensed something was wrong the moment he had ridden through the gates of Dunnbea. Peter, Wallace, and Bowen were busy gathering men and horses in the bailey, their faces grim. Eric had not even bothered to dismount, just ridden over to where Bowen stood.

"James?" he asked, fear for Bethia a tight knot in his belly.

"Aye, the lad too."

"How in God's sweet name did William get into Dunnbea?"

"He didnae. The lass and the bairn had gone out to gather some herbs. They took two men with them. They werenae complete fools. Weel, now one of those men is dead and the other sorely wounded. Peter's wife Grizel is nay sure he will live." Bowen mounted the horse Peter brought to him. "We are going out to hunt for them. Are ye with us?"

"Of course."

"Old Helda and poor Dougal have told us where to begin our search and that will help some," Bowen said.

As the men rode out of Dunnbea, Eric fell in next to Wallace, with Bowen and Peter close behind. "What possessed the lass to leave the safety of the walls?" he asked when they slowed their pace upon entering the wood.

Wallace shrugged. "I dinnae think she believed it was completely safe to leave, but certainly safe enough to go for a short wander with two armed men. William appeared to have withdrawn from the chase, to be just pleading his right to become guardian to the lad through long, tediously polite messages. That fool uncle and aunt of mine were actually considering the matter, which terrified Bethia more than the chance that William might still plan outright murder."

"It certainly terrifies me." Eric glanced at Thomas, who was searching for a trail for them to follow. "Is he good?"

"The best, I think. A few of the neighboring clans have actually borrowed the mon when they had some important tracking to be done. Thomas can find a clue in the bend of a blade of grass."

"I hope he finds the trail quickly. Bethia and James have already been in William's hands for too long."

Wallace frowned. "Do ye think the bastard still means to kill them?"

"Oh, aye."

"It makes no sense. Everyone would ken that he had done it and why."

"I am nay sure he has the wit to see that, and even if he did, he is arrogant enough to think that he can explain it all away and maintain his grasp upon Dunncraig."

"Dinnae worry, mon. We will find her."

"I hope so. I havenae been wed but a fortnight. I have no wish to become a widower."

* * *

Bethia was aware of two things as she started to wake up: The strong smell of horse filled her nose and she could hear James whimpering. Then her head began to throb and the memory of her capture came back to her with sickening detail. Cautiously, Bethia sat up, fighting the nausea that swept over her. Although the pain in her head made her vision blurry, she looked around for James. Her heart skipped with fear when she saw that Iain, the most brutish of William's sons, held the baby before him on his saddle.

"Ah, awake, are ye?" William grinned at her as he rode up beside her. "Head hurt, does it?"

"Oh, why dinnae ye just curl up and die," she grumbled, lifting her hand to rub her forehead only to discover that her wrists were tied together and lashed to the pommel. "We all ken that ye have won. 'Tis naught but childish for ye to gloat about it."

She could tell by the scowl on William's face that his good humor had quickly faded and she was glad. A vicious, stupid William was far easier to understand than a pleasant one. This was the man she recognized.

"I have a right to gloat," William snapped. "All of ye Drummonds, so proud and haughty ye are. Ye all thought I should be so cursed grateful because ye let me take on the name. But that was all ye would give me."

"That was more than ye had when ye married Robert's poor besotted aunt. Ye and your loathsome sons would have been ragged and starving in some filthy hovel if she hadnae taken ye in."

"Dunncraig is mine. I earned it."

"Doing what? Standing about and boasting about what a fine mon ye are?"

"Finer than any Drummond. Where are they for all their

pride? All their beauty and fine ways? Dead. As ye will soon be. As that cursed brat will soon be.''

Despair washed over her as he left her side and rejoined his sons. She fought against it, for it made her weak. Although she could see little chance of escape, especially as long as William kept her and James apart, she knew she had to keep hoping. Without the spark of hope, she would go to her death like a lamb to the slaughter and, worse, take poor little James along with her.

Bethia glanced up at the sky and tried to judge how close it was to sunset. It was not something she had ever been very good at and the pain in her head was not helping her to concentrate, but she felt sunset must be drawing near. Then Bowen would come looking for her. It would be close, but if she could somehow delay William and Bowen was particularly impatient, there was a small chance of rescue. Bethia suspected it was such a small hope, it was a false one, but it gave her something to cling to.

She took several deep breaths and struggled to push aside the pain in her head and her jaw. That pain clouded her thoughts and she needed a clear head. Somehow she was going to have to keep William talking—talking so long that Bowen arrived to cut his murdering throat and she was still alive to cheer him on.

By the time Bethia got her pain under control enough so that she could think without wincing, William ordered a halt. As one of the men untied her and yanked her out of the saddle, she kept her eyes on James. The feeling was just painfully returning to her hands when James was shoved into her arms.

"Get over here and kneel down," William ordered from where he stood in the middle of the small clearing.

"Ye wish me to just meekly submit? Ye are mad," Bethia said and shook her head.

Then she bolted. She knew she had no chance at all of escaping so many men, especially carrying James as she was, but miracles could happen. It also wasted time—time in which Bowen might come looking for her. No matter how much she darted and veered she found every route out of the clearing blocked by one of William's men. Finally one man simply charged her and she was not quick enough to get out of his way. Bethia concentrated simply on holding James out of harm's way as the burly man slammed into her and brought her down, hard, onto the ground.

Even as she was yanked to her feet, gasping for air, Bethia struggled to quiet a screaming James. She knew he was mostly terrified, not badly hurt, but the look on William's face told her that James had better stop crying. William looked as if he was more than ready to kill the child immediately. James's noise would also make it hard for her to get William talking and keep him talking. She sent up a silent prayer of thanks when James was quickly subdued to soft hiccoughs and shudders.

"That was verra foolish," William said. "Where did ye think ye would go?"

Bethia cursed softly as she was forced down onto her knees so hard that pain shot through her already battered body. "Mayhap I ne'er intended to go anywhere. Mayhap I just did it to annoy you."

"Aye, I can believe that. Ye have been naught but a thorn in my side since the day ye rode into Dunncraig."

"Ye killed my sister and tried to kill her child. Did ye expect me to thank ye?"

"I expected ye to be as dim-witted as your sister. She and her foolish husband ne'er guessed my plan. How did ye ken it?" William frowned at her. "Mayhap ye are a witch. Aye, with those eyes, ye probably are."

He sounded very much like a petulant child, and Bethia wished her dagger had not been taken away from her. She ached to bury it deep in his heart. William spoke as if her efforts to stop him from murdering a child were little more than rude or unkind. It showed that he considered James, as well as the child's parents and his own wife, as nothing more than obstacles on his path to riches, insignificancies to be kicked aside. A man like that was, if not already mad, probably very close to it.

She tossed her head to get the hair out of her eyes because, recalling his remark that she was a witch, she had an idea. Toying with the fear so many had of things they did not understand could be dangerous, for it could get her killed very quickly. If she could make them think she had some power they could hesitate, however. It was foolish for people to think she was evil or had strange powers just because her eyes did not match, but Bethia had felt the sting of that fear before. Now she might actually be able to gain some benefit from it. She stared straight at William, not really surprised when he tensed and took a small step back before he could stop himself.

"It was nay hard to see your foul plans written on your black heart," she said.

"I kenned it," he said, his triumph over being right tainted with a hint of fear. " 'Twas the only way ye could have escaped me, the only way ye could have kenned which meal held the poison."

If I am so clever I can read thoughts, what am I doing here? she wanted to rage at him. The man was such a complete fool she was astounded he had stayed alive long enough to torment her. It also enraged her that such a stupid man had succeeded in killing Sorcha and might well succeed in killing her and James. That simply did not seem fair. She did nothing to keep the disdain she felt for him out of her expression. After all, she mused, if she was really such a powerful witch, she would certainly view such a man with utter contempt. Bethia prayed someone would come to help her, for by playing this game, she could easily talk herself into being set afire instead of just having her throat cut. Shaking away that morbid thought, she concentrated on what she should say next.

* * *

Moving through the wood as fast as possible without making noise, Eric and the men from Dunnbea trotted toward the sound of James's crying. Then abruptly all was quiet and Eric felt chilled. "He has stopped."

"That doesnae mean he is dead," Bowen reassured him. "Bethia may have just succeeded in calming the lad."

"They are but a few yards ahead," Peter said as he rejoined them after scouting ahead.

"Alive?" Eric demanded.

"Aye, though 'tis clear that he means to kill them both. They are in a small clearing. Bethia and the lad are kneeling on the ground and William and his men stand in front of her. About a dozen."

Bowen quickly instructed his men to encircle the clearing, placing his two skilled archers at William's back. Wallace and Eric moved toward the place that would put them behind Bethia and James. Once the attack started, it would be important to get Bethia and the child out of harm's way as fast as possible. Eric tried to find comfort in Wallace and Bowen's assurances that Bethia would know what to do once the attack began, but he was too afraid for her to be reasonable. When he heard what she was saying to William, his fear grew and so did his confusion.

"What game does the lass play?" he muttered as he sprawled on his stomach next to Wallace, using the thick undergrowth of the forest to hide himself.

"William is obviously one of those fools who think Bethia is a witch just because her eyes dinnae match," Wallace replied in a voice as soft as Eric's, barely loud enough to be heard by the man at his side and easily hidden by the noise of men and horses in the clearing. "I am nay sure how she thinks it will help her though."

"It could just get her killed all the quicker. 'Tisnae wise to toy with a mon's fears."

"I ken what ye plan now," Bethia said, keeping her voice low and hard.

"Aye, I plan to kill ye and the bairn and claim Dunncraig," William snapped. "That wasnae hard to guess."

"Ye will ne'er hold Dunncraig." Bethia was pleased with the power of her voice and the way William paled slightly. "Do ye really think my clansmen or my husband will believe the bairn and I were killed by thieves or vagabonds?" The way William's eyes widened and his sons looked at her in gaping astonishment told her that she had guessed his plan correctly. "They ken weel how ye are trying to murder your way into the laird's chair at Dunncraig."

"They have no proof."

"My word on it is good enough. Ye kill me or this bairn and my clan and my husband will hunt ye down. Aye, and your loathsome sons. They will kill ye—slowly. And ye will welcome death, for ere the life's breath leaves my body, I shall curse ye, your sons, and all who help ye. Ye will be covered in great, oozing sores, the stench of which will be so great that no one will be able to abide your company."

"Shut your filthy mouth, witch," William yelled.

"Then all of your hair shall fall out. Next your teeth." William's sons and his men started to mutter. "Ye will be fair crippled by stabbing pains in all of your joints."

"Shut her mouth, Father," Angus bellowed, hastily crossing himself.

"I warn ye, woman," said William, pointing his sword at her. "If ye dinnae cease I will cut your cursed tongue out."

"For every drop of blood that falls from my body or James's, ye will ken a new torment. Your fingernails and toenails will blacken and fall off. Your monhood will become twisted and—''

A scream pierced the air, silencing her. For one brief moment, Bethia thought she had actually put the fear of God into one of William's men. Then she saw a man fall, an arrow in his back. Even as a second pain-filled cry sounded, she grabbed James and ran away from William and his men—and straight into Eric and Wallace.

"Are ye all right?" Eric asked, lightly touching the large bruise on her face.

"Aye," she replied in a shaking voice, reeling from the miracle of her timely rescue.

"Watch her, Wallace," he ordered and strode away to join the battle between William's men and her clansmen.

Wallace grinned at her. "Your monhood will become twisted?"

"It seemed one of those curses that might frighten a mon," she murmured and shrugged.

"Oh, aye, that it would."

Although she did not really wish to distract Wallace, who stood alert and ready to defend her and James if any threat came their way, there was one thing Bethia had to know. "How did ye find us?"

"Luck was with us or, mayhap, with ye and the lad. One of the horses ye took eluded capture by William, but stayed near at hand. Dougal survived, dragged himself onto the horse, and hied back to Dunnbea. We werenae that far behind ye."

"And of course, ye had Thomas to find the trail."

"Aye." He lightly ruffled James's bright curls. "And this wee laddie's voice to follow for a wee while."

"I was so afraid I had failed him, had led him straight to his death."

"Nay, lass. William fooled us all. We thought he had gone back to Dunncraig too, or we would ne'er have let ye and the lad ride outside of the walls of Dunnbea. Your mon was nay pleased to find out we had done so.''

Bethia frowned toward Eric, but quickly looked away, unable to watch him fight without feeling choked with fear for his safety. She wondered if she should allow herself to see some clue to Eric's feelings for her in his anger over the fact that she had left the safety of Dunnbea, then told herself not to be a fool. He had sworn to protect her and James and had done so again when he had wed her. Eric was a knight, a man of honor. He had left her at Dunnbea, thinking her safe, only to return and find her in danger. That was all that stirred his anger. She glanced once more toward Eric, saw him fighting his way toward William, and hastily closed her eyes. She stopped worrying about what he did or did not feel for her and started praying for his safety.

Eric swore as he cut down the man standing between him and William only to have another shoved into his path. William was throwing away the lives of his men just to save his own. It was hard for Eric to control his fury as he saw how close the man was to reaching his horse and the chance to escape.

"Stand and fight like a mon, ye filthy bastard," Eric yelled even as he fought the man William had pushed into the fight.

"I dinnae plan to die here," William replied as he struggled to get hold of the nervous horse. "Nay, that bitch has caused me to lose my sons and the lands that should have been mine. I intend to live long enough to make her pay dearly for it."

Cursing viciously, Eric knocked the sword out of his opponent's hand, then glared at the white-faced man. "Get out of my way," he snarled and was not surprised when the man bolted, making no attempt to pick up his sword and return to battle. "Ye brought yourself to this end," Eric said as he darted around the men still fighting and the bodies of the slain.

"Dunncraig should have been mine!" Wallace screamed as he swung up into the saddle and kicked his mount into a gallop, heedless of anyone who was in his path.

"Wallace!" Eric yelled in warning even as he ran after the fleeing William.

Wallace cursed as he saw William bearing down on them, his sword raised. "Move out of the way the moment I yell *now*, Bethia."

"Sweet Jesu, does he mean to run us down?" she whispered, holding James close and wondering how she could protect him.

"Now!" Wallace met and deflected William's deadly swing, but the force of the blow staggered him.

Although it felt cowardly to do so, Bethia darted behind Wallace as William tried to control his panicked mount. Twice more he tried to cut down Wallace and get to her. Then he looked beyond her and cursed. A quick glance over her shoulder told Bethia why. Eric and the others were racing toward them. William could not fight them all, and what few of his own men had survived were using the distraction to run for their lives.

"This isnae o'er yet, bitch," he yelled at Bethia.

"Ye have lost, William. Give it up," Bethia replied, frightened by the look of madness twisting his features.

"Nay. Ye must pay for the lives of my sons. Ye and the bratling."

William galloped away, disappearing into the wood. Bowen sent two men after him, but Bethia could tell by the expression upon his face that he did not hold out much hope of catching the man this time. She trembled as Eric stepped up beside her and put his arm around her shoulders. After a quick look showed her that he had no wounds, she leaned against him. He smelled of sweat and blood, but for the moment, she did not care. She needed his strength to calm her fears.

It had been a near escape, too near. Worse, Bethia knew that it was still not over. With so many witnesses to his attempt to kill James and her, William could no longer work from the strength of Dunncraig. He was now a hunted man. She believed his threats, however. Being stripped of everything—his sons, lands, coin, and fighting men—would not stop William. Now he would hunt her not for greed, but for revenge. And now that he knew his plots for gain were known, he would do his hunting from the shadows.

"What were ye thinking of to leave the safety of Dunnbea?" Eric asked after taking a long drink from a wineskin Wallace gave him and then offering some to Bethia.

After a quick glance around revealed the men of Dunnbea at the grim task of stripping the dead of all that was valuable, Bethia took a long drink of wine and decided to fix her attention only on Eric. "I fear I believed in the false trail the mon had laid. I thought he was at Dunncraig."

Wallace muttered a curse and nodded as he accepted his wineskin back. "We ne'er thought to question or spy upon his messenger." Wallace took a drink, glanced around, and then pointed to one of the dead men with an arrow in his back. "That is him right there."

"Do ye recognize any of these men as Drummonds from Dunncraig?" Eric asked.

"Nay," replied Bethia, "but William had obviously replaced Robert's men with his own, most of them base hirelings."

"Men who wouldnae be troubled fighting for a mon who gained his land and wealth through cowardly murders. The true men of Dunncraig might also have had some qualms about attacking other Drummonds, true Drummonds."

"There were a few who were ready to betray their clan, their blood, and aid that usurper in the hope of some reward. I didnae see any of them here, however. They will probably have to be cleared out of Dunncraig." She glanced in the direction William had fled and shivered. " 'Tis nay o'er yet."

"Weel, if any of those curses ye hurled at his head should take, he will be verra easy to find," Eric drawled, and he grinned when Wallace laughed. "It should be quite easy to find a bald, toothless, pain-ridden mon who limps and has blackened toenails and fingernails."

"Ye heard it all, did ye?" Bethia felt somewhat embarrassed.

"Right up to the threat of a twisted monhood." He chuckled when she blushed deeply, but then grew serious. "What were ye thinking of, my heart? Ye were pushing those men hard, stirring up their darkest fears. They were aching to cut ye down."

"Actually, I was hoping that they might hesitate to murder me out of fear. They were clearly more than ready to believe I was some witch. Aye, and all because I didnae eat the poisoned food William had sent to me and James."

"They could just as easily have killed ye a lot sooner than they had planned to."

"All I could think to do was to gain some time," Bethia said quietly. "I had already gotten him to boast of all his crimes and argued over the wisdom of killing James and me. Then he mentioned that he thought I was a witch. It gave me the idea of trying to make him think it was dangerous to kill me. After all, if he was fool enough to even think I was a witch, surely he was fool enough to believe my claim that I was and to fear my great powers. I wasnae sure rescue would come, for I thought both my guards were dead, but I was compelled to try to gain enough time for someone to come and rescue me. Bowen had told me that I must be back by sunset and I kenned he would set out to find me as soon as that time had passed. I was trying to hold off the execution William had planned for me and James."

"Weel, as a plan it wasnae perfect, but it served its purpose," Eric said, nodding a greeting to Bowen as he joined them.

"Time to leave this dark place," Bowen said, briefly touching a sleepy James's curls.

"Aye," Bethia agreed. " 'Tis a place of death, those promised and those fulfilled."

Bowen nodded as he started to walk toward where the men from Dunnbea had left their horses. "And witchcraft."

Bethia sighed and shook her head as all three men laughed. "I shall ne'er hear the end of this, shall I?"

"Nay." Bowen bent to kiss her cheek, then laughed again. "Twisted monhoods, eh? Jesu, that was terrifying."

When all three men laughed yet again, Bethia decided to just ignore them. She allowed them to have their fun. It was good to hear the laughter, for she doubted it would last long. William was still out there and now he wanted revenge.

Chapter Twelve

"At least ye didnae get any of our men killed with your foolishness," said Lord Drummond.

Bethia inwardly sighed and filled her trencher with food. She had succeeded in avoiding her parents when she had first been brought back to Dunnbea. Eric had skillfully gotten her upstairs and into their bedchamber, where she had had a calming bath and a rest before her parents had even seen her. By the time he had returned to take her to the great hall for the evening meal, she had hoped that enough time had passed to dull the bite of her parents' tongues. It made her sad to discover that had been a foolish hope.

Her parents obviously did not want to admit that they had been wrong about William Drummond. It would also require them to admit that she had been right about the man, and that was evidently something they could not abide to do. Somehow it had all become her fault, as if she had set out to get herself brutally murdered just to spite them. Not once had they asked if she had been hurt. What really troubled her, however, was that they had not asked after James either. Their only grandchild had been held at swordpoint and they said not a word. It was as if the child did not exist.

"I am sorry," she said. "At least we have reduced the number of our enemies to one."

"And just how is it that he got away?"

That question carried a criticism of Eric, Wallace, Bowen, and Peter, and Bethia could not allow that. The laird of Dunnbea sat on his well-rounded backside, safe inside the walls of Dunnbea, and then dared to belittle the efforts of his men. Even as that thought passed through her mind, Bethia nearly gasped in shock. Never had she had such an angry, almost disloyal, thought about her father. All she could think of was that her need to defend the men who had so gallantly rescued her and James had briefly overwhelmed her, prompting such wicked thoughts. Her father was the laird, she sternly told herself. He had every right to question his men. Bethia wondered why that reminder did not fully kill her anger, then decided that she was simply too tired to be reasonable.

"He used his men as his shield," Eric replied. "We were unable to kill them fast enough to reach him."

Lord Drummond grunted and gave Eric a cross look before returning his attention back to his overfilled trencher. Bethia breathed a silent sigh of relief and tried to eat something. Her father did not like to be criticized, no matter how subtly, and that was just what Eric had done. Worse, she could sense a cold anger in Eric. Although she understood his sense of insult—for himself and for the other men—she prayed he would keep it controlled. She did not want to be caught in the middle of a quarrel between her husband and her father.

A few more remarks were made about her rescue and the threat William still posed. Her father not so gently criticized, and Eric and Wallace not so gently defended themselves while rebuking him. There was no outright argument, but Bethia soon found it all very hard to bear. The food she had managed to eat now sat like lead in her stomach, and she completely lost her appetite.

"I believe I will seek my bedchamber now," she said to Eric, but loudly enough so that her parents could hear.

Eric kissed her on the cheek. "I will join ye soon."

"Eric," she whispered, sensing his lingering anger at her father and fearing he might unleash it once she was gone.

"Dinnae fret, my own. I willnae allow myself to be too provoked."

She nodded and walked out of the great hall. It was both pleasant and unsettling that he could so easily guess her concerns. Bethia hoped it was because he understood her well and not because her face was too easy to read. After all, if he could too easily read her emotions in her expressions, so could others, and she did not want her parents to see the occasional surges of anger and resentment she found harder and harder to control.

"Ye didnae stay verra long in the hall," Grizel said as Bethia entered her chamber.

"I couldnae eat another bite," Bethia replied as Grizel began to unlace her gown. "Father isnae happy to discover he was so completely wrong about William and I fear he tries to find fault with the men. That makes Eric and Wallace angry. The food I was eating began to sit like a rock in my gullet as I waited for someone to cease being politely angry and become truly enraged."

"I would suspect no mon likes to hear the battle he just fought at risk to his own life being demeaned and criticized by a mon who hasnae lifted a sword in o'er a dozen years."

The sharpness of Grizel's tone surprised Bethia; then she recalled that Peter had been one of her rescuers. In a way, her father was heaping scorn upon Grizel's husband as well. Bethia wished her father would be more cautious in his criticism, then decided it was probably too late for the man to change his ways. The fact that so many men lingered in service to Dunnbea despite her father's constant complaints was probably out of loyalty to Wallace and Bowen. They simply waited patiently for the day when Wallace would be the laird of Dunnbea.

"I am sure my father doesnae completely scorn their efforts," she murmured and ignored Grizel's snort of disbelief. "How is James?" Bethia asked as, dressed only in her shift and a thick robe, she sat on a stool in front of the fire so that Grizel could brush out her hair.

"Sleeping like the wee, sweet bairn he is," replied Grizel. "Your mon and I looked him o'er weel, from his soft curls to his tiny toes, and found naught but a few bruises."

"I had hoped that was the way of it. Ah, Grizel, how could anyone, mon or woman, even think of murdering that bairn?"

"Greed, lass. Pure unreasoning greed. Peter and Bowen are enraged that adder slithered out of their grasp."

"So am I. I am also terrified." Bethia shivered and wrapped her arms around herself. "If ye could have heard him threaten me and James as he fled, ye would be too. I dinnae think he was ever fully sane. How could he be and even consider killing five people o'er some land—people who had done him no wrong? But now he is mad. I could see it in his ugly face as he glared at me."

"Dinnae fret. Ye and the lad are weel guarded."

"But how weel can one be guarded against such insanity?"

"With strong, weel-armed men," Grizel said firmly. "Not only will ye and the lad be watched, but that bastard will be hunted." She set a jug of wine and a goblet on a little table next to Bethia. "Now ye set here afore the fire and sip some wine. 'Twill relax ye ere ye get into bed."

"Aye, I am a little weary despite the rest I had earlier."

As the door shut behind Grizel, Bethia poured herself some wine and stared into the fire as she sipped it. She needed to calm herself, not only because of the ordeal of her capture, but the ordeal of dinner in the great hall. Bethia realized she had thought her parents would welcome Eric once he had married her, but that was not happening. Eric was certainly pretty enough to suit them, perhaps even prettier than Robert. The more she thought about it, however, the more she realized that there was one very large difference between Eric and Robert. Eric was a strong man. Robert had been sweet and easily led, just like Sorcha. Eric obviously did not take well to being led, at least not by her parents. It was probably time she, Eric, and James left Dunnbea, and as soon as Eric joined her, they would discuss the matter.

"What are ye doing here?" Bowen asked as Wallace and Eric entered Bowen's small cottage just outside the walls of Dunnbea. " 'Tis late." He winked at Eric as he poured his unexpected company some ale. "I would have thought that, after having been away for a fortnight, ye may have a word or two ye wanted to say to Bethia."

Eric grinned as he sat down on the bench at the rough table. "If she goes to sleep ere I get there, I suspect I can wake her up." He laughed briefly with the men, then grew serious. "I plan to take Bethia to the king's court with me in a day or two."

"So ye will be wanting some men to ride with ye," said Bowen.

"Aye, but my greatest concern is that I also plan to leave James here."

"Dinnae worry o'er the lad," Wallace assured him. "E'en if my uncle is too great a fool to see the threat to the lad, we do. The bairn will be watched verra closely, day and night."

"Thank ye, but there is more that I would ask." Eric took a deep drink of ale to calm himself, not sure of how his next words would be received. It was one thing for members of the laird's own clan or family to criticize the man, quite another for an outsider to do it. "I would prefer it if the laird and his lady have as little to do with the child as possible while Bethia and I are gone. It was my hope that Grizel would share in the care of the lad with his nurse and thus keep the lad quietly tucked out of sight,'' Eric said.

Bowen nodded. "He will be.''

"It may require verra little as the laird and his lady dinnae seem verra interested in the lad. Jesu, I am nay sure they e'en recall his name.''

Wallace frowned and rubbed his chin. "I noticed that. In truth, seeing how much the lad looks like his mother, I was a little afraid they would take o'er his care, doting on him as they had doted on Sorcha. Ye are right, though. 'Tis as if they looked him o'er, decided he wasnae perfect enough, and promptly forgot him.''

"Mayhap they dinnae like looking at the proof that their wee angel actually bedded a mon,'' drawled Bowen.

Eric's eyes widened in surprise. "Ye may just have the right of it. Weel, it matters not how their strange minds work, so long as they dinnae taint James. Now I will be able to reassure Bethia when I tell her the bairn will be left behind.''

"Are ye sure ye wish to travel to the king's court now?''

"I would prefer to wait until William is dead, but, aye, now would be a good time. I have the acceptance and support of the MacMillans, and that will add weight to my claims upon the Beaton lands. Also, to be blunt, if I stay here much longer, I will probably put my fist down your laird's throat—mayhap his lady's as weel.'' Eric smiled crookedly when the other men laughed. "I dinnae want to fight with Bethia's parents, dinnae wish to put her in a position where she might have to choose between us. That would be a trial for any new bride, but, I think, it would be especially hard for Bethia.''

"Go to court. The lad will be shielded from William and Bethia's parents,'' Bowen vowed. "Get the lass away from here. 'Twill do her good to get out from under their bootheels for a wee while.''

Eric suspected Bowen was right. As he walked to his bed-chamber, he considered several different ways of telling Bethia his plans and how to get her to agree with them. He smiled faintly as he entered their room and caught her nodding off in front of the fire. Quietly, so as not to startle her, he walked over and lightly touched her on her shoulder.

"Oh, Eric, 'tis you." Bethia quickly put her hand over her mouth to hide a huge yawn.

"To bed with you, my wee wife, ere ye tumble off your stool and into the fire," he teased as he helped her stand and nudged her toward their bed.

Bethia shed her robe and climbed into bed. Simply getting up and moving was enough to rouse her. She suspected the wine and the heat of the fire had made her so somnulent.

As she watched Eric strip down to his hose and wash up, she decided she could stay awake for a little while longer. She had missed him, missed his touch. After staring death in the face today, she also needed him to hold her, to make her blood flow hot and her heart pound, to make her know she had truly survived.

When he got into bed and tugged her into his arms, Bethia cuddled close to him, then frowned. He had brushed a kiss over her forehead and idly rubbed her back for a moment, then no more. After two long weeks of an empty bed, she had expected quite a bit more than that. For a brief moment, she feared he had sated himself on so many willing women at Bealachan that he had no interest or strength left; then she forcefully reminded herself that she had sworn to trust him. She moved her leg until it rested over his groin and found hard proof that he still had plenty of both.

So why was he lying there like a lump? she mused. Realizing she was drumming her fingers against his chest as her irritation rose, she quickly stopped. Bethia took a deep breath and forced back her demons—the ones that would have her believe he no longer desired her. For some reason, Eric was treating her gently and had obviously decided not to force his desire upon her. Then Bethia recalled all she had been through and almost laughed at herself. Eric probably felt she needed rest and care, not passion. She started to think of all the ways she could change the foolish, if gallant, man's mind.

Eric gritted his teeth against a surge of desire as Bethia moved her small, soft hand over his stomach. He wanted her so badly he did not think there was a part of him that did not ache. She had been hit, kidnapped, and then threatened with death, had even had to endure the fear that James was about to die as well. She needed rest, not some lust-crazed fool pounding into her body, trying to slake a hunger that had gnawed at him for two long weeks. It would be a good time to discuss going to court, he decided.

"I have decided that we will leave for the king's court in a day or two," he abruptly announced, grabbing her hand to stop its tormenting progress up his thigh.

Bethia was immediately distracted from trying to seduce her husband. "So soon?"

"Aye. The MacMillans now fully accept me."

She leaned up and brushed a kiss over his mouth. "I am so pleased for you, Eric."

He swallowed the urge to hold her close for a fuller, more passionate kiss. "It did feel good to be accepted. I am content to be a Murray. I wanted for naught at Donncoill, but a small part of me was pinched by the fact that my own blood had turned their backs on me. The moment I rode up to the gates of Bealachan only to be questioned by the guard if I was truly a Murray and not a MacMillan, I realized I had erred in not coming to them sooner. One look was all the laird needed. He clearly saw his sister in me. He had been convinced by the Beatons that I was just some opportuning bastard. They didnae e'en read the letters I sent them."

"If the mon loved his sister, he would have found dealing with such trickery verra painful."

" 'Tis what he said. His lady wife also said that there was a subtle threat made by the Beatons as weel—something about how they would take it as a personal affront if the laird tried to deal with me in any way. 'Twould be the same as crying the laird of Dubhlinn a liar.''

"Clever."

"The Beatons have e'er been that. But now that the Mac-Millans accept me, now that they believe the tale of murder and lies I told them, they are ready to stand with me as I press my claim for Dubhlinn. They sent word of their support to the king whilst I was there. I feel it would be wise to follow that as soon as I can."

Eric decided it was best not to mention that the MacMillans had also offered him men and arms if he was forced to fight for Dubhlinn. Bethia seemed to accept that he had a right to all that had been his father and mother's. It was the possible need to go to battle to gain it that troubled her. For now he would only talk of petitions. He could only hope that, by the time it came to go to battle—and he was sure that time would come—Bethia would understand that it was far more than some greed for lands that caused him to pick up his sword.

"Weel, I have been learning what I could about the ways of the court," she muttered, "so mayhap it willnae be so verra great an ordeal." She smiled faintly when Eric laughed. "Dinnae forget, I have ne'er really left Dunnbea and have had little training."

"Ye will be fine." He took a deep breath, readying himself for any argument, and added, "I think we should leave James here."

Bethia raised herself up on her forearms and frowned slightly. "Do ye think it will be dangerous to go to court now?"

"No journey is ever completely safe and William still lurks in the shadows. It would be difficult to keep a close watch on James amidst the crowds and confusion that can reign in the king's court. Here, at Dunnbea, he can be guarded day and night and no stranger could e'er draw near unseen."

"That is true." She sighed, then grimaced. "I just dinnae

like leaving him in the care of my parents for too long. 'Tis probably just that they are still so grief striken o'er Sorcha's death that they have found dealing with her child verra painful.'' Bethia frowned briefly, certain that, out of the corner of her eye, she had seen Eric roll his eyes. "They appear to ignore him and that isnae good for the boy. He is a loving child who needs plenty of attention and love.''

"I have spoken to Bowen, and I will speak to Grizel. Bowen and Wallace have already sworn that they will protect the lad and see that he doesnae fall under the care of your parents.''

"It would appear that ye have thought of everything,'' she drawled, eyeing him with suspicion.

"I tried,'' he admitted. "When I feel what I am going to say may cause an argument, I do try to think it through so that I have my thoughts clear and my answers ready. Otherwise I might be reduced to simply repeating my demands, too caught up in the quarrel to indulge in any reasoning or explanation.''

"Ah, and thus begin to sound like the arrogant laird, setting up the hackles of your opponent.'' Bethia smiled crookedly. "Especially if that opponent is a woman. I suspect ye discovered this during your many years as a rogue.''

"Actually, I learned it from watching my brothers with their wives. Standing outside of an argument at times makes it easier to see how it went wrong. It didnae take long to see that making sweeping demands didnae set weel with women who had both spirit and wit.''

"Ye think I have spirit and wit?'' Bethia asked, surprised and deeply flattered.

"More than I think ye ken yourself.'' He lightly touched the bruise on her face, wishing he could have made William pay for that. "Ye faced William with no fear.''

"Eric, I was fair sick with fear for myself and especially for poor wee James.''

"Aye, but ye didnae let it rule, didnae let it turn ye into some cowering, stupid sheep ready for the slaughter. That is spirit."

Bethia was so moved by his praise she felt close to weeping, so she kissed him. He tried to halt her at a brief brush of the lips, but she would not allow that. She teased his lips with her tongue and he quickly gave in, wrapping his arms about her and giving her the passionate kiss she craved. To her disappointment and annoyance, however, he found the strength to stop with but one kiss.

"Enough of that, lass," he said in an unsteady voice as he held her away from him, "or I shallnae let ye rest."

"Husband, do my eyes look as if they are being weighted closed with sleep?" She opened her eyes very wide and stared at him.

Eric smiled faintly. "Nay, ye look quite wide awake. Howbeit, ye have been through an ordeal today."

His voice cracked slightly on the last word, for his slender wife was wriggling down his body, kissing his chest and stomach and rubbing her lithe, warm body against his in a way that made desire throb through his veins. He groaned when she curled her long fingers around his erection. This was more temptation than any man should have to endure.

"Aye, I was punched, kidnapped, and threatened with death." She licked him, smiling with triumph when he cried out softly and threaded his fingers in her hair. "Howbeit, last I looked, naught was broken or cut."

"My heart, after a fortnight of sleeping alone, I am nay sure I will be able to be verra gentle with you." Eric was surprised he could still talk with her mouth and tongue caressing him so intimately.

"Good. After a fortnight of sleeping alone, I am nay sure I will be able to be verra gentle either. And, mayhap, after facing death, a little wild, rough loving is just what I need to make me certain that I survived. 'Twill certainly make me glad that I did.''

She enclosed him in the moist heat of her mouth and Eric ceased to fight. Before he lost all control, he pulled her away and pushed her onto her back. He soon had her in a frenzy equal to his, leaving no part of her silken body untouched or untasted. When he finally joined their bodies, he held still for a moment, eager to savor the feel of her body encircling his.

"Eric?" Bethia called softly as she ran her hands up and down his sleek back.

"Dinnae move, dear heart. I but wished to enjoy the feel of your heat for a moment." He brushed his lips over hers. "I have spent too many long, lonely nights thinking about it." He felt her muscles clench around him and groaned, knowing he could wait no longer. "Weel, mayhap later."

Bethia laughed briefly, then softly cried out her pleasure as he began to move. This was what she needed. She just wished she had the will to make it last longer, she mused, and then succumbed to the force of her release. Eric's cry a moment later told her he joined her in that heady fall and it added to her pleasure. She held him close as they both slowly recovered their senses, wondering a little sadly if she would ever be able to tell him what he meant to her.

"Do ye feel alive now, wife?" he asked as he finally eased the intimacy of their embrace, rolled onto his back, and tucked her up against him.

"Oh, aye." She sleepily patted his smooth, hard chest. "Ye did good, husband." She smiled when he laughed.

"Ye are too kind, madam." He yawned, then grimaced ruefully and shook his head. "As I rode here from Bealachan I had some verra grand plans to spend the night loving ourselves into a stupor."

"I think we have done that."

"Aye, I just hadnae expected it to take only one time."

"Ah, weel, ye hadnae planned on hieing to my rescue ere ye had even had a chance to dismount."

Eric tightened his arms around Bethia slightly, clearly recalling his fear for her. "Nay, and I have an urge to lock ye in a tower surrounded by armed men."

" 'Twould keep me safe, yet somehow, to do so would almost be the same as letting William win."

"Aye, and 'twould make ye unhappy. Both reasons stop me from giving into that urge."

Bethia kissed his shoulder, then rubbed her cheek against it. " 'Tis terrifying to think that the mon lurks out there craving my death. Aye, and especially for things that were his own fault. I cannae let that fear guide my every step, however. Always watching o'er our shoulders, trying to flush him out of whate'er hole he hides in, will be trial enough."

"I ken it." He kissed the top of her head and closed his eyes. "We will find the bastard and then we will kill him."

"I am sorry, Eric."

"For what, my heart?"

"Bringing ye such trouble. Making ye have to kill a mon."

"None of it is your fault. The mon is long o'erdue for killing. 'Twill be naught but justice. Rest now, dearling. Ye will need your strength for the journey to the king's court."

For a long while, Bethia lay in his arms, listening to his breathing slow, feeling his arm grow heavy around her as he fell asleep. Although her body cried out for sleep, her mind was too busy to let it conquer her. Only a month or so ago, the greatest worry she had was whether the garderobes smelled fresh or if she could finally put a meal on the table that her father would not find fault with. Now she had a madman hunting her, a husband, and a child.

The guilt she felt for putting Eric in danger was hard to push aside. It was undoubtedly a cause any true knight would fight for willingly, but Eric now had no choice. She wrapped her body around his a little more tightly. Bethia knew that, if anything happened to Eric, the guilt and fear she felt now would seem like a pinprick next to the desolation which would sieze her. All she could do was pray that his honor and sense of justice did not cost him too dearly. It seemed a pathetic weapon to wield against a madman.

Chapter Thirteen

Bethia grimaced as the maid entered the room to help her dress for the evening feasting. Court was not proving to be very exciting. It consisted mostly of gossip, ceremony, and eating. And women who did not seem to understand that adultery was a sin, she thought crossly. She had only gotten to dance once as well.

She slowly sat up from where she lay gracelessly sprawled on the bed. Sitting very still, she clutched the edge of the bed tightly and took several deep breaths to still the nausea and dizziness that briefly assailed her. They had been at court for almost a month, and in the last week, this illness had struck every evening about the same time. Bethia wondered if she was being made ill by too much rich food and intrigue.

"I can get ye a potion for that, m'lady," said the maid as she helped Bethia into her deep blue corset and skirt.

"A potion?"

"Aye, to rid yourself of the bairn."

"The bairn?" Bethia's eyes widened as she considered that possible explanation for her strange malady.

"Oh." The maid blushed. " 'Tis your husband's child then, is it?"

Bethia looked at the plump young maid and shook her head in amazement. That the girl would so blithely offer her a potion to prompt a miscarriage and, worse, seem a little surprised that she might actually be carrying the child of her rightful husband said more about the immorality at court than Bethia really wanted to know. This was not a way of life she could ever become accustomed to. She was a little surprised that Eric seemed so comfortable, but began to suspect that he simply paid it all very little attention. Men, she decided, often showed a true skill at being oblivious to what went on around them.

"I fear there is no delicious intrigue here," she told the maid, Jennet, smiling faintly. " 'Tis my husband's child. It could be no other's." She frowned as Jennet tugged hard on the laces of her pale blue surcoat. "That is, if I am truly with child. I am nay sure."

"Have ye had your courses as ye should?"

"Nay. Not since before I was married."

The maid nodded as she gently pushed Bethia down onto a stool and began to force her hair into one of the intricately braided hairstyles so popular at court. "And ye feel sick and light-headed every day at about the same time."

"Aye, right now. Although last eve, when they set that odd-smelling egg dish right in front of me, I certainly didnae feel too weel."

"Some women do find that some smells and foods are verra hard to endure when they get with child."

"It seems too soon."

The little maid giggled. "Some women get with child on their wedding night."

Bethia placed her hands over her stomach. It was certainly possible that she was with child. She felt excitement course through her veins, then fought to control it. It was still too soon to know for sure. A great deal had changed in her life lately, and she was living under a constant threat. Such things could easily affect her courses. Although she hated to even think about it, she reminded herself that many women lost their child in the first few months. She decided to say nothing until she was certain that she was with child and that it was well set in her womb.

"I havenae said anything to my husband yet," she said.

"No one shall hear it from me, m'lady."

"Good. I should hate gossip to give my husband such news ere I could share it with him."

"And such a fine, handsome mon ye have too"

"Thank ye." Bethia smiled, then glanced in the polished metal mirror at her elaborate hairdo of coiled braids. She prayed she did not look as foolish as she felt. "I certainly find him so," she murmured, then easily turned the maid's attention to fashion and hair.

Once readied to go to the great hall for the nightly feast, Bethia sent the maid away. She poured herself a tankard of wine and drank it down. It helped brace her for the night ahead. Bethia smiled ruefully as she set the tankard down and left her room. If she and Eric stayed at court too much longer, she could become a drunkard.

Eric met her even as she stepped into the great hall and led her to their table, To Bethia's dismay, Lady Catriona MacDunn seated herself directly across from them. The woman had become a complete nuisance since her arrival only a week ago. Lady Catriona made no secret of her desire to pull Eric into her bed. Bethia could not seem to find Eric alone outside of their bedchamber and, she thought glumly, if Lady Catriona could find a way to get in there, she would.

When Lady Elizabeth MacFife sat down on the other side of Eric, Bethia nearly groaned. Lady Elizabeth also spent far too much time flirting with Eric. Glancing at Lady Catriona,

Bethia caught a fleeting look of anger on the woman's pretty face. That woman obviously did not like Lady Elizabeth's flirtations either. Bethia wished she could find some satisfaction in that. Instead, it looked to be a long, upsetting meal ahead. If she did not already have stomach troubles, this meal would undoubtedly give her some.

Bethia reminded herself that Eric was in her bed every night. He also spent a great deal of his time trying to get the king to heed his case against William and the Beatons. The way he treated the ladies who pursued him revealed no more than simple politeness, a cool courtesy that offered no encouragement. That did not help. Calm and reason were hard to cling to as the meal dragged on, and the only conversation Bethia managed to have with her own husband was if she rudely interrupted the other two women.

She was just thinking of giving up and going to her bedchamber for a hearty sulk when Eric kissed her on the cheek. Bethia prayed he had not done that because she already looked as if she felt sorry for herself. The highly annoyed glances the other two women sent her way soothed her bruised feelings a little.

"Do ye mind returning to our chamber on your own, my heart?" Eric asked. "Lord Douglas signals to me, and I must go and see what he wants. Mayhap he has finally decided to aid me. If he has, I will soon gain what I seek and we can leave this cursed place."

"I think I should like that," she murmured, smoothing her hand over the fine embroidery decorating the front of his jupon.

Eric smiled, his gaze soft with sympathy. "I ken that this is a tedious, unkind place."

" 'Tis where ye must be to gain what is rightfully yours. I do miss wee James though."

"Aye, so do I." He stood up, then bent to kiss her on the forehead. "Just dinnae let any of these lustful rogues distract you."

"Nay, I have found a good stout club to beat the hordes back," she drawled.

He laughed and shook his head, then hurried away to meet with Lord Douglas. Bethia was sweetly unaware of the men who tried to flirt with her. A few tried to lure her from his side out of spite or just to try to claim the coup of cuckolding him, but many were truly intrigued with Bethia's looks and air of innocence. Eric could not completely quell a sense of pride and satisfaction when, each time she entered a room, her gaze sought him and only him.

A grimace crossed his face as he glanced back at their table and watched the ladies Catriona and Elizabeth, both of whom he had once dallied with. He had thought the affairs ended long ago and amiably, but both women seemed to see Bethia as a challenge. Bethia did not plague him with fits of jealousy, but he knew the games the women played were hard for her to bear. It was just another good reason to get her out of there as soon as possible. The very last thing he needed was for some of his old lovers to start regaling Bethia with tales of their affairs or false claims about any continued association. Even he could understand that there was only so much a wife could tolerate and, whether or not Bethia trusted him, had little to do with it.

Bethia sighed as she watched Eric disappear into the crowd. She prayed that he was right, that Lord Douglas was about to help him get what he wanted. Although she would stay if it was necessary, Bethia really wanted to go home. Her home or Eric's home—it did not matter. She had had a bellyful of court life.

When she stood up to leave, she was dismayed to see Lady Elizabeth and Lady Catriona do the same, appearing united for the first time that evening. She had the sick feeling that the women wanted to talk to her privately. Although Eric had said nothing about either woman, Bethia felt sure that, at one time, he had been far more than some coolly polite courtier to them. She did not really wish to have her suspicions confirmed. Knowing Eric had bedded other women in the past could be accepted and set aside. Hearing sordid details about those love affairs could not be so easily dismissed, might even linger in her mind and heart to act like a slow poison upon her marriage.

"We will escort ye to your chambers, Lady Bethia," Lady Catriona said, smiling sweetly.

" 'Tis kind of you, but not necessary," Bethia murmured as she stepped away from the table.

" 'Tis no great imposition," said Lady Elizabeth as she and Catriona flanked Bethia. "We must pass your room to reach ours."

"Ye must tell us how ye came to meet our dear, bonny Eric," Catriona said.

Resigned to a long, possibly grueling walk to her bed-chamber, Bethia told them the tale that she and Eric had agreed on. It was the truth to say that she and Eric had met on the route to Dunnbea and that he had been invited to join her entourage because he traveled alone. The lie was in the implication that her entourage had consisted of the usual armed men and maids, and not just herself and James. Nor was it a complete lie to imply that a love match had ensued, for she, at least, was deeply in love.

"So romantic," murmured Catriona, "but then Eric was always a mon of strong passions."

"Oh, aye," Elizabeth agreed, those two words heavy with meaning.

"A much sought after lover, but he was so discriminating." Catriona patted her elaborately coiffed blond hair and then, after a quick glance at Bethia's chest, fleetingly played at smoothing out some unseen wrinkle upon her well-filled bodice.

Not verra subtle, mused Bethia, trying hard not to feel like some child as she walked along between the two taller, far more shapely women.

"Verra discriminating," agreed Elizabeth. "Many men were verra jealous of Eric's conquests, but, I suspect, ye have already suffered some because of that. I have noticed a few of Eric's enemies attempting to woo you."

Frowning at the woman, Bethia almost said that she had not noticed anyone flirting with her. The implication that a man would do so only to avenge himself upon Eric was insulting, however, so she just nodded. She wondered idly if one of Elizabeth's current lovers or one she sought to capture had shown some fleeting interest in her. The fact that she had not responded, had not even noticed the man's interest, would not matter to Elizabeth. Bethia suspected Elizabeth was one of those women who took a man's wavering interest as nothing less than an insult.

"True," agreed Catriona. "Few men were able to tolerate Eric's weel-kenned skill as a lover. Sir Lesley Moreton was quite enraged when Eric began to woo me. One must always beware of jealous men," Catriona told Bethia with an air of a dear friend imparting some great wisdom.

"Aye, 'twas the same with Lord Munroe when Eric turned his beautiful gaze my way."

Bethia wondered if the two women often sat together over wine discussing their mutual lovers, then scolded herself for being nasty. She then wondered if she could claim a sudden violent illness and race ahead to her chamber. They were going to start to tell her all about their affairs with Eric. She could see the unwanted confidences trembling on their lips and dreaded them.

She tried to remain calm, even polite, as Catriona and Elizabeth congratulated her on capturing such a wondrous lover. Their apologies for being too personal, their occasional gentle queries about whether or not they were distressing her with their revelations, were all that was polite and blatantly false.

They told her of Eric's wooing, of their many trysts, even of the sweet love words he had used to so skillfully seduce them. Bethia was so happy when they reached the door to her chamber that she almost cheered aloud. The women had exhausted every aspect of their affairs with Eric that could be spoken of with some subtlety, and Bethia feared they were about to tell her such things as just how often Eric had bedded them and how. It was, as far as she could see, the only things left to discuss.

"I do envy you, Lady Bethia," Catriona said. "Just how do ye manage to hold on to such a glorious mon?"

Looking at the two women who thought nothing of describing their exploits with a lover to the man's own wife, Bethia was suddenly furious. It did not help her temper any to hear, in the very tone of her voice as she had asked the question, that Catriona obviously felt she had to have some strange hold on Eric or he would not be with her. She had done nothing to these women. And despite their less than subtle hints, she knew Eric would not have given them any false promises. They tried to hurt her—that was all. Whether it was from spite, stung pride, or jealousy did not matter. They were being unneccessarily cruel, and at that precise moment, she hated them for it.

"I hold him firmly by his pintle," she said in a voice so sweet it nearly sickened her. "Surely the two greatest whores in all of the king's court would understand that."

She stepped into her room and slammed the door shut on their shocked faces. Pressing her head against the wooden door, she listened to them walk away, not able to hear exactly what they said, but recognizing the fury in their voices. Now she had given them a real reason to hate her. Bethia wondered why she did not feel better about it.

Deciding not to ring for the maid, Bethia undressed to her shift. After a quick wash, she decided she did not feel like taking down her hair, so she simply loosened the coiled braids and crawled into bed. Bethia sprawled on her stomach, buried her face in her pillow, and decided it was time to indulge in a sulk. The evening she had just endured cried out for one.

Try as she would, she could not dismiss what Catriona and Elizabeth had said. They were both fulsome, fair-haired women, and it was painfully easy to see them as Eric's lovers. It was also painfully easy to compare her slight form to their lush curves and begin to feel sadly inadequate. Bethia suspected their skills in the bedchamber far exceeded hers as well.

Telling herself that Eric still sought her bed and none other, that his passion still ran hot for her, did not make her feel all that much more confident. They were but newly wed, lovers for such a short while. What would happen when that newness faded? What would happen if her body grew round with the child she might be carrying?

The sound of the door opening and shutting, and Eric's distinctive tread on the stone floor, pulled Bethia from her dark thoughts. She turned her head just enough to peer at him with one eye. He came to a halt by the side of the bed, put his hands on his hips, and frowned at her.

"Are ye sulking, Bethia?" he asked.

"What makes ye ask that?" The man's ability to guess her moods was not always welcome, she mused. It would be nice to be mysterious.

"Mayhap the way ye are lying there trying to smother yourself in the pillow," he teased and started to undress. "I begin to think that ye actually enjoy a hearty sulk from time to time."

"I suppose I might. I hadnae expected ye back so soon, so I thought I had the time to indulge."

"My meeting with Lord Douglas was quick, but we didnae need to say much to each other. He has agreed to support me."

"That is wonderful." The thought that they would soon be able to go home was enough to give her voice the appropriate touch of delight.

"Poor Bethia." Eric kissed her cheek and, tossing his jupon

and shirt on a chest, moved to wash up. 'What has put ye into a sulk?''

"Eric, how come ye have ne'er given me flowers?'' she asked, then inwardly cursed herself for revealing her weaknesses and doubts.

"There are none about and willnae be until spring. I might be able to find ye some heather blooms, but that would be all.'' He watched her closely as he rubbed himself with a drying cloth. "Those two bitches had a wee talk with you, didnae they?''

She stared at him in some surprise. "That seems a harsh way to speak about your lovers.''

"Old lovers and, my heart, ye must ken that a mon doesnae need to like or respect the women he beds. Ere I met you I looked only for comely and willing. Catriona and Elizabeth were both. I wooed my way into their beds, and, trust me, it took verra little wooing to lift their skirts, took what I wanted, and left. I had thought I had played the game as weel as their former lovers, but perhaps not. 'Tis clear that they wish to cause me trouble through you.''

"I think they are just a wee bit piqued that ye married me—a lass they dinnae believe shines as brightly as they do.'' She frowned as Eric got into bed beside her. "I think their pride has been pinched.'' She cast him a guilty look as he tugged her into his arms. "I fear I have made it worse.''

"Aye? What did ye do?''

"Weel, they walked me to our chambers.'' Bethia nodded as he grimaced. "Dinnae worry. I got here ere they could be too precise in their tales. But I suddenly got verra angry.''

"I am sorry, Bethia. I wish I could rub out my past.'' Eric lifted his brows in surprise when she placed her fingers over his lips.

"I wasnae angry with you, or e'en about the fact that ye bedded women ere ye met me. True, I dinnae like meeting them, but as ye told me, no one held your name or your heart.

Ye were a free mon and ye didnae e'en ken who I was. Nay, I was angry at them. There was no reason for them to tell me such things. I have ne'er done them any wrong. And yet, they sought to hurt me, mayhap e'en cause trouble in this marriage by stirring up jealousies and doubts. I fear I said something they will find hard to forgive, and now that I think on it, it wasnae verra kind to speak of ye in such a way.''

When Bethia hesitated and blushed deeply, Eric's curiousity was aroused. ''So? What did ye say?''

Bethia took a deep breath to steady herself, told him what Catriona had asked her, and then what she had replied. Eric stared at her in shock for a moment, and Bethia feared she had gone too far, had perhaps even thoroughly disgusted him. Then he started to laugh.

''Oh, lass, ye must have left them speechless,'' he finally said, tugging her back into his arms.

''At least for as long as it took me to get back inside this room and shut the door. It wasnae good of me, though.''

''It wasnae so verra bad and they deserved it. In their arrogance, they looked at you, saw a wee, sweet-faced lass, and felt they could grind ye beneath their slippers. Ye are right. They were most unkind. There was no reason to tell ye anything about what happened in the past. They deserved whate'er ye wished to say or do to them.''

''Mayhap.'' She moved her hand over his taut stomach. ''Weel, they willnae e'en feign a liking for me now, and perhaps, that isnae such a bad thing. In truth, it may be as much honesty as I will e'er get from such women. I pray I willnae have to worry o'er them for verra much longer. Will I?'' she asked.

''Nay, not for verra much longer. Now, about what ye said—''

''Eric, I didnae mean it. I was just so angry.''

''Ah, that is a shame.'' He grabbed her hand and placed it

over his hardened manhood. "I was rather hoping ye would lead me about tonight."

Bethia laughed and kissed him, knowing that, at times, the passion they shared controlled him as firmly as it did her. She soon had to wonder who led and who followed as they exchanged kisses and caresses with an equal fervor. They crested the heights of passion together and, her doubts banished for the moment, Bethia fell asleep even before Eric had left her body.

Eric held Bethia close and slowly undid her braids, idly wondering what possessed women to do their hair up in such complicated ways. He had brought her to court, not only because he wanted her at his side, but to get her away from her parents' poison. Some time away from that constant criticism and denigration could help Bethia gain some pride and confidence. At least, that had been his plan, and it had seemed a good one. Instead, he had thrown her into the midst of the often cruel, petty intrigues of court.

He had considered the possibility of her hearing of or even meeting lovers he had known in his past, but Eric realized he had not really seen such women as the threat they could be. Even a strong, self-assured woman would have found Elizabeth and Catriona's jealous talebearing hard to tolerate. Bethia was not self-assured, however, but had spent her whole life being ignored, compared unfavorably to her sister, and, when noticed, heartily criticized. For such a woman, it had to have been painful to listen to two beautiful, fulsome women boast of having shared her husband's bed. No wonder Bethia had felt a need to indulge in a sulk.

A little smile curved his lips as he kissed her forehead and combed his fingers thorough her now loosened hair. He found it oddly attractive that Bethia liked to indulge in what she called *a good sulk*. She was endearingly honest in her emotions, good and bad. It was yet another reason why she was finding life at court hard to bear.

As Eric let sleep wash over him, he promised Bethia that he would push harder to get what he wanted so that they could leave. He had allowed himself to be nudged aside. He had politely accepted excuses for delays and repeated himself again and again, believing that his king simply wished to be sure of his facts before he passed judgment on William Drummond and Sir Graham Beaton. It was time to stop being so gentle, so well mannered. He wanted Bethia away from women like Catriona and Elizabeth before their poison could begin to do more than cast Bethia into one of her sulks.

Bethia stretched, then frowned as her outstretched hand touched cool linen instead of Eric's warm chest. She opened her eyes and knew from the dim light seeping into the room that it was barely past dawn. As she reached over to steal his pillow something crinkled and she picked up a message left there. She smiled faintly as she read his apologies for slipping away so early, but she was gratified by his expressed intention to press his case even harder. It was difficult to understand the king's hesitancy when the proof against William and Beaton was so strong. These were not men the king needed as allies.

She stretched again, then cautiously eased out of the bed and rang for a maid. By the time she had bathed, washed, and dried her hair, it was time to break her fast. Bethia subdued the cowardly urge to have her meal brought to her room. It had been her own words that had angered Elizabeth and Catriona. She had to face the consequences. If she was very fortunate, she mused as she walked to the great hall, it was still far too early for either of the women to be out of bed.

As she walked through the heavy doors of the great hall, Bethia nearly walked into Catriona and Elizabeth. Elizabeth did not say anything or openly snub her, but her look was cold. It was no more than Bethia had expected. Catriona, however, smiled pleasantly, and that made Bethia very uneasy.

"Dinnae look so wary, child," Catriona said, putting her arm around Bethia's shoulders and aiming a kiss into the air near Bethia's cheek. "Ye were angry. 'Twas our own fault. We should have guarded our words more carefully."

" 'Twas nay an excuse for me to be so unkind," Bethia murmured, deciding that she could be generous. She and Eric were leaving soon.

"To show that all is forgiven, we will break our fast with you, and then go to the market together."

"I really dinnae need anything at the market," Bethia protested as she was dragged over to a table.

"Dinnae be shy, Lady Bethia. Every woman enjoys going to the market. We shall all have great fun."

Bethia found herself pulled into Catriona's plans. No excuse was accepted and Bethia was hesitant to be blatantly rude. She had already deeply offended the woman once. There was no knowing whom the woman knew or what power she might wield. Bethia did not wish to risk all Eric had worked for by angering Catriona so much that the woman worked against him. Like it or not, she thought with a sigh, she was going into the town. She just wished she did not feel so uneasy, almost frightened about the little trip.

Chapter Fourteen

"Catriona? Elizabeth?"

Bethia frowned as, looking around her, she saw neither woman. Market day had drawn a large crowd, however, and she told herself not to let their apparent disappearance make her nervous. They could easily have wandered off to look at something else and forgotten to tell her or she had not heard them do so. Carefully counting out her money, she paid the woman who had been helping her for the ribbon she had picked out and started to look for the two women.

It was difficult to see anything over the heads of the people milling around. Bethia cursed her lack of height and walked toward a bench in front of the alehouse. Smiling nervously at the people gathered there, she nudged her way through the men and rough women and finally got to the bench. Bethia hesitated a moment, not sure it was proper to stand on the thing, then decided she had no choice. If she was to find the women she had to be able to see through or over the crowd, and that required some added height. Hoping no one who knew her as Eric's wife chanced to see her, she climbed onto the bench.

It took several minutes, but Bethia finally spotted the elaborate headdresses of Catriona and Elizabeth. She frowned, for it looked very much as if the women were hurrying back to the castle. Leaving her stranded in the market seemed a remarkably childish thing to do, but as she got down off the bench, Bethia told herself she should have expected something. It was unlike Catriona and Elizabeth to let the insult she had dealt them go unpunished.

Although she found it annoying, Bethia also decided it was for the best. The women had been gently taunting her and insulting her the whole morning in the guise of friends helping her to become more of a lady, more worthy of her husband. She began to think they had taken lessons from her parents, then scolded herself for her unkind thoughts concerning her parents. It was difficult to know how much longer she would have been able to hold on to her temper.

"Are ye all right, Lady Bethia?" asked a voice Bethia did not recognize for a moment.

Turning slowly, Bethia recognized the little maid Jennet, who had helped her dress for the evening meal nearly every night since she had arrived. "I have just lost my companions," she replied.

"Ah, those two." Jennet nodded and took Bethia by the arm. " 'Tis nay good for ye to be wandering about the market alone and I suspicion they ken it. They are nay verra nice ladies, m'lady. Ye should be wary of them."

"I begin to see that most clearly."

Eric was going to be furious, Bethia thought with a sigh. When she had left the castle, she had been with four others: Elizabeth, Catriona, a maid, and one man-at-arms. It had seemed more than enough protection, and she had assured Eric of that in the note she had left for him. When she returned alone, he was going to wonder if she had lied or had done something silly, like get herself lost. For a brief moment, she considered telling him exactly what had happened, then sighed. It would serve no purpose. He could not do anything about it, and the two women would most certainly deny it. She supposed she would have to settle for telling him she had simply become seperated from her companions.

"I could take ye back right now, if ye wish, m'lady," said Jennet.

"It would be best if I return to the castle with someone, but I am more than willing to follow about after you until ye are ready to leave," said Bethia.

"I dinnae have that much left to do. I shouldnae be too much longer."

"Enjoy yourself. I havenae really finished seeing all that is being offered."

"Will your husband nay be looking for you?"

"I told him where I was, but I dinnae think he will return to our room ere I do. He has a great deal of work to do."

Jennet nodded. " 'Tis said that he has several causes to plead before the king, and to tell ye the truth, m'lady, the king is e'er verra slow to decide on any cause, no matter how righteous. I sometimes think our king likes to have the great men of the land begging him for things and makes it last longer than it needs to." She gasped and looked at Bethia a little warily. "But I am just a wee maid. What do I ken about kings and such?"

Bethia wanted to say that the girl understood a great deal more than some men, but she just smiled. Jennet was afraid she had spoken recklessly, might even have put herself in danger, at least of losing her place at the castle. It was kindest to just let the moment pass and never mention it again.

To put the maid even further at ease, Bethia began to ask her advice on matters of fashion. Jennet relaxed quickly as she helped Bethia decide on what colors were best for her and even advised her on certain types of cloth that were the best to use as they wound their way through the crowded market. Although Bethia had never had to worry about such things before, she was now the wife of a laird or soon would be if the king recognized Eric's claim, so it was probably time to learn a few things.

She hoped Eric did not return to find her gone or, worse, see Catriona and Elizabeth at the castle without her after she had said she was going to the market with them. He would start to worry and he had enough trouble at the moment. When she had first found herself alone, she had felt a little afraid, but now, walking with the very talkative Jennet and surrounded by people enjoying market day, she began to feel at ease. Her only real enemy was William and he would have a hard time stealing her away or murdering her in such a crowded place.

"I dinnae like this," Elizabeth muttered as Catriona ordered their maid and guard to stay behind and dragged her into a tiny, dark alley on the road to the castle. "I still think the best way to get revenge is to bed the little bitch's husband and let her ken it."

"Eric isnae interested," Catriona snapped. "Mayhap it is because he is still but newly wed and she is unusual, but he has no eye for the ladies at the moment."

"Ye just say that because he hasnae responded to your wiles. Mayhap 'tis just ye he isnae interested in."

"He isnae interested in you either. Considering what a passionate mon he is, I find that a wee bit odd, dinnae ye?"

"Mayhap he is in love," Elizabeth said, her tone of voice indicating that the words nearly gagged her.

"With that too thin, strange-eyed wench? I dinnae think so. 'Tis naught but her innocence that intrigues him, but that will soon pale."

"Then let us destroy that in his eyes, as I suggested," Elizabeth urged as they stopped, waiting for the man they had agreed to meet.

"I have watched the wench since I got here, and trust me, she isnae one who can be seduced. We would have to tell pure lies about her—tales without a grain of truth to them. Eric would have no trouble seeing through such things." Catriona crossed her arms over her chest and tapped her foot in a gesture of growing impatience. "Where is that fool?"

"Right here, m'lady."

Elizabeth stepped closer to Catriona when that raspy voice came out of the shadows, followed by a bulky man badly in need of clean clothes and a bath. "I dinnae like this," she whispered and winced when Catriona jabbed her hard with her elbow.

"We were about to leave, Sir William," Catriona said in a cool voice. "I dinnae like to be kept waiting."

"Ye should learn the skill. Patience can bring one such rich rewards. Where is the lass?"

"Left alone in the market just as I promised. She is dressed in a soft green gown with a dark green surcoat. She wears no headdress."

"Do ye remember what to say if her husband asks after her?"

"Aye, that she insisted upon staying behind to look at lace. I should do whate'er it is ye want to do as quickly as ye can for I dinnae think that wee tale will hold him long. The mon keeps a close eye on her."

"Dinnae worry. I will need but a moment or two."

Elizabeth shivered again as the man disappeared into the shadows. "I like this even less now."

"I didnae ken ye were so weak spirited, Elizabeth."

"How did ye find that mon?"

"One of my men-at-arms met him lurking outside of the alehouse. I have kenned for two days that he was looking for that little bitch. I just wasnae sure how to use that knowledge until last eve.'' Catriona started to leave the alley.

Hurrying to catch up, Elizabeth said, "I think he means her some harm.''

"Oh, I do hope so.''

"I mean that I think he may wish to kill her.''

"So?''

"I am nay sure I wish to have a hand in a murder.''

"Try to soothe yourself with the knowledge that there may soon be a heartbroken widower who will need consolation.''

Eric frowned as he read the note Bethia had left on his pillow. It troubled him a little that she had gone off with Catriona and Elizabeth. After Bethia had insulted them, he had to question the motives of the two women in asking Bethia to join them on a trip to the market. The very last thing they would wish to do was make friends with his wife.

He told himself not to be so cautious. The women would only try to further torment Bethia with tales of past affairs and maybe insult her a little. If Bethia had thought she could not manage such abuse, she would not have gone. He just hoped they did not tell her anything too intimate. Eric did not really like the idea of his wife knowing exactly what he had done in the beds of other women.

Shrugging aside that worry, for there was little he could do about the matter, Eric went to the great hall to partake of a noon meal. He had hoped to have Bethia join him so that he could share the good news he had, but there would be plenty of time for that when she returned. The moment he stepped into the great hall, he forgot all about food, however, for sitting at a table were the very women Bethia was supposed to be with.

As he fought to calm himself, to push aside a sudden sense of foreboding, he walked over to where Elizabeth and Catriona sat laughing with two young courtiers. "M'ladies," he murmured, nodding a greeting to the men. "Is my wife not with you?"

"Why, nay, should she be?" asked Lady Catriona.

"She left me word that she had gone to the market with you."

"Ah, and so she did, but she didnae return with us."

"And why not?"

"She was having trouble deciding what ribbons she wanted. Is that nay right, Elizabeth?"

Elizabeth nodded and muttered, "Aye, but 'twas lace she looked at."

"Did no one stay behind with her until she was done?" Eric asked.

"Nay. Was that necessary?" Catriona asked. "She insisted we go on our way and said she would join us shortly. She must be in your room."

"Nay. I have just come from there."

"Then I fear I cannae tell ye where she might be."

It was hard, but Eric resisted the urge to shake Catriona until she told him that she knew exactly where Bethia was and that she was safe. Although he had the feeling that Catriona was not telling him everything, he knew she would not understand why it was so important for him to know where Bethia was or why it was so dangerous for his wife to be alone.

He curtly bowed to the small group and hurried out of the great hall. Eric planned to check his bedchamber one more time and then he would go to the market to hunt down Bethia There was always the chance that, childishly, Catriona and Elizabeth had just left Bethia there alone, intending no more than to alarm her a little and make her feel the sting of their abrupt desertion. If Bethia had been silly enough to do as they said she had—to send them on their way and purposely leave herself alone and unprotected—he would make very sure that she understood how foolish that was before he let her out of his sight again.

Bethia frowned and glanced into the shadows of the small alley she stood near. Jennet and the man she was trying to buy her herbs from were having a fierce argument about the price of his stock. It had been amusing for a while, but Bethia had finally stepped away, if only to give her poor abused ears a rest. The sudden urge she had to rejoin the maid and listen to the bickering all over again did not make sense.

Just as she decided she would obey whatever instinct was telling her to move away from the alley, a hand closed over her mouth and she was dragged backward into the shadows. Bethia clawed at the hand that nearly smothered her and heard a man curse. The rough voice so close to her ear made her blood run cold.

"Ye little bitch," William growled as he moved his arm to around her neck. "Ye will pay for all ye have cost me."

His strangling grip on her throat made it impossible for Bethia to do any more than whisper. "Ye must be mad to think ye can kill me here. Everyone will ken it was you."

"Do ye think I care? Your husband is working to make me an outlaw—a mon any other mon can kill without hesitation, a mon who must spend his life running and hiding. Let him ken who killed ye and then let him try to protect the boy."

Bethia did everything she could to slow William down as he dragged her away from the market square, but she was unable to completely stop him. "So run and hide. At least ye will be alive."

"Nay for long, but I mean to have the satisfaction of kenning that ye are dead ere I meet my fate."

"Lady Bethia?" Jennet called.

Bethia tried to call back but her voice was little more than a croak. "Ye willnae e'en get out of town."

"Who is that?"

"My maid."

"As if I fear some stupid little bitch. I ken that your husband isnae near. Those two women assured me that he is at court and thinks ye safe. One maid isnae enough to save you."

Bethia was a little surprised that Catriona and Elizabeth had arranged this, although those were the only two women he could possibly be referring to. She had not thought that she had angered them enough for them to want her dead. Sending a murderer after her seemed a very harsh punishment for an insult.

"Lady Bethia? Are ye down there?"

Please, Bethia prayed, as she started to weaken and William was able to move faster. Even little Jennet would be a help. The thought of dying was hard enough, but the thought that she could be taking her unborn child with her was more than she could bear.

Eric heard Bethia's name being called and shoved his way through the crowd to the woman doing the yelling. It took him a minute to recognize the little maid. He struggled to recall her name as he reached her side.

"Jennet, where is my wife?" he demanded.

"Oh, Sir Eric, I am so glad to see you," Jennet said. "I saw her standing here but a moment ago and now she is gone."

"Did ye see anyone with her?"

"Nay. I think she went down there although I cannae imagine why."

Even as Eric looked down the dark alley he heard a soft sound as if someone or something was being dragged along. Pulling his sword, he started down the alley. He was halfway down before he saw them and softly cursed. It was not going to be easy to get Bethia away from the man.

"Ye have been caught, William. Let the lass go," Eric called as he drew closer.

"Ah, the great Sir Eric. Ye are just in time to watch me cut her throat."

"And yours will be cut ere she hits the ground."

"Ye have had me declared an outlaw. I am already a dead mon."

Eric wondered how William knew that. "Ye could buy yourself a little more time if ye just let the lass go."

"And give ye an easier target?" William laughed. "How big a fool do ye think I am?"

Bethia felt William's grip ease on her throat as he pulled his sword, preparing to meet Eric's possible charge. She took several deep breaths as cautiously as she could, not wishing to let William know that she was recovering from his choking grasp. It was clear that Eric was helpless to act as long as she was in the way. Eric's presence, and the return of air to her lungs and head, helped Bethia clear her mind of fear for a moment. Then she recalled something Bowen had taught her.

Praying that Eric could move fast enough if she managed to loosen William's hold on her, Bethia balled up one fist and punched William in the groin as hard as she could. His bellow of pain nearly defeaned her. He loosened his grip as he instinctively covered himself and she fell to the ground. She tried to move away from him, but was too weak to do more than crawl. The moment she heard him making a loud, stumbling retreat, she collapsed.

"Bethia?" Eric sheathed his sword and knelt by her side.

"Go after him," she rasped.

"Jennet! Get in here and help your mistress," Eric yelled, and as soon as he heard the maid hurrying over, he took off after William.

"M'lady," Jennet cried as she knelt by Bethia and helped her sit up. "What has happened to you?"

"I will be all right," Bethia said, her voice little more than a hoarse whisper.

"Jesu, ye sound as if ye have been strangled."

Bethia almost laughed as Jennet helped her stand up. "I was."

Bethia was not really surprised when Eric rejoined them before they even got out of the alley. She only needed one glance at the black look on his face to know he had lost William. The man was proving alarmingly hard to catch.

It took a few moments to convince Eric not to carry her all the way back to the castle. With Jennet's help, they got her back to her bedchamber. Eric left to send his men out to hunt for any sign of William, and Jennet helped Bethia have a bath, then get into bed. The maid was just giving her a drink of spiced ale heavily sweetened with honey to soothe her throat when Eric returned.

Bethia sat sipping her drink as Eric pressed several coins into Jennet's hand and thanked her for her help. As soon as the maid left, he came and sat beside Bethia on the bed. He looked at her throat and Bethia could tell by the murderous look in his eye that she was badly bruised.

"I ache to kill that bastard," he muttered as he briefly hugged her and pressed a kiss against her hair.

"Aye, so do I," Bethia murmured.

"Why did ye stay alone at the market?"

There was more confusion in his voice than anger and Bethia wished she could tell him the whole story. She really had no proof that Catriona and Elizabeth were behind the attack by William, however. All she knew was that they had purposely left her alone and unprotected and William had mentioned the aid of two women. Eric was not without enemies. Someone else could easily have thought to strike at him through her and seen William as the perfect way. She could not bring herself to accuse the women of having a hand in an attempted murder when she had so little proof.

"I became seperated from the others," she replied, trying to stay as close to the truth as possible. "As I was headed back to the castle, I met with Jennet and decided that staying with her would be better than going on alone."

"Catriona and Elizabeth said ye had trouble deciding what lace ye wished to buy and had told them to go on back without you."

"They probably saw that ye were upset and didnae wish to have ye get angry with them."

"Mayhap." Eric had the feeling she was not telling him everything, but decided not to press her.

"They didnae ken some madmon was about trying to kill me. They couldnae ken that it was dangerous to leave me alone. We havenae told verra many people. Ye saw them and decided to come looking for me, did ye?"

"Aye. I admit I was a little puzzled that ye had gone with them in the first place."

Bethia smiled faintly. "I didnae want to, but I decided I had insulted them enough. In truth, I suddenly wondered if either of the women might know people who could cause ye trouble. Since we were soon to leave here, I felt it would be best if I didnae antagonize them any further."

"And we are indeed soon to leave here."

"Truly?" she asked, the mere thought of going home enough to make her feel better.

"Aye." He smiled and brushed a kiss over her mouth. "I was hoping to leave on the morrow, but . . ."

"I will be fine."

"Of course. Nearly being strangled is naught to worry about."

Bethia ignored Eric's sarcasm. "Did ye get what ye wanted?"

"Aye. William has been declared an outlaw. He was right to say he is already a dead mon, although I am curious as to how he kenned he had been condemned, for I have but recently been told myself."

"He had probably heard that ye had requested it and didnae doubt that ye would get what ye wanted."

"That could be the way of it. He must have been lurking around here for a while to have found ye so easily. I am having thoughts of locking ye away again," he muttered.

"And I am beginning to think I just may agree soon. What of the other things ye wanted?"

"I am the laird of Dubhlinn. Sir Graham Beaton has been formally asked to leave, to hand the keep and the lands o'er to me. If he doesnae, he too could find himself declared an outlaw. And the last thing I asked for will be a pleasant surprise, I hope. I didnae tell ye about it beforehand as I didnae want ye to be disappointed if I didnae get it."

"And what is that?"

"I have been named James's guardian."

Bethia was speechless, surprise and delight stealing her ability to say any of the things whirling in her mind. She felt tears sting her eyes, and hastily setting her drink down on the table by the bed, she threw herself into Eric's arms. He laughed softly and hugged her.

Eric kissed her on the cheek, felt the dampness of her tears, and said, "That was supposed to make ye happy."

"Oh, it has." She rubbed her hands over her cheeks in a vain attempt to brush away her tears. "I was so afraid of what would happen to James now that he is a laird, but too young to take his place at the head of the clan. I just tried not to think of it much. It pained me too much to ken that I might lose him. Now he is ours to raise. Ye could have given me no finer gift."

"Except, perhaps, to go home and tell the lad the good news?" He smiled at her when she looked at him and slowly began to grin.

"Aye, except that."

Chapter Fifteen

"And ye are arrogant enough to think ye can do a better job of raising Sorcha's child than we can?" Lady Drummond demanded.

Bethia stared at her parents and barely stopped herself from sharply replying aye. She had only been back at Dunnbea for an hour, just long enough to clean the dust of three days of travel away and kiss James. It was true that she had requested this meeting with her parents, but she thought it somewhat inconsiderate of them to demand she meet them in the solar so soon after her arrival from court. She had not even had a chance to tell Eric, who had gone to settle their men and oversee the unpacking. Bethia wondered if that had been her parents' intention.

"Eric and I are young," she began.

"We arenae in our graves yet."

"I ken it, Mama. 'Tis just that ye have already raised two children—three, if ye include Wallace. 'Tis the time of your life when ye should be at your ease. A lively child like James can be a trial, even with a nursemaid and others to help.''

''Ye dinnae e'en ken where ye will live yet,'' her father said. ''That mon has ne'er told us where he means to take ye and the bairn. I think we should ken where our grandson will live ere ye **take hi**m away.''

''He will **live** at Donncoill,'' Eric said as he walked in and moved to stand beside Bethia. '' 'Tis a fine, strong keep south of here. 'Tis held by the clan Murray. My brother Balfour is the laird there.''

''Your brother? I thought ye were a MacMillan.''

Bethia stood quietly as Eric gave her father a cool, succinct explanation of his lineage. She could not believe her father did not know all of that already. Eric must have told him something but her father had obviously not cared enough to listen. It appeared that her father had not really been concerned about whom she had married except that it was the man she had been found in bed with. She supposed she should not be surprised. Her father had already revealed his disdain for her and her marriage, even for her husband in some ways, by not offering even the meagerest of dowries for her.

''So ye will be the laird of Dubhlinn soon?'' Lady Drummond asked, scowling at Bethia before turning her cross look upon Eric.

''Aye, and weel able to raise James to become laird of Dunncraig.''

''Weel, I hope ye can hold on to his lands better than ye held on to your own.''

Taking Eric's hand in hers, Bethia tried, silently, to ease the sting of her mother's insult. She did not understand why her parents treated Eric so poorly. He was a man many parents would be glad to have as a husband for their daughter. He was handsome, strong, and wealthy—a laird with a rather impressive bloodline. The marriage had brought the Drummonds new allies. Yet her parents often spoke to him, when they deigned to acknowledge him at all, as if he was some baseborn pauper.

"I have already asked my cousin, Sir David MacMillan, to hold Dunncraig for James until he comes of age," Eric replied in a cold, hard voice that revealed his barely controlled anger. "The mon is not only a kinsmon of mine, but one of your oldest allies. I believe we can trust him."

A few more questions were asked, a few more complaints and insults tossed at their heads, and then Bethia and Eric were coldly dismissed. Bethia felt ashamed as well as confused. She also realized that, not once, had her parents ever called James by his name. She glanced up at Eric as he walked her to the nursery so that she could have a longer visit with James, and she winced when she saw the anger on his face.

"I am sorry, Eric," she said. "I dinnae ken why my parents treat ye so"—she hesitated, searching her mind for the right word—"unkindly. It makes no sense at all."

Eric bit his tongue to control the angry words aching to spill from his mouth. He wanted to tell Bethia that her parents did not like him because they knew he saw them clearly as the coldhearted, arrogant fools they were. That he saw how cruelly they treated their own daughter and how they gave no thought at all to their own grandson until it became clear that Bethia wanted the child. Saw too how they resented him for depriving them of the dutiful, meek servant they had turned Bethia into, or at least had tried to. Such truths would only hurt Bethia, and no matter how much he wanted her to break free of her parents' cruel hold, to see that they were wrong to treat her as they did, he would not hurt her by forcing her to see it. He was sure she was beginning to see it on her own and when that revelation finally came, she would be hurt enough without him adding to it with his anger.

"Mayhap they havenae forgiven me for seducing you," he finally said, even though he believed that only troubled them because it had forced a marriage.

"Many parents would be secretly glad," she said and gave him a shy smile. "I chose a rich, handsome laird to lead me into sin and thus get him dragged before a priest. I am surprised no other lass has been so clever."

"A few have tried, e'en before there was talk of my becoming laird of Dubhlinn. I learned quickly to recognize the dangers."

Bethia was about to ask why he had not recognized that danger in her, but they entered the nursery and James's squeals of welcome quickly distracted her. The nursemaid smiled and quietly left her and Eric alone with the child. Bethia sat on the floor and watched Eric play with James. He was going to be such a good father, she thought with a sigh.

"Does something trouble ye, lass?" Eric asked as he gently bounced a giggling James on his knee.

"Nay. I was but thinking, yet again, how glad I am that ye were named his guardian. Ye will be such a good father to him."

"Thank ye. Although it should have been ye who were named as his guardian. Ye are his mother's twin, after all."

"No one would give a wee lass a guardianship. And e'en if they wanted to, James is destined to be the laird of Dunncraig. No court or king would entrust such a lad to a mere woman."

"Aye, sad and unfair, but true." Eric took a deep breath to steady himself and said, "I want us to go to Donncoill."

"Of course. I have been expecting the journey. 'Tis your home," she said quietly.

"Now. I want us to leave as soon as possible. I would leave today if I could."

"Is it safe to travel? 'Tis the time of the year when the weather can worsen verra quickly."

"I think we are being blessed with a verra mild season. Are ye nervous or afraid to go to a strange place?"

"Of course I am nervous. But I have just survived a month in the court of the King of Scotland. I believe I can meet a few Murrays and nay wilt." Bethia grinned when he laughed.

"They will love you," Eric reassured her. "Are ye certain about leaving Dunnbea? 'Tis your home, after all, and once ye are away with me to Donncoill, then settled as the lady of Dubhlinn, ye willnae see this place verra often."

Bethia looked deep into her heart and found no regret about leaving her home, not even much reluctance. There were people she would miss, deeply so, but they could always come to visit her. The more she looked into herself, the more Bethia realized that there lurked within her an eagerness to leave Dunnbea, nearly a joy at the thought that she would soon be free. Free of what, she was not really sure.

"There are people I will sorely miss," she confessed, "but that is all. I am your wife. I go where ye go—always."

Eric briefly kissed her. It was no vow of love, but her word held a calm, heartfelt conviction that pleased him. There was no sense of only duty there, although he had no idea what other emotion lurked behind her readiness to stay at his side. For now, however, it was enough.

"Mayhap ye need not miss all of them for too long," Eric murmured, smiling at her.

Before Bethia could ask what he meant, Wallace arrived to tell him that they were ready to begin a search for William. She took James from Eric, hugging the child close as he left with her cousin. Simply the name of her enemy was enough to bring a chill to her heart. She tried to find some comfort in the fact that, despite William's elusiveness and his attempts to kill her, he had not drawn close to James since his sons had died.

Eric shifted in his saddle and dragged his fingers through his hair. He wanted to scream out his frustration. There were signs that William was near, that he had followed them here from court, but no sight of the man himself. Even Thomas had failed to find a trail he could follow to the end.

''I begin to think the bastard can fly,'' Wallace grumbled as he rode up beside Eric.

''Or fades into the air whene'er it suits him,'' Bowen added as he paused on Eric's other side. ''Poor Thomas fears his skills have faded. He is sorely dispirited.''

''I didnae think the mon was this clever,'' Eric said, shaking his head. ''Mayhap it was arrogance, but I really didnae think he would be this much trouble to hunt down and kill. He certainly hadnae shown any great wit or skill before this.''

''Nay,'' Bowen agreed. ''He used poisons, a coward's weapon, and his success was more because he dealt with blind fools than because he had any wits. 'Tis the madness.''

''Ye think that he is mad?''

''Aye. I think he always has been. 'Tis the only explanation for murdering so many people. 'Tis certainly the only explanation for why he continues to hunt Bethia and James now. Any other mon would have fled by now, accepted that he had lost, and tried to save his own neck.''

''He just accepts that he is a dead mon,'' Eric murmured, recalling what the man had said when he had held Bethia in the alley. ''E'en before I got him outlawed, he simply accepted it. All he seems to want to do is take Bethia with him. He speaks of James as weel, but I am nay sure he really thinks of the lad much anymore. 'Tis Bethia he seeks.''

''She was the one that put a stop to all his plans,'' Wallace said. ''He blames her for his failure.''

''Nothing,'' Thomas grumbled as he walked up to them. ''I find a sign and then it disappears or appears to. I cannae find the cursed mon.''

Eric almost smiled as he watched Thomas walk to his horse and mount. The man's whole body was set in an expression of despair and anger. When Thomas said nothing else, just started to ride back to Dunnbea, Eric turned to look at Bowen.

''I believe the hunt for William has just ended for the day,'' Eric drawled. He smiled faintly when both Wallace and Bowen laughed. "I begin to fear that Thomas will ne'er forgive me for this."

"It has sore bruised his pride," Bowen agreed as he and his companions turned their horses back toward Dunnbea.

"We shall have to keep an even closer watch upon Bethia," Wallace said.

"Aye." Eric sighed. "I intend to go to Donncoill verra soon if the fine weather holds."

"There is a good chance William will follow ye there."

"I ken it, but he will be on unfamiliar ground. Mayhap that will aid in his capture. It matters not. I need to get Bethia away from here."

" 'Twill do the lass good," said Bowen. "And ye are her husband. She should go where ye go."

"Verra true, but Bethia wasnae raised to go anywhere, was she? Unlike most lasses, she has ne'er been readied to leave her home, to have her own family. Nay, Bethia was raised to do the work her mother should be doing."

Wallace grimaced and nodded. "Aye, ye have the right of it. 'Twas clear to see whilst Bethia was verra young. Sorcha was to make the good marriage and Bethia was to be the one who stayed behind to tend to her parents' needs. 'Tis odd that they often seem verra ungrateful for that, e'en though 'tis what they wanted." He glanced at Eric and grinned. "And ye will ne'er be a favorite of theirs for ye are taking her away."

Eric laughed as they rode through the gates of Dunnbea. "Oh, I saw that from the verra start. Nay, I will get Bethia away from here, and mayhap she can finally shake free of their hold on her."

"Will ye be needing men to fight for Dubhlinn?"

"Aye, I will."

"Then ye shall have some."

"And I suspect ye may be needing some men to work at your new keep," Bowen said as they dismounted and handed their horses over to the stable lads.

"Aye," Eric said carefully, glancing at Wallace as he added, "And any mon who seeks to stay shall be weel settled, with good pay and housing."

"Then me and Peter may be joining ye. We will certainly be fighting for ye, if only because it will get the wee lass a keep of her own."

"I will be pleased to have ye and I dinnae think that it needs to be said that Bethia will be delighted." Eric watched Bowen walk into the stables, then turned to Wallace as they started toward the high, heavy doors of the keep. "And what do ye have to say? Ye will be losing two good men if they plan to stay with me at Dubhlinn."

"That I will, and I think a few others will go if ye find yourself as short of trustworthy and able men as ye think ye will." Wallace smiled a little sadly. "Bowen and Peter were ne'er my men or e'en my uncle's. They have always been Bethia's men. Aye, they have had the training of me, and I am most grateful, but they must go where they feel they will gain the most for their labors. That isnae here."

"Dunnbea isnae a poor keep."

"Nay, which is why we have so many healthy people. And that means there arenae as many deaths as there are in other places. Especially since we have done little fighting here for many years. 'Tis a peaceful place now. There are more hands to do work than there is work for them to do. And since there are really too many people depending upon Dunnbea, it means some dinnae do as weel as they might elsewhere. Nay, I will let Bowen and Peter go if they choose to, because they deserve a chance to gain for their skills and labor and there is no gain for them here."

"Nor gratitude for their efforts," Eric murmured as they entered the keep and were barely acknowledged by the laird and his lady as they passed them on the stairs.

"That has e'er been in short supply."

* * *

"Ye didnae find him, did ye?" Bethia said as Eric entered their bedchamber.

She was not surprised when he shook his head and then began to ready himself for the evening meal in the great hall. There had been a grim, disappointed look upon his face that had been all too easy to read as he had walked in. Bethia pushed aside her own disappointment and anger and turned her attention to Eric.

As she helped him get his dusty clothes off, she talked about James and how much he had grown. She made him smile with her tales of all the new skills and words the boy had learned. By the time he was ready to walk her to the great hall, she felt she had cheered him. Then he pulled her into his arms and gave her a quick, hard kiss before leading her out of their bedchamber.

"What was that for?" she asked as she struggled to calm her racing pulses.

"For working so hard to help me cast off my dark mood," he answered.

"Oh." She grimaced. "Ye guessed what I was doing, did ye?"

"Dinnae look so guilty. I think that may be one of the things wives are supposed to do. I am almost tempted to send ye to Thomas, because that mon was verra beset with wounded pride and anger."

"How does Wiliam keep slipping away? I would ne'er have believed he could be so skilled at it or so clever as to elude us for so long."

"Neither did I believe it, but Bowen thinks madness sharpens his wits."

"Aye, that is possible. 'Tis sad that madness can make a mon stronger than most, sly and devious when they ne'er have been before. Mayhap we need to lure him into a trap,'' she said, frowning in thought.

"A trap requires bait and if ye are thinking of offering yourself as that bait, I should pause a moment to think again."

"It might work," she grumbled, a little annoyed that he had cast aside her idea before she had even had a chance to speak of it.

"And it might get ye killed. We arenae dealing with the mon we thought we were, or the mon William used to be. He appears and disappears. E'en Thomas cannae follow the mon, and Thomas could track thistledown. William's trails seem to start, then stop, then start somewhere else as if he is leaping o'er the land. Aye, setting ye out in the open, apparently unguarded, would certainly draw him out, but I am nay longer certain we could stop him from killing ye and getting away again."

Bethia shivered and walked a little closer to his side as they entered the great hall. Her mind was so consumed with the problem of William that she took her place at the head table beside Eric and barely noticed her parents' customary scowls of greeting. Next to the threat William posed, her parents were but a small irritation. They had a true skill for making her feel useless and for hurting her feelings, but William could kill her.

"So 'tis nay enough that ye have taken all of your sister's gowns," Lady Drummond began in her cold, hard voice, "or that ye are taking away our grandson, but now ye plan to take some of our men as weel."

"I havenae taken any of your men," Bethia said, pulled from her thoughts about William so abruptly that she did not really understand what her mother was complaining about now.

"Wallace has kindly offered me some of the men of Dunnbea to help me take and hold Dubhlinn," Eric said.

That seemed to hint at fighting and Bethia frowned. She had not allowed herself to think about how Eric would get Dubhlinn away from Sir Graham Beaton. The king had given it to Eric and told Sir Graham to leave. Bethia supposed it had been extremely naive of her to think that was the end of it. Sir Graham had refused Eric his rightful place for thirteen years. He probably would not calmly ride away from the land now.

" 'Tis the wrong time of the year for a battle," Lord Drummond said.

"I dinnae mean to ride to the gates tomorrow and demand that Sir Graham leave or fight." Eric took a long drink of wine to steady himself, refusing to let them anger him. "I, and your daughter and grandson, will need men at our side as we travel to Donncoill, however. And since spring is soon to be here, it seemed reasonable to hold the men Wallace gives me until then. That will allow them to train with the men the MacMillans are sending as weel as my brother's men."

"I wasnae consulted on this."

"The Murrays are our allies now, and the MacMillans have always been," Wallace said. "I didnae think we had any reason to refuse their request for aid in this matter."

Bethia could tell that that calm reasoning annoyed her father. Although she dreaded even the thought of a battle, she could not understand his reluctance to offer aid. She knew Dunnbea would not be left unmanned and certainly would not have its purse depleted by much.

"I will do my best to see that your men arenae carelessly thrown into a needless battle," Eric said, "and that they are returned to you as swiftly as possible."

He chanced a look at Bethia, but could tell little by her expression. She always assumed a calm, meek look when in the presence of her parents. He realized he had grown to dislike that look intensely. Right now, he was eager to see how she was taking the talk of battle. It was something he had tried to keep away from her. Since there was nothing to be read in her face, however, he decided he would have to wait until they were alone to talk about it.

Bowen entered at that moment and brought Sir David MacMillan with him. Bethia was a little astonished at how much the young man looked like Eric. It was no wonder everyone had begun to question Eric's claim of being a Murray from the moment he had drawn near to the MacMillans' holdings. After the introductions were made, Sir David sat across from her and Eric, and Bethia found herself subjected to even more talk of a possible battle to gain Dubhlinn.

She sighed to herself as she struggled to finish her meal. None of the men sounded particularly bloodthirsty, but it was evident that they held some degree of anticipation for a battle. They saw it as a good cause, right being on their side. Bethia wished she could too. All she could see, however, was that men, including the man she loved, were about to risk their lives and the lives of others for a piece of land.

"Mayhap ye should leave the laddie and Bethia here until this is all settled," Lord Drummond said.

"Nay," Eric replied firmly, his voice a little sharp as he reached out and took Bethia's hand in his. "My wife and James travel with me."

To Bethia's complete surprise, her father did not argue. "Are we to leave soon?" she asked quietly.

"Aye, tomorrow, if the weather holds," replied Eric.

Bethia opened her mouth to argue, then quickly shut it. She would not question Eric in front of her parents. Instinct told her that they would try to take advantage of any hint of disagreement and that would only add to the tension she could feel in her husband. In truth, she had no real complaint about when they would leave. She had simply reacted to the tone of command Eric had used. That in itself surprised her a little, for she had grown very good over the years at bowing to that tone of indisputable command and arrogance. Her father and mother used it a lot.

"Weel, lass, it seems your husband insists on thrusting ye right into the middle of his troubles," her father said. "I hope ye are ready to behave as a wife should. 'Tis time to cast aside all of your recklessness and disobedience and follow your husband.''

''Recklessness?'' Bethia murmured, wondering when she had ever given her father the idea that she was reckless.

Lord Drummond looked at Eric and said, ''I fear we have nay prepared the lass weel for marriage. Ne'er thought a mon would have her since she is such an odd-looking thing. But I am sure ye can teach the child what she needs to ken to be a good wife. We did our best. 'Tis to our shame that it was ne'er enough.''

Eric stood up abruptly and dragged Bethia to her feet. ''I think ye did more than enough. We will leave at dawn. Mayhap we will see ye to say our fareweel then.''

Bethia stumbled after Eric as he dragged her out of the hall. Something had made him furious and she had a feeling it was her father's remarks about her. She was so accustomed to such complaints about her looks and behavior that she had not paid them much heed.

''Mayhap I should begin to pack,'' Bethia said as Eric pulled her into their room.

'' 'Tis nearly done,'' Eric replied sharply, then sighed and pulled her into his arms. ''I am sorry. 'Tis nay ye I am angry with.''

''I ken it, although I am nay sure what has made ye so furious.'' She wrapped her arms around his waist and glanced up at him.

''That ye are so used to hearing such things said about you that ye feel no anger at all only adds to mine.''

''Father was disappointed with me from the day I was born, or at least from the day he saw that I wasnae exactly like Sorcha. If I heeded his remarks too much I should have gone quietly mad by now.''

He smiled faintly and began to nudge her toward the bed. ''And I shall go mad if I must stay here and continue to swallow such insults to you. So for the sake of our sanity, 'tis best if we leave as soon as possible.''

Bethia laughed, then gasped with amused surprise as Eric tumbled her down onto the bed. ''If we are to begin traveling so soon on the morrow, I think we had best get a lot of rest,'' she said, but did not stop him from removing her clothes.

''Oh, we will,'' he murmured against her breast. ''After.''

Chapter Sixteen

Huddled in a blanket and pressed close to Grizel, James tucked up between them, Bethia stared out at the men riding with them. They looked as cold as she felt. For three days, they had ridden as hard as they dared, always watching for the weather to turn against them. Instead it had remained no more than cold, although Bethia was beginning to think that was becoming as great a danger as any snow or icy rain would be.

She was going to be glad to reach Donncoill. Any shyness or uneasiness she might have felt about meeting Eric's family had already been frozen right out of her. Her first concern was going to be getting warm.

The cart started to slow down and Bethia leaned forward enough to look at the sky. It was late and she realized with a groan that they were going to have to spend one more night outside. The large fires the men built, the tents, and the way people all huddled together had eased some of the chill, but Bethia was eager to crawl into a nice warm bed.

"Only one more night, my heart," Eric said as he rode up behind the cart.

" 'Tis all right, Eric," she said as she grasped his outstretched hand and let him pull her up in front of him on his horse. "Connor shall be verra glad of his stable though," she murmured as she patted the mount's neck.

"If we had even as much as that at the moment, he would have to fight the men for some room."

"At least there has been no storm. I keep reminding myself of that each time I feel inclined to complain."

"Aye, I have been doing the same." Eric shook his head as he started to ride away from the camp the men were setting up. "Still, it may not have been wise to travel now. I probably should have waited."

"Ye were eager to get home. I am sure everyone understands that."

"Come, lass. Ye ken that part of my need to ride home now was because I was angry with your parents."

Bethia sighed and pressed closer to him, murmuring her enjoyment when he wrapped his plaid around her and pulled her into its warmth. "I ken it. Father is a hard mon to get along with."

"Wallace manages."

"Nay, Wallace just ignores him most of the time." She smiled when Eric laughed. "And Wallace doesnae have to put up with much, for he sleeps with the men a lot, and since he has already been named my father's heir, my parents are reluctant to criticize him too much. After all, that could steal away the men's confidence in Wallace, and my father might have to lead the men into battle himself."

Eric almost kissed her. There was a definite bite to her words, and for once, she did not immediately rush to apologize for what she had said or try to excuse her father in some way. He did not want her to come to hate her parents, but he was very pleased at this sign that she was starting to look at them more clearly. Once she began to see their faults, she would begin to see that they were wrong in what they had believed about her and what they had raised her to believe about herself.

"Where are we going, Eric?" Bethia asked as she realized

he was riding far enough away from their camp to be out of sight of the others.

"I wanted to show ye Dubhlinn," he murmured, touching a kiss to the top of her head.

" 'Tis near here?"

"Just through these trees."

" 'Tis odd that we can draw so close without being challenged."

"We have been seen. Word has already reached Sir Graham that the king has accepted my claim. He darenae cause me trouble. Not yet, leastwise."

Bethia glanced back at him. "I dinnae suppose he has already fled the keep."

"Nay." Eric kissed the tip of her cold, reddened nose. "He still sits inside. I will give him some time to leave, but nay much. He has bled these lands of all their worth for too long already."

She said nothing and Eric was a little disappointed. He wanted her to openly support him when he had to go fight. He sympathized with her belief that people should not die for the sake of land or coin. For the most part, it was a belief he shared. There was more to the taking of Dubhlinn than that, however. It was for that reason that, despite the cold, he was showing her the land he now claimed but did not yet hold.

"There sits the keep," he said as he reined in.

Bethia frowned toward the large, dark keep. It sat in the middle of barren ground—that emptiness enhanced by the cold deadening of the land winter brought. The gates were closed and no one lingered in the open. She pressed even harder against Eric. Dubhlinn did not look welcoming. In truth, it gave her a chill.

"Ye truly want that place?" She was almost relieved to see the hint of movement on the top of the encircling wall, even though it meant that Dubhlinn was well guarded, for it was a small touch of life.

Eric briefly chuckled. "I ken that it doesnae look verra warm and inviting. 'Tis built for defense, after all. And winter steals the softening green of the fields that surround it. For all of my life and many years before that, this keep has been little more than a place for carrion to roost and feed on the surrounding people.''

"Those carrion being the Beaton lairds?"

"Aye. I fear that, for now, the place reflects the darkness of its masters. I stayed there but once, when my father captured me. He still thought I was naught but a bastard, but he needed a son. He had bred no others and he was ill, thought he was dying. He didnae want to leave the keep to some distant kinsmon. So he took me and planned to make me into the mon he thought I should be.''

"And ye didnae take to his training."

"I spent most of the time in the dungeons until he captured my half sister Maldie and she got us out. The thing I can most remember—the time that still haunts my dreams—is when he made me watch him kill one of the Murray men. I was but thirteen and had lived a somewhat sheltered life. He tortured that mon to death and I was forced to watch each pain inflicted, forced to hear every scream. He felt this would harden me.''

"It made ye hate him, didnae it?" Bethia whispered, horrified by the tale he told and fighting the urge to weep for the boy he had been then.

"It did. After seeing just how cruel he could be I was nay pleased to find out that he really was my father.''

"Ye arenae afraid that ye are like him in any way, or could become so, are ye?"

"Nay, although it did worry me for a wee while." Eric turned his mount and rode toward the village. "It helped to watch another who carried his seed, to see that none of his poison marred her. Aye, especially since she had lived a far harder life than I had and her mother wasnae fit to raise a child. Even with the bad on both sides, Maldie carried no taint. So how could I?"

" 'Tis why ye continue to call yourself a Murray, isnae it? Ye cannae abide to use the mon's name.''

"Nay, I cannae, and those who went before and after him deserve no honor either. My grandfather was so evil, my father was driven to kill him." Eric shrugged when Bethia gasped with horror. "I also remain a Murray because I feel like one. I have kenned no other life, no other family.''

"Then a Murray ye shall stay." Bethia looked at the few villagers who were not huddled inside their homes as Eric and she rode slowly through the village. "Do ye plan to make all of these people claim the name as weel?''

"Nay. They can call themselves what they will. There will be a strange mix of people and names here for a while. Some MacMillans will undoubtedly stay and so will some Drummonds. And if needed, a few Murrays will join us.''

"A new beginning.''

"I hope so.''

Bethia looked down at the village when Eric stopped at the top of a small rise at the end of the rough, narrow road. Although she was not much of a judge, since she had rarely left Dunnbea, she felt there was something very sad and neglected about the place. Even though it was late in the day and cold, there should have been some sign of activity. The only movement there was was the scurrying of a few people into their houses. The passage of a man and a woman sharing a horse was enough to send the villagers into hiding.

Despite the increasing shadows, Bethia looked a little closer. There were no horses at the stables, no sound of animals at all. Only a few of the houses emitted smoke, revealing that a hearth fire was lit. Several cottages had only part of the roof left. The village was dying. Bethia began to think that Sir Graham had bled it dry.

"I begin to think that ye will be taking on more trouble than gain if ye get this place," she murmured as Eric turned their mount back toward the camp.

"I ken it. 'Twill be a while ere I see any gain.''

It was hard not to think about all she had seen as they returned to camp. It was sad to see what could have been a prosperous place brought to near ruin. There was little life left at Dublinn—as if it had all been choked out of the place.

As they dismounted in the camp, Bethia hurried over to sit with Grizel and James before a very large fire. She ate the meager, but filling meal of porridge, telling herself that tomorrow she would feast. The men stood guard, their tense stances telling Bethia that they were not alone, not unwatched.

"Ye dinnae think the Beatons will try to attack, do ye?" Grizel asked, frowning toward the wood her husband had just disappeared into.

"Eric doesnae think so," replied Bethia.

"Ah, so Sir Graham is just going to hand over the land?"

"Nay, I dinnae think that will happen. He just willnae attack Eric here and now. He should ken that he has lost by now, but he obviously needs time to decide how and if he will fight."

Grizel sighed. "Weel, I am nay surprised. No mon likes to give up land and wealth. Sir Graham may have no right to this place, but he does hold it, and I think it will have to be wrested from his hands."

"It will be," Eric agreed as he paused by their campfire to kiss James good night.

"Are ye standing guard?" Bethia asked Eric, returning his quick kiss.

"Aye, for a while, and then I will find the biggest of the fires and curl up in front of it."

Bethia just smiled, then watched him walk away. She helped Grizel get James cleaned up after his meal, then joined her maid and nephew in the wagon. Someone had drawn it very close to the fire, and once the covers were tied off, it was almost warm inside.

"I could almost feel guilty for being here whilst the men

are out there," Grizel said as she settled into her bed of blankets next to James.

"Almost," Bethia agreed and exchanged a grin with Grizel as she too crawled into her pile of blankets. She lay on her back and stared up at the wooden frame that held up the little wagon's tentlike cover. "I will still be eager to crawl into a proper bed on the morrow. Mayhap I willnae e'en wait until the sun sets."

"I think I shall find whate'er bed they give me and Peter and crawl right in, dirt and all. Ha! I shallnae e'en wait for Peter. Nay, the only thing I shall do first is light a verra big fire."

"Actually, I think I shall drag my bed right up close to the fire." They both laughed softly and then Bethia sighed. "Although ye and James are warm enough, I will also be glad to have Eric back beside me."

"Aye, I ken what ye mean. Noisy, hairy things though men be, they can be verra fine to curl up with." Grizel exchanged a grin with Bethia over James's head. "Are ye worried about meeting your mon's family?"

"A wee bit. I come with some trouble"—Bethia lightly touched the sleeping James's curls—"and already burden their kinsmon with a child."

"A burden he seems more than happy to bear. The way Sir Eric acts with the lad and the other children tells me that Donncoill is a place that will accept another bairn with open arms. A mon isnae so good to a lad nay his own unless he has been raised to appreciate the gift that the wee ones are."

"I believe ye have the right of it. Ah, weel, we will be there on the morrow. 'Tis good to feel sure that the wee laddie will be welcomed. I just pray the people of Donncoill are willing and able to accept a wee lass as weel."

Looking around as she rode into Donncoill seated in front of Eric on his horse, Bethia immediately saw the differences between it and Dubhlinn. Here was life and warmth. Men hurrried forward to take the horses and see to the men who had ridden with Eric. There was noise. There were the smells that came with horses, fires for heat and cooking, and a lot of people. Some of those smells were not always the best, but this time Bethia welcomed them as readily as they welcomed her.

Just as Eric helped her down, Grizel hurried over and handed her James. The maid just as quickly disappeared back into the crowd, undoubtedly searching out her husband and making sure that they got a warm place to sleep. Wallace and Sir David joined them and followed closely as Eric led her to the huge iron-studded doors of the keep. She was a little startled when they were thrown open even as Eric reached the steps leading up to them.

Holding tightly to Eric's hand, Bethia found herself and the others hastily ushered into the warmth of the keep, introduced to several people: a large brown man named Balfour; his tiny, beautiful wife Maldie; a man named Nigel, who was nearly as handsome as Eric; and his beautiful, pregnant wife Gisele. Bethia was just getting that clear in her mind when maids and pages hurried them all up to the bedchambers to get clean, changed, and warm. Bethia was bathed, dressed, and left sitting before a large fire with a goblet of heady mulled wine in her hand almost before she knew what had happened.

Eric laughed as he sat down next to her, helped himself to some of the wine, and kissed her frowning mouth. "Ye look a wee bit stunned, lass."

"I dinnae think I have e'er arrived, said a greeting, and been ushered to a bedchamber with such speed." She grimaced and shook her head. "Of course I havenae. I have ne'er been anywhere until I met you."

"Weel, it was done swiftly. E'en I was impressed. I sent a lad ahead to tell them we were coming and that we were verra cold after three days and nights of no shelter. I think it was the thought of how cold we must all be that did it. Gisele especially hates the cold.''

''Ah, Gisele. The pregnant one. Nigel's wife,'' she muttered, then asked, ''Is she related in some way to Maldie, the laird's wife?''

''Nay. That similarity in looks did cause a wee bit of trouble in the past, for Nigel once believed himself in love with Maldie, left for seven years, and came back with Gisele.''

''Oh, dear.''

''Aye. Oh, dear.''

'' 'Tis a verra fine keep.'' Bethia curled her toes into the soft sheepskin rug before the fireplace, then hastily redonned her slippers.

''This is what I want Dubhlinn to become.''

Bethia looked around at the tapestries warming the walls, the huge fireplace warming them, and the rugs warming the floor. Then she eyed Eric a little warily. ''I ken that ye arenae without some coin, but do ye have this much?''

''Nay, but only because I believe a lot of what I have will be spent on such things as roofs for the cottages, plows, seed, and other such necessities. This will come.''

''Of course. I wish my father had nay been such a tightfisted mon. Ye should have been given some dowry for taking me and it could have helped.''

''Ye will help. That is all I need.''

''Have ye told your kinsmen the whole truth about us?''

Eric nodded, stood up, and grasping her hand, tugged her to her feet. ''There is no need to play the game we did at court.''

''That wee tale made us look a wee bit more weel behaved than we were. It wasnae such a bad story.''

''Ye need not fear that ye will be faulted for how we got married. Believe me when I say that the way we met and wed was probably the most common and boring way a Murray has met his wife in quite a while.''

Bethia was not sure she believed that, but she did not argue.

She clung tightly to Eric's hand as he led her down to the great hall, where a welcome feast had been laid out, if the smells coming from that direction were any indication. Her stomach started to growl and she started to blush, only to giggle when Eric's did the same.

Once in the great hall, food became more important than conversation for a while. Bethia was surprised at how much was said despite the noise of so many hungry people eating. It was not until the sweet and mulled wine was brought round that the true conversation began, however. She sat enjoying a stewed, honey-sweetened apple and sipping her wine as Eric told his family all that had happened since he had left them.

A lot was said quickly, for he had kept them well informed, but then came the subject of William and the problem of Beaton and Dubhlinn. The hunt for William would go on. Bethia wished she could believe that he would be found soon. There had been too many failures, however—failures by good, quick-witted, skilled men—for her to be too confident. To think of William also meant that she had to face the fact that she badly wanted a man dead. Although few men deserved it as much as William did, that did disturb her.

When the men began to talk of ousting Sir Graham from Dubhlinn and the battle that would surely have to be fought, Bethia lost what remained of her appetite. Yet again, she listened as good men, men she would never consider bloodthirsty or greedy, talked of fighting to regain a piece of land. Here too was that hint of anticipation, that near excitement over the possibility of fighting a battle that had right on its side.

"I should try nay to listen, if I were you," Maldie said, moving closer to Bethia after Gisele quietly left to go to her bed. "That is what I do."

"It might be wise. These are things I cannae understand, m'lady."

"Please, call me Maldie. We are sisters now, ye ken."

"Thank ye, Maldie. Do ye understand all of this?"

Maldie shrugged her slender shoulders. " 'Tis a just cause. Dubhlinn should be freed of the yoke of too many bad Beaton lairds. Why the men almost seem to enjoy the thought that Sir Graham will make them fight for it? Nay, that does puzzle me, but 'tis the way of men. They probably wonder how I can get so excited o'er a finely turned-out dinner or a new potion I have found. I think men and women are doomed to confuse each other from time to time."

"I dinnae want them to fight. I dinnae want people to die o'er a piece of land."

"Neither do I, Bethia, but 'tis the way of things."

Deciding that even this pleasant woman could not seem to understand how she felt, Bethia turned the subject. "Eric told me ye are a healer."

"I do what I can. I dinnae wish to sound vain, but I believe I have some skill and knowledge."

" 'Tis nay vain to recognize what one can do. 'Tis just that I have begun to learn what I can. Old Helda, the healer at Dunnbea, taught me some things, but I should like to learn more. I begin to think that Dubhlinn shall have to be rebuilt in many ways, not only in mortar and stone or new plows, but in skills."

"I shall be glad to teach ye all I can before ye go to your new home."

It was late before Eric took her back to their bedchamber. Despite all the talking Bethia had done with Maldie, it had been impossible to completely ignore the talk of war. As she watched him shed his clothes, she found herself wondering how many places there were on his fine body that could be pierced and how many would become fatal wounds. She softly cursed and crawled into bed. When Eric slipped beneath the covers and pulled her into his arms, she remained tense against him for a moment, before the warmth of him and her body's response to his touch could make her relax.

"It looked as if ye and Maldie found a lot to talk about,"

Eric said, smoothing his hands over her back and wondering why she seemed upset, almost distant.

"She is going to teach me about healing. I thought it might be a useful skill when we reach Dubhlinn."

"Ah, Dubhlinn. Bethia, I dinnae want to fight," he began.

"Nay"—she kissed him to stop his words—"dinnae say anything. There has been enough talk of Dubhlinn and Sir Graham and righteous fights tonight. We havenae shared a bed for three long, verra cold nights. I can think of better things to discuss, cannae you?"

"Aye, but soon we really must talk about this."

Bethia placed her hands on the side of his head and pulled his face down for a kiss. She put all of her need for him, all of her increasing fear into the kiss, and soon they were both breathing heavily. Passion made her feel better, made her happy, and with her head filled with men talking of war, she wanted the forgetfulness it also brought her. That blissful oblivion was very short-lived, but she craved it.

Eric soon found himself dragged along beneath Bethia's passionate assault. He sensed that she was using him and the passion they shared in some way, but he was too afire to care. He wrestled with her over each caress, each kiss, over the matter of who would dominate whom in the lovemaking. It was a battle he loved to fight with her, for he was usually too lost in pleasure to care if he was the victor. As he joined their bodies and felt the sense of rightness only she could give him, he decided that, so long as it brought him to this sweet point, he was always the winner.

Drained and happy, Eric flopped onto his back and tugged an equally limp Bethia up against his side. "Welcome to Donocoill, Bethia Murray," he drawled and grinned when she giggled.

Chapter Seventeen

"I dinnae think your wee wife likes this," Balfour murmured as he watched Bethia hurry away from the training ground.

Eric sighed and took a long drink from the wineskin Bethia had brought him. "Nay, she doesnae. I have tried to talk to her about it, but"—he grimaced—"she is verra good at distracting me."

Balfour laughed and nodded in complete understanding. "At least she doesnae berate ye or weep all o'er you trying to change your mind. Just what doesnae she like about all of this?"

"Aye," Nigel said as he walked up beside them and accepted a drink from Eric's wineskin. "What could trouble her about this fight? 'Tis a righteous one."

"She sees it as a fight o'er land, and she doesnae like people fighting and dying o'er such things," Eric replied. "In most such instances, I might agree with her."

"Are ye saying that she doesnae accept your claim to Dubhlinn?"

"Oh, she accepts that. She has no doubt that Sir Graham is

wrong, that he has no claim at all to Dubhlinn, and that he should give it to me."

"Ah, I see." Balfour laughed softly. "And somehow this will all happen without any of us having to lift a sword."

"A foolish thought and I ken that Bethia isnae a foolish lass. Nay, she thinks with her heart in this matter and that makes it verra hard to reach her and reason with her."

"Then leave it be. Let her sort it out in her own mind and heart."

"That may be for the best. She kens the facts of the matter. I have e'en shown her how bad it is at Dubhlinn. There is nay more I can say. If she is to accept this, she must do it on her own."

"There is that or"—Nigel smiled as Gisele waddled over to him followed by Maldie—"there is getting like minds to speak with her."

Bethia frowned as Maldie and Gisele entered her bedchamber. She had thought the soft knock had been Grizel, for the last she had seen of the two women they had been going to visit with their husbands. Setting aside the tiny shirt she was making for James, she poured them each some wine and pulled the stools over in front of the fire. In the month since she had arrived at Donncoill, this was the first time the women had purposely sought her out and she was a little nervous as to the reason why.

"Is everything all right?" she asked as she sat down beside Gisele, but angled enough to see both women clearly.

"Aye," Maldie replied, then she sighed. "And nay."

"I have done something wrong?"

"Why do ye always think that?"

"What do ye mean?"

"Each time there is even the smallest thing amiss, ye apologize, or if one of us seeks ye out to have a talk and, mayhaps as now, looks a wee bit serious, ye always ask if ye have done something wrong.''

"It has been my experience that that is quite often the case,'' Bethia murmured.

"Bah,'' Gisele snapped. "I have seen no great fault in you since you came here. Eric certainly sees none. You do not trip. When you have helped around the keep you show true ability at managing, and you are always very kind. People have been trying to make you think you are a nothing and you should ignore whatever they said, eh? They were clearly very stupid people.''

Bethia almost smiled. Gisele sounded so fierce. It was also very flattering to have the woman talk of her abilities.

"Ye do both look verra serious though,'' Bethia said.

"We have come to speak to you about Eric. I think you do not mean to, but you make him unhappy.''

Maldie frowned. "That wasnae the best way to put that, Gisele.''

"Why? He is unhappy. Not with you,'' Gisele hastened to say when she saw the look of distress on Bethia's face. "With something in your head, something you think.''

"Bethia,'' Maldie said, reaching out to pat Bethia's clenched hands, "your distaste for the battle that is to come has, in some ways, hurt Eric.''

"Has he sent ye to tell me this?''

"Nay, our husbands did. Eric thinks we but mean to talk only of the battle and try to help you see that it is, if nay all right, at least nay as bad as ye think it is. He believes ye are seeing it all with your heart and, mayhap, thought women could best discuss it with you. After all, in his wee mon's mind''— she exchanged a quick grin with the other two ladies—"he has told ye everything. Since he has and ye still dinnae see the matter as he does, he is at a loss.''

"And this hurts him?''

"He didnae say that. He talks about how he doesnae like

the way it has upset you. But, aye, I believe he is a wee bit hurt. He understands, but he also wants ye to stand fully behind him.''

Bethia sighed and took a bracing drink of wine. "I will ne'er go against him.''

"That was well said," Gisele murmured.

"Come, lass, dinnae try to play with us," Maldie said and smiled gently. "We have been married too long. The answer that isnae an answer and the promise that isnae really a promise is a game we ken verra weel and can quickly recognize. Just tell us exactly what is in your head and mayhap we can help ye reach some compromise, some place where ye willnae be so upset by all of this and Eric's poor bruised feelings will be soothed.''

"I cannae like people fighting and dying o'er land," Bethia said.

" 'Tis more than that and I think ye ken that. Dubhlinn belongs to Eric. He has every right to it. It will be Sir Graham refusing to obey the king's orders to give it up that will cause the battle.''

"And that isnae fighting o'er land?''

"In a way, but doesnae he have a right? And ye saw how it is at Dubhlinn. The people are sick at heart. The past three lairds have cared naught for the people who depend upon them. They have beaten them, starved them, tossed away their lives in useless squabbles with neighboring clans, and kept them terrified, hungry, and poor until they are little more than sheep.''

"I think you know all of this," Gisele said. "Mayhap you should look more closely at why you are so upset about this battle. I wonder if it is less the why of the battle and more about who shall have to go and fight it.''

"Of course I dinnae want Eric to go and fight. Nay, nor Bowen, Wallace, or Peter. Yet I have ne'er felt it was right for people to die in a fight o'er land. 'Twas a greed for land that cost my sister her life, and the lives of her husband and his aunt. And 'tis the same greed for land that has set a madmon on my trail. Can ye blame me for nay liking it?''

"Not at all," said Maldie. "But ye dinnae really think Eric is like that mon, do ye?"

"Nay, of course not."

"Yet, that may be what ye are telling Eric when ye let him see how much ye dislike this."

That thought horrified Bethia. "I have told him that I dinnae think he is anything like William."

"Aye, but sometimes just saying so isnae enough."

"Ye are trying to make me feel guilty."

Maldie smiled. "A wee bit. All I ask is that ye look into your heart and try to see the true reason ye dinnae like the idea of Eric fighting for Dubhlinn. I think Gisele is right. I think 'tis a fear for Eric and the others more than the reason for the battle."

"Weel, I will admit that, when I do think of the battle to come, I am nay thinking of the men with Eric or the people of Dubhlinn. I think only of Eric, my cousin, Peter, and Bowen. I couldnae bear it if anything happened to them, if they died fighting for a piece of land." She grimaced. "Which is just what Gisele said, isnae it?"

"Verra nearly," said Maldie. "I dinnae think we have eased your fears at all, but mayhap ye could cease speaking of how ye feel. If ye must say anything, express only your fear for the safety of those you care about."

"Ye want me to hide what I feel?"

"Just the part that has Eric thinking ye condemn what he may be forced to do."

Bethia thought about that for a moment. Her fear for Eric and the others was a deep part of why she hated the battle that was to come. It would not be that hard to fix her mind upon that and push her dislike for the reasons to the back of her mind. It would not be quite the same as lying to Eric.

"Then that is what I will do," she finally agreed. "If ye

feel ye must tell him something about this talk, then tell him that. Mayhap if he hears it from you, he willnae press me to talk about my feelings.''

"At which time ye may say the wrong thing." Maldie nodded as she stood up and helped Gisele to her feet. "I understand. We are all afraid, Bethia. None of us wants to see our mon ride off to fight for we ken that someone will be trying to kill him. Ye arenae alone in that fear."

The moment they left, Bethia hurried over to lie down on the bed. Evening approached and her head and stomach began to feel very uneasy. As she lay there, she thought over all that the women had said. The very last thing she wanted to do was hurt Eric or make him feel that she had nothing but disdain for him concerning this battle he would be forced to fight.

She had been selfish, she decided. She had been so concerned with how she felt that she had given no thought to the feelings of others. Bethia sighed and felt embarrassed. It was time to cease being such a child. The other women at Donncoill also faced the loss of their men, of the husbands, lovers, and kin that would soon ride off to fight Sir Graham and his men.

She decided it was far past time that she showed a little of the courage they did. It did not mean she had to be false to herself, only that she had to keep some of her feelings to herself out of kindness for others. However, she mused, she would still pray every night that some fierce attack of gallantry overcame Sir Graham and he handed over the lands of Dubhlinn to their rightful owner without a fight.

"Ye are with child," Maldie said as she wiped the sweat from Bethia's face.

Deeply embarrassed that she had become ill in front of Maldie, Bethia could only nod. This attack had come in the morning instead of the evening and thus had taken her completely by surprise. Bethia was glad that she had only just let Maldie into her bedchamber, that Eric was gone, and that she was not in some well-crowded hall or bailey. As she slowly sipped from the goblet of cider Maldie served her, she wondered how well Eric's sister would take her request for silence.

"I havenae told Eric yet," she said.

"Ye didnae need to tell me that. Eric wouldnae be able to keep such news to himself. What I cannae understand is why are ye hiding it?"

"Probably for verra silly reasons. I wanted to be sure I was with child and then I wanted to be sure I would stay with child."

"Nay so foolish," Maldie said as she sat down on the edge of the bed. "Weel, ye must be sure now."

Bethia laughed softly, then frowned. "While I was at court, and for a while here, this illness came in the evening. 'Twas verra faithful. Just before I was to go and dine I would feel weak, dizzy, and nauseous. Do ye think something has gone wrong and that is why it has begun to strike in the morning?"

"Nay, I doubt it. It may have decided to come now instead of later. Ye may find that it still comes in the evening. Twice a day isnae so unusual. Or it could just be that something ye ate last night didnae sit weel in your belly. Being with child can sometimes make the mildest of foods a torture on one's digestion. How far along do ye think ye are?"

"Two months, mayhap a wee bit more. I fear I cannae be certain when the last time was that I had my courses. All I am sure of is that I havenae had them since I met Eric."

"Then I would count from the first time ye and he lay together. 'Tis nay so unusual for a lass to get with child the first time she beds with a mon, but e'en if ye didnae, 'twas probably soon after."

"Then I probably approach three months' time."

"And soon ye willnae get sick anymore. Most women cease to empty their bellies in the third or fourth month. Then all ye have to do is sit back and get verra fat."

"There is something to look forward to."

"So when do ye tell Eric?"

Bethia sighed and rubbed her hand over her stomach. "I believe I will wait a wee bit longer. I am nay sure it is something one should tell a mon practically on the eve of battle. In truth, I have been with child for the whole six weeks I have been here and he hasnae noticed. I think I would like him not to be so preoccupied and so busy elsewhere when I tell him."

Maldie laughed and stood up. "Aye, 'tis news that ye want to tell at the right time and in the right place. There is a lot of trouble surrounding the two of you though. So keep in mind that that time and place may be a long time in coming and 'tis always best if ye tell him ere he finds out for himself. Men can sometimes have some verra unkind thoughts when they think ye have been hiding something this important from them. Ye certainly dinnae want the moment ruined by an argument."

As she watched Maldie leave, Bethia decided that was advice she would be wise to remember. She had heeded the last advice Maldie and Gisele had given her concerning her feelings about the upcoming battle and that had proven sound. Eric might not feel as if he had her complete approval for what he would do to get Dubhlinn, but she was sure he no longer felt that she hated what he was about to do. The few times her fears and unease were noticed or mentioned, she referred to no more than her concern for his safety.

In truth, she was beginning to realize that that was exactly what it was. The more she kept her mind on her fear for him, the less she fretted over the why of the fight. Bethia decided she had let herself get her fears and her opinions all mixed up. In her heart, she knew that Eric had no choice and that there was no comparison between what he was about to do and what Sir Graham and William had done. Sir Graham was the thief and it was past time that he gave up his ill-gotten gains.

There were still a few weeks left before the time of year was right to have a battle, she mused as she closed her eyes.

She would never be able to send Eric off to fight with a kiss, a smile, and a wish for good luck, but she felt she could begin to let him see that she believed in his cause.

Time at Donncoill passed quickly and, to Bethia's great relief, peacefully. She played with James and Eric's nieces and nephews, studied healing with Maldie, and attempted to learn French from Gisele. Although she still could not bring herself to openly approve of the battle the men so diligently prepared for, she had tried to let Eric know it in small ways.

There were two shadows dimming the joy she might have felt. William lurked close at hand. It was now certain that he had followed them from Dunnbea. Despite the fact that he was on unfamiliar ground, however, he remained elusive. Every hunt for him proved fruitless, leaving Eric increasingly frustrated, a feeling Bethia shared wholeheartedly.

The other problem she had was in her marriage. She and Eric stayed where they had begun, passionate and companionable, but with no real indication that his feelings for her had deepened beyond that. At times she could comfort herself with the knowledge that very few married couples had more than that—that many had a great deal less. Then she would watch Eric's brothers and their wives, see the deep love they shared so openly with each other, and feel eaten alive with jealousy and envy. That was what she wanted yet it continued to elude her.

Bethia put down her needlework and moved to stare out the window of the sewing room. The hint of spring was already in the air. The days grew longer and warmer; the ground softened and was quickly churned up into mud by men and horses. Even the chatter of the women in the sewing room with her had become livelier. It was a time of the year she had always loved. This time, however, it meant that soon Eric would be riding off to fight with Sir Graham.

Slowly, she put her hand over her womb as the child growing within her began to move. She was at least four months along, yet Eric still did not notice any change in her. If the movement within her womb grew much stronger, however, he would have to feel it. The time to tell him about the child they had created was drawing very near. Bethia had hoped to gain some hint of a return of the love she felt for her husband by now, imagining some very romantic, tender moments as they spoke of love and she told him he was to be a father. She finally accepted the fact that she was simply going to have to tell him, plainly and quickly. Yet again she was going to have to bite back the words of love she so ached to tell him.

"Come, spring is a wondrous time," Maldie murmured as she moved to stand next to Bethia.

"Aye, I have always loved it, despite the mud and the bugs." Bethia briefly returned Maldie's smile. "This time it but signals the start of the war with Sir Graham. He refuses to leave Dubhlinn and openly challenges Eric to come and take it."

"Weel, the Beatons were always arrogant fools."

" 'Tis a shame they arenae so cowardly that they run the minute they see Eric and his men riding toward them." She held up her hand when Maldie began to speak. "I ken it willnae happen, and just lately, I have actually found some comfort in seeing how hard the men prepare for this fight."

"And fight they will. Is that what has ye looking so sad?"

"Nay, I was just thinking that little has changed between Eric and me and I had hoped for more by now."

"Ah, ye want him to love ye as ye love him."

"Wouldnae any woman want that? But it hasnae happened."

"Are ye sure?"

"He hasnae spoken of love. I dare not try to guess what he feels. If I let hope make me guess wrong I should be hurt." She patted her stomach and smiled faintly. "I had some verra foolish dreams about how it would be when I told him of this child."

"I ken the sort of dreams. Something like him falling to his knees and declaring undying love, claiming ye are all the world to him, and that the child is but the miracle born of that love?"

"I would allow him to stand," Bethia drawled and laughed along with Maldie.

"Mayhap it willnae be that sweet, but ye need not fear that Eric will be anything but pleased to ken he will be a father."

"I ken it." She sighed. "And that is no small thing. 'Tis just that, weel, I want what ye have."

"A big brown mon?"

Bethia was surprised into a laugh. "Maldie, I dinnae think ye are taking me seriously."

"Oh, I understand and sympathize. There is just nothing I can tell ye except to keep loving the mon as ye do. Eric has often said that he too wants the sort of marriage Balfour and I have. That means he is willing to try. He may be trying right now. Ye just havenae noticed. Eric stepped into this marriage far too calmly for it to be just passion. Ye havenae been married for too long. Sometimes it takes a wee while to get all ye desire. And none of this is really making ye feel better, is it?"

"Aye, actually, it is. I think I just need to be pulled from my melancholia now and again. In truth, mayhap 'tis time to go and indulge in a good sulk."

"Pardon?" Maldie asked, half laughing.

"Weel, I havenae done it since I got here, but I fear I actually enjoy going and having a hearty sulk now and again. I lie there and think o'er all that I believe is wrong and makes me unhappy, wallow in that misery for a wee while, and then feel quite refreshed."

Maldie grinned. "I am nay sure what it says about me, but I find that that makes sense." She laughed along with Bethia, then hooked her arm through hers. "Let us go and see the children, and when our ears ache from the noise they make, we shall go and see how our husbands fare."

Bethia allowed herself to be pulled along. Maldie was good

company, and despite the dozen years age difference, Bethia felt they had grown close. She realized that, unlike when she left Dunnbea, she would feel quite sad when she had to leave Donncoill. The only consolation she had was that Dubhlinn was not that far away. Since Eric was close to his brothers and sister, Bethia suspected there would be a great deal of visiting back and forth.

For an hour, they played with the children. James had quickly adapted to having so many other children to play with and Bethia felt it was helping him learn how to talk better. More and more she could actually understand what he was trying to say. When she moved to Dubhlinn, she would make sure that he was not left alone in his nursery, but was allowed the company of other children even if they were not equal in birth.

An hour passed before Maldie dragged her away. With so many children talking and demanding attention, Bethia realized an hour was about all she could take as well. She loved children, but the nursery at Donncoill was so crowded with lively children of all ages that one began to feel very overwhelmed.

"Now we go to find our husbands," Maldie announced as she started down the stairs. "I was wondering how your sickness is? Gone yet?"

"Nay. For a wee while, it came in the morning and at night and that was a bit of a trial."

"Ye should have said something. I could have given ye something to ease it."

"And I should have thought of that, but I didnae. Now 'tis just in the morning, and I think it may be easing some. 'Tis still there but it doesnae leave me so weak anymore."

"It must be hard to hide it from Eric."

"It would be if I woke up when he did, but I have been sleeping verra late. And deeply. He gently complained that I must be working too hard, for I am difficult to rouse in the morning." She laughed along with Maldie, for they both knew exactly why he would be trying to wake her up.

As they stepped out into the bailey, Bethia took a deep breath. She could almost smell the rapid approach of spring. Winter had not been too hard to bear, but she was more than happy to see it pass.

A commotion at the gates caused Bethia and Maldie to pause. Her eyes widening, Bethia watched a small, elaborately decorated cart roll into Donncoill, three well-armed, burly men escorting it. Her heart sank as she recognized the voice of the woman sharply ordering people around.

Eric, Balfour, and Nigel moved to greet the visitor, and Bethia had to fight the urge to race over and grab her husband. Locking him in their bedchamber suddenly seemed like a very reasonable thing to do. She cursed as Lady Catriona got out of her cart and threw herself into Eric's arms.

"And who is that?" said Maldie.

"Lady Catriona, one of Eric's old lovers."

"What in God's sweet name is she doing here?"

"Obviously, God felt I needed a challenge. Lady Catriona has arrived with the spring mud to do what she did at court— something she does so verra weel."

"And what is that?"

"Make me utterly miserable."

Chapter Eighteen

"Just look at her," Gisele grumbled, glaring across the great hall at Catriona.

"Disgusting," Maldie muttered and then she joined Gisele in frowning sternly at Bethia. "Weel? Arenae ye going to do anything?"

Bethia sighed and watched Catriona fawn all over Eric. It seemed she did that a lot. In the week since the woman had arrived uninvited at the gates of Donncoill, Bethia saw her husband only when he joined her in their bedchamber. If he was not training his men or hunting for William, Catriona was draped all over him. It brought back some very unpleasant memories of her time at court.

"What do ye think I should do? Go over there and kick her right in her pretty smile? Mayhap knock out a few of those beautifully white teeth?" Bethia asked.

"I would," Gisele said, one small hand clenched in a tight fist at her side, while she smoothed the other gently over her child-rounded belly.

" 'Twould be tempting,'' Maldie agreed. "Howbeit, that would lack manners.''

"You think that slut shows good manners by trying to seduce a man right in front of his wife?''

"This sort of thing always makes Gisele a wee bit crazed,'' Maldie explained to Bethia. " 'Tis the French, I think.''

"Oh?'' Gisele eyed Maldie narrowly as she said, "Blithely ignoring a woman licking your husband as if he is a sweet just because you fear being rude sounds very English to me.''

"English?'' Maldie hissed. "Are ye accusing me of acting like a cursed Sassanach?''

"If the slipper fits,'' Gisele murmured, then shrugged.

The two women started to argue, and Bethia turned her attention back to Catriona. Maldie and Gisele argued a lot. It had not taken Bethia long to realize that they thoroughly enjoyed it. One thing Gisele had said, however, stuck in her mind. Catriona might not actually be licking Eric as if he was a sweet, but she was very close to it. Surely the woman had to be stepping over some line, even if it was only the one that marked the difference between good manners and bad.

It was the complete audacity of the woman that truly stunned Bethia. Catriona acted as if she had some right to Eric. The woman constantly hinted that she and Eric had been almost betrothed. Catriona also seemed to forget that she had played a large part in William's attack upon Bethia while she and Eric had been at court. The more Bethia had considered the events of that day, the more guilty Catriona had looked, yet the woman acted the complete innocent, as if the incident was and should be forgotten. Bethia had no idea of how one should deal with such a woman.

"Ah, listen to us,'' Gisele said. "We argue while poor Bethia's heart is being torn to shreds.''

"Actually, I think she looks a wee bit confused,'' Maldie murmured.

"That is exactly what I was feeling,'' Bethia said and shook her head. "The audacity of the woman is beyond understanding. She implies that what she and Eric once shared was more than lust, that a betrothal was in the offering." She nodded in agreement when both women muttered strong denials. "I ken that that is a lie. E'en so, she cannae think that he would set me aside. He and I were wed by a priest. So is she willing to settle for just an affair again? That makes no sense. Then there is what happened at court." Bethia told them all about Catriona's part in the attack William had made on her. "Yet here she is, expecting me to welcome her, to act as if naught has happened."

"Did ye tell Eric what she did?" Maldie asked.

"Nay, I really have no proof. In truth, sometimes I wonder why I think it. Yet, instinct tells me that she was a part of it."

"Aye, I can believe it. Ye have to fight for the mon, Bethia."

"Fight for him? Have ye taken a good look at Catriona?" She paused and both women nodded. "And a good look at me?"

"So? Aye, that bitch is verra fair and has a more fulsome shape. She also set ye in the hands of a murderer, has had more lovers than she can probably count, and tries to tempt a mon into adultery in his own home in front of his wife. My brother isnae a fool, Bethia. He sees the rot beneath the fair face. Howbeit, e'en though ye ken that ye can trust him, ye do yourself no favors by standing back and letting that woman do as she pleases. What do ye think that tells Eric?"

Bethia sighed. "That I simply dinnae care. I ken it and 'tis certainly not what I wish him to think. Howbeit, I have no wish to play the jealous shrew either."

"No one is telling ye to do that," said Gisele. *"Non,* that would be very bad. You should at least let him know that you are not completely ignoring this insult. And let that slut know it too."

"A wee hint of jealousy isnae a bad thing," Maldie said. "Believe me, ye would be seeing it in Eric if ye had some mon hanging all o'er you like Catriona is hanging all over him.''

Recalling how Eric had pressed her to say that she was his before they were married, Bethia nodded. ''Aye, Eric can be a wee bit possessive. I suppose it wouldnae hurt to show him that I am too. And it might not hurt to let Catriona ken that I willnae abide this nonsense quietly.''

''Mayhap now would be a good time to tell him that you love him,'' Gisele suggested.

''Now why do ye think I love the fool?'' Bethia sighed when both women looked at her in disgust. She had, after all, already confessed it to Maldie. ''Ye dinnae think everyone sees it, do ye? I dinnae really like the idea that I am walking about with a lovesick look upon my face.''

''Nay,'' Maldie said and patted Bethia on the shoulder in a gesture meant to comfort and calm. ''Eric doesnae see it.''

Bethia decided it would be a waste of time to argue that it was not just Eric she was worried about, especially since they all knew it was. ''I think it would be a bad time to talk of love. Eric might think the words were prompted by jealousy, that I am only saying them in the hope of tearing him away from Catriona. If I e'er say those words to him, I would like them to be believed even if they arenae returned.''

''Aye, Bethia is right, Gisele,'' Maldie agreed. ''Saying such things now could weaken the importance of the words.''

''Mayhap you could just give him a little more loving, remind him a little more often of the passion you can share,'' Gisele said.

''If I remind him of the passion we share any more than I do now, the mon willnae be able to walk,'' Bethia drawled.

''That would work.''

Bethia and Maldie stared at Gisele for a moment and then all three women laughed. Her sisters by marriage offered several more suggestions about how Bethia could draw Eric out of Catriona's grasp, some of them quite silly, making them laugh again. In the end, she decided she would just go and stand with her husband. As she started toward Eric, Bethia prayed Catriona did not say or do anything that would nudge her barely leashed temper too hard. The jealous shrew she did not want to be was lurking just below the surface of her calm, eager to spring forward and do Catriona some serious harm.

Eric was suddenly flanked by his brothers. Balfour draped an arm around his shoulders while Nigel distracted the annoyingly tenacious Catriona. Hoping he was not about to get a lecture on the sanctity of his marriage vows, thus being insulted by the implication that he was considering breaking them, Eric eyed his eldest brother a little warily.

"I believe ye may be in some serious trouble, laddie," Balfour said.

Not sure what the man referred to, Eric asked, "How so?"

"Maldie and Gisele have been consulting with your wee wife, advising her, I am thinking."

Looking toward the three women and seeing their scowls before they quickly looked away, Eric murmured, "Ah, I see. Do ye think I should summon an armed guard for Catriona?"

"She would probably just bed them and then they would prove useless as guards." Balfour smiled briefly when Eric laughed. "Nay, Nigel and I thought we ought to warn you. When our two wives get together, they can brew enough trouble for a dozen men. I dinnae ken your lass verra weel, but since Maldie and Gisele like her, I can only believe she would add to that brew. Ah, it looks as if they are nearing some decision. I believe Nigel and I will just return to our chairs now."

"Afraid your fine clothes will be spattered with my blood?"

"Actually, laddie, it wasnae yours I was afeared would be spilled."

"Cowards," Eric murmured just loud enough for them to hear as his two brothers hastily deserted him.

Eric watched his wife nod to Gisele and Maldie, then start to walk toward him. The moment Nigel left her side, Catriona latched on to his arm and started telling him, in great detail, about a very public, very violent, love affair that had recently scandalized the court. Eric nodded and murmured politely as he studied his approaching wife and tried to figure out what sort of mood she was in.

The only thing he was sure of was that Bethia neither liked Catriona nor wanted the woman at Donncoill. Maldie and Gisele felt the same, and they did little to hide their displeasure. Catriona was oblivious to it all or simply did not care. What Eric was not sure of was the true source of Bethia's dislike. Was it jealousy or simply because Catriona was such a disagreeable person, something Eric was surprised he had not noticed much before now?

When Bethia reached Eric's side, he smiled at her and closely studied her face. Whatever emotion she was feeling, it was a strong one. Her eyes were hard and they glittered faintly, yet she wore the calm, stupidly sweet expression she donned for her parents. Although he did not want a scene or an argument, he thought that some hint of jealousy might be nice.

"Ah, Bethia," Catriona murmured. "I see ye have finally left the company of the matrons."

Since Catriona was closer in age to Maldie and Gisele than to her, Bethia thought that comment was a particularly foolish thing for the woman to say. "I dinnae think it would be wise to call them that within their hearing," Bethia said as she slipped her arm though Eric's.

"Forgive me. With so many children between them, I may have mistaken their ages." Catriona glanced at Gisele and was unable to fully hide her distaste. " 'Tis clear that at least one of them is still young enough to breed again."

No, Bethia thought as her last doubts about the truth of some of Catriona's claims faded away, Eric would not have spoken of marriage with this woman. He loved children and Catriona did not have the sense to hide her utter distaste for them. Eric had told Bethia that no woman had held his heart or his name. She had believed him then and would continue to do so.

"Ye ne'er said why ye stopped here, Lady Catriona," Bethia said, leaning against Eric and idly rubbing her cheek against the sleeve of his fine linen shirt.

"Weel, I heard that Eric was soon to go to war with Sir Graham," Catriona replied.

"Ah, and ye were afraid that ye would miss the bloodletting." Bethia was thrilled when Eric took her hand in his, gently entwining his fingers with hers.

"Certainly not," Catriona snapped, then ruined her pose of outrage by asking a little too eagerly, "Do ye think it will be a verra fierce battle?"

"I still pray that Sir Graham will flee and give Dubhlinn to Eric without a sword being drawn."

"That willnae happen. Why should Sir Graham give up land that he already holds?"

"Because the king commands it and the land rightfully belongs to Sir Eric."

"Ah, of course." Catriona smiled brilliantly at Eric. "Ye will make a fine laird, Eric."

"Thank ye, Catriona," he murmured, then looked at Bethia. "What were ye, Gisele, and Maldie talking about for so long?"

Bethia bit back the urge to tell him the truth, even to repeating Gisele's suggestion that he needed to be bedded more. She could tell he knew they had been discussing Catriona and her blatant pursuit of him. There was no need to give him the satisfaction of telling him that he was right. The fact that she was standing there hanging on to him almost as much as Catriona was all the stroking she intended to give his vanity.

"Breeding"—she smiled sweetly—"and good manners"— then unable to resist, she looked right at Catriona—"and broken teeth." She heard Eric choke back a laugh. "Gisele was particularly interested in the broken teeth."

"I can imagine," Eric said, well aware of Gisele's temper.

"Does Lady Gisele have trouble with her teeth?" Catriona asked.

When Eric stared at Catriona with a look of disbelief, Bethia was relieved. She did not want to think that she believed Catriona was stupid just because she was jealous. The woman either did not realize how much she infuriated other women or was too arrogant to give the animosity she stirred up so effortlessly the attention it deserved. Catriona knew how to use her beauty to seduce men, and she had the lack of morals to be a deadly enemy. But Bethia began to think the woman did not know much else.

"Er, nay," Eric muttered, idly musing that it obviously had not been Catriona's keen wit that had drawn him into her bed. "I believe Gisele's teeth are just fine."

"Good. Bad teeth can be such a trial, quite ugly and painful. I was blessed with verra good teeth."

"Aye, we can see that," Bethia said. "Why, as I stood across this great hall, I could see the tidy whiteness of your smile. In truth, when the light from the candles hits it, it can be quite blinding. I admit, I was quite dazzled."

"Bethia," Eric murmured in warning, but laughter trembled in his voice.

Seeing the angry look upon Catriona's face, Bethia decided to heed his warning. Courtesy demanded that she not insult her guest, even if that guest was uninvited, unwanted, and unmannered. She also saw that she had finally pierced Catriona's thick hide, and while she found some pleasure in annoying the other woman, she did not wish to make a scene.

A few moments later, Bethia decided she had endured quite enough. Her presence might tell Eric that she did not have any intention of letting some other woman have him, but it seemed to inspire Catriona to new heights of outrageousness. The only comfort Bethia found was in the fact that Eric looked very uncomfortable. She supposed she ought to rescue him from a situation he was so obviously finding more and more uncomfortable, but Bethia excused herself to go to her bedchamber. It was either that or punch Catriona right in that smile she was so proud of, and Bethia suspected Eric might find that even more embarrassing.

After stripping down to her shift, Bethia poured herself some wine and crawled into bed. As she drank the wine, she struggled to calm her temper, for she did not wish to inflict it upon Eric. When he entered the room, she sipped her wine and watched him get ready for bed. She could not really blame Catriona for wanting him, she thought and sighed.

"Dazzled, were ye?" Eric said as he stood by the side of the bed, took her goblet, finished the wine, and set it down.

"I admit I was beginning to lose my temper," Bethia said as he slipped into bed beside her.

"I dinnae blame you. She is verra hard to bear." He kissed the hollow by her ear, smiled against her skin when she shivered, and quickly removed her shift. "I was thinking earlier that I must have been particularly blind when I kenned her, for she is a thoroughly unlikable woman and, despite her slyness and seductiveness, not particularly smart. I dinnae ken what I saw in her."

"Oh, I can think of two rather large things that might have caught your lecherous eye."

"Ah, those." Eric curved his hands around Bethia's small, firm breasts and teased the nipples to hardness with his thumbs. "Fools that we men are, we often think that bigger is better." He lathed the taut nipples with his tongue. "But bigger is definitely not sweeter."

Bethia sighed with pleasure and threaded her fingers in his thick hair as he lathed and suckled at her breasts until she squirmed with eagerness beneath him. He kissed his way down her body, then down one leg and up the other. When he touched his lips to the curls between her thighs, she briefly tensed, still uneasy about such intimacy. With but one stroke of his tongue he quelled her shyness. She tightened her fingers in his hair and opened to his kiss. He toyed with her, keeping her balanced precariously on the very edge of release until she thought she would scream.

When he moved to sit next to her and picked her up, Bethia quickly eluded his attempt to set her astride him. She sprawled on her stomach between his legs and took him in her mouth. For as long as she could, she tormented him as he had tormented her, struggling to prolong the pleasure. He finally growled her name, grabbed her under her arms, and set her upon him. It did not really surprise her when they both shuddered with the strength of their releases but a moment later, for they had each pushed the other too close to the edge to linger there very long.

After washing them both clean and chuckling mercilessly at Bethia's blushes, Eric sprawled on his back and pulled her into his arms. "Ye do ken how to exhaust your mon, my heart."

She sleepily kissed his shoulder. "Odd, that was one of Gisele's suggestions for keeping ye out of Catriona's reach. She said I should give ye a wee bit more loving." She smiled when he laughed softly.

"Lord, Bethia, if ye gave me any more, I wouldnae be able to walk."

"I told her that," she said and exchanged a grin with him. One thing she was sure of was the passion they shared.

"And what did Gisele say?"

"She said, 'That would work.' " Bethia laughed with him.

"Ah, I am sorry about that fool wench, Bethia."

" 'Tisnae your fault she is here."

"Not completely, but I obviously misjudged her character. When I was playing the rogue at court, I was arrogant enough to think I kenned which lasses to avoid, to ken which could be trouble later. Ye see, I always kenned that I would marry and end my roaming and I didnae want the past to intrude into my life with my bride. Weel, it has done that with a vengeance, hasnae it?"

The way he spoke of his dalliances—as if they were part of some game played by a young, lusty, free man—eased her lingering concerns about his past. It was unpleasant to think of him lying like this with any other woman, but Bethia knew those women had never meant anything. He had used them as they had undoubtedly used him.

"I am sure she will go away when she realizes the game she plays willnae gain her anything."

"Weel, I fear I am nay that patient," Eric said. "After all, I made it clear that I didnae play those games any longer while we were still at court. She is either too vain or too stupid to believe it. The laws of hospitality willnae let me toss her out into the mud simply because she annoys everyone." He smiled when Bethia giggled. "Howbeit, they dinnae say that I must politely tolerate any and all of her nonsense. I have tried to be both polite and kind. Now I see that she will only use both to try to gain her own ends. So now I will be neither."

"If ye think that is best," Bethia murmured, but inside she grimaced. Catriona would not tolerate that behavior very long before she made a scene.

"What have ye told him about me?"

Two days, Bethia mused as she turned to face an angry Catriona. She was rather surprised that the woman had taken so long to react to Eric's change of attitude. Glancing at Catriona's mud-splattered gown, Bethia decided that the woman must be truly furious to have hunted her down outside, for Catriona was usually ridiculously precise in her appearance. As Bethia folded her hands in front of her, she hoped Catriona would not enact too long a scene. She had finally found the time to come out and carefully study Maldie's herb garden so that she could make one like it at Dubhlinn. She certainly did not want what time she had grasped stolen away because Catriona was having a tantrum.

"I am nay sure I understand what ye are talking about,"
Bethia said.

"Eric has changed toward me, grown cold, almost rude, and
I ken that it is your fault," Catriona snapped.

"Mayhap he but grew weary of being embarrassed by your
unwanted attentions."

"Unwanted? I will have ye ken that—"

"I ken it all," Bethia cut her off. She was surprised at how
calm yet nasty she sounded. She decided she had just had her
fill of the woman and could no longer even feign politeness.
"Ye and Eric were great lovers, he adored you, the passion ye
shared was sublime, and ye were almost betrothed. Weel, I
dinnae believe ye were anywhere near becoming betrothed.
When Eric wed me, he told me that no woman had held his
heart or his name. I prefer to believe him."

"Oh, aye, ye would. Ye are far too naive to understand that
men will say anything to get what they want."

"Obviously, so will women. Where is your pride, Catriona?
He doesnae want you."

As the two women argued, they were unaware of Eric's
approach. Still out of sight, he paused and stared at his former
lover and his new wife. He had been a fool not to realize that
Catriona would blame Bethia for the cold rebuffs he had been
giving her. A part of him wanted to step in before Catriona
said something that would hurt Bethia, but he hesitated. Instinct
told him that there was more behind Bethia's dislike of Catriona
than jealousy and he wondered if, somewhere in the midst of
this confrontation, he might discover what that was.

"He did. And why shouldnae he?"

"Because he is now married?" Bethia said in a tone of voice
that implied she was trying to explain something to an idiot.

"To you. Look at yourself. Ye are skinny, your hair is an
odd sort of not brown but not red, and your eyes dinnae match."

"I have good teeth," Bethia murmured.

Catriona ignored her. "What mon would turn from me to hold on to to you?"

"Mayhap I am verra good in bed. Light, easy to move about into the right position. Men like that, I think."

"Now ye are just being silly. Nay, ye have turned Eric against me by telling him what happened that day in the market."

"Ah, the day ye led me straight to a mon who wished to kill me."

"Now, the mon didnae say he wanted to kill you. He just wanted to find ye alone."

"Please at least try to be honest," Bethia said, her voice heavy with disdain. "Ye didnae care what he had planned for me."

"Nay, I didnae," Catriona snarled. "He should have cut your cursed throat. Ye insulted me." Catriona's last word ended on a high, strangled note as Eric suddenly walked up to stand between her and Bethia.

Eric stared at the two women, then fixed his gaze upon a pale, terrifed Catriona. Now he knew why Bethia had such strong feelings about Catriona. As soon as the woman was gone, he intended to find out just why his wife had not told him the truth about that day in the market.

"Ye were willing to see my wife dead because your vanity was pinched?" he asked, fury and disbelief roughening his voice.

"Nay, Eric m'love"—she reached out to grasp him by the arm—"ye misunderstood."

He yanked free of her grasp. "Nay, I think not. I want ye gone from Donncoill—now!"

"But, Eric, 'tis late in the day," Catriona began.

"Now." He spared a sharp glance for Bethia. "I want to talk to ye later. The women's solar. One hour."

Bethia did not believe he could get Catriona out of Donncoill that fast, but after an inadequately short study of Maldie's garden, she made her way to the ladies' solar. She was surprised when she had to wend her way around maids rushing to throw Catriona out. When Eric said *now,* he obviously meant it, she thought. Knowing that he had learned the whole ugly truth about Catriona, and that she probably would never have to see the woman again, made Bethia feel that she could easily endure the scold Eric so plainly intended to give her.

It was less than an hour later when Eric strode into the solar and slammed the door shut behind him. Bethia sat very straight in her chair and watched him pace in front of her. She hoped he was trying to walk off some of his anger before he talked to her. When he suddenly stopped and faced her, she jumped slightly, startled by his abrupt movement.

"Why didnae ye tell me that she tried to hand ye over to William?" he demanded.

"I had no proof," she replied. "All I had was the fact that she and Elizabeth acted strangely friendly even though I had insulted them. They took me to the market fair, and then they deserted me. When William grabbed me, he mentioned something about two women helping him find me. Aye, it certainly seemed to have been Catriona and Elizabeth, but it could have been someone else."

"Ye still should have told me."

"Mayhap, but we were leaving. I assumed that would be the last we e'er saw of her and, I saw no benefit in stirring up a lot of trouble." She eyed him warily when he leaned toward her, placing his hands on the arms of her chair and caging her there. "I just wanted to leave that cursed place and felt that, if accusations were made, we might not be able to leave."

"Fair enough, but ye must ne'er keep such a secret from me again."

Bethia nodded, but inwardly cursed herself for a liar. She was keeping two secrets from him at that very moment: secrets about the child she carried and how much she loved him. She hoped that, when she told him those secrets, he would understand why she had kept them. Realizing he was just standing there staring at her, she met his gaze and frowned.

He reached out and tugged her bottom lip down with his fingers. "Ye are right," he murmured. "Ye do have good teeth."

"Oh, no," Bethia groaned, suddenly realizing how long he had stood there listening to her and Catriona and what he must have heard.

"There was something else ye said that has me wondering." He started to grin when she softly cursed. "Light, ye said, and easy to move about."

Easily recognizing the gleam in his eyes, Bethia ducked under his arms and slipped out of the chair. She laughed as she ran to the door and escaped the solar, for she could hear him right behind her. She decided she would not make him chase her for too long before she let him catch her. The herb garden could wait for another day.

Chapter Nineteen

It was hard, but Bethia tried not to yell at Eric. She did not think she was asking for much. All she wanted to do was go to the village with Maldie. They had agreed to taking half-a-dozen armed men with them. As she watched Eric pace their bedchamber, she wondered if he was being too protective or if she was foolishly ignoring just how big a threat William was.

"Ye dinnae need anything," Eric said as he stopped pacing to frown at her. "And if ye do, we could send a maid to get it."

"There will be six armed men with us. Do ye really believe one mad fool could get to me through them, or past Maldie, or e'en all the villagers?"

Eric cursed and dragged his hands through his hair. He did not know what was the matter with him. William seemed to have taken on mythic proportions in his mind. It was foolish, but the thought of Bethia being outside of his sight made him gnash his teeth. She was right. There would be a lot of people watching her. If William could get to her through her guards, her companions, and a crowd of curious villagers, then the man could reach her anywhere, even within the walls of Donncoill.

"I dinnae like it," he grumbled, "but ye may as weel go."

Bethia moved to hug him, then stood on her tiptoes to brush a kiss over his mouth. "Thank ye."

"Oh, aye, ye can be so verra sweet now since ye have gotten what ye wanted," he drawled.

"Aye," she admitted and laughed when he gave her a very fierce and very false scowl. "Eric, dinnae think I disregard the threat William poses. I have seen him, have listened to his ravings, and have twice nearly been killed by him."

"And yet ye wish to go outside these walls?"

"I do, but nay alone or unprotected. 'Tis spring," she said and grimaced at the meagerness of that explanation. "At Dunn-bea, before William cursed our lives, I would be more outside the walls than in at this time of the year. I ken I cannae go prancing through the fields or go hunting, but I want to."

"Ye want to prance through the fields?" he asked, grinning widely.

"Eric, pay attention," she said firmly, but she had to fight the strong urge to grin back. " 'Tis just that I feel as if he has made me his captive. Donncoill is a wonderful place and the people who live here are all that is kind, but no matter how beautiful a place is or how gracious the captors, 'tis still a prison if ye arenae allowed to leave it. Weel, I am nay so foolish as to flee to the outside and dare the mon to catch me, but must I allow him to keep me chained with fear?"

"Nay, my heart." He cupped her face in his hands and gently kissed her. "Go, but watch your back."

Bethia hurried away before he could change his mind. It was just a short ride over to the village that claimed the protection of Donncoill and the village was small, if prosperous. While she might well buy something, the true purpose of the trip was so that she could try to see why the village was prosperous.

She also wanted to see what the village had that caused Maldie and Gisele to say that it served almost all of their needs. Eric would do his best to bring the village back to life at Dubhlinn, but he might not understand what would make it an attractive, useful place for a woman.

There was also the simple matter that she needed to get out from behind the walls of Donncoill. She suspected her need to ride out, no matter how short the journey, was increased because she was not allowed to do so freely. When she saw Bowen holding her horse, she beamed at him. She had seen little of him lately.

"So he is letting ye go," Bowen said as he tossed her into the saddle.

"Aye. Are ye going to be one of my *six* armed guards?" she asked, as she straightened out her skirts.

"I am. I am nay sure I like this since we have seen a few signs that the bastard is lurking about, but I think ye need it. A wee trot to the village and a look around may ease the dangerous restlessness ye are suffering."

Bethia nodded. "I do feel, weel, confined. I am nay used to it."

"I ken it. Dinnae worry. The bastard cannae hide from us forever," he said as he mounted and led them out through the gates of Donncoill.

"I understand just how ye feel, Bethia," Maldie said as she rode up beside her. "I was let to run free as I grew. When I first settled here, became the laird's wife, and thus required a guard of some sort every time I went anywhere, I found it all verra hard to bear. The big change was that I went from a place where no one cared where I went or what I did to a place where people care enough about me to worry about me and want to keep me safe."

It was almost too difficult for Bethia to simply nod. She felt weak, stunned by the revelation that had just swept over her. Maldie probably did not even know the importance of what she had just said, but Bethia saw it all too clearly. From the time she had learned how to walk, she had been allowed to run free, to go and do whatever she wanted to. Only Bowen and Peter, and then Wallace, had tried to maintain some control over her. She had seen it as freedom, but now realized that it was pure neglect. Her parents had simply not cared what happened to her. Bowen and Peter had raised her and Wallace, kept them safe, cared for them. Sorcha had barely been able to step out into the bailey without someone watching over her. Bethia had sometimes thought that was sad, but now she saw that her parents were cherishing Sorcha with their protection.

And that really hurts, Bethia thought as she fought a sudden urge to weep. She had always thought that her parents' criticism was simply how they showed their displeasure with her. In truth, they had shown their disdain from the first day they had allowed her to toddle out into the bailey without even the spit boy to watch her. She had spent her whole life struggling to please them, but she had never had a chance—not from the day shortly after her birth when they had looked at her, deemed her imperfect, and set her aside. Sorcha had been the cherished one and poor, thin Bethia with her mismatched eyes had been cast aside. Bethia began to think that her parents' constant criticism, their continued efforts to denigrate her, had been done because she had kept reasserting herself into their lives, had refused in her own childish way to be forgotten.

Despite her strenuous efforts not to, Bethia found herself wondering what it all said about Sorcha. The answer came with a heartbreaking swiftness. Sorcha had cared for her as little as her parents had. Sorcha—her twin, the sister of the womb, the one person in the whole world who should have loved her without question—had not given Bethia much more thought than she had her maid. The kind words and smiles Bethia had seen as sisterly affection, she now recognized as the well-learned courtesies of a well-trained lady. While she had sat elegantly gowned in her soft bedchamber waiting for the maid to style her hair, Sorcha had looked down on her dirty, ragged sister and felt nothing at all. The only time in her whole pampered life that Sorcha had reached out to Bethia was when she had needed someone to help her son.

"Are ye all right, Bethia?" Maldie asked.

How did you tell someone that, no, you were not all right, that you had just discovered how cleverly you had lied to yourself for your whole life? How did you say that you wanted to rage and scream because you had been such a fool? How did you say that you had just realized that your parents and your beautiful sister had not been ignoring or insulting you your whole life because they were selfish and unkind, but because they just did not want you around? Bethia suspected that, if she said all that, poor Maldie would think she had gone mad.

"I am fine," Bethia said, not surprised to hear how rough her voice was.

"Are ye sure ye arenae going to be ill?"

"Nay. I just had an unpleasant thought."

"Is that all? To make yourself look so gray, it must have been verra unpleasant indeed." Maldie reached across their horses to pat Bethia's hands, which were clenched, white knuckled, upon her reins. "We could go back and do this another day."

Bethia took a deep, steadying breath and shook her head. "Nay, I will be fine. I was just thinking of a spring day much like this one and suddenly recalled something that stole all the warmth from my blood. One of those dark memories ye try so hard to bury, but it has the ill manners to creep up on you now and again. 'Tis gone again and I will recover from it."

"One of those I dinnae really want to ask about?"

"Especially not now when I have banished the wee demon."

"I pray it wasnae some kind of omen."

"Nay, I dinnae believe so."

Maldie was still watching Bethia closely by the time they

reached the village. But soon Bethia was able to lose herself in the study of the houses and shops. It was not hard to see that it was a very prosperous little town, even if she had not had the dismal village at Dubhlinn to compare it to. Bethia followed Maldie as she went from shop to shop, stopped to speak to several of the villagers, and even admired a new baby. All the while, six armed men stomped along behind them. Bethia thought they must make a very odd sight.

As Maldie talked to the woman selling ale, Bethia looked for Bowen. Her eyes widened slightly as she saw him scowling down at a selection of ribbons a woman held out for him. She moved to his side.

"If ye are thinking of getting one for your wife, Bowen," she said quietly, "I think she would like the red ones."

"Are ye sure? My Moira wears verra plain colors," he muttered, cautiously reaching out to touch the red ribbon with one callused finger.

"I dinnae think she has much choice. A bright cloth is a great deal more dear than, oh, a brown one, and she spins a lot of your cloth herself. Now, with her black hair and dark eyes, I think the red ribbon would look verra fine. Aye, or some red thread, for then she could put some colorful stitching on her clothes."

"The lass has the right of it, sir," said the woman. "I have the thread if ye wish to see it."

"Ye will have to bring it to me here." He briefly frowned at Bethia. "I must keep an eye on this lass."

"Weel, this lass is going to go back to Maldie," Bethia said as the woman hurried away to get the thread. "Is she still talking to the alewife? I cannae see her o'er the ones standing around the place."

"Aye, lass, although I would say that she is more arguing with the woman than talking."

"Maldie likes a good argument."

Bethia could almost feel Bowen watching her as she nudged

her way through the people gathering to listen to Maldie and the alewife argue over the price of a barrel of ale. Bethia gasped as she felt a sudden stinging pain on her arm. She cursed and put her hand over the pain, felt a dampness there, and pulled her hand away to stare in horror at the blood staining her fingers. When she lifted her gaze to search the crowd, she stared straight into the glittering eyes of William Drummond.

Then there was an ear-ringing bellow. A moment later, Bowen was there, his sword drawn. He wrapped his free arm around Bethia's waist and held her tightly against his side as the men from Donncoill and several people from the crowd chased William. Bethia tried to follow William's flight through the village, but quickly lost sight of him.

"I dinnae think they will catch him," she said as Bowen carried her to a bench in front of the alewife's cottage and set her down. She winced when Maldie tore her sleeve so that she could look at the wound. " 'Tis but a scratch."

"Aye, 'tis," Maldie said as she bathed it with water the alewife fetched for her. Then she bandaged it with a strip torn from her own shift. "Does the fool mean to kill ye with little pinpricks like this?"

"Nay. I think he wanted me to turn around so that he could stick his dagger in a more deadly place." When one of the other Donncoill men returned to stand by her and Maldie, Bethia looked at Bowen. "Go and get your gift for Moira."

"Oh? Look what happened the last time I took my eyes off you," he grumbled, glaring at her bandaged arm.

"He willnae be back. He makes his attempt, then flees when the cry goes out and he kens that he has been seen."

"Dinnae move," Bowen ordered and hurried back to the woman selling the ribbons.

"Does he think I mean to rush off and dance in the streets?" Bethia muttered, casting a quick frown at the guard standing by Maldie, for she was sure she had heard the man laugh. "Weel, I shall surely be locked in the tower now."

"What do ye mean?" Maldie asked as she sat down next to Bethia and gave her a tankard of ale.

"The last time that madmon nearly killed me, Eric said he had an urge to lock me in a tower and surround it with armed men."

"That is rather sweet."

"Sweet?"

"He wants to protect you, that is all. And I truly doubt he would do it."

"Mayhap not, but I dinnae think I will be let out of Donncoill again until William is dead." She sighed with resignation when Maldie offered her no reassurances.

"I should lock ye in a high tower and surround it with armed men," Eric yelled as he lifted Bethia off her horse and set her down in front of him.

Bethia glanced at Maldie and cocked one eyebrow. Maldie clapped a hand over her mouth and hurried across the crowded bailey to the keep. Eric put his arm around Bethia and held her close to his side as Bowen told him what had happened.

"Do ye think it is worth going out to try to hunt him down?" Eric asked Bowen.

"Probably not," Bowen replied. "But we may as weel. I should hate to nay do so and discover later that he was seen near at hand or that some trail was left that we could have followed."

Eric nodded and, seeing that Grizel had arrived, gently nudged Bethia toward the maid. "Go and rest, Bethia." He sighed and shook his head. "I dinnae think I will be gone verra long. I hold little hope of finding anything, but feel I must at least look."

There was nothing Bethia could say to give him hope. She did not have any within her to share with him. Giving him a brief smile of encouragement and a quick kiss on the cheek, she followed Grizel into the keep, entering just as Nigel and Balfour hurried out to join Eric. With so many men looking for William, it was very hard to understand how he kept escaping. Maybe *he* was the witch, she thought.

By the next morning, Bethia realized that she had been right. Eric was not going to let her step one foot outside of Donncoill until William was dead. She listened patiently to him explain all she should do and why she was being made a virtual prisoner as she sat in the great hall to eat her morning meal. It was not Eric's fault, nor was it hers, but she hated it.

The moment he left her, she stood up and started back to her room. It was time to have a good sulk. She winced a little as she walked. Eric's lovemaking last night had been exhilarating, but a little rough, filled with something very much like desperation. Bethia realized that he was honestly and deeply afraid for her. That seemed to imply that it was a lot more than duty and his promise to protect her and James, which was behind his almost relentless search for William.

She stepped into her room, smiled briefly at Grizel, who was changing the linen on the bed, and went to look out of the window. The men were training hard. She watched Eric and his cousin David fight for a while, the clash of their swords making her wince. Eric was good, quick, and obviously strong, and those traits gave her some comfort. Of course, his cousin was not trying to kill him. Then she saw the pile of weapons being stacked up by the armorer's shed and tensed.

"They will go soon," Grizel said as she moved to stand beside Bethia and stare down at the men.

"How soon?" Bethia asked, fear taking the strength from her voice.

"Within a few days, mayhap sooner. They but wait for a few of Lady Maldie's kinsmen to join them. Peter says the

Kirkcaldys are verra eager to fight the Beatons. 'Twas the old laird's sister who was seduced and abandoned by a Beaton.''

"Aye. Eric's father and Maldie's mother. Weel, at least there will be a large, strong army behind Eric when he rides off to let the Beatons try to kill him.''

Grizel smiled faintly. "I am fair sick with worry too, though I think ye have a more clever bite to your words than I do when I spit them out. I spend a great deal of time reminding myself that 'tis a just fight my mon will be joining in.''

"Aye, 'tis just, but 'tis still just land when all is said and done.''

"So speaks one born to own it or marry it. Aye, 'tis just land. 'Tis your laird's land and 'tis his right to get it back. My Peter fights for ye and for Sir Eric, but he also fights for us, him and me. He marches in this battle because at the end of it is a chance for a better life for him and me and our bairns. A cottage with more than one room. Mayhap a few coins in his purse. A chance for him, and mayhap his son if we are blessed with one, to become more than just another one of the men-at-arms.''

"I didnae think ye had such a hard life at Dunnbea," Bethia said quietly.

"Nay, it wasnae hard. It was ne'er going to change though. My Peter is near thirty and has ne'er been knighted. When he and Bowen first came to Dunnbea, there was a lot of fighting. They risked their lives again and again to protect Dunnbea and its people.. Aye, they are bastards, but they arenae baseborn men. Their fathers were knights. I dinnae think they expected too much to think that your father would see them knighted.''

"Nay. I was but a child, but e'en I recall how important Peter and Bowen were to the defense of Dunnbea.''

"Weel, they didnae get it. Nay then. Nay once in all the years since. Your father lets Bowen and Peter lead his men, e'en train his men. He thinks them good enough for that, but 'tis clear he doesnae find them good enough to make them knights.''

"But Eric will."

"Aye, if they serve him weel, he will see them knighted." Grizel shrugged. "Setting a sir afore their names willnae make them rich, but 'twill make them proud, give them respect e'en from those who dinnae ken them. Oh, I am cold to the heart just thinking of my mon going into battle, but I willnae try to hold him back. He hungers for that knighthood. I willnae deny him the chance for it by shackling him to the hearth with my fears.''

When Grizel left, Bethia sprawled on her stomach on the clean bed and buried her face in the pillow. The battle with Sir Graham Beaton was becoming more complex by the moment. Eric fought to regain his birthright. The Murrays would fight to help him and to rid the neighboring keep of a mon no one trusted. The MacMillans fought for Eric, but also to repay Sir Graham for his lies—lies that had made the laird of Bealachan deny his own nephew. The Kirkcaldys would fight because a Beaton had dishonored one of their kinswomen and because Eric was the half brother to another of their kinswomen. The Drummonds would fight for her, for if Sir Eric became laird of Dubhlinn, she would be his lady. Men like Peter and Bowen would fight for honors long denied them— honors that would gain them and their families a better life. Bethia suspected a few others fought for that same reason, just as she suspected some joined the battle out of a pure love of fighting.

Thinking of how Bowen and Peter had been denied honors they had earned long ago brought her thoughts to her father, to her family. Tears stung her eyes as she fully accepted the painful fact that they had never been her family. She had been cast from the nest long ago, but had been too blind, too stupid, to see it. Bethia suspected most everyone else had seen it. It explained the anger Eric often felt toward her parents—the same anger Bowen, Wallace, and Peter had sometimes revealed. That made her feel an even greater fool.

She became so sunk in her misery that it took her a moment to realize that someone sat beside her on the bed and rubbed her back. Even before she turned to look, she knew it was Eric. Bethia hurriedly wiped the tears from her face with the sleeve of her gown, but she knew it was too late to hide the fact that she had been weeping.

"Does your arm pain you?" he asked as he brushed a kiss over each tear-dampened cheek.

"Nay. Truly," she insisted when he frowned. " 'Twas but a scratch."

"Did I catch ye in the midst of a verra big sulk then?"

"Oh, aye, a verra big one. So big that I am nay sure how long I have been at it."

" 'Tis time for the midday meal."

"Jesu!" Bethia scrambled off the bed. "Just let me tidy myself a wee bit first."

Eric watched her wash her face, smooth out the wrinkles in her gown, and fix her hair. He wanted to ask her why she had been weeping, but was afraid of the answer he would get. Earlier he had seen her watching them training for battle and now he found her weeping. Whenever he tried to speak of the battle to come, she responded by saying she simply suffered a woman's fears for the safety of those she cared about. He believed her, but felt that was not all of it.

He sighed and admitted that he was a coward. If Bethia still felt the battle was only for land, still felt that it was a wrongful waste of life, he did not want to hear it. Especially not on the eve of battle.

"Tomorrow?" Bethia gasped, sitting up in bed and staring at Eric in shock, "Ye ride to Dubhlinn tomorrow?"

"Aye, at dawn."

That explains a lot, Bethia thought as she continued to stare at him. After they had shared a meal at midday, he had disappeared. Her spirits still depressed, she had spent the rest of the day playing with James and sewing clothes for him. When Eric had brought their meal to his room, she had thought it very nice that he had wanted to spend time alone with her. Now she suspected he had wanted to keep her from hearing the talk in the great hall or discovering that the Kirkcaldy men had arrived. It certainly explained the speed with which he had gotten her into bed and the fierceness of his lovemaking. He had probably hoped she would be too sated and sleepy to fully react to his news.

"Lass, what are ye thinking?" Eric finally asked, a little uncomfortable beneath her steady look.

"I am thinking ye are a verra sly fellow," Bethia murmured.

It took all of her strength, but Bethia subdued her urge to yell at him, to demand that he not go. Her blood ran cold at the mere thought of it, but she had to face the fact that this could be the last night she spent with him. She would not ruin it with tears, pleas, or recriminations.

"Bethia, I have to go." He frowned when she silenced him with a kiss and tentatively wrapped his arms around her.

"I dinnae wish to speak of it," she said quietly.

"Ye cannae just ignore this, my heart."

"Aye, I can for tonight. I wish it gone from my mind."

"I am nay sure how ye can do that."

"Weel, ye will have to help me. I want ye to love me into a stupor. I want ye to keep my mind so clouded with passion that I cannae think of anything but you. And I want ye to love me until I fall into an exhausted, dreamless sleep."

Eric smiled, willing to play her game. It was certainly more to his liking than tears or arguments. The memories he would take into battle on the morrow would be sweeter too.

"I want ye to love me into forgetfulness," Bethia said. "Make me so weary that I had best kiss ye fare thee weel now, for I might nay be able to crawl from this bed to see ye leave. And when I do wake up on the morrow, I want to have been so weel loved that my first thought will be the sweet memory of that passion. Can ye do that for me, Eric?''

''Oh, aye, I believe I can,'' he said as he nudged her onto her back and kissed her.

Chapter Twenty

"Where is your wife?"

Eric grinned slowly at Maldie and Balfour, then at Nigel, who stepped up to join them in front of the door to the keep. He could tell by the looks upon their faces that they feared Bethia was making a show of her disapproval. They had all discussed her feelings and they all sympathized, but he also understood his family's opinion that she should at least make an effort to appear as if she fully supported him. Although he would like that too, would be elated if she gave him her complete, heartfelt support, he could still find some enjoyment in telling his family exactly why Bethia was not there.

"Gisele isnae here," Eric pointed out, unable to resist teasing them a little.

"Gisele is verra pregnant," Nigel said. "She still sleeps. I didnae feel inclined to linger for the hour or so it would take to wake her." Nigel smiled faintly when Maldie laughed and his brothers grinned.

"Ah, weel, my wee wife is asleep as weel. Aye, and I think it would take an army to rouse her."

"Is she with child too?"

"Not that she has told me. Nay, I fear this exhaustion is caused by my dutiful fulfilling of her request."

Balfour rolled his eyes. "So, ye said fare thee weel to your lady in the same manner so many others did. Nay need to boast." Balfour gave his very alert wife a mock frown. "Ye look verra wide awake," he grumbled. "Do ye resist my vigor?"

"I suspect she didnae ask ye to love her into a stupor." Eric nodded at the stunned looks upon their faces. "Aye, no jest. She specifically asked me to love her into a state of mindless exhaustion. I, being a kind, dutiful husband"—he ignored his brothers' grumbles, which contained several coarse references to wee lads choking on their own vanity—"complied. Indeed, once she succumbed to exhaustion, she said that I had done weel and that she was indeed so exhausted she probably wouldnae be able to lift an eyelid until weel after the battle was o'er and won."

"Let us pray ye havenae done so weel that ye have no strength left to wield your sword against Sir Graham," Nigel said, nudging Eric toward the horses Bowen and a stableboy held ready for them. "Mayhap we could ask Beaton to hold back until ye have had a wee rest."

Maldie distracted them from their bickering by kissing each of them on the cheek and wishing them luck. A moment later, they were all riding out the gates of Donncoill. With dawn's light painting everything with soft, warm colors, it was hard to accept that, within a few hours, they would all be caught in the midst of a battle, facing death and dealing it out to others. Eric felt a strange mix of exhilaration and sadness. He knew the former was that strange, taut excitement all men of battle felt when they faced a good fight. Some of the latter feeling, however, was undoubtedly due to Bethia's lingering disapproval.

As he rode, he tried to push aside his hurt over her refusal to accept what he was doing. A few times she had even made him question his reasons for what he was about to do. Yet search his heart as he would, he found no taint of greed. Eric did not believe Bethia saw any there either. Dubhlinn was his. He could bring the lands back to the prosperity they had once enjoyed before too many venal lairds had bled them dry. Eric felt Bethia had to agree with that too.

Yet she still offered him no clear sign of support. It made no sense to him. He was not sure why it troubled him so, even hurt him. He was right. The fight was just. That should be enough to satisfy him no matter what whim his wife clung to.

"For a mon who spent a long night dutifully pleasuring his new wife into a mindless stupor, ye have a verra dark look upon your face," Balfour drawled as he rode up beside Eric.

"Mayhap he is just recalling that it wasnae his wondrous skills as a lover that sent her into a deep sleep," Nigel said as he flanked Eric, "but that knock upon her head when she slammed into the headboard as he was so vigorously pleasuring her." He grinned when Balfour laughed.

"Such wits." Eric sighed and shook his head. "I fear I was just feeling a wee bit sorry for myself because I have failed to win Bethia's respect."

"What makes ye think ye havenae got her respect?" Balfour asked.

"She still hasnae supported me in this."

"Does she condemn ye for it in word or deed?"

"Weel, nay, but—" Eric began.

"I havenae seen her looking at ye or acting toward ye in any way that would make me think she lacks respect for you. Have ye, Nigel?"

"Nay." Nigel half smiled at Eric. "Ye might have tried talking to the lass for a wee bit first last night."

Eric grimaced. "Aye, and I thought I would, but when she asked me to love her into a stupor so she wouldnae e'en think about the morrow, I was distracted." He briefly grinned as his brothers laughed, then he sighed and shook his head. "In truth, I wanted to be. Part of me wanted the truth of her feelings, but a greater part didnae want to hear it."

"Weel, I think ye worry o'er it all far too much," Balfour said. "Just because she doesnae want this battle fought, doesnae mean she lacks respect for you or questions your reasons. Maldie said Bethia is verra adamant in saying that ye are nay like that bastard William nor are ye akin to Sir Graham in any way. And where did ye e'er get the idea that she should support everything ye do or agree with all ye say in every matter just because she married you?"

"That isnae it. I have ne'er expected that. Nay, nor would I wish for it. 'Tis just that I have worked for this for half my life. Every letter written, every petition sent, every visit to the king's court, and every alliance made was made with the thought that this day would come. I have grown to monhood struggling to gain this right. 'Tis all part of being recognized, I suppose. Aye, and I have tried to get it all by peaceful means. I suppose I wanted Bethia to understand all of that, wanted her to be a full partner in the culmination of thirteen years of work."

"Mayhap she will be, once she kens that the end of the fight willnae leave ye, or the others she cares for, dead or wounded."

"Be at ease," Nigel said. "Set your mind on beating Sir Graham as cleanly and as quickly as possible. Put aside your concerns about how Bethia feels until later. She will still be at Donncoill. The lass may not have wished ye to go and fight this battle, but I ken, without a doubt, she will be waiting for ye, wanting ye to come back to her, with open arms. Sir Graham, however, will be waiting for ye with a sword and arrows."

* * *

Eric stared at the men lining the parapets of the tightly barricaded Dubhlinn and cursed. All during the ride to its gates, he had nourished the small hope that Sir Graham would give up peacefully. In the last message he had sent only three days earlier, he had given the man one last chance to surrender the lands as ordered by the king. He had even listed all of his allies. Even the realization that so many clans had banded together against him had not made the man see reason. The man clearly intended to cling to the death to lands he had so decimated Eric doubted they could produce enough coin to pay his hirelings. Eric could not blame Bethia for questioning such insanity.

"He means to stand and fight," Nigel said, scowling toward the walls as he tried to judge the strength of the keep. "It willnae be easy to get inside those walls."

"Nay, but we must," Eric replied. "Mayhap, if we strike first and hard, hurting him sorely, some of his hirelings will decide that he isnae worth dying for."

"Aye," Balfour agreed. " 'Tis worth a try. Only a brief one though. I cannae stomach using men as nay more than arrow fodder. If we dinnae see an immediate weakening, I will stop the assault."

"Agreed," Eric said, fully agreeing with Balfour's opinion. He had always been sickened by the wasteful hurling of men against well-manned walls until the dead piled up so high at the foot of the walls the callous laird could simply climb that pile and step over the ramparts.

The first assault upon the walls of Dubhlinn was indeed swift and brutal. It was ended just as swiftly because the men were met with a thick shower of arrows. Fortunately, few were lost or wounded, for they had been well trained in how to use their heavy shields. Getting up and over the walls while holding a sword and a shield over one's head was impossible, however.

Next they tried the siege weapons they had brought with them. The boxed-in ladders saved the men from the deadly sting of the arrows, but proved no defense against fire, boiling water, or scalding oil. A few more men were lost before the retreat was called and heeded. Eric knew their refusal to waste men's lives was seen as a weakness by Sir Graham, one to be used against his attackers, but Eric could not regret it.

"It appears we will have to lay siege," Sir David said as he walked up to where the Murray brothers stood glaring at the solid walls of Dubhlinn. "If we cannae beat them, we must wait them out."

"He is weel prepared for an attack," said Eric. "He may be weel prepared for a siege."

After glancing around at fields that had obviously seen little or no care for a long time, David asked, "With what?"

"Aye," Nigel muttered after he too looked around. "Dubhlinn has slid deeper into ruin than I would have guessed. Are ye sure ye want the place?"

" 'Tis mine." Eric muttered a curse and, lifting his helmet, dragged his fingers through his sweat-dampened hair. "By refusing to heed the king's decision, Sir Graham commits treason. He is a dead mon already."

"Then mayhap we should alert the king to his transgressions, and let the king's army come and tear him out of there."

"We would still have to lay siege, holding the place and the traitor inside until the king's men could arrive. And I have fought in the king's army. They willnae leave much standing nor have a care for the innocent. 'Twill nay be only Sir Graham whom they will consider a traitor, but all who are a part of his clan, whether they actually fight for him or cower in hiding, praying they will survive this."

"They are nay all cowering," Bowen said as he approached them, a plump, gray-haired woman walking steadily at his side.

"This be Mistress Leona Beaton. Been a maid at Dubhlinn all her life."

"Aye," the woman agreed. "Began my training when I was but a wee lass of seven years. So 'tis forty years now that I have spent behind these cursed walls."

"So ye were a maid when my mother was there?" Eric asked.

"If ye be Sir Eric, aye, I was."

Apologizing for his lack of manners in not introducing himself and the others, Eric hastily rectified the omission. "Ye have been here through it all then?"

"Aye. I was still but a child when your father killed the old laird, your grandfather, and I was here when ye Murrays killed that evil mon, may God forgive me for speaking ill of the dead."

Although his claim had been accepted, Eric knew it was mostly because of the support he had finally rallied to his side. Many still questioned his legitimacy. This woman spoke as if she knew the truth and Eric felt excitement tingle through his veins. Such a witness, a Beaton by birth, and one who had born witness to so many years of ill deeds by her lairds, would silence most of those lingering doubts.

"Ye called Sir William Beaton my father. Do ye do so only because the king now gives me the right to the land?"

"Nay, laddie. My eyes told me the truth years ago. I was maid to your mother. Beaton ne'er kenned it, but I kenned all about your poor, sad mother's affair with that rogue, the old Murray laird. I also kenned when it ceased. There was but a verra wee chance that ye were seeded by that rogue. I slipped into the birthing room to steal a wee peek at you after ye were born and saw the mark ye carry. That mark told me clearly that ye were Beaton's son." She brushed a tear from her cheek with the back of her hand as she added, " 'Twas the last time I saw ye or your mother alive until ye were captured that time thirteen years ago."

"Ye ken the mark I carry? Ken that it is the mark of a Beaton?"

"Of a Beaton laird," she said firmly and nodded. "Aye. I had the bitter misfortune of seeing it on your father several times, though he ofttimes tried to hide it. The mon treated the women unfortunate enough to be within the walls of that keep as if they were his own private breeding stock. I bore the bastard three daughters, two of whom still live. Their close blood relationship saved them from this laird's attentions, but he did naught to keep them safe from his men. That sad brutality took the life of one of my lasses and has hurt my other two in their minds and spirits—and given them two bastards each."

"I am sorry for the wrongs done to ye and yours," Eric said quietly, knowing he had had no part in it all, but feeling the pinch of guilt because he shared blood kinship with the commiters of those crimes. "More half sisters," he murmured and smiled faintly.

"Aye, eight of them within those walls and a few more in the village. A few nieces and nephews too. I am sorry I couldnae save ye, lad. I tried. When I realized what had been done, I slipped away to find ye, but the Murrays had already done so. I admit I did naught to correct your father's belief that ye were a bastard. I felt ye were safer where ye were, especially after he murdered your mother and the midwife. When I learned how ye sought your birthright, I thought to help ye. I planned to go to the king myself and affirm your claim. I couldnae. This laird kens that he sits upon a stolen seat. He would let none leave Dubhlinn. If any slipped away, he was cried a traitor and his family suffered for it. I watched Sir Graham have a mon and his two wee sons slain before the mon's wife because she had slipped away to visit kinsmen and was gone but two days. I couldnae risk my daughters' lives, nor those of their bairns. I just wasnae that brave." She shook her head. "That poor woman stood in that bailey and stared at the bodies of her loved ones for hours; then she slashed open her wrists and laid herself down beside them and died. I feared there was no end to the darkness at Dubhlinn, then the word came that the king had given it all to you, that ye would be our new laird. And so I have waited. Now I can help you.''

The tale she told so shocked and moved Eric that it took him a moment to find enough voice to ask, ''How, mistress?''

Mistress Leona smiled. ''I shall get ye inside those walls the same way I got myself out.''

''Are ye sure we ought to trust her?'' Nigel whispered as they followed the woman through the shadowed wood.

Eric shared Nigel's wariness, but it was not strong enough to make him refuse her aid. They had waited until nightfall, using the torturous hours of waiting to lay out their plans. Then, leaving Wallace, Peter, and Balfour behind to direct the men, Eric, Nigel, and David had gathered nearly two dozen men and followed Mistress Leona. They were taking a risk, one that could get them all slaughtered, but Eric preferred to follow his instincts. They told him that the woman could be trusted.

At the very edge of the wood, still a fair distance to the walls of Dubhlinn, Mistress Leona stopped them. Eric's eyes widened as, with Nigel's quickly offered help, she lifted what appeared to be the remnants of a lightning-shattered tree stump. It was a hatch. The woman held her sheltered lantern in front of her and descended the narrow steps her light revealed. She waved them to follow her, and Eric hesitated only a moment before doing so. Somehow, the fact that Sir Graham—mayhap even his father—had built such an incredibly long tunnel to help himself, and the very few people he trusted, escape an enemy made him feel more confident. Sir Graham trusted no one. Eric could not believe he would have revealed such a deep, useful secret to a mere maid, to a mere woman, no matter what gain it might promise him.

''Where does this lead to?'' Eric whispered as he moved

close to Mistress Leona's side while she led them along the tunnel.

"To the laird's own bedchamber," she replied in an equally soft voice.

"That doesnae seem a particularly wise place to visit."

" 'Tis the best place right now. I have survived through the reigns of three lairds. During one of the many squabbles the Beaton lairds provoke with their neighbors, a battle the Beatons werenae winning, I noticed that the laird had disappeared from the fray. That got me to thinking that the bastard had a way out. It has taken me years, but I found his wee bolt-hole. I also noticed that, whilst in the midst of a battle, a Beaton laird stayed with his men unless he felt an urge to rut. Then he would grab a lass, bed her, and leave her quickly to return to the walls. Either way, the way out of this should be clear for us."

Once inside of the laird's bedchamber, Eric felt more certain of success. He sent the youngest of his men back out with word for Balfour and with orders and to escort Mistress Leona to safety with the Murrays. There was only one thing lacking.

"Mistress Leona," Eric said as her youthful guard tried to pull her inside the tunnel, "what about your family? If ye could describe them, mayhap we could protect them or lead them to safety."

"I have already done so. The moment I decided that I had to help, I slipped my daughters and their children out through this tunnel. They are huddled in a damp, dark shieling high in the hills with my cousin Margaret. If ye win, they will return. If not, they will flee with or without me."

"A woman who kens weel how to survive," Nigel murmured as Mistress Leona disappeared into the tunnel. "I wonder why she didnae flee this dark pit ere now?"

"Mayhap she wished to stay and help me. Mayhap she didnae feel she could get far enough away ere her absence and that of her family was noticed. This battle and the confusion that

will follow it will give her the time to get verra far away,"
Eric answered. "Now let us go and open these gates."

As they left the laird's bedchamber and made their way
through the keep, Eric knew they were being watched. Once
or twice he caught a fleeting glimpse of a servant, but no one
cried out against them. Sir Graham had obviously not bred
loyalty or love amongst his people. He would soon pay dearly
for his arrogance and his cruelty.

Sir Graham's men fell quickly, since their attention was on
the men outside the walls. They had never anticipated an attack
from behind. A few, Beaton by name and blood, surrendered
to Eric and his men on sight. A slender young man named
Pendair Beaton even helped them open the gates for the others.

Once the gates were opened, Balfour led the rest of the men
into Dubhlinn's bailey swiftly and loudly. The war cries they
screamed as they pushed through the gates and set upon Sir
Graham's men with a vengeance even set Eric's hair on end.
Several times Eric saw Sir Graham himself and fought to reach
the man. Sir Graham was trying desperately to cut his way
through his enemy and get back inside the keep, to his no
longer secret bolt-hole.

Eric looked from Sir Graham to the keep, trying to judge
the best place to put a stop to the man's flight, and froze. He
stared at the man half way up the stairs to the heavy door of the
keep. When he realized it was indeed Sir William Drummond he
saw, and that the man was close to escaping, he broke free of
his stupor and raced toward him, only faintly aware of Bowen
and Peter swiftly moving to protect his back.

A cry of pure rage escaped him when William disappeared
inside the keep. Even as Eric bounded up the blood-slick steps,
Sir Graham raced inside, but he was unable to bar the door.
Eric shoved it open, causing Sir Graham to stumble backward,
but the man quickly recovered and faced Eric. Over Sir Graham's shoulder, Eric saw William going up the stairs. He fought
to regain some sense of calm, knowing that he could not give

into the urge to relentlessly pursue William. An able fighter, Sir Graham stood firmly between Eric and the man he so ached to kill.

"Drummond, ye cowardly bastard," Sir Graham bellowed. "Get back here and fight!"

"Nay, ye are on your own," William yelled back. "Ye said ye could beat this fool. That is what I sought. Ye were to rid me of the ones who stand between me and that wee bitch. Weel, ye havenae done it. Aye, ye have lost this battle. I mean to flee ere I die with ye." William disappeared up the stairs.

A moment later, Peter followed William while Bowen stayed to guard Eric's back. Eric forced his attention to Sir Graham, pushing aside his disappointment and fury. He knew he had lost William yet again, knew in his gut that Peter would fail to catch the man, but his fight was with Sir Graham now.

"Ye were a fool to ally yourself with that madmon," Eric said as he and Sir Graham warily circled each other.

"He told me he could sway the Drummonds, if nay to join me, at least to nay fight against me."

"That mon has no sway o'er the Drummonds. His hands are too stained with their kinmen's blood."

"Aye, I wondered on that. Howbeit, he was verra good at tormenting you and he might have finally succeeded in killing your wee wife. That would have pleased me. 'Twas worth the risk."

"Ye should have left this place while ye had the chance." Eric lunged and took careful note of how Sir Graham protected himself against his sword, noting the weariness evident in the man's movements.

"Dubhlinn is mine. I have held it for thirteen long years."

"Ye have held nothing. Ye claimed what was ne'er yours."

"This land is mine!"

"Since ye love it so dearly, I will be sure to leave ye enough to bury ye in."

The fight was short, if fierce. Sir Graham had skill, but he had not kept it well honed. He was soft, his strength lost to drink and debauchery. When Eric finally pierced the man's heart with his sword, he felt no real sense of victory. He had not really wanted to gain Dubhlinn by spilling the blood of his kinsmen, no matter how much that man deserved killing. As he knelt to close Sir Graham's sightless eyes and cleaned his blade upon the man's jupon, he felt almost sad. It appeared that the only Beatons he could trust were the poor ones of low birth and the bastards his father had bred so freely.

"Peter?" Eric called as he watched that man come down the stairs, but he was not surprised when the man reported his failure with one curt shake of his head. "Curse the bastard. Will I ne'er catch him?" he grumbled as he stood up and sheathed his sword. "Get out the word that Sir Graham is dead and that a new laird holds Dubhlinn," he ordered his two men.

"I should stay and watch your back," Bowen protested.

"I will be fine. And as soon as the people hear that Sir Graham is dead, I believe the fight will end immediately."

"Aye," Bowen agreed. "These men willnae fight now that the promise of pay has been snatched from their grasp."

As soon as Bowen and Peter left, Eric took a look around. By the time he had finished touring the keep, he had a small group of wide-eyed terrified servants following him from a safe distance. This tentative sign of acceptance eased a little of the dismay he felt upon seeing the poor state of the keep. He gave his brothers a faint smile when he descended the stairs and found them waiting for him.

"No sign of William?" Nigel asked and cursed when Eric shook his head.

"Not much sign of anything else either," Eric reported.

"Aye, from what little I have seen, if there was wealth here, it has been completely stripped away."

"There is indeed verra little left and what there is hasnae been kept weel at all."

"Ye will have a lot of work to do."

"When I saw William here I had thought I could end all of my troubles in but one battle. Now I have my lands, but I will have to fight to bring them back to what they were, what they could be again. And William still hunts Bethia."

Balfour draped his arm around Eric's shoulders. "One battle at a time, lad. Ye have won this fight. Ye will soon win the other. William may disappear like a ghost, but he is still naught but a mon. He can bleed and he can die."

"And he can go to hell, which is where I mean to send him as soon as possible," Eric vowed.

Chapter Twenty-one

"Cease this pacing or I shall tie ye to the chair," Maldie warned.

Bethia sighed and sat down. She, Maldie, Gisele, and several other women had gathered in the great hall to await the return of the men. They had done the same the previous day until late into the night. Although she had finally retired to her bed along with the others, Bethia had slept too fitfully for it to have been restful. Now she sat at the table, picking at the food set out for their morning meal, still tense and desperate for some word from the men. Bethia was amazed at how well the other women appeared to maintain their calm. She feared that, if she did not hear something about Eric's fate very soon, she would start tearing her hair out.

"Are ye sure 'tis nay a bad sign that they didnae return yesterday?" she asked Maldie.

"Aye, verra sure," Maldie responded.

"Once I realized I wouldnae be granted my wish that Sir

Graham would just give up and that the battle must still be fought, I had hoped that it would be a verra short one.''

"It could have been. Howbeit, if it wasnae, that doesnae mean verra much. Balfour and his brothers are always verra careful with the lives of their men. Such caution can slow the progress of a battle. They could even have decided it was best to place Dubhlinn under siege.''

"Oh Jesu,'' Bethia groaned. "That could take months. I shall be naught but bones by then.''

"Aye, it could take months,'' Maldie said, but her tone was gentle with understanding. '' 'Tis better than hurling men against weel-protected walls and watching the dead and wounded pile up. And from what Eric told me of Dubhlinn, I dinnae think a siege will last for months.''

"Sir Graham refused to give up Dubhlinn despite orders from the king himself. I dinnae think a mon who spits in the eye of his liege, who risks charges of treason, will be brought to his knees by a siege. And from what I saw of Dubhlinn, a wee touch of starvation willnae deter him either.''

"Non,'' Gisele agreed; then she added meaningfully, "Not the starvation of his people or even his men.''

"But he willnae be able to long abide his own pangs of hunger or thirst,'' Bethia finished the thought. "But how can we ken that he will suffer them? Dubhlinn 'tis a verra sad place. Oh, do ye ken, I saw no animals.''

"Which means they have all been sold or eaten,'' Maldie said. "The mon has either filled his purse with the unwise selling of all his stock or eaten so much naught has been left to adequately replenish that stock. True, 'tis the wrong time of the year to be certain, but Eric said the fields looked as if they had been verra poorly managed, mayhap not e'en planted in a long while. Nay, the mon willnae be weel supplied in his keep, I am thinking.''

"What of the people of Dubhlinn?''

"The people of that cursed land have learned how to protect

themselves. Aye, they learned it long ago. They dinnae throw their lives away fighting either. After all, what care they who the laird is? They have gained naught but misery and pain from the last three lairds. They hide and they are verra skilled at it.''

''There are so few of them, or so it appeared when we paused near the place.''

''There are certainly a lot fewer than when my accursed father held the land, but I doubt they were killed in battle. Nay, cruelty and hunger, both inflicted by their lairds, have decimated their numbers.''

Bethia smiled suddenly, casting Maldie a faintly scolding look. ''Ye are nay so subtly trying to make me see that Dubhlinn will be weel served by the removal of the laird. Nay need to be so clever. I ken Eric will be better for them all.''

'' 'Tis odd. Dubhlinn has been brought to near complete ruin, the clan little more than a handful of ragged, terrified paupers who spend a lot of time hiding, and their one chance of survival lies with Eric, the supposed bastard of the previous laird. The Beatons will be saved by a mon who refuses to carry their name, by the true heir to Dubhlinn, who was cast out to die in the hills. In truth, all Eric should wish to do is raze that place to the ground.''

''And spit upon the ashes,'' Gisele added, then slowly eased herself out of her chair. ''I am to bed.''

''Are ye all right?'' Maldie asked.

''*Oui,* I just do not sleep well.'' She smiled as, with a nervous maid keeping close by her side, she started to walk out of the great hall. ''I know it looks as if I sleep a lot, but I merely lay this bulk upon the bed a lot and pray for sleep. Wake me when Nigel returns.''

''Nay, I will send the mon to ye and let him take the risk or nay as it pleases him.''

''She is all right, isnae she?'' Bethia asked after Gisele left, her mind briefly distracted from worrying about Eric.

''Aye. 'Tis her last month and she finds it hard, always has.

She carries large and has verra active bairns," Maldie said with a faint smile. "The poor woman finds it uncomfortable to sit, to walk, e'en to lie down. And she sleeps fitfully; thus she is e'er tired. She will be glad to be brought to her birthing bed."

Bethia surreptitiously smoothed her hand over her still very small stomach, then caught Maldie grinning at her. "I but wondered if I will be so verra uncomfortable in a few months."

"Every one of us carries differently, but once ye ken what ye will or willnae suffer, ye can always find a woman to compare ills with"—Maldie briefly exchanged a grin with Bethia—"or learn from. When are ye going to tell the mon?"

"Ah, a good question." Bethia sighed and shook her head. "I ken that ye warned me, but I really didnae think the right moment would be so cursed hard to find. When he returns"—she took a deep breath to steady her sudden rush of fear for Eric—"and I ken what is to happen next, I will pick a time and I will tell him—e'en if I have to tie him down. Oh, aye, and make sure he cannae murmur sweet words or touch me until I have finished speaking." She smiled when Maldie laughed. "He is certain to notice soon, and again ye are right: 'Twould be best if I can tell him ere he guesses for himself."

"The two of you badly need some time when ye arenae surrounded by kinsmen or fighting someone."

"Aye. This will settle the trouble with Sir Graham. That leaves only William." Bethia shivered faintly at the mere mention of the man and cursed the fear he had bred in her. "I find it hard to bear, but I dearly want that mon dead."

" 'Tis the only way ye will be free of him. Dinnae find fault in yourself for seeing that dark truth. Nay, the mon chose his own path the day he decided to use murder to steal what wasnae his."

Before Bethia could respond, she became aware of a growing noise. A moment later, she recognized it as the sound of excited voices. She exchanged a brief glance with Maldie, then started out of the hall, the other women quickly following. They nearly

ran down the boy sent to tell them the good news. By the time
Bethia went through the doors of the great hall, she was running.
The men had returned and she was desperate to see that Eric
had returned, if not completely unharmed, at least only mildly
wounded. She was more than happy to accept a scar or two on
his fine body, even a limp—anything so long as he was alive—
and she needed to see him breathe with her own eyes before
she dared to hope.

Once in the bailey, Bethia was forced to slow down. Chaos
ruled. Men, horses, and women looking for their men crowded
the place. Then Bethia saw Eric dismounting near the stables
and she started to run again. Now that she knew he was alive,
she was desperate to touch him. It was hard not to curse and
flail at everyone and everything in her way.

Eric turned toward her even as she cleared the last cluster
of people between her and her husband. Bethia flung herself
into his arms so forcefully she knocked herself breathless and
caused him to stagger back a step. She pressed her ear to his
chest and shuddered with relief at the strong, steady beat of
his heart.

"Lass, are ye all right?" Eric spared a brief smile for Maldie
as she hugged Balfour; then he turned his concerned gaze upon
Bethia. " 'Tis o'er and done with, Bethia."

"Are ye hurt?" She released him enough to glance at his
clean linen shirt and equally clean plaid. "Ye dinnae look as
if ye have e'en been in a battle."

"I am fine, as are the others ye are about to ask after. We
took the keep after dark. We were led inside by a Beaton
woman. Since we couldnae ride home until dawn, I had a
chance to bathe and change," he explained. "I had to kill Sir
Graham."

Hugging him tightly again, Bethia nodded. "Aye, he left ye
no choice."

Eric smiled as he tucked her up against his side and started
to walk toward the keep. He had seen nothing in her expression

as she had raced toward him except pure, unhidden relief. Now, as he confessed to having killed Sir Graham, she shrugged the slaying aside, referring to it only as the unpleasant necessity it was. He did not believe she had had some sudden change of heart in such a short time, so he began to think he had misread her.

She clung to him, smoothing her hand over his chest, often pausing to hold it over his heart for a moment, before starting her stroking all over again. Eric began to wonder if he had allowed himself to be so concerned with her feelings about the battle with Sir Graham that he had missed seeing a lot of things. Bethia cared for him. It was there in her touch, in the looks she was giving him. She had obviously spent hours deeply afraid for his safety and was unable to hide her deep pleasure over his safe return.

In fact, Eric decided as they entered the keep, he was almost sure that Bethia loved him and did not believe it was vanity that made him think so. It would be good to have his wife love him, he mused. There would be no more concern about the passion they shared fading away. She would stay with him forever, tied to his side by the strong bond of love. It occured to Eric that he ought to take a good, hard look at why he wanted Bethia to love him, why the thought that she might thrilled him, and why he was always so concerned that she be firmly marked as his. Determined to find the time to thoroughly examine his own feelings, he started into the great hall, only to be halted by Bethia's strong hold on his arm.

"I thought to have some ale to wash the dust from my throat," he said, trying to read the expression on her face, his eyes widening as he suddenly recognized the warm gleam in her eyes.

"I have some verra fine wine in our bedchamber," she said, a little surprised at the huskiness in her voice and the heat in her blood, for the man had not even kissed her.

"Good. We may e'en find a moment to drink some." He grabbed her by the hand and headed up the stairs.

Bethia was not sure what ailed her, but it produced a pure hot need in her and it called out loudly for Eric. She made no protest about his speed even though she had to trot to keep pace with him. In fact, she found herself wishing she had longer legs so that they could move even faster. It shocked her, but she realized she was going to find it difficult to wait until they reached their bedchamber.

The moment Eric tugged her into their room and shut the door, Bethia flung herself into his arms. She kissed him with all of the hunger that raged inside of her. He stumbled back against the wall next to the door and returned her kiss with a need equal to her own. Bethia started to unlace his shirt, quickly examining each newly exposed patch of skin for any sign of injury before kissing it.

"The bed"—Eric began, only to help her undo his plaid.

"Do ye need one?" Bethia asked as she helped him shed his shirt.

"Nay." He began to unlace her gown, groaning as she kissed his chest and curled her long, slender fingers around his erection. "I dinnae think I have the wit left to find it."

Bethia smiled slightly as she lowered her kisses to his taut stomach. He looked glorious standing there in his soft deerhide boots and naught else. Bethia was stunned at how wild she was acting, but found it exciting. Eric's vocal pleasure as she knelt in front of him and took him into her mouth only excited her more.

A cry of surprise escaped her when, but moments later, he yanked her to her feet. He stripped her down to her shift so hastily she heard a few distinct tearing sounds, but she could not make herself care if her clothes were ruined. Eric turned and pressed her against the wall. When he knelt before her, pushed her shift up to her waist, and began to repay her intimate kisses in kind, Bethia groaned and shuddered with delight. She was too desperate for him to endure such play for long, no matter how sweet it was. Despite her pleas, he took her to her release with a kiss, then started her on that heady climb all over again. When he stood, picked her up in his arms, and urged her to wrap her legs around his waist, she did so and rubbed herself against him greedily. Eric groaned and quickly joined their bodies. It was rough, fast, and feverish, but Bethia delighted in it, crying out his name as a second release tore through her body. She wrapped her body tightly around his as he held her against him and shuddered with his own release.

It took them a few moments to regain some semblance of calm. Eric eased out of her body, smiling faintly at her murmur of regret, and carried her to the bed. He dropped her on the bed and sprawled on top of her, pillowing his head on her breasts and idly moving his hand up and down her thigh.

"Are ye satisfied that I havenae damaged anything, lass?" he finally asked when he recovered enough strength to talk.

Bethia wearily patted his head before combing her fingers through his thick hair. "Aye, ye did weel, husband."

He grinned, finding that he really liked those teasing words. "Ah, weel, ye being so light and small and easy to move about." He grunted when she lightly punched him in the side. "My heart, one thing that made those words so amusing is that there is some truth to them."

"Are ye saying that ye like me being such a wee lass?" Bethia smiled faintly, both flattered and amused.

"Aye, I find it verra pleasing indeed."

"Good, for I dinnae think I will be growing much." She shivered with pleasure when he chuckled against her skin. "So Dubhlinn is now yours, is it?"

"I hold it now. I left Bowen and Peter and a few men there."

"Do ye think there will be any trouble?"

"Nay. The few people who dared to come out of hiding were pleased to see that I had won. After so many years of

Beaton lairds who were not but cruel, greedy, and cared naught for their people, it will take time to win their trust.''

Bethia sighed and nodded, smoothing her hand up and down his warm back. ''But they accept that ye have the right to hold Dubhlinn and claim yourself as their laird?''

''They all ken the tale about me and that the king granted me the lands, naming me the rightful heir.'' He propped himself up on his elbows, smiled at her, and kissed the tip of her nose. ''And a woman named Leona, who was my mother's maid, is telling all who will listen that I am no bastard. It seems that she saw the Beaton mark upon my shoulder when I was born and had seen the same upon my father''

''And she ne'er said anything? If she had come forward at the start, ye would have been spared all of this.''

''Aye, and I might have been raised by my father.'' Eric nodded when Bethia gasped softly in dismay. ''She went to try to find me when she realized they had cast me out to die; then she held silent when she kenned that the Murrays had found me. She felt I would be safer there, and though she didnae say so directly, I believe she felt it better if I wasnae tainted by the darkness which enshrouded Dubhlinn. She even thought to go to the king on my behalf.'' He told her how Sir Graham dealt with those he considered traitors; then he kissed her in a vain attempt to soothe the horror caused by his tale.

''She was right. 'Tis best that ye were raised here. Mayhap she hoped ye would become just the mon ye are, the laird Dubhlinn needs so badly.''

He had to kiss her for that; then he sighed as he readied himself to tell her the bad news. ''William was there.''

Fear coursed through Bethia's veins and she briefly clung to Eric. It took longer than she liked, but Bethia soon softened the sharp edge of her fear. Bethia hated that fear and loathed William for filling her heart with it.

''He got away though, didnae he?'' she asked quietly, already knowing the answer.

"I fear so. I saw him fleeing into the keep, knew he was headed to the bolt-hole we had used to sneak into the keep, but Sir Graham was between me and William. While I was caught facing one enemy, the other fled to safety."

"So that is where he has been hiding whilst he was in this area. But what would Sir Graham have wanted with him?"

"William had him somewhat convinced that he might be able to dull the swords of the Drummonds. Sir Graham also said that the way the mon tormented us was reason enough to ally himself with him, to give him a safe place to hide as he did so."

"We have us some verra strange enemies. At least 'tis only mine who is left."

"William is my enemy too, Bethia. He tries to hurt what is mine. For that he will die. Aye, I badly wish to kill the mon myself, but I will accept his death however it comes, e'en if 'tis just that he falls off his horse and breaks his filthy neck."

Although they were dark words of vengence and death, Bethia was moved by the feeling behind them. There was a chance that Eric was beginning to truly care for her. It would help if they did not spend a lot of their time looking over their shoulders for a killer, but she was pleased with this hint of caring. She would find the time to make it more.

"Do we go to Dubhlinn then?" she asked.

"Ye dinnae change a subject with much subtlety, my own."

She grinned briefly, then grew serious. "There is nay much to say about William Drummond. He wants me dead, mayhap still wants James dead as weel, and I suspect he wouldnae mind seeing ye dead too. We hunt for him and he hunts for us. One day we kill him. There really isnae any more to say, and in truth, e'en thinking about him gives me a chill."

"Then, aye, we will be going to Dubhlinn," Eric replied and returned her grin. "There is a lot of work to be done, my heart."

"I could see that when ye rode around the lands ere we came here."

"The same neglect and barrenness is inside the keep as weel."

" 'Tis sad. If Sir Graham hadnae been quite so greedy, he could have had a good keep, fine lands, and plenty of coin. Instead, he filled his hands with coin faster than the poor land and people could produce it."

"I will take a few days to gather what I can to send there. 'Twill make our life a wee bit easier."

She kissed him. "Dinnae fret. I dinnae need much."

"Weel, your mon does."

"Oh, aye? What?"

Eric leapt out of bed and lightly slapped her on the backside. "I need some food."

"Actually, I am feeling rather hungry myself." Bethia got up and started to dress. "Do we take James with us right away?"

"Aye," he said as he donned his plaid. "He will be as safe at Dubhlinn as he is here—especially since Bowen and Peter will have closed up that bolt-hole by the time we get there. Once we are sure the mon is dead, we can open it again. But for now, 'tis just a way for him to get to you or James."

"Bowen and Peter were a lot of help during the battle, were they?" she asked as she tidied her hair, then glanced over her shoulder and caught Eric grinning at her.

"They will soon have those knighthoods your father never gave them," he said and laughed when Bethia hurried over to him and kissed him. "Mayhap I should have teased ye with it, waited to see what ye would have tried to do to get me to do as ye wanted."

"Ah, too late." She started out of the room. "Now ye will ne'er ken just how good I am at groveling." As Eric caught up with her and linked his arm through hers, she said, "I suppose I had best begin to pack."

``Aye, and ye might think of what ye would want to be comfortable at Dubhlinn.''

"Shouldnae that wait until we get there and I can see what is lacking?''

"Bethia, believe me when I tell ye that everything is lacking.''

"Oh, dear. Then the little hunt for herbs Maldie and I plan to take on the morrow will be even more important.''

She started to count to ten and never even reached five before he protested—loudly.

Chapter Twenty-two

"Ye would think we were going on a raid," Maldie said, frowning at the half-dozen armed men riding with her, Bethia, and Grizel.

Bethia smiled and shook her head. "Eric is verra protective."

"And so he should be. I but like to complain. S'truth, I doubt these men wish to be riding along to watch us collect medicinal plants. Howbeit, William still lurks out there thirsting for your blood."

"Ah, aye, but do ye think ye could be a wee bit less, er, colorful when ye speak of the mon." Bethia grinned briefly at a giggling Grizel.

"Oh. Pardon. Balfour is e'er telling me to watch what I say. I fear I became caught firm in the drama of it all." Maldie sighed with pleasure as she looked around. " 'Tis the coming of spring as weel, I think. It makes me giddy, a wee bit foolish."

"I can understand that," Bethia said and Grizel nodded her agreement. "And it would explain why Gisele was actually thinking of coming with us e'en though I think the horses would have all shied from the thought of carrying her.''

Maldie laughed with them and then nodded. ''Poor Gisele is so round with this child.'' She gave Bethia a quick looking over. ''Ye will definitely have to tell Eric soon,'' she said quietly so that the men riding with them could not overhear. ''I am so surprised that he hasnae noticed any changes in you yet—or e'en suddenly realized that ye havenae had to deny him because of your courses.''

''I have decided to tell him when we get to Dubhlinn, to our new home.''

''Aye, 'twould be a fitting place.''

''He must be ready to take us there soon. It took me a week to convince him to let me do this and I truly thought we would have left by now. There are days when I think he is in danger of emptying Donncoill because he has sent so much to Dubhlinn.''

''Weel, that sad place needs a lot of supplies, coin, and verra hard work.''

''I dread to think of what I will find inside the place. The outside looked so barren and meager, even accounting for the time of the year, and Eric says the inside is just as bad.''

''True. The Beatons bled it dry of coin and of people with petty raids and fighting.'' Maldie pointed to the line of trees a few yards ahead of them. ''Just beyond those trees is one of the best places to find the plants we seek. 'Tis still early in the year but there will be something for us. Ye shall have enough herbs and potions to cure a city ere we are through.''

Bethia nodded and nudged her horse to a slightly faster gait in order to keep up with Maldie. As they rode through the trees, Bethia felt a chill of fear creep down her spine. She looked at the women with her, then at the strong-armed men guarding them, and relaxed a little. There was no need to worry. This was no village where the crowds could hide William. William could not get near her unless she did something foolish and she had absolutely no intention of putting herself at risk in any way. She briefly touched her gently rounded stomach. There was entirely too much at stake now.

After they dismounted and waited patiently for the men to thoroughly check the area, Bethia and the other women collected their small sacks and began hunting for the plants they wanted. Over the past weeks Bethia and Grizel had learned a lot from Maldie. Rarely did they need to question whether a certain plant was really the one they wanted or if it was ready to be harvested.

Just as Bethia was testing the readiness of some moss, she tensed. A quick glance around showed her that she was not far from the others, still well within their view and almost within their reach. Deciding she was letting her fear rule her too closely, she looked back down at the moss and watched in growing horror as a large, filthy hand ripped it from the ground and held it out to her.

"William," she whispered, knowing that it was going to take her a moment to get the fear she felt to ease its grip on her enough to allow her to scream. "I am nay alone."

"Aye, I can see that. Two wee bitches and a half-dozen Murray cowards."

"Run, William. Ye might still save yourself."

"Run to where? I am an outlaw. Your husband made me one. No place is safe for me. Even that fool Sir Graham failed me. I might have hidden there for a long while, but once I got myself settled comfortably, the idiot went and got himself killed."

"Just like you, he tried to take what wasnae his." Bethia's voice grew stronger as she struggled to calm herself. Even if no one heard her talking to the man or saw her acting strangely, she would soon be able to let out a scream they would hear all the way back to Donncoill.

"It should have been mine!"

Her eyes widened, for William had screamed those words. Even as she realized that he no longer cared about being caught, she could hear the men from Donncoill yelling and running toward her. Then she saw the dagger in William's hand and knew they would not be in time. She screamed and mindlessly placed her hands over her belly as he threw the knife. The knife buried itself in her right shoulder, causing a pain strong enough to bring her to her knees. William started to draw his sword and she stumbled back. Then a Murray man stepped between her and William and, with one fierce sweep of his huge sword, took William's head from his shoulders.

"Dinnae look," Maldie said as she knelt by Bethia and, placing a hand on her cheek, turned her face toward her.

"He is dead," Bethia said, swaying slightly. Then she felt Grizel at her back, steadying her.

"Aye. Get a sack, Robbie, and take the head back to Donncoill so that Eric might see it."

"That is verra bloodthirsty of you."

Maldie smiled, then studied how the knife was placed in Bethia's shoulder. "Ye have been hunting that mon for a verra long time. Eric needs to ken that he is dead. He will be sorely disappointed that he didnae kill the bastard himself."

"I am always disappointing Eric."

"If ye werenae in so much pain that ye probably wouldnae feel it, I would slap ye for being such a fool."

Bethia started to laugh, then gasped from the pain it caused. "Is it a bad wound?"

"Weel, he missed your heart, which must have sore annoyed him."

"I think William was tired of hunting me. He didnae e'en try to hide or run away. All he wanted was to kill me."

"He was mad," Maldie said. "There is nay understanding the mad ones. I am going to take the knife out now, Bethia."

"That is really going to hurt, isnae it?"

"Aye, I fear it is. If God is kind, ye will faint as the pain first strikes ye."

"Will this make me lose the bairn?" Bethia asked, finally

voicing the fear that had gripped her from the moment William
had thrown the dagger.

"Not if I can do anything about it."

"Dinnae tell Eric."

Maldie did not answer. She just grasped the knife and yanked
it out. Bethia opened her mouth to scream, but blackness over-
took her before she had even finished taking a breath. Grizel
swayed slightly as Bethia sagged in her hold, but she kept a
firm grip on the other woman as Maldie worked to stop the
bleeding.

"Eric is going to be displeased," Robbie said as he returned
to stand by the women.

"Displeased, is it?" Maldie muttered as she tied a bandage
around Bethia's wound. "Somehow I dinnae think that is a
strong enough word. Let us get her back to Donncoill so that
I can tend this wound as it must be tended."

Eric stared at the group returning to Donncoill and felt his
blood run cold. Bethia's horse was riderless. He then saw her
with Robbie, the limpness of her body terrifying him. William
had won, he thought, and he wanted to scream out his rage.
Balfour reached his side and clasped him on the shoulder. The
grasp was both a comforting gesture and a silent command to
hold steady until he knew exactly what had happened. When
Robbie rode up in front of him and tossed a bloody sack at his
feet, Eric finally started to pull free of the tight grip of fear.

"The bastard is dead," Robbie said. "His head is in the
bag. Here is the wee lass. She isnae dead."

Eric moved quickly to grab hold of Bethia as Robbie handed
her down to him. Eric's terror eased a little when he saw that
Bethia's wound was high on her shoulder, although it appeared
as if she had lost a lot of blood. She looked too pale and far
too delicate to endure such an injury.

"How did he get to her?" Balfour demanded.

"We looked o'er the place, but saw no sign of the fool. Then he just walked up to her and tried to kill her." Robbie shook his head. "He didnae try to hide or run away. I reached him ere he could e'en draw his sword to finish her."

"Eric," Maldie said as she reached his side, a pale Grizel right behind her. "We need to get Bethia to her room. The wound needs to be better cleaned and then closed."

"Eric?" Bethia called, opening her eyes and staring at him through a haze of pain. "I am sorry."

"So ye should be," he said, surprised at how calm he sounded as he carried her into the keep. "Ye shouldnae have impaled yourself upon the fool's dagger." He found some comfort in the way she smiled fleetingly.

"That is the funny thing. I looked at it whilst it was still stuck in me and realized that he had stuck me with my own dagger."

"Ah, the one ye lost on the day we killed his sons."

"Aye. Do ye ken what else was funny?"

"Ye found a lot of humor in nearly getting killed, did ye?"

"Weel, nay, for it does hurt a bit. Nay, 'tis just that I saw his hand first. His fingernails were black."

"Oh, God, lass," he muttered, laughing shakily.

Bethia fainted again as Eric set her down on the bed. As Maldie collected what she would need, he helped Grizel strip Bethia. Although Maldie nudged him out of the way when she began to clean and stitch Bethia's wound, Eric stayed close by. The moment Maldie touched her needle to Bethia's skin, he was needed to hold his wife steady. Each cry of pain she uttered, each pass of the needle through her soft skin, cut at his heart as sharply as the dagger had cut through her flesh.

When the stitching was done, Eric stepped away to allow the two women to clean Bethia up and slip on her night rail. He was not surprised to find his hands shaking as he helped himself to a large tankard of wine. Just as Maldie finished forcing a potion down Bethia's throat, he dragged a chair over to the side of the bed, sat down, and took Bethia's hand in his. He barely managed a thank-you for Grizel as she left.

"She looks verra pale," he said, glancing at Maldie who stood on the other side of the bed.

" 'Tis but the pain and the loss of blood."

"Will she die?" he whispered.

"Nay, Eric, for if she dies that means that bastard has won and ye really dinnae think I would allow that, do ye?"

Eric found a small thread of strength in Maldie's words. He sent her off to get some food and rest. Slowly, as he sat there and watched Bethia sleep, he began to get some control over the fear he felt.

He loved her. Eric was astonished that it had taken something like this to make him see it. The knowledge made everything so clear. It explained the sense of rightness and possession he had felt from the start. It explained why he had found her parents' treatment of her a source of such anger. It also explained his need to know that she approved of his taking of Dubhlinn and the hunger he felt to know what was in her heart. He had always been searching for some sign that she felt more than passion for him and now he knew why. His heart had demanded it.

Now all he needed was the chance to tell her. He smiled at his own cowardliness, for he knew that, if she recovered, he would hesitate. Even though he knew his own heart now, he wanted to know how she felt before he bared his soul.

By dawn, Bethia was caught firmly in the throes of a high fever. Eric helped Maldie bathe Bethia with cool water, force potions down her throat, and hold her still when her thrashing threatened to open her wound. The battle to try to keep her alive demanded all his strength and attention. He calmed her fears, kissed away her tears as she relived some pain in her fevered mind, and talked to her when she slipped into too deep a sleep. After one grueling hour of listening to the hurt child Bethia had been, Eric looked up to find Maldie crying.

"Her parents are cruel bastards, arenae they?" Maldie said as she rubbed the tears from her cheeks with the sleeve of her gown.

"Aye," Eric agreed. "They made Bethia Sorcha's shadow."

"I think it was e'en worse than that. She was set in Sorcha's shadow, then constantly told she wasnae even worthy enough to be there. And Sorcha—her womb sister, the one person in this world who should have been close to her—should have stood by her, but did naught to change it."

"Nay." Eric sighed. "I think Bethia begins to see that for herself now. She is stronger, more sure of herself, but I think the scars will be a verra long time in healing."

"Aye, but having a bonny laddie like you ever eager to share her bed should help." Maldie smiled faintly. "Ye Murray men do have a softness for poor wounded sparrows, dinnae ye?"

"Mayhap we just have an eye keen enough to see what will be there when the bandages are removed."

Maldie stepped over to him and kissed him on the cheek. "I am going to curl up with my big brown mon for a wee rest. Be sure to fetch me if there is any change. And"—she pointed at the tray of food Grizel had brought in earlier—"eat something before I am forced to be nursing ye as weel."

It was on the afternoon of the fourth day that Eric heard Bethia curse. He bent forward, prepared to deal with another fevered dream, but the eyes looking up at him were clear. His hand unsteady, he rested his palm on her forehead and found it cool. He took several deep breaths to calm the emotion swelling up inside of him, afraid that he was close to bursting into tears. Not only would that embarrass him, but he had the feeling it would seriously alarm Bethia.

"Why am I so wet?" Bethia asked, wincing as she realized her throat was so dry it hurt to speak.

Eric poured her some of the sweet mead Maldie had left by the bed and helped her drink it. "Ye have been fevered for four days, lass."

"Oh." She slumped against the pillows he hastily plumped up behind her, the simple act of drinking making her feel weak. "At least that explains why, when I first woke up, I didnae understand why my shoulder hurt. Ah, weel, William is dead and that ordeal is o'er."

Bethia became acutely aware of how uncomfortable she was. She wanted her night rail changed. She also needed to relieve herself. Casting an embarrassed look at Eric, she knew she could not let him take care of such personal needs, even if he had been doing so while she had been ill. Bethia also had a need to speak to Maldie. She was terrified of what four days of fever could have done to the child she carried.

"Is Maldie near at hand?" she asked.

Guessing what she wanted, Eric smiled. "Shy, Bethia? While ye have been so ill, I, your wondrous husband, have—"

"If ye are about to tell me how often ye infringed upon my privacy, I should think again," she said, scowling at him. "I appreciate your care," she added hastily, "but I really dinnae want to learn all ye did whilst I was insensible."

He laughed and touched a kiss to her fever-dried lips. "I will fetch Maldie and Grizel."

By the time Maldie and Grizel arrived, Bethia was nearly frantic. She did not think she had lost the child, but she could not feel it either. The moment the door shut behind the women and no Eric followed them in, she began to try to sit up.

"Maldie," she said, grasping the woman's hand tightly when she reached the side of the bed. "What about the bairn?"

"Ah, so that is why ye are so upset and afraid." Maldie held on to Bethia and eased her into the chair by the bed so that Grizel could change the bed linen. "Ye still carry the child. The few times I could do so without Eric seeing me, I felt for the bairn and felt movement. Aye, and a good strong movement just this morning."

"Thank God," Bethia said as Maldie helped her move to

the chamber pot to relieve herself. "I was so afraid. He is obviously just being a quiet lad now."

"Since ye can feel the bairn move and I could feel it, ye havenae much time left before Eric does too."

Bethia was unable to reply as Maldie and Grizel took off her night rail, washed her down, and tugged on a clean one. By the time they got her settled back into her clean bed, she was almost too exhausted to swallow the broth Maldie forced into her. The wound and four days of fever had badly sapped her strength. Since their ministrations had caused her shoulder to throb, Bethia reluctantly agreed to drink Maldie's rather sour potion. It would ease her pain and help her sleep. Bethia knew that was important now, but decided that this was the last time she would take it. She was not sure what it might do to her child.

"Rest, lass," Maldie said as Grizel left with the dirty linen. "That is what will make ye stronger. Strong enough to tell Eric he is to be a father."

Bethia smiled weakly. "Aye, I will have to do it verra soon. I was just hoping I would ken better how he felt about me ere I told him."

"That mon has sat here day and night, barely eating and taking a rest only when his brothers forced him to. Now, I cannae say that he loves you, for I cannae see into his heart, and e'en though I am his sister, he hasnae confided in me. But I swear to you, it wasnae simply duty that held him in that chair. Aye, that I will swear to."

"It will have to be enough."

Maldie's smile held a wealth of sympathy and understanding. " 'Tis hard when ye love the fool so, but mayhap 'tis time to take a chance. Trust me in this, and Gisele will tell ye the same, sometimes men can be bigger cowards than we are when it comes to speaking of what is in their hearts."

"Ah, Balfour and Nigel were slow to confess their feelings, were they?"

"Painfully slow. And men are sometimes verra slow to e'en see how they feel. Ah, I hear the thud of your husband's big feet," Maldie said even as the door opened and Eric walked in.

"Big feet?" he muttered, sending Maldie an injured look.

"Actually, I have always thought he had verra nice-looking feet," Bethia said; then she blushed when she realized what she had just confessed.

Eric grinned and kissed her cheek. "Thank ye, my heart."

"Weel, this is all too revolting for me to witness. I will return in one hour, Eric, and ye will then leave and go to bed. Ye need rest as much as Bethia does," Maldie ordered even as she left the room.

"Once upon a time," Eric said as he sat in the chair and took Bethia's hand in his, "my brother Balfour was the laird here." He smiled when Bethia giggled sleepily. "Maldie poured one of her potions down ye, did she?"

"Aye. My shoulder did ache some after they had moved me about and changed my night rail. I dinnae like the way it makes me sleep whether I wish to or nay," Bethia complained.

"This time it will do ye good to rest. I ken what ye mean though. I have had to swallow that poison a time or two, and just as ye start to go to sleep, ye feel quite helpless, for ye ken that ye cannae stop yourself." Eric brushed a kiss over Bethia's knuckles. "I feared we would lose you."

"Has James been troubled by this?"

"Some. He is too young to ken the danger ye were in, but he sensed that something was wrong. I only brought him in to see ye once, just to show him that I spoke the truth when I said ye were ill and had to stay abed. Later, when ye have rested for a while, I will bring him in to see that ye are getting better."

Even though Bethia knew she would lose the battle in a few minutes, she fought to keep her eyes open. "Ye can ne'er tell what a child that young sees and understands. They cannae tell ye, can they?''

''Grizel has stayed close to him. In truth, he rather clings to her.''

''Ah, the poor lad. He has been frightened then. Mayhap, in some small way, he kenned his parents' illness and how that led to them going away. Or e'en how it led to him being taken from his nursemaid.''

''Sleep, lass. As I told ye, I will bring the lad to see ye so that ye can soothe his fears as soon as ye have rested. Ye will need your strength to do that.''

''I ken it. One good sleep should be enough. I just want to be able to smile at him so that he kens I am getting better. 'Twill do, I think.''

Eric reached out to trace the delicate lines of Bethia's face, which were made even finer due to her illness. He smiled faintly when he realized that she had fallen asleep. ''Aye, 'twill do. It was enough for me.''

''When are ye going to tell her?''

Eric started, hastily made sure that his abrupt movement had not disturbed Bethia, then glared across the bed at his brother Balfour. ''Ye didnae knock.''

''I didnae feel there was much chance that I would be interrupting anything.'' He crossed his arms over his broad chest. ''I was right. Ye were talking about the lad. So I ask again: When do ye plan to tell her?''

''Tell her what?'' Eric could see by Balfour's mildly disgusted look that he was not fooling the man at all.

''Mayhap that ye are sick with love for her?''

''I am nay sure sick is the word I would have chosen. Blind, for a while, aye.''

''And now just a wee bit terrified,'' Balfour drawled.

''Recognize the symptoms, do ye?''

''Ye ken that I do, and Nigel is no stranger to them either.

Now, ye were always the smartest. Dinnae prove us wrong for thinking so. Tell her.''

"Mayhap I but wait for some hint that she would welcome such feelings.''

Balfour shook his head. "She let ye seduce her. There is your hint.'' He held up his hand when Eric started to speak. "Aye, I ken that ye have been able to seduce a lass with little more than a smile since ye were nay more than a lust-hungry lad, but this lass isnae one of those foolish girls. For her to bed down with ye, she had to see more than your bonny face. I think ye ken that.''

"I do, but then I fear I am wrong. Nay, no more advice. I will tell her. William is dead and Dubhlinn is mine. Our troubles have been cleared away. Howbeit, please allow me to pick my time and place.''

"And some time to work your courage up.''

"That too.'' Eric met Balfour's grin with one of his own. " 'Tis strange how such a wee lass can make a grown knight tremble in his boots.''

"Ah, weel, take comfort in the knowledge that ye arenae the first and ye certainly willnae be the last.''

Chapter Twenty-three

Bethia waited until the door had shut behind Eric, then she cautiously got out of bed. Nothing happened. She felt no dizziness, her stomach did no more than loudly announce its emptiness, and she did not suddenly break out into a chilling sweat. In the week since they had settled in at Dubhlinn, she had not been sick once. For a moment, she fought the urge to dance around their huge bedchamber in a foolish expression of delight. Instead, she greeted Grizel's entry with such a beaming smile, the woman eyed her with suspicion.

"Ye are in verra fine spirits," Grizel said as she set down the large bowl of heated water she had brought up. "What are ye up to?"

"Four months," Bethia replied, grinning when Grizel looked confused for a moment, then rolled her eyes as Bethia moved to wash up and clean her teeth.

"Ah," Grizel muttered as she changed the linen on the bed. "Ye are keeping a close count, are ye?"

"Of course, although I think I may be a wee bit off, for I havenae really begun to show much yet."

"When it starts, it will happen verra fast."

"I ken it. Also four months is when I thought it would be safe."

"Safe?"

"Aye. I wanted to be verra sure and, I think, verra certain that I could carry the child, nay lose it. Weel, for nearly a fortnight now, I havenae been troubled with that sickness, and I can feel the movement within me so strongly now, I canne doubt the life there." She giggled when Grizel hurried over and put her hands on her stomach. "Soon James will have someone he can play with." Thinking of all the children residing within the walls of Dubhlinn, Bethia added, "Weel, someone of his own blood."

Grizel laughed. "This keep fair to squirms with bairns, doesnae it? So now ye will tell the laird?"

"Tonight." Bethia's smile wavered as she suddenly felt nervous. "I think he will be pleased." Bethia's eyes widened when Grizel muttered some very colorful curses and glared at her. "Do ye really think ye ought to speak to the laird's wife that way?"

"Nay, but ye were ne'er good at reminding me of my place. Dinnae think either of us truly kens what that is." She exchanged a brief grin with Bethia, then quickly became stern again. "Ye do that bonny mon an unkindness with your thoughts, lass. Aye, ye do. After what happened at court, how can ye keep doubting the mon?"

"Ye mean the way all those women, many of them his past lovers, fairly flung themselves at his feet should make me feel safe and sure?"

"Nay, but the fact that your bonny, wee mon ne'er once looked their way should."

"He isnae wee," was all Bethia could think to say.

"Lass, only the bairns look wee to one as tiny as ye are."

She ignored Bethia's scowl. "Your mon had more temptation set afore him in those few weeks than most men see in a lifetime, yet he ne'er turned from your side."

"I ken it. I should be pleased. Eric is a verra honorable mon who holds true to his vows," she said as she sat down on the bed; then she saw the look on Grizel's face. It was not a friendly one. "I have said something wrong again?"

"Whye'er would ye think that?"

The sharp sarcasm in Grizel's voice made Bethia wince. "Because ye have a certain look upon your face."

"What look?"

"Like ye want to bang your head against something hard."

"Talking to ye makes me feel that way sometimes. And 'twould be your head I would be banging against something hard."

"Grizel, have ye taken a good look at my husband?" It annoyed Bethia that no one seemed to understand or sympathize with the uncertainties that plagued her.

"Aye, he is one of the bonniest men I have e'er seen. Just looking at him can make a lass's heart flutter."

"Exactly. Now look at me."

Grizel pulled Bethia to her feet and started to help her get dressed. "Ye are bonny."

"Ye are my friend. Ye may not see me as others do. My eyes dinnae match, my hair is neither red nor brown, and I am so short and thin, it looks as if I forgot to finish my growing."

" 'Tis obviously enough to stir the laird's blood or ye would-nae be with child now, would ye?" Grizel grinned briefly at Bethia's deep blush. "Lass, I ken ye willnae like to hear this, but I think ye have had your eyes opened a wee bit in these last few months. Ye have let your parents and sister convince ye that ye arenae worth much. I am nay saying they did it a-purpose, but 'tis what they accomplished. 'Tis past time ye ceased to see yourself through their eyes, for ye ken now that they werenae seeing clearly. Your mon isnae seeing ye as they did. Nay, that bonny mon looks at you and sees a lass he is sore eager to roll about in the heather with.''

"He does seem to want to do that a lot." She smiled, then sighed, when Grizel started giggling so hard that she had to sit down on the bed. "I do ken that, weel, something wasnae right in the way my family treated me. They were wrong to cast me aside, to treat me as little more than Sorcha's shadow and a poor one at that. But that doesnae mean I am a beautiful woman. It just means that I am nay as bad as they let me think I was."

"Lass, ye are more beautiful than Sorcha e'er was or e'er could be. Nay''—Grizel held up her hand to stop Bethia's protest—''I dinnae mean in face or form, though there is naught wrong with the ones ye have. I mean in your heart. No one followed the beautiful Sorcha when she left Dunnbea, did they? But near to two dozen couldnae pack fast enough to follow you. Bowen and my Peter were settled comfortably at Dunnbea yet they have dragged their families here to be with you. If Wallace wasnae going to be laird of Dunnbea, he would have come here too, although, in truth, he is here more often than not. For all of her beauty, Sorcha ne'er stirred that kind of loyalty."

"But people loved her."

"They loved what they saw, but aside from Robert, who was much akin to her and your fool parents, name me one person who kenned her weel who expressed any love or loyalty for her. Ye cannae, can ye? And dinnae name yourself.''

Bethia tried, but could not, and that saddened her. "I dinnae think that it was all her fault," was all she could say.

"Nay, she was raised to be nay more than a beautiful woman. Your parents cherished her outside, but nay nurtured her inside. No one e'er taught her how to love or care for anyone but herself."

"I think she loved Robert. Aye, and James."

"As much as she was able, aye. And think on this: Who did Sorcha call out to when she finally realized that her son was in danger? Nay her parents, as one would think she would, nor any of those fine, strong men so captivated by her beauty. Nay, she sent for you. Sorcha kenned that you—the one she and your parents tossed aside—were the one who could protect and care for her son. In the end she acknowledged your worth. Can ye nay see that your mon does too?''

"Ye are making me want to cry."

"Lass, ye are with child. Near anything could make ye want to cry." They exchanged a brief grin.

"So ye think my husband may care for me."

"I dinnae think anything I can say will truly make ye believe it, for ye have believed yourself near worthless for too long. But I believe he does. The mon cannae keep his hands off of you. Aye, and dinnae forget how he was when ye were wounded and like to die. That tells ye something. He cares for ye a lot, lass. So when ye tell him about the bairn, I think ye should tell him how ye feel about him. Tell him how much ye love him." Grizel stood up and, grabbing Bethia's hairbrush, started to fix her lady's hair. "The way he replies could end all of your uncertainties."

" 'Tisnae easy to hand a mon your heart when ye are nay sure he wants it or is of a mind to make ye an equal trade." Bethia sighed. "I fear how I will feel if I tell him how much I love him and he says little more than thank ye."

"I think he will say a great deal more than that and all the words it would do ye good to hear, but 'tis your choice."

Bethia was still considering all Grizel had said when, after breaking her fast alone in the great hall, she went in search of her husband. Fear and indecision knotted her insides, but that began to annoy her. She did not like to be such a coward.

She saw Bowen near the stables mending a harness, and she walked toward him. "Have ye seen Eric?" she asked.

"He is in the village again. There is a lot that needs repairing," Bowen answered with a shake of his head. "Those fools did verra little to care for the lands they were so eager to cling to.''

''Aye. After a little wariness, the people seem pleased to have a new laird.''

''They ken he is a good mon.'' Bowen glanced at Bethia's middle. ''When are ye going to tell him about the bairn?''

''Ye ken?'' Bethia gaped at her friend in utter surprise.

''Lass, I come from a verra large family and I have five bairns of my own. Ye have the look.''

''Eric hasnae seen it.''

''Weel, I think ye are verra good at hiding a lot from the lad.''

She sighed. ''He is such a bonny mon.''

Bowen laughed and nodded. ''And that sore troubles ye, doesnae it?''

''A wee bit. Do ye think he cares for me, Bowen?'' she asked abruptly and blushed beneath his look of disgust.

''Ye can be such a foolish wee lass. He wed ye.''

''Ye had a sword at his throat.''

''I took it away ere he said the vows.'' He nodded at her look of surprise. ''I didnae want ye bound to a mon who would hurt ye. I asked him if he really wished ye for his wife and he said aye. I gave him the chance to run. He stayed.''

Bethia was still wondering over that when Eric returned from the village. He told her all about his plans as they went to the nursery to visit James. She realized that he did not hesitate to ask her opinion and truly listened when she gave it. Bethia realized that he had always truly listened to her, even argued with her as if he considered her an equal. Accustomed to such treatment from Bowen, Peter and Wallace, she had not really noticed, but Eric was no mere man-at-arms or childhood friend and cousin. Eric was born and bred to be a laird. For him to treat her so was a surprise.

It took only a moment of watching Eric play with James for her to lose the last of her concerns about how he would feel about the baby. Eric loved children; he treated James as if the child was his own. She had seen that from the beginning, but had let her own doubts about herself make her forget. The news about their child would undoubtedly please Eric, and she was sure that he would care little if she bore him a son or a daughter. Or even, she thought with a warmth that spread throughout her body, if the child was bonny.

Her eyes now opened, Bethia watched Eric for the rest of the day. She noticed how often he touched her, as if he could not be within reach of her without doing so. He sought her out several times to talk over some plan he had. She watched how the children followed him, how every man and woman with a problem felt free to come to him. No matter how hard she looked, she saw no hint of discontent in her husband.

By the end of the day, Bethia felt both stupid and ashamed. She cursed herself for a fool and worse as she prepared for bed. Just as her parents and so many others had done, she had seen only Eric's beauty, had let that taint her every thought and feeling, had let it feed her doubts and fears. The men who talked to him about the defense of the keep were not doing so because he was bonny. The villagers who sought him out to discuss repairs and trade were not doing so because he was bonny. The children who skipped after him, or came to him with their hurts, probably would do so if he was covered in warts and had three eyes. They saw what her heart had always seen, but unlike her, they did not let their minds become clouded with his fair looks.

Sir Eric Murray was a very good man. His beauty went to the bone. That was why she loved him. That was why the diverse group now living at Dubhlinn all loved and respected him. Eric might not love her as she did him, but he liked and trusted her. It was far more than her parents had ever given her. Caught up in her own doubts, she had not completely returned the gift. She suspected he might even truly care for her. Bethia had wondered about it when she had been wounded and he had cared for her so well, but again, she had let her own lack of confidence smother that hope. If any man deserved to be loved, Eric did, and Bethia decided it was past time for him to know how his own wife felt.

When Eric entered their bedchamber, Bethia watched him prepare for bed. She smiled faintly as he washed, stripped off his clothes, and sprawled on his back on the bed, his hands crossed behind his head. If Eric had a fault, it was his complete lack of modesty. Still dressed in her thin linen shift, she sat beside him on the bed, watching him as she brushed her hair. As always, the sight of his lean body made her blood warm, but she struggled to subdue her heedless desires. They needed to talk.

"Ye are staring at me," Eric said, clenching his hands against the urge to tangle them in her soft, beautiful hair.

"Weel, mayhap I am nay used to having so much naked mon in my bed," she drawled.

He grinned briefly, then grew serious again. "Ye have been in an odd mood all day."

"I have?"

"Aye, ye have. Ye have been staring at me all day, watching me as if ye thought I might disappear on the wind."

Although Bethia had hoped Eric would not notice, she saw no reason to deny it. "Aye. In truth, I would say that I have been looking at you, truly looking. I havenae really done that, have I? For some reason, I couldnae get much past your bonny face and fine body."

Eric turned on his side and gave in to his need to touch her, idly trailing his fingers up and down her thigh. The way she sat cross-legged with her thin shift riding high up on her beautiful legs told him that the intensity of her modesty had waned a little, and he was pleased. It also appeared that she was about to be honest concerning at least some of her feelings, and he felt himself tense. For the first time in his life, he was unsure about a woman. Although he liked the fact that Bethia could puzzle him, he ached to have at least some knowledge of what she felt for him beside passion. She held his heart in her small hands and he felt vulnerable. It was a new feeling for him and one he did not really like.

"And what were ye looking for?" he asked.

"Ye. Eric, ye do ken that I am nay here just because ye are bonny, dinnae ye?" she asked in a soft voice, suddenly shy and uncertain of how to say what she wanted and needed to say.

"Aye, lass. I have become verra good at judging who stands by my side just because they think me bonny. In truth, I believe that, at times, ye are almost afraid of it, would much rather I were a plainer mon." Eric smiled faintly when Bethia cast him a brief, guilty look. " 'Tis odd, for once, to find my face more a curse than a blessing. 'Tis but a face, my heart, a lump of flesh that can be torn, scarred, or broken and made verra ugly indeed. For now, why cannae I find some pleasure in the fact that I have a face my wife might be pleased to look upon? I am always pleased to look upon yours." He lightly caressed the blush upon her cheeks with his fingertips.

"Thank ye, but if our bairn has a choice of faces, I hope it gets yours."

"Ah, my own, ye are fair, and I eagerly await seeing that sweetness in the face of one of our bairns."

"Weel, ye may nay have as long a wait as ye think." Bethia smiled at Eric when he sat up and grasped her by the shoulders for the look upon his face told her, clearer than any words could, that he would welcome their child.

"Ye are with child?"

"Aye, near to four months gone. Ye will soon see what face our child carries."

She laughed softly when Eric hugged her almost too tightly. When he urged her down onto the bed, she offered no resistance. Bethia could think of no better way to celebrate the wonder of their child than to make love. And perhaps, she mused as he tugged off her shift and tossed it aside, she might find the courage to speak her heart while caught in the heat of passion.

Eric smoothed his hands over her midriff, then rested one hand against her stomach as he gave her a slow, gentle yet seductive kiss. "I should have noticed," he murmured, sliding his hands up her body to cover and weigh her breasts. "I ache to make love to you."

Bethia frowned, for it sounded as if he was hesitant to do so. "I believe, nay, I am certain I havenae protested the idea."

He smiled and brushed a kiss over her mouth as he teased her nipples to an aching hardness with his thumbs. "I dinnae wish to hurt the bairn."

When he started to move away, she wrapped her arms and legs around him and held him close. "Ye cannae hurt the bairn."

"Ye are so small, sweetling."

"Your brothers' wives arenae verra much bigger than I, yet I suspect your brothers didnae leave their wives alone at such a time."

The way his tiny, slender wife was clutching him, as if she could somehow hold him against his will, made him smile. She was right, however. Now that he had cleared his mind of a sudden fear for her, he knew there would be no harm done if he made love to her. Eric did think, however, that he might continue his pose of hesitancy for just a little while longer. It could be amusing, and undoubtedly delightful, to see how Bethia might try to change his mind.

"But my brothers' wives havenae been dragged from keep to keep, chased and wounded by some mad fool." Eric closed his eyes and bit back a groan of pleasure as she trailed her soft hands down his back and lightly caressed his backside.

Bethia traced his collarbone with short, wet kisses. She sensed that he played a game, that his protests were not heartfelt, but she was more than willing to play. The moment he relaxed against her, she shoved him away. He tumbled onto his back at her side and she quickly straddled him. She placed her hands on his shoulders, lightly pinning him to the bed. Bethia knew he could break her hold swiftly and easily but he did not move.

"I was with child whilst all of those things were happening to me," she said as she trailed kisses over his broad chest and down to his taut stomach. "Naught would shake this fruit from the tree." She glanced up at him when he gripped his hands in her hair a little too tightly.

"Ye could have lost the bairn when ye were wounded and fevered." His voice was hoarse as he realized that she had been in even more danger than he had realized. If she had miscarried their child, it surely would have been enough to kill her.

"Aye, but the bairn still thrives." As soon as his grip on her hair eased she began to cover his strong legs with kisses. "I am hale, Eric. E'en the sickness has passed."

Eric wanted to ask her why she had waited for so long to tell him of the child, but then her tongue lightly stroked his manhood. He groaned his pleasure as she loved him with her mouth. Despite all of his efforts to control his passion so that he could enjoy her attentions for a long time, his control was shattered soon after she enclosed him in the warmth of her mouth. With a soft growl of need, he grabbed her under her arms and dragged her up his body.

"Ride your mon, my own," he said, his voice hoarse and unsteady from the force of his passion as he eased their bodies together. "Ah, my heart," he rasped as she slowly moved upon him, "there can be no sweeter place for a mon."

Bethia cried out his name as her release tore through her. She was faintly aware of his echoing cry as he grasped her by her hips and held her tight against him. Still trembling, Bethia slowly collapsed against him, enjoying the way he enfolded her in his arms and touched her face and hair with languid kisses.

The sweetness of their lovemaking still warming her blood, Bethia kissed his ear and whispered, "I love ye, Eric Murray."

Her eyes widened when his whole body trembled once. He grabbed her by the arms and shoved her into a sitting position so quickly she felt her head snap back. Cursing softly, she rubbed the back of her neck, soothing the faint, taut pain caused by the wrenching he had inadvertently given her.

"What did ye say?" Eric demanded.

"Weel, I am nay sure I can repeat it now that ye have fair snapped my neck," Bethia muttered.

"Repeat yourself."

She studied him for a moment. His gaze was fixed unwaveringly upon her face. To her surprise, she caught a gleam of uncertainty in his eyes, the hint of a fierce hope. The man had to feel something for her if he was so interested in her emotions. Eric might not yet return her love, but it was evident that he was anxious to hear about hers. For now, that would serve. She would make it serve.

"I love ye, Eric," She gasped when he yanked her back into his arms. "If this is how ye act when I speak those words, I believe I will have to use them sparingly or I will be forever suffering from a wrenching pain in my neck."

Eric laughed shakily, then turned so that she was sprawled beneath him. It did not surprise him to see his hand tremble as he gently brushed her tangled hair from her face. Emotion raged through him like some caged animal frantic to break free. The news of their child had given him joy, but it paled compared to what those three words had stirred within him.

"When did ye ken it, lass? Today? Is that why ye stared at me so?" he asked.

"Nay, I told ye I was but looking at ye closely, with my eyes open and all my doubts and fears ruthlessly reined in. My heart was already set firmly in your hands. I was sure it wasnae just because ye were bonny, but after seeing the bitter truth about my family, I sometimes feared I was more like them than I was aware of." Bethia traced the perfect lines of Eric's face with her fingers. "Oh, I do love looking at your bonny face, but I finally realized it wasnae your eyes or your smile that captured my heart, but ye, the mon. This beauty could be savaged in your next battle, and though 'twould grieve me some, I kenned ye would still hold my heart in your hands. I kenned ye were my love when ye fell ill after your wee swim in the river. The fear I felt for ye was verra strong, and I kenned that, if ye died, it would tear the heart right out of me." She smiled and welcomed his kiss.

"Why didnae ye tell me ere now?"

"I wasnae sure ye would wish to hear the words."

"Ye can be a verra foolish lass," he said so gently it took all of the sting from his words.

"I ken it. Ye were right, Eric. At times, your fine looks troubled me deeply. I kept wondering how or why such a mon seemed to want me."

"Because he loves you."

Bethia blinked, unable to speak or move for a moment. There it was. All her heart's desire spoken quietly, without warning. Finally, giving a soft cry, she kissed Eric. Despite all of her efforts not to cry, tears trickled from her eyes.

"When did ye ken it then?" she asked, smiling as he kissed each tear-dampened cheek.

"I think I kenned it for a long time, but I finally confessed it to myself when I feared ye would die."

"Ye ne'er said anything."

"Ah, my wee bonny wife, I feared ye wouldnae believe me. Then there were your concerns about how I was seeking my inheritance." He kissed her fingers when she set them against his lips to silence him.

"It troubled me, but I was ne'er able to convince myself that ye were like William in even the smallest way. Nay, nor like Sir Graham."

"I soon kenned that ye didnae condemn me. When I returned

from unseating the Beaton laird, the way ye welcomed me home assured me that ye no longer doubted my right to do what I did. I dinnae ken why I have held silent. I am a coward. I didnae ken what ye felt and didnae want to bare my soul ere I did. But it may have helped ye o'ercome your doubts about yourself if I had told ye and—"

"But ye didnae wish to bare your soul and meet only disbelief or gain naught but a polite thank-ye. And though it pains me to admit it, ye may have gained naught else from me. I needed to ken my own mind and heart first. Aye, I saw clearly that my family had treated me poorly, saw it shortly after reaching Donncoill, but it took me a little longer to truly see that they were wrong to do so. I needed to take that last step out of Sorcha's shadow. I needed the courage to love you e'en if ye didnae return that love."

Eric brushed a kiss over Bethia's lips. "My heart, 'tis returned tenfold." He grinned when she frowned and started to speak. "Do ye mean to argue with me o'er which of us loves the other the most?"

"That could take a verra long time."

"Years. Our whole life."

"Then I shall make a promise to you, my bonny knight. Promise me your love for always, as I now promise ye mine."

"For always and 'tis a promise easily made."

"And easily kept," she whispered against his mouth.

Epilogue

Yuletide—1445

"James, I really dinnae think your cousin Bega wishes to be sat upon," Bethia said, biting back a smile as she lifted the giggling boy off his cursing cousin. Gisele's delicate little girl certainly had a colorful way with words, she mused.

"Bethia, I think our wee lass is going to win this time," Eric called.

Glancing at her husband, Bethia exchanged a look that was an equal mix of amusement and exasperation with Gisele and Maldie. Her daughter Sorcha had just begun to crawl and Gisele's child Brett, although five months older, still crawled more than he walked. Nigel and Eric had taken to racing them against each other, some of the men even making bets. Bethia suspected it was not quite proper, but it kept the men and the older children entertained.

As she set James down and moved to sit next to Eric, ready to catch her daughter as she reached the end of her run, Bethia looked around the great hall. All of Eric's family had gathered at Dubhlinn to help them celebrate their first Yuletide in their new home. There was Balfour and Maldie and their seven children, Nigel and Gisele and their four children, and even a few of Gisele's French relations. Bowen and Peter were there with their wives and Bowen's lively children. Wallace and Gisele's cousins, Sir Guy and Sir David, sat together laughing at the antics of the children. Her parents were not there, but Bethia realized it no longer mattered. This was family, she thought and grasped her husband's hand even as their sturdy little daughter reached them.

Eric laughed and hugged his daughter, then grinned at Nigel, whose son stood up and staggered the last few feet into his father's open arms. "The lass is fast," Eric said.

"She only bested my lad because he cannae decide which he wants to do: crawl or walk," protested Nigel.

"Weel, we will have to race them when they are both steady on their feet."

"Eric!" Bethia cried, laughing and catching her daughter when the little girl flung herself into her arms.

"I jest, my heart."

She might have believed him if she had not caught the look he exchanged with Nigel. Bethia decided not to argue the matter now. Sorcha was making it known a little too clearly that she was hungry, and although almost weaned, she was hungry for her mother's nourishment. Blushing slightly as Sorcha tugged on her bodice, Bethia quickly excused herself and hurried away to her bedchamber.

Once settled comfortably against the pillows on her bed, Bethia put her daughter to her breast and sighed with contentment. She had thought that her child would be a boy, as Gisele's had been, but she was not in the least disappointed. Not even when she had seen that her child had her mismatched eyes. Little Sorcha was a charming mixture of both of her parents. She lovingly touched her daughter's thick red-gold curls, studied the features that already held the promise of a lovely delicacy, and smiled. She and Eric made beautiful babies, she mused with a sense of pride.

"And what has ye smiling?" asked Eric as he entered their bedchamber, walked over to the bed, and sprawled at her side.

"I was just thinking that we make beautiful babies together," she replied and met his grin with one of her own.

"Aye, that we do, my heart." He ruffled his child's silken curls and kissed Bethia on the cheek.

"Do ye ken, I really thought I was carrying a son as Gisele did."

"Dinnae fret, lass. Ye will give me a son yet. And if all ye bear me is lasses, I willnae complain. I have more nephews than I can count and we have James to raise. Aye, and if the lasses are all as bonny as this wee one, I shall be run ragged keeping the rogues and lusty lads away from our door."

Bethia set her daughter against her shoulder, rubbing her tiny back even as she leaned over and kissed Eric. Although she had been delighted to have a healthy child, regardless of the sex, she had at first worried that Eric would be disappointed that she had not given him a son. He had quickly dispelled that worry. His pride in and love for his little daughter was and continued to be obvious to all.

"What was that for?" he asked.

"Because I love ye and ye have given me a wondrous family."

Eric laughed, for the noise from the great hall could be heard even in their room. "Mayhap too big a one."

"Nay, ne'er that. 'Tis what I have e'er dreamed of," she said softly, "when I allowed myself to see that something wasnae right with my own. And this Sorcha will ken the beauty of it. So will wee James."

"Aye, my own, a family. Whate'er else we have or dinnae have, that much I can give you. Aye, a family and all the love ye could possibly need. I promise ye that."

"As I promise ye, this bairn, wee James, and any other bairns we are blessed with."

They kissed, but the sweet solemnity of the moment was abruptly shattered. Little Sorcha belched so loud Bethia jumped with surprise and felt her daughter's tiny body rock with the force of it. Her daughter then sighed with contentment and giggled. Eric laughed as he stood up and took his daughter into his arms.

"Do ye ken," he murmured as he started toward the door, "I think that was louder than any Nigel's lad Brett has made. Hah! I bet my lassie can win at that too."

"Eric!" Bethia cried and was redoing her gown even as she hurried after her laughing husband.

THE MURRAY FAMILY LINEAGE

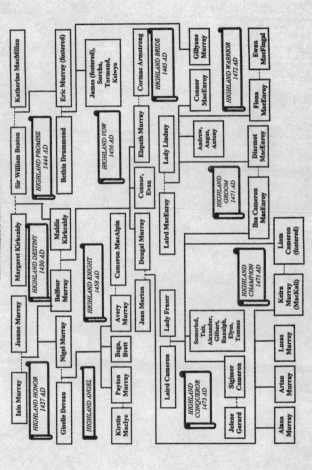

Please turn the page for an exciting sneak peek of
Hannah Howell's newest Highland romance
HIGHLAND LOVER
coming in June 2006!

Scotland, Spring 1475

"Oof!"

Oof!? Dazed and struggling to catch her breath, Alana decided she must have made that noise herself. Hard dirt floors did not say *oof*. It was odd, however, how the rough stone walls of the oubliette made her voice sound so deep, almost manly. Just as she began to be able to breathe again, the hard dirt floor shifted beneath her.

It took Alana a moment to fully grasp the fact that she had not landed on the floor. She had landed on a person. That person had a deep, manly voice. It was not dirt or stone beneath her cheek, but cloth. There was also the steady throb of a heartbeat in the ear she had pressed against that cloth. Her fingers were hanging down a little and touching cool, slightly damp earth. She was sprawled on top of a man like a wanton.

Alana scrambled off the man, apologizing for some awkward placement of her knees and elbows as she did so. The man certainly knew how to curse. She stood up and stared up at the three men looking down at her, the light from the lantern they held doing little more than illuminating their grinning, hairy faces.

"Ye cannae put me in here with a mon," she said.

"Got no place else to put ye," said the tallest of the three, a man called Clyde, who she was fairly sure was the laird.

"I am a lady," she began.

"Ye are a wee, impudent child. Now, are ye going to tell us who ye are?"

"So ye can rob my people? Nay, I dinnae think so."

"Then ye stay where ye are."

She did not even have time to stutter out a protest. The grate was shut, and that faint source of light quickly disappeared as the Gowans walked away. Alana stared into the dark and wondered how everything had gone so wrong. All she had wanted to do was to help find her sister Keira, but none of her family had heeded her pleas or her insistence that she could truly help to find her twin. It had seemed such a clever idea to disguise herself as a young girl and follow her brothers, waiting for just the right moment to reveal herself. How she had enjoyed those little dreams of walking up to her poor, confused brothers and leading them straight to their sister. That had kept a smile upon her face and a jaunty spring in her step right up until the moment she had realized that not only had she lost her brothers' trail, but also had absolutely no idea of where she was.

Feeling very sorry for herself and wondering why her gifts had so abruptly failed her just when she needed them the most, she had been cooking a rabbit and sulking when the Gowans had found her. Alana grimaced as she remembered how she had acted. Perhaps if she had been sweet and acted helpless, she would not be stuck in a hole in the ground with a man who was apparently relieving himself in a bucket. Maybe it would be wise to tell the Gowans who she was so that they could get some ransom for her and she could get out of here. Appalled by that moment of weakness, Alana proceeded to lecture herself in the hope of stiffening her resolve.

Gregor inwardly cursed as he finished relieving himself. It was not the best way to introduce himself to his fellow prisoner, but he really had had little choice. Having a body dropped on top of him and then being jabbed by elbows and knees had made ignoring his body's needs impossible. At least the dark provided a semblance of privacy.

He was just trying to figure out where she was when he realized she was muttering to herself. Clyde Gowan had called her an impudent child, but there was something in that low, husky voice that made him think of a woman. After she had landed on him and he had caught his breath, there had also been something about that soft, warm body that had also made him think of a woman despite the lack of fulsome curves. He shook his head as he cautiously stepped toward that voice.

Despite his caution, he took one step too many and came up hard against her back. She screeched softly and jumped, banging the top of her head against his chin. Gregor cursed softly as his teeth slammed together, sending a sharp, stinging pain through his head. He was a little surprised to hear her softly curse as well.

"Jesu, lass," he muttered, "ye have inflicted more bruises on me than those fools did when they grabbed me."

"Who are you?" Alana asked, wincing and rubbing at the painful spot on the top of her head, certain she could feel a lump rising.

"Gregor. And ye are?"

"Alana."

"Just Alana?"

"Just Gregor?"

"I will tell ye my full name if ye tell me yours."

"Nay, I dinnae think so. Someone could be listening, hoping we will do just that."

"And ye dinnae trust me as far as ye can spit, do ye?"

"Why should I? I dinnae ken who ye are. I cannae e'en see you." She looked around and then wondered why she bothered, since it was so dark she could not even see her own hand if she held it right in front of her face. "What did they put ye in here for?"

Alana suddenly feared she had been confined with a true criminal, perhaps even a rapist or murderer. She smothered that brief surge of panic by telling herself sharply not to be such an idiot. The Gowans wanted to ransom her. Even they were not stupid enough to risk losing that purse by setting her too close to a truly dangerous man.

"Ransom," he replied.

"Ah, me too. Are they roaming about the country plucking up people like daisies?"

Gregor chuckled and shook his head. "Only those who look as if they or their kinsmen might have a few coins weighting their purse. A mon was being ransomed e'en as they dragged me in. He was dressed fine, although his bonny clothes were somewhat filthy from spending time in this hole. I was wearing my finest. I suspect your gown told them your kinsmen might have some coin. Did they kill your guards?"

Alana felt a blush heat her cheeks. "Nay, I was alone. I got a little lost."

She was lying, Gregor thought. Either she was a very poor liar or the dark had made his senses keener, allowing him to hear the lie in her voice. "I hope your kinsmen punish the men weel for such carelessness."

Oh, someone would most certainly be punished, Alana thought. There was no doubt in her mind about that. This was one of those times when she wished her parents believed in beating a child. A few painful strokes of a rod would be far easier to endure than the lecture she would be given and, even worse, the confused disappointment her parents would reveal concerning her idiocy and disobedience.

"How long have ye been down here?" she asked, hoping to divert his attention from how and why she had been caught.

"Two days, I think. 'Tis difficult to know for certain. They gave me quite a few blankets, a privy bucket which they pull up and empty each day, and food and water twice a day. What troubles me is who will win this game of ye stay there until ye tell me what I want to know. My clan isnae really poor, but they dinnae have coin to spare for a big ransom. Nay when they dinnae e'en ken what the money will be used for."

"Oh, didnae they tell ye?"

"I was unconscious for most of the time it took to get to this keep and be tossed in here. All I have heard since then is the thrice-daily question about who I am. And I am assuming all these things happen daily, not just whene'er they feel inclined. There does seem to be a, weel, rhythm to it all. 'Tis how I decided I have been here for two days." He thought back over the past few days, too much of it spent in the dark with his own thoughts. "If I judge it aright, this may actually be the end of the third day, for I fell unconscious again when they threw me in here. I woke up to someone bellowing that it was time to sup, got my food and water, and was told about the privy bucket and that blankets had been thrown down here."

"And 'tis night now. The moon was rising as we rode through the gates. So, three days in the dark. In a hole in the ground," she murmured, shivering at the thought of having to endure the same. "What did ye do?"

"Thought."

"Oh, dear. I think *that* would soon drive me quite mad."

"It isnae a pleasant interlude."

"It certainly isnae. I am nay too fond of the dark," she added softly and jumped slightly when a long arm was somewhat awkwardly wrapped around her shoulders.

"No one is, especially not the unrelenting dark of a place like this. So, ye were all alone when they caught ye. They didnae harm ye, did they?"

The soft, gentle tone of his question made Alana realize what he meant by *harm*. It struck her as odd that not once had she feared rape, yet her disguise as a child was certainly not enough to save her from that. "Nay, they just grabbed me, cursed me a lot for being impudent, and tossed me over a saddle."

Gregor smiled. "Impudent were ye?"

"That is as good a word for it as any other. There I was, sitting quietly by a fire, cooking a rabbit I had been lucky enough to catch, and up ride five men who inform me that I am now their prisoner and that I had best tell them who I am so that they can send the ransom demand to my kinsmen. I told them that I had had a very upsetting day and the last thing I wished to deal with was smelly, hairy men telling me what to do, so they could just ride back to the rock they had crawled out from under. Or words to that effect," she added quietly.

In truth, she thought as she listened to Gregor chuckle, she had completely lost her temper. It was not something she often did, and she suspected some of her family would have been astonished. The Gowans had been. All five men had stared at her as if a dormouse had suddenly leapt at their throats. It had been rather invigorating until the Gowans had realized they were being held in place by insults from someone they could snap in half.

It was a little puzzling that she had not eluded capture. She was very fast, something often marveled at by her family; she could run for a very long way without tiring, and she could hide in the faintest of shadows. Yet mishap after mishap had plagued her as she had fled from the men and they had barely raised a sweat in pursuing and capturing her. If she were a superstitious person, she would think some unseen hand of fate had been doing its best to make sure she was caught.

"Did they tell ye why they are grabbing so many for ransom?" Gregor asked.

"Oh, aye they did." Of course, one reason they had told her

was because of all the things she had accused them of wanting the money for, such as useless debauchery, and not something they badly needed like soap. "Defenses."

"What?"

"They have decided that this hovel requires stronger defenses. That requires coin or some fine goods to barter with, neither of which they possess. I gather they have heard of some troubles not so far away, and it has made them decide that they are too vulnerable. From what little I could see whilst hanging over Clyde's saddle, this is a very old tower house, one that was either neglected or damaged once, or both. It appears to have been repaired enough to be livable, but I did glimpse many things either missing or in need of repair. From what Clyde's wife said, this smallholding was her dowry."

"Ye spoke to his wife?"

"Weel, nay. She was lecturing him from the moment he stepped inside all the way to the door leading down here. She doesnae approve of this. Told him that since he has begun this folly, he had best do a verra good job of it and gather a veritable fortune, for they will need some formidable defenses to protect them from all the enemies he is making."

Alana knew she ought to move away from him. When he had first draped his arm around her, she had welcomed what she saw as a gesture intended to comfort her, perhaps even an attempt to ease the fear of the dark she had confessed to. He still had his arm around her, and she had slowly edged closer to his warmth until she was now pressed hard up against his side.

He was a very tall man. Probably a bit taller than her overgrown brothers, she mused. Judging from where her cheek rested so nicely, she barely reached his breastbone. Since she was five feet tall, that made him several inches over six feet. Huddled up against him as she was, she could feel the strength in his body, despite what she felt like a lean build. Considering the fact that he had been held in this pit for almost three days, he smelled remarkably clean as well.

And the fact that she was noticing how good he smelled told her she really should move away from him, Alana thought. The problem was he felt good, very good. He felt warm, strong, and calming, all things she was sorely in need of at the moment. She started to console herself with the thought that she was not actually embracing him, only to realize that she had curled her arm around what felt to be a very trim waist.

She sighed inwardly, ruefully admitting that she liked where she was and that she had no inclination to leave his side. He thought she was a young girl, so she did not have to fear him thinking she was inviting him to take advantage of her. Alone with him in the dark, there was a comforting anonymity about it as well. Alana decided there was no harm in it all. In truth, she would not be surprised to discover that he found comfort in it, too, after days of being all alone in the dark.

"Where were ye headed, lass? Is there someone aside from the men ye were with who will start searching for ye?" Gregor asked, a little concerned about how good it felt to hold her, even though every instinct he had told him that Alana was not the child she pretended to be.

"Quite possibly." She doubted that the note she had left behind would do much to comfort her parents. "I was going to my sister."

"Ah, weel, then, I fear the Gowans may soon ken who ye are e'en if ye dinnae tell them."

"Oh, of course. What about you? Will anyone wonder where ye have gone?"

"Nay for a while yet."

They all thought he was still wooing his well-dowered bride. Gregor had had far too much time to think about that, about all of his reasons for searching for a well-dowered bride, and about the one he had chosen. Mavis was a good woman, passably pretty, and had both land and some coin to offer a husband. He had left her feeling almost victorious, the betrothal as good as settled, yet each hour he had sat here in the dark, alone with his thoughts, he had felt less and less pleased with himself. It did not feel *right*. He hated to think that his cousin Sigimor made sense about anything, yet it was that man's opinion that kept creeping through his mind. Mavis did not really feel *right*. She did not really *fit*.

He silently cursed. What did it matter? He was almost thirty years of age, and he had never found a woman who felt *right* or *fit*. Mavis gave him the chance to be his own man, to be laird of his own keep, and to have control over his own lands. Mavis was a sensible choice. He did not love her, but after so many years and so many women without feeling even a tickle of that, he doubted he was capable of loving any woman. Passion could be stirred with the right touch, and compatibility could be achieved with a little work. It would serve.

He was just about to ask Alana how extensive a search her kinsmen would mount for her when he heard the sound of someone approaching above them. "Stand o'er there, lass," he said as he nudged her to the left. "'Tis time for the bucket to be emptied and food and water lowered down to us. I dinnae want to be bumping into ye."

Alana immediately felt chilled as she left his side. She kept inching backward until she stumbled and fell onto a pile of blankets. She moved around until she was seated on them, her back against the cold stone wall. The grate was opened, and a rope with a hook at the end of it was lowered through the opening. The lantern this man carried produced enough light to at least allow them to see that rope. Gregor moved around as if he could see and Alana suspected he had carefully mapped out his prison in his mind. She watched the bucket being raised up and another being lowered down. As Gregor reached for that bucket, she caught a faint glimpse of his form. He was indeed very tall and very lean. She cursed the darkness for hiding all else from her.

"We will need two buckets of water for washing in the morn," Gregor called up to the man, watching him as he carefully lowered the now-empty privy bucket.

"Two?" the man snapped. "Why two?"

"One for me and one for the lass."

"Ye can both wash from the same one."

"A night down here leaves one verra dirty. A wee bucket of water is barely enough to get one person clean, ne'er mind two."

"I will see what the laird says."

Alana winced as the grate was slammed shut and that faint shaft of light disappeared. She tried to judge where Gregor was, listening carefully to his movements, but she was still a little startled when he sat down by her side. Then she caught the scent of cheese and still-warm bread, and her stomach growled a welcome.

Gregor laughed as he set the food out between them. "Careful how ye move, lass. The food rests between us. The Gowans do provide enough to eat, though 'tis plain fare."

"Better than none. Perhaps ye had better hand me things. I think I shall need a wee bit of time to become accustomed to moving about in this thick dark."

She tensed when she felt a hand pat her leg, but then something fell into her lap. Reaching down, she found a chunk of bread, which she immediately began to eat it. Gregor was obviously just trying to be certain of where she sat as he shared out the food. She did wonder why a small part of her was disappointed by that.

"Best ye eat it all, lass. I havenae been troubled by vermin, but I have heard a few sounds that make me think they are near. Leaving food about will only bring them right to us."

Alana shivered. "I hate rats."

"As do I, which is why I fight the temptation to hoard food."

She nodded even though she knew he could not see her, and for a while, they silently ate. Once her stomach was full, Alana began to feel very tired, the rigors of the day catching up to her. Her eyes widened as she realized there was no place to make up her own bed and doubted there were enough blankets to do so anyway.

"Where do I sleep?" she asked, briefly glad of the dark, for it hid her blushes.

"Here with me," replied Gregor. "I will sleep next to the wall." He smiled, almost able to feel her tension. "Dinnae fret, lass. I willnae harm ye. I have ne'er harmed a child."

Of course, Alana thought and she relaxed. He thought she was a child. She had briefly forgotten her disguise. The thought of having to keep her binding on for days was not comforting, but it was for the best. Thinking her a child, Gregor treated her as he would a sister or his own child. If he knew she was a woman, he might well treat her as a convenient bedmate or try to make her one. She brutally silenced the part of her that whispered its disappointment, reminding it that she had no idea of what this man even looked like.

Once the food was gone, Gregor set the bucket aside. Alana heard him removing some clothing and then felt him crawl beneath the blankets. She quickly moved out of the way when she felt his feet nudge her hip. After a moment's thought, she loosened the laces on her gown and removed her boots before crawling under the blankets by his side. The chill of the place disappeared again and she swallowed a sigh. Something about Gregor soothed her, made her able to face this imprisonment with some calm and courage, and she was simply too tired to try to figure out what that something was.

"On the morrow we will begin to plan our escape," Gregor said.

"Ye have thought of a way out of here?"

"Only a small possibility. Sleep. Ye will need it."

That did not sound promising, Alana mused as she closed her eyes.

Chapter 2

Alana grimaced as she finished washing, patted herself dry with a cloth, and began to don her clean but damp clothing. The Gowans catered to her and Gregor's need to keep clean, but there was nothing they could do about the all-pervasive damp. Or the chill, she mused, wrapping her damp plaid around her shoulders. After three days in the dark hole the Gowans had tossed her into, Alana felt as if that chill had settled deep into her bones. The only time she felt even partly warm was when she was curled up in Gregor's arms, pressed close to his warm body.

And that was beginning to be a pure torment, she thought as she brushed and braided her hair. All too often she had to sharply bite back the confession that she was a woman, not a child. Alana did not understand how she could be so hungry for a man she had only known for a few days, one she had never seen and who told her very little about himself. In most ways, he was a complete stranger to her, and yet, she felt as if she had known him for years. Each time she felt that hard length pressed against her backside, she wanted to move against it and ached for it to be born of a desire for her, not for some chimera in his dreams or a need to relieve himself. It was utter madness. Worse, she could think of no way to cure herself of this insanity.

It was past time for the man to devise a plan of escape, she decided, especially since she had not come up with one. Since he had spoken of it the first night she had joined him in the pit, he had never really spoken of it again. The few times she had ventured to mention it, he had said only one thing—patience, lass. Just how patient was she supposed to be? If he had a plan, he could share it with her, and if he did not, why did he not just admit it? She would be disappointed but would not fault him for not being able to find a way out of a very deep hole in the ground.

"Best ye move to the bed, lass," Gregor said. "Our meal is arriving."

Alana cautiously groped her way toward their rough bed. She doubted she would ever learn to move about in the dark as easily as Gregor did no matter how long she stayed here. Stumbling into the bedding, she quickly sat down and watched as the faint shaft of light appeared overhead.

"Ready to tell us who ye are?" asked the Gowan man who was lowering down the clean privy bucket.

"Nay," replied Alana, proud of how she resisted the growing urge to scream out her full name, give precise directions to her people, and demand to be pulled out of the darkness.

She frowned a little when Gregor's response was little more than a grunt of agreement to her words as he exchanged the clean bucket for the soiled one. He stood as he had for the last three days, staring intensely at the rope as the Gowan man raised the privy bucket and then lowered down their food. And again as he exchanged the dirty water for clean water. It puzzled Alana, for he was far too intense in how he watched the whole tedious process. Although she could not see his face, she almost felt his concentration and could see it in the taut stillness of his lean form.

Their guard left, taking that faint light with him, and Alana shivered with fear as she always did. She fought for calm, but still sighed with relief when Gregor sat down next to her. Each time that light disappeared, her fear of the dark reasserted itself. It embarrassed her that she required Gregor's presence to harness it again. It seemed so cowardly, yet it was not a fear that could be reasoned with. She could only hope that Gregor was not aware of how deep and strong that fear was, although why that should be important to her Alana did not know.

"I have a plan now, lass," Gregor said as he divided the food between them, carefully placing her share in her lap.

"And just when did ye devise this plan?" she asked calmly even though her pulse quickened with hope. "Before or after ye assisted in changing the privy bucket?"

"So sharp for one so wee," he murmured, grinning. "I was watching the raising and lowering of the buckets."

"I noticed that. I cannae see much in that wee flicker of light, but it did seem that ye were most interested in that."

"I was studying it all verra closely. It took me a while to decide on the best way to judge it."

"Judge what?"

"The distance up to that hole."

"Too far for either of us to reach it."

"Aye, but, mayhap, nay too far for the two of us."

Alana took a moment to think about that as she finished the bread she had just filled her mouth with. "What do ye mean by the *two* of us?"

"How tall are ye, lass?"

"Five feet."

"And I am six feet and a few inches."

"How proud ye must be," she muttered, and then sighed out her irritation, "but how does that matter?"

"Your height added to mine must be enough to get ye up to that opening."

"To do what? Gnaw through the thick iron bars?"

"The grate isnae locked or barred." He could feel her grow tense even though she was not sitting up against him.

"Are ye certain of that?"

"Aye. Why should they bother? 'Tis too high to reach, or so they believe. And these walls cannae be climbed. I tried several times ere ye arrived and got naught for my effort save more bruises. I am a verra good climber, but e'en I need the odd niche or outcrop or so to grab hold of as I climb. The few there are are too far apart and not easily grabbed hold of."

"So how do ye plan to get us out of here?"

"I think that if ye stand upon my shoulders, ye will be able to reach that grate."

Alana looked up, envisioning the grate in her mind since it was too dark to see it now. It was made of a very thick iron. Barred shut or not, it would be difficult for her to move it, especially since she would be standing on a man's shoulders and not firm, steady ground. She was also not that fond of heights but felt she could overcome that unease if offered the chance to escape. Alana was just not sure this plan gave them much chance.

"'Tis a heavy thing to try to push up and out of the way," she murmured.

"I ken it, and t'will be a struggle for such a wee lass, but there is no other choice. I cannae stand upon your shoulders."

"Quite true. 'Tis worth a try."

"T'will probably take several tries because of the lack of light. 'Tisnae easy to do anything in this dark. We should give it a try after we sup."

"Why wait?"

"If we succeed, 'tis best if we try to leave the keep come nightfall. After the last meal is delivered, we can also be certain no one will be coming down here for hours. If we fail, it will also give us time to hide all possible sign of what we were trying to do. After having come up with a plan, I dinnae want it to fail simply because the Gowans caught us at it and secured the hatchway better."

"Should we attempt to hoard a little food?"

Gregor sighed. "We should, but I still worry o'er attracting the rats."

"I certainly dinnae want them for company, but I havenae heard much scratching about within the walls. Mayhap they have given up since ye have been here nearly a week and we havenae left anything out for them."

"True. It may also be that, since the Gowans have only recently begun to play this game, the vermin havenae discovered a way in here. We shall give it a try. Mayhap if we wrap it securely in cloth and keep it close they willnae sniff it out and come ahunting for it."

The mere thought of rats crawling about their prison made Alana shiver. She loathed the creatures. Unfortunately, she and Gregor did need to at least try to hoard a little food for their escape. If they got free of this place, they would have to move swiftly and stealthily, which would make hunting for any food very difficult. She had little doubt that the Gowans would set out after them. Although she did not believe the Gowans would follow her and Gregor too far, there would probably be several days during which she and Gregor would spend a lot of their time running and hiding. For that they would need food, if only to keep up the strength needed to run fast and hide well.

"'Tis a shame we willnae be able to get the horses," she murmured.

"Aye," agreed Gregor. "Howbeit, I think e'en these fools would notice if I tried to slip a horse or two past the gates."

Alana laughed softly and then frowned as a sudden complication in his plans occurred to her. "If I can get up there and open the hatch, how do we both get through it? Once open, I can pull myself up and out, but I cannae pull ye up after me."

"Ah, weel, that is a weak point in my plan."

Hannah Howell

"'Tis nay a weak point, Gregor. 'Tis a gaping hole."

"Sarcasm is unbecoming in a female," Gregor said and grinned when she muttered a curse in response to that pious and condescending remark.

"So is punching someone offside the head," she muttered.

He ignored that. "I think we could use one or two of the blankets as a rope of sorts if ye can find naught to use up there. Once we ken if ye can move that lump of iron, we can tie the blankets about your waist ere ye climb out of here. If I recall it aright, above us are several things ye could tie the end of a rope to."

"Ah, that may serve."

"The first problem we need to solve is how to hold ye steady enough upon my shoulders so that ye can open that cursed grate. How much do ye think ye weigh?"

"Seven stone, mayhap a little more."

"I can lift that easy enough, but I have ne'er tried to balance such a weight upon my shoulders. But dinnae worry. I will catch ye if ye fall."

Alana did not feel particularly comforted by that reassurance. Six feet was not a great distance to fall, but the ground was hard. She still had bruises from landing on Gregor when the Gowans tossed her into the dungeon. Obviously unwilling to damage their prize too much, they had lowered her down by her wrists first, but it had still hurt when the man holding her had let her go.

For a brief moment, she battled the urge to tell Gregor that she could not do it, but then she lectured herself sternly to banish that surge of cowardice. They needed to escape this place and not just to save their families the expense of ransoming them. She needed to get out of the unrelenting dark before she began to cling to Gregor like some terrified infant. Each time the Gowans brought that blessed shaft of light and took it away again, she drew closer to that point. Her fear of the dark grew sharper and took longer to shake free of.

It was also necessary to escape the chill and damp of their prison. Alan was surprised that Gregor was still so hale and strong after spending a week in such a dismal place. The man appeared to be annoyingly untouched by conditions she knew were slowly robbing her of the good health she had enjoyed before entering the prison. If fear of the dark did not drive her to attach herself to Gregor like a leech, then the chill creeping into her bones would.

The thought that she was a pathetic weakling settled itself in Alana's mind. Cold and damp were ever pervasive, annoyances she had thought herself inured to. She hastily shook that troubling thought aside. There had always been fires to warm one and dry clothes at hand. They were blessed with neither in this dark pit. If one could not get warm and dry from time to time, it was only to be expected that the cold and damp would settle in deep and hard. It was also not surprising that Gregor held up better than she did, for he was much bigger and had more meat on his bones.

"What are ye scowling about now?" asked Gregor as he carefully packed away some of their food, a simple chore that was proving very difficult to do well in the dark.

"How do ye ken what expression is upon my face?"

"Ye make a little noise when ye are irritated."

"A little noise?"

"A soft, weel, grunt, or the like."

"Ladies dinnae grunt."

"Of course not. My mistake."

She ignored that remark, for the words were heavily weighted with amusement. "What are ye doing?"

"Attempting to secure some food. A simple chore. Or it would be, if we had a wee bit of light," he grumbled and then asked, "So, what has annoyed ye?"

Alana sighed. "I was just thinking on what a puling weakling I am." Gregor made an odd choking noise and she decided it was probably flattering that he would find such a statement amusing. "I always told myself the dark *unsettled* me. Weel, I cannae lie to myself anymore. It frightens me. As for your plan to escape? Standing on your shoulders to try to open a way out of here is a good idea and I shall do my best, but thinking of how high up I will be also frightens me. I am weary of the cold and the damp, can feel it in my verra bones. Each time one of those fools asks if I will now say who I am, I have to fight verra hard to say nay. A part of me wants to cry out my name, where I am from, give them a clearly drawn map to get to my people, and demand that they be quick in the doing of it. And that part gets bigger every day. 'Tis a coward I am."

Gregor had to bite back a laugh as he sat down next to her and put his arm around her slim shoulders. She sounded extremely irritated with herself. He could understand that well enough, for he had battled with a few of his own fears in those days he had been alone. Being alone in the dark with no way out and nothing to do made one think about oneself and see oneself far too clearly. Gregor suspected few people would find that comfortable.

"I suspicion many people are made uneasy by the dark and by being up high," he said. "Each is a fear I think we are all born with and we ne'er fully shake free of. There is naught wrong with being afeared of something, only in letting it control you. As for the cold and the damp? There is naught wrong with ye for feeling that. So do I and I grow most weary of it."

"Ye have been here longer than I have."

"And I have a lot more flesh for it to sink its teeth into. Takes a lot longer for it to burrow down into my bones, but 'tis there. Nay, lass, ye are no puling weakling for that either. Ye havenae wept, or needed a wee sharp slap to restore your wits, or complained incessantly."

Alana said nothing, just subtly pressed a little closer to him. For warmth, she told herself. She was not sure she believed all his kind reassurances, but they were comforting all the same. The urge to have a screaming, hair-pulling fit lurked inside of her, but his presence helped cage it. Alana did not think it would be wise to tell him so, however. If nothing else, it would not be fair or kind to put the weight of such a responsibility upon his broad shoulders. There was a good chance he was using her presence in a similar way, so there was no need to belabor the matter.

For a fleeting moment, she wished she had never left home, and then she accepted the fact that she simply could not have continued to wait for some word form her sister. Hearing that Keira was a widow, that her home had been taken by a man whose evil reputation was widespread, and then hearing nothing from her for months had been hard to bear. Her fear for her sister had grown stronger with each day that passed without word or sight of Keira, only more rumors and all of them bad. The only thing that had kept Alana from blindly rushing off to find her twin immediately was the feeling that Keira was still alive. That and her dreams.

She frowned as she realized she had had no dreams of her twin since setting out after her brothers. That should trouble her more than it did, yet she simply could not believe that Keira was dead. Alana still felt drawn toward her sister and suspected she would begin to sense in exactly what direction to go once she was free again. Yet it was odd that, in all other ways, she had lost that bond she and Keira had shared all of their lives. It made her feel intensely alone, and she pressed even closer to Gregor.

"Troubled, lass?" he asked.

"Nay, not truly," she lied, still uncertain if she sould tell him exactly why she had been alone and such easy prey for the Gowans. "I think the chance to escape is so tantalizing, I fear to let myself believe in it too much."

Gregor idly rubbed his hand up and down her slender arm. "I think I ken what ye mean. Now that we have a plan, we must face the daunting possibility of failure."

She nodded, feeling the soft wool of his plaid rub her cheek.

Alana knew just how bitter failure tasted. Her arrogant plan to lead her brothers to their sister had been a failure of monumental proportions. It was something that still stung her pride and puzzled her as well. She really should not have failed so badly. All her skills and gifts had deserted her, and that made no sense. It was as if whatever power had granted them had abruptly taken them away, but she did not understand why.

Alana inwardly shrugged. She could still sense that her twin was alive, could not believe that the other half of her was gone forever. There had to be some purpose to it all, some reason God and fate were conspiring to keep her from joining her sister at this time. Perhaps Keira needed to pass some test, to learn some great truth about herself, and having her twin at her side could make that difficult. Or, she mused, perhaps *she* needed to pass a test. Alana did not like that idea at all and hastily asked for Keira's forgiveness for hoping it was her sister who was being tested. Keira was pretty, kind, and clever, much more able to pass such a test of her spirit and courage.

Although she loved her sister dearly, felt that Keira was truly her best friend and ally, Alana ruefully admitted to herself that she often suffered the pinch of envy concerning Keira. Keira was the one who looked so much like the matriarch of their family, being vividly beautiful with her black hair, fair skin, and green eyes. Alana was little and brown. Keira had the true gift of healing whereas Alana was just a good healer, using knowledge and skill well but lacking the touch and strong instincts Keira had been blessed with. Keira had the sight. Alana only had a bond with her twin that occasionally stirred dreams and strong intuitions. Although neither of them had a bad temper, Keira was the gentler one, the sweeter one. Alana knew her tongue could be as sharp as a knife's edge. Although she knew it was nonsense, knew she was as beloved by her family as Keira was, Alana occasionally felt that, as the second born, she had entered the world in Keira's shadow and had never left it. She sighed, dismayed by her own foolishness.

"That was a mournful sound, lass," Gregor said. "Are ye sure ye arenae troubled?"

"Nay, I am just thinking on how long we must wait until we may try to escape," she lied, embarrassed by her thoughts.

Gregor did not need to see clearly to know he was being lied to, but he did not press her. "Weel, what say ye to a game of chess to pass the time?" he asked, leaning back against the wall and tugging her along with him.

"Aye, I am prepared to beat ye soundly yet again," she said. "Ye may make the first move."

"How gracious ye are," he drawled, suspecting her confidence was warranted as he had not won a game yet.

He closed his eyes, pictured his much-prized chess set in his mind, and struggled to decide upon his first move. If he was very lucky, he might take longer to lose this time. His victory could then be found in keeping them both well occupied during the too-long wait ahead of them.

ABOUT THE AUTHOR

Hannah Howell is an award-winning author who lives with her family in Massachusetts. She is the author of nineteen Zebra historical romances and is currently working on a new Highland historical romance, HIGHLAND LOVER, which will be published in June 2006. Hannah loves hearing from readers and you may visit her website: *www.hannahhowell.com*. Or write to her c/o Zebra Books. Please include a self-addressed stamped envelope if you wish a response.